A delightfully entertaining story of love.

For romance, drama, humor, spirituality, and total entertainment value, Call to Arms is a novel difficult to top. It is a skillfully written blend of serious drama with some comic relief. It's light enough to lift your spirit, heavy enough to touch your heart and soul.

This is a story of true love between a man and woman torn apart and tested by the tragedy of war; a classic tale of good versus evil, masterfully woven between the actual pages of Civil War history.

The plot has several unique and unexpected twists and is enhanced by a cast of colorful characters. Its profound perspective on life and love almost qualify it as a self-improvement book.

Reviews

"I really, really love it. It's written very well . . . wonderful job."
—Susan Duke,
author of more than a dozen published books

"A valuable document that will historically inform, teach, edify, and even encourage the reader toward a high moral standard . . . contains powerful truths to fortify our souls, stimulate our minds, and provide a path to ease a troubled spirit. Well done."
—Anonymous publisher

"I was totally stunned at how well it was written and how good the storyline was. I didn't want to put it down to go to sleep."
—Ronnie Ward,
a connoisseur of historical and western novels

"Thank you for reminding me of the important things in life. The way you weaved God into the book was masterful."
—Kalen J. Finefrock,
army reserve captain and Civil War student

"I'm impressed with how much imagination went into the story. And what great characters . . . fun and delightful. There isn't a dull page in it."
—Sue Hamlett, a Gone with the Wind buff

Call to Arms

Call to Arms

A Civil War Tale of
Trauma, Tragedy, Triumph and True Love;

The kind of dynamic story Mel Gibson
would be pleased to take to the silver screen

CLAUDE WAYNE

Library of Congress Control Number: 2005902422
ISBN: Hardcover   978-1-4134-8298-0
                 Softcover   978-1-4134-8297-3

This is a work of fiction. Names, characters, places and incidents either are the product of the author's imagination or are used fictitiously, and any resemblance to any actual persons, living or dead, events, or locales is entirely coincidental.

This book was printed in the United States of America.

To order additional copies of this book, contact:
Xlibris Corporation
1-888-795-4274
www.Xlibris.com
Orders@Xlibris.com
Xlibris is a strategic partner of Random House, LLC, and a subsidiary of Random House, Inc.
27823

Contents

❋Foreword❋

This book is one of those rare literary pieces that was written backward. By that, I mean the story was originally written as a motion-picture screenplay. Books are usually made into movies, seldom the other way around. How did that happen? I would like to acknowledge a business associate of mine, Chuck LeGette, and credit him with being responsible for the reverse circumstance, and the inspiration for my even attempting the project. For a good many years, Chuck was a successful broadcasting and media magnate in my hometown of Louisville, Kentucky. He also operated his own advertising agency, and I did most of his creative work on a freelance basis—writing, producing, directing, and quite often, starring in hundreds of radio and television commercials. I also wrote and produced commercial musical jingles, much of his print materials, and did artwork too, even creating a cartoon strip which ran in ads for one of his clients.

Chuck was not the easiest guy in town with which to work. He was very soft spoken and always a gentleman, but could be very demanding. Because of that, I dubbed him "Mr. Immediate." When he wanted something, he wanted it right now, and almost always had me working against near-impossible deadlines, not to mention wanting something that was a near-impossible creative premise. There were many times this led to a strained relationship, but I must say Chuck LeGette was responsible for pushing me to the point of perfecting my creative talents even more. Often, things I thought were going to be creative disasters I was able to make work, and we turned out many advertising campaigns that, if they weren't award-winning, were certainly unique enough to stand out with impact in the marketplace.

One thing that gave Chuck the incentive to use me for his creative work was the fact that I have a variety of talents, including doing over 350 voice impressions. One example of how we applied this made a car dealer in Nashville somewhat of a celebrity in television commercials, by making him look like he was doing impressions of famous movie stars. Actually, I would give him directing instructions on the visuals and I would lip sync the voice in an editing session, whether it was Rodney Dangerfield or Bugs Bunny. It worked so well no one knew the car dealer wasn't doing the impressions. In fact, the car dealer was approached by a talent agent saying he had too much talent to be wasting his time in the car business. He became so popular I heard that Hank Williams Jr. once asked the car dealer for his autograph.

Chuck had wanted to be a movie producer for a long time and, in the late nineties, moved to Nashville, Tennessee, investing in and producing a film with an independent film company. Later he branched out on his own and moved to the Charleston, South Carolina, area. When he approached me to write a Civil War movie script for him, I flatly refused, saying it would take up too much of my time. Well, Mr. Immediate was also Mr. Persuasive. He wouldn't let up, frequently calling me and encouraging me with all manner of incentives, including complete creative freedom to develop the story.

Finally, I told him I would write it only if I could think of something really good. I didn't want to waste my time on some ordinary or trashy movie. Chuck suggested we ought to pray about it.

I then remembered that when I was in high school I had the desire to write a book as good as *Gone with the Wind*. So I would think of ideas for a plot. Of course, the plots involved the Civil War era. I never wrote any of the ideas down. I just kept them in the back of my mind in the event I ever wanted to write a novel, never dreaming someday someone would actually ask me to write such a story. So I mentally dusted off those old ideas and thought of many new ones, and after a week or so, I felt I had enough thoughts together to start writing. The result was a motion-picture screenplay under the working title *Call to Arms*. Other than being a story woven amongst the historic pages of the Civil War, it bears no resemblance to *Gone with the Wind* whatsoever. But after reading it, Chuck called me back to say he thought it was a masterpiece that definitely belonged on the big screen. We were both pleased.

However, a series of unfortunate extenuating circumstances forced Chuck to postpone producing the film. Nevertheless, I then decided to write the story as a novel. It's designed to please readers who enjoy a good story with an interesting plot, colorful characters, charm, drama, adventure, intrigue, and spiritual values with a positive message of love. It has a serious side (with some scenes that may bring a tear to the eye), yet it is spiced with comic relief. This is a story designed to take the reader on a rollercoaster ride of emotions and adventures that will entertain and uplift you.

A movie can enhance a story with visuals set to mood music and songs and make for a condensed presentation that is highly entertaining for a short period of time. But a book can take time to give you a much broader insight into the plot, scenes, situations, and characters of a story. The book has episodes that go beyond the motion-picture screenplay. So I would like to invite you to take the time to enjoy *Call to Arms* in detail.

Claude Wayne

Preface

The American Civil War was a serious time of conflict, bloodshed, and suffering that brought a great nation to its knees and brought about change. While the following fictional story sometimes takes a lighthearted view of that time in history, it nevertheless is not intended to demean or ignore the seriousness of the conflict, or the sacrifice of those who suffered and died.

However, don't expect *Call to Arms* to be primarily a comedy. It is primarily a Civil War adventure and romance novel often spiced with comic relief, ranging from light to heavy humor to none at all. Some portions of the tale are very serious. Sometimes the story is historical, other times hysterical. Sometimes it's tragical, other times magical, but always classical, interesting, and entertaining. Overall, it is the ultimate love story that encompasses not only the erotic love of a man and a woman, but love of God, love of country, and brotherly love as well. It has an overall positive message based on popular cultural attitudes and spiritual beliefs of that period in American history.

This story is set in a time period when Christian beliefs in God were revered and respected without question, and dominated not only public society but were the very foundation of the government of the United States of America, including the Declaration of Independence and the Constitution of the United States. Fundamentals of the

Judeo-Christian belief were the mainstream of American culture from the time of the landing of the pilgrims through the mid-twentieth century when the Supreme Court began to make decisions that have inhibited and shifted the mainstream of American culture and beliefs more to the left. The religious content of *Call to Arms* is based on religious beliefs more as they existed during the time of the Civil War.

Acknowledgments

M y special thanks to the kind and helpful staff of the Danville, Virginia Public Library for the research materials they have provided to help me write this fictional story.

Some portions of the story are based on actual persons, places, and events. The most unbelievable parts of this novel are based, in part, on true Civil War stories.

❈Chapter 1❈

NORTH TO SOUTH

By 1860 the prevailing winds of time were already revealing signs of conflict on the horizon for the nation, much as dawn's early light reveals the inevitable coming of a new day. Tension was in the air too, as cool north winds were being heated by southerly breezes drifting in this first week of April, when the carriage of John William Van Worth Jr. rolled along the rugged streets of Columbus, Ohio, with his son John William Van Worth III at his side. The younger was nearing the age of thirty and had always affectionately been referred to as "Johnny" by his mother to cut down on confusion caused by the similar names. Three generations of Van Worths had built a very successful business, although the grandfather and founder of the company had passed away several years earlier.

Johnny was nothing like his father or grandfather, both of whom were very serious, stern, and long suffering in their dutiful attention to business and their social standing in the community. Johnny was more carefree and debonair with a keen sense of humor, always looking for a reason to laugh. Traveling home together after putting in another hard days' work at the family-owned Van Worth Hardware and Supply Company, the conversation would often turn from the business of the day to more personal matters, which frequently accented this clash of personalities. The contrast was amusingly apparent even in their faces. The stony-faced father in his midfifties, tall, thin, and distinguished, wearing a felt hat with hints of gray brushed through his beard, leaning forward, handling the reins with squinty-eyed intenseness. And the handsome son leaning back, arms crossed, wearing a mischievous grin and a porkpie hat cocked to one side. Johnny's dark-colored hair and refined features were inherited from his attractive mother, Clara. We can assume his well-groomed mustache was more a product of his father's genes.

The mood was slightly altered as his aristocratic father glanced up at the trees, took a deep breath, inhaled the refreshing spring breeze, and slowly exhaled with a slight smile.

"*Aaah.* Spring is in the air, Johnny! And what does a young man's fancy turn to?" Johnny seized the opportunity to turn his father's words into a moment of jesting. With tongue in cheek, Johnny announced, "*Uh* . . . well, Dad, I want you to be the first to know. I'm gonna get married!"

His father's eyes lit up and he beamed a broad smile.

"What? Well, it's about time! Who? When?"

Almost yawning to keep from laughing, Johnny continued what to him was a humorous barb.

"Yep. Gonna get married . . . *uh* . . . to *somebody* . . . *someday*!" He laughed.

Johnny succeeded in amusing only himself. His father gritted his teeth, tossing a disgruntled glare at his son. This particular subject had been a point of contention between them for some time. Johnny's moment of teasing his father would have led to a verbal badgering all the way home, but the stress of the moment was halted by a salutation from the mother of Johnny's most recent romantic interest. She waved as the carriage passed by her on the street, her face framed in a stylish light blue bonnet and matching hoop-skirted dress.

The lady addressed the elder Van Worth with an air of cordiality, "Good evening, Mr. Van Worth!" She snubbed Johnny with a brief glance flashing away with a look of disdain. Johnny's father barely noticed the spurning and replied, "Good evening, Mrs. Miller!" He then addressed his son with a suspicious tone in his voice, "How's your courtship going with Mrs. Miller's daughter? You haven't said anything about her for quite a spell now."

Glancing away momentarily, Johnny hesitated, took a deep breath, exhaled with his mouth shut and lips loose, imitating the lip-fluttering of a horse's snort, "*Pppuuuh!* I . . . *uh* . . . I believe it ended when she slapped me and went home."

His father's mouth dropped open as his head turned back and forth between looking at his son and watching the roadway. Then his stern eyes squinted at Johnny.

"And what horrid thing did you do to cause that?"

"I was just trying to pay her a compliment. I told her I thought she had eyes almost as pretty as Opal Anderson's. Everyone knows Opal has the most beautiful eyes of any woman in the county." Then he showed exasperation, tossing his palms upward. "I don't understand it!" Johnny's father rolled his eyes in despair at the thought of his son not understanding that women get jealous hearing a man talk about the attributes of some other woman.

In a pitying tone he said, "Oh, Johnny! I sent you to college, son. You should have better sense. Maybe if you had graduated from Yale you'd be smarter. But you fouled that up too."

Johnny retorted, "Oh, come on, Dad. We've been through this a hundred times. So I had to transfer to Ohio University. I graduated, didn't I?" In a low pleading tone his father responded, "I want my eldest son to carry on the family name. You're darn near thirty years old. Do you realize that if you were a woman you'd be an old maid now?" With a shocked expression on his face, Johnny glanced over at his father. He lowered his head, recognizing his dad's concern, and realized the comment was a bit humorous, but it was too close to the truth to laugh about. He had inadvertently avoided marriage, not because he chose to do so, but because he was the apple of so many ladies' eyes that he played the field and had a hard time choosing just one of them. His romances often ended with a jealous slap.

His father observed the hurt look on Johnny's face and for a moment they rode silently and the horse's clopping along the street and the mating calls of the birds were the only sounds to be heard. Johnny's grin began to fade as the tension between them slowly sizzled.

In a slightly defensive, yet apologetic tone, he assured his father, "I'll get married someday, Dad. I just haven't met the right girl, that's all!" They rode the rest of the way home with little more to say to each other. Johnny with his arms crossed somewhat defiantly and his smile diminished to a near pout. His father exuding serious concern and wishing things were different. He wondered, *Where did it all go wrong with Johnny?*

Being the heir of a wealthy family, Johnny was the product of a spoiled childhood that made him more the forerunner of a twentieth-century man than one of the age in which he lived. He had little need for ambition and tried to cope with the everyday stresses of life by turning serious moments into laughing matters. Even as a boy he had been handsome and grew up always sporting a playful grin. It earned him an air of confidence with his fellow man and made him popular with the ladies, who saw him as a very eligible bachelor. However, in latter years, his nonchalant manner was worked into play primarily as a cover-up for his prankish past, which included being expelled from Yale University for cheating on tests. It had not been a case of Johnny's having low mentality. He was highly intelligent, but was easily bored with studying things he knew he would never be able to apply to real life. So his studies took a backseat to having a good time, and he saw getting answers from his more studious peers as a clever short-cut to getting a legitimate education. Johnny's casual and outgoing personality made him popular with his fellow students, who eagerly assisted him with his short-cutting endeavors, albeit leading to an early demise of his elite private college education in his sophomore year.

Johnny's father, being a proud, well-respected member of the community, of course, did not take the news well at all. Keeping his son's failure as much of a family secret as possible, he used his influence to get Johnny "transferred" to Ohio University in Athens. "So the boy would be closer to home and the family business." Johnny was very popular there too, entertaining his dorm mates with such suggestions as making petticoat raids on the dormitories of the nearest ladies' finishing school. They never did, but the thought made for a frequent, amusing, and titillating joke to the young college men of that time.

Johnny's father wasn't aware of most of his son's college pranks, but he knew Johnny hadn't shown much interest in the business. Although he did a good job of serving customers and keeping track of the inventory, his father knew his son's heart wasn't in it. Perhaps that was why Johnny was always pulling practical jokes, especially on his friends and workers around the shop. John William thought something needed to happen to change his son, something to mature him and make him more responsible. But what could that be?

When they arrived home at the Van Worth mansion, Clara Van Worth was busy preparing the evening meal, her face flushed from the radiant heat of the crude cooking facilities. Although she had maid servants who could do all of it, she took great pleasure in cooking meals for her family. As her husband entered the kitchen, she focused her warm brown eyes on him and, with a loving smile, said, "I'm cooking a roast tonight. It'll be a little while longer." John nodded his approval with a mild smirk of appreciation. She continued stirring vegetables in the iron pot hanging in the hearth of the huge stone fireplace so typical of finer kitchens of the era. Brushing her curled brunette locks back from her temples with the back of her forearm, she went on to tell her husband, "In the meantime, you can read the letter that came today from your brother. It's on the living room mantle. Fred wants to sell the farm in South Carolina and move back here with us."

This was not what John wanted to hear. "What? He needs to keep that farm. It's a family inheritance! Besides, I don't want Fred and Elsie living here with us."

Clara stopped stirring and wiped her hands on her apron while looking at her husband, pondering the thought and wondering what to say. Finally she relented. "I'm sure you'll think of something." Then she went back to her cooking chores.

John had not totally outgrown sibling rivalry with his younger brother, leaving their relationship prone to personality clashes. Fred moving back to Ohio was quite contrary to John's plans for a peaceful future retirement. He sat down at his desk and began reading Fred's letter.

In 1855, Fred Van Worth inherited a one-hundred-acre farm in South Carolina from his Aunt Isabel who took pity on Fred because he was the younger, more pitifully puny of her two nephews. Her will granted Fred her property because she knew John would get the family mansion in Ohio. But after working the land himself with little help except for a few slaves, which he purchased from the neighboring Brown family plantation, he made some mistakes in the care of his cotton crop for two years running. Boll weevils and blight finished off the rest of it. This was the only cash crop Fred and his wife Elsie had, and though they raised most of what they needed for food, this was a devastating blow to their economic status. After the winter of 1859-60, they were even running low on food they stored from autumn. It was a desperate situation. That's why Fred was considering the prospect of selling the farm and asking to move back to the family mansion in Ohio.

After reading the letter, John William began massaging his temples, searching for a solution that would keep Fred and Elsie in South Carolina and save the farm as a family property. He wondered how he could help Fred. Of course, the first thing would be to send him some money to survive. But his brother needed someone who was healthy who could help manage the place since Fred had been in poor health for some time. John could send his brother currency to buy more slaves but John William didn't believe in slavery. So that was out. Besides, that wouldn't solve the management problem.

He heard Johnny in his upstairs bedroom. Suddenly it clicked in his mind. Johnny loved his Uncle Fred and Aunt Elsie. He was young and healthy and would be perfect for helping Fred organize things once he knew what to organize. He reasoned that a change of scene and responsibility would do his son good. He started writing a check. His stern voice rang out as he shouted, "Johnny! Come here!"

John had been irritated for some time that Johnny had muffed all of his romances and was still living at home. He was pleased with himself that he was about to propose a solution as Johnny scurried down the ornate Victorian staircase two and three steps at a time and sauntered into the living room in his typical casual manner, unaware of what awaited him.

He eagerly asked, "What is it, Dad? Dinner ready?"

"No, it's not ready, you bonehead, but I'm ready!"

Johnny's eyebrows raised at the tone of his father's voice, which was a little more stern than usual, as he fired back, "Ready for what?"

"Ready to make you a proposal!"

"Aw gee, Dad, you don't have to do that just because I've run out of girlfriends. Besides you're not my type and . . . hey! You're already married, aren't you?"

His father bristled at Johnny's attempt to make light of the situation. "Isn't it about time you got serious about life?"

In spite of the anger Johnny kept on grinning.

"Your Uncle Fred and Aunt Elsie had a bad cotton crop last year, and they're thinking about selling the farm and moving back here."

"Hey, that's great! I haven't seen Uncle Fred and Aunt Elsie in four or five years," came Johnny's enthusiastic reply.

"I have a better way for you to see them," his father scowled. "I want you to go down there and help your Uncle Fred get back on his feet so he can keep the farm."

Suddenly, Johnny felt the need to get seriously defensive, blurting out without thinking, "Come on, Dad! You know I don't know a cotton pickin' thing about pickin' cotton!"

His father grinned at the poor choice of words, weakening Johnny's defensive posture.

"You don't have to. Just do what your Uncle Fred says. He needs help, that's all." Reaching into his coat pocket his father pulled out his bankbook. "I've written a draft you can cash tomorrow. That should be enough for your travel expenses and money to hold Fred and Elsie over 'til they can harvest a crop."

Johnny started to protest, "Oh, Dad, I don't want to go down there—"

But he was cut short by his father's stern voice and sweeping gesture, telling him, "You're going!"

Johnny knew his father's mind was made up, and since the only job he had ever known was working at the family wholesale hardware and supply business while living in his father's house, he decided he didn't have any choice. He thought he'd prove himself to his father, get Uncle Fred on his feet, and come back home in about a year or so. After all, Johnny had confidence in his ability to figure out a short cut to whatever end he had in mind. So he prepared to say goodbye to his mother Clara, his kid brother Jeremy, his scowling father, and his job, to head South.

The next day they all gathered on the front porch of the mansion with the carriage hitched and ready to take Johnny to the bank and the nearest stage pickup point and then east to Wheeling, where he would take the B&O Railroad to Baltimore and on to Washington DC. From there he would travel again by coach to Richmond, Virginia, and by rail again to Charleston, South Carolina.

With tears streaming down her face, Clara sobbed because she knew she would miss her son just as she had during his college years. Johnny and his mother were very close. She was greatly responsible for spoiling him and most influential in shaping his personality, teaching him many life lessons including how to live by the golden rule. She also shed tears out of worry, aware that travel was hard and hazardous in those days. Twice they had read about wooden railroad bridges collapsing in Virginia, with the engine and crew toppling into a gorge. Plus, there was always the danger of ruthless thieves holding up stages and trains. With a mother's intuitive powers, she felt the need to give her son a serious warning.

"Johnny! Promise me you'll be careful and stay on the alert for danger."

"Now, Mother! You know I will. I came back from Yale unscathed after that coach robbery, didn't I?" Clara closed her eyes and squeezed her arms around him even tighter as she thought about his former accounts of the incident. It provoked her to say, "Yes, but you were lucky then. Faking a gun in your coat pocket with your finger. Oh, the very idea! You don't know how many nightmares I've had over that. You could have been killed! Oh, Johnny, please don't do anything that foolish again!"

Johnny put his hands on his mother's shoulders and leaned her back to look her in the eyes. He gave her a reassuring smile. "I got him to drop his pistol, didn't I? But don't worry, I'm carrying a real one now."

She embraced him tightly and whispered, "I'll be praying for you."

He kissed her cheek and held her close, looking down into her face. "Now you're talkin'! You keep praying and I'll be just fine." Looking at his mother's tear-soaked eyes, he began to feel moisture building in his own. Feeling it to be an affront to his masculinity, he quickly turned away and, glancing down to hide his sensitivity, instructed his teenaged brother, "Take care of her, Jeremy!" The seventeen-year-old Jeremy put an arm around his mother and said, "I will," as Johnny sauntered toward the carriage with his father and rode away from the elite Van Worth mansion.

Once they reached the stage line, Johnny's father got down from the carriage and waited with his son. They talked without much contention for the first time in many a year. Even though John had used his sternest, most demanding tone of voice to make Johnny understand, he had no choice but to make tracks South, he was now mellow and almost sentimental in seeing his son off. John impressed his son with the idea this would be a good thing for him. They talked of manly things and politics. They discussed the new Republican Party and wondered who would be the next president of the United States to be elected in the fall. The tall, gangly senator from Illinois, Abraham Lincoln, had established a reputation with excellent speeches and was a front-runner to be nominated by the Republicans. The northern Democrats favored Vice President John C. Breckinridge of Kentucky, while the southern Democrats were leaning toward Senator John Bell of Tennessee. They considered the differences in politics and the attitudes of most people in the South, especially regarding slavery. They recalled portions of a speech made by Abraham Lincoln when he was running for senator against Stephen A. Douglas of Illinois. Lincoln stated,

A house divided against itself cannot stand. I believe this government cannot endure, permanently half slave and half free. I do not expect the Union to be dissolved. I do not expect the house to fall. But I do expect it will cease to be divided. It will become all one thing or all the other. Either the opponents of slavery will arrest the further spread of it, and place it where the public mind will rest in the belief that it is in the course of ultimate extinction; or it's advocates will push it forward till it shall become alike lawful in all the States—old as well as new, North as well as South.

For the most part, slavery was an accepted way of life in the South after many generations grew up with it. Not many Southerners questioned the customs of their society. They were taught those attitudes from early childhood so that their minds were marinated in the thought that their social mores were just the way life had always been and should always be. Anything else was considered insulting to elders. But these attitudes were challenged by the writings of Harriet Beecher Stowe who authored a novel published in 1853 titled *Uncle Tom's Cabin*. It focused on the plight of slaves and the evils of slavery and made an impassioned plea for people of faith to resist a "system which confounds and confuses every principle of Christianity and morality." Her book had a profound effect on shaping opinions that began to divide the nation into conflicting viewpoints. Johnny and his father had read it.

Johnny expressed himself in a serious fashion for a change. "I agree with you, Dad. I don't see how Uncle Fred could go along with buying even one slave. I guess he's more desperate than we figured, and influenced by the way of life around him. After I've had a chance to look things over, I hope I can convince him he can make it without slaves."

His father nodded in agreement and went on to verbalize his thoughts. "I hope you can work it out that way too, son. But I'm trusting you to have the good judgment to do whatever is necessary to keep the farm. You've shown good judgment in managing the store." He softened the pitch of his voice and squinted to say, "I wish you had as much sense in managing your courting of women."

Johnny grinned and came to his own defense, saying, "Aw, come on now, Dad. Let's not talk about that. I want to leave in peace, you know."

"Well, who knows? Maybe you'll do better with those charming Southern ladies."

"Yeah. Maybe." Johnny wondered, "You think they really are more charming?"

"For your sake and mine, I hope they're more charming . . . *and* desperate for a husband."

"All right! You're embarrassing me now, Dad."

Putting one hand on Johnny's shoulder and shaking his hand with the other, John wished his son the best. "Good luck, son. And Godspeed!"

"Thanks, Dad. I'll do my best to get Uncle Fred going . . . and I'll be back . . . Soon, I hope."

His father was not prone to showing affection, but as the stagecoach approached, he gave Johnny a hardy hug, something he hadn't done since Johnny was a child. It showed Johnny that under that crusty personality his dad had a soft spot he didn't often admit was there. Johnny thought perhaps he got a hug too because his father feared for his safety.

He paid the driver, loaded his travel bag on top of the stage, and the guard tied it down with a rope. Then he climbed aboard, shut the door, and waved at his father with a wink and a thumbs-up gesture. Johnny wondered *just what really did lie ahead* as the driver cracked the whip and shouted out the starting command to the team of horses, "*Heaaah!*"

His father wondered the same thing as he watched the stage creak and clatter forward, slowly at first, then faster to a steady pace, fading away in the distance down the rugged road—the first link of Johnny's trek from North to South.

❋Chapter 2❋

DREAMS AND SCHEMES

Even though travel posed many dangers, it stirred an excitement for adventure in Johnny's heart. He realized how bored he had grown with the daily routine of working the family business and was glad to get away and enjoy the passing countryside as the stage rumbled over the crude dirt roads of eastern Ohio, sometimes slowing to a near halt to wade through shallow streams or climb hills. Occasionally, they passed through a covered bridge with a thundering roar echoing from the floor timbers and off the walls so that all conversation had to be halted until they reached the other side. He enjoyed the beauty of nature, the mixture of earth and rocks, trees, grass, and shrubbery, all providing homes and roaming grounds for animals of all sorts.

He gazed out the window for much of the early hours of the trip, ignoring the other three passengers aboard, a young married couple and a middle-aged businessman. He was having too much fun enjoying the scenery and activity along the ever changing landscape before him. He observed many deer bolting deeper into the wooded areas, obviously frightened by the noise of the approaching stage, the occasional crack of the driver's whip and clopping horse's hooves.

The clatter of their approach also put other creatures on a run across the thicket now beginning to bud in a variety of hues from emerald to lime. He delighted in watching rabbits and squirrels, raccoons, opossums, chipmunks, ground hogs, and foxes darting and dancing among the dandelions and purple violets on forest floors and in fields along the roadway. And he observed many birds marking their territories, building nests, and singing their love songs.

He threw an occasional glance at the newlyweds seated across from him, observing how they seemed so happy exchanging adoring gazes and smiles. They were adorable in many ways. Almost constantly, they held hands and the groom often had his arm around her to seemingly protect her from every jostle of the carriage.

The joy of the newlyweds made Johnny aware he was missing out on something he had never experienced before: the magical togetherness of being in love. He was thinking he really did have a need to meet a lovely lass sometime soon in his life before life started passing him by. Now that he was free of the prodding of his father, he began to realize his father was right, and he was now feeling the need to prod himself to make a commitment to marriage before many more years rolled away.

Johnny's interest gradually drifted to the conversation within the carriage, most of which emanated from the businessman Walter Moneypenny, a banker returning to Zanesville, Ohio. He was an opinionated man, with reddish hair protruding from the sides of his hat, who took himself much more seriously than his clownish appearance would imply while talking to the couple.

"Yes, if I were you I'd invest in railroad stock. As soon as they complete the bridge across the Ohio River . . . why, the B&O will race across Illinois, Indiana, and Ohio nonstop to Baltimore and Washington DC. They've already laid much of the track. By next year we'll be making this trip by railroad.

Mark my words!" Just then, the carriage bumped up hard, rolling over a tree limb that had fallen across the road, bouncing all passengers into the air and crashing them back into their seats again. Mr. Moneypenny continued to dominate the conversation, reaffirming his opinion.

"See! That wouldn't happen on the railroad. It's a much smoother way to travel."

Johnny quipped, "Well, let's look on the bright side. On a train you wouldn't get all of these free massages!"

They chuckled at his sense of humor. Johnny had introduced himself when he got aboard so they were acquainted only with his name.

Until now he had been very quiet, enjoying the beauty of nature, shyly ignoring the boring Mr. Moneypenny and the newlyweds who were traveling to Niagara Falls for their honeymoon.

The banker addressed Johnny. "Well, Mr. Van Worth, we haven't heard much from you. Don't you agree with me that the railroads are going to spearhead great economic growth for the country?"

Johnny really hadn't thought about it and had no opinion at all, so he awkwardly replied in a shaky uncertain manner, "*Uh*, well, yeah . . . railroads . . . *uh*, sure. They'll get you where you're goin'. I mean . . . it's sure a good way to make tracks."

The young newlyweds laughed heartily but Mr. Moneypenny just managed a weak smile. It wasn't so much what Johnny said but the way he said it, his expressions and gestures, that made people laugh. In his desire to create laughter, he had perfected a sense of timing that would often make people giggle even if what he said wasn't even funny. But he had a deep serious side too and a good common-sense attitude toward life that gave him a perspective to balance heaviness with lightness.

He continued to amuse his passengers all along the trail. When Mr. Moneypenny got off at Zanesville and new passengers came aboard, Johnny enjoyed making the journey easier with more light conversation. At one point they went across a wooden bridge and Johnny imitated the rumbling of the wheels with his voice, and the horse's hooves by slapping his cheeks with his mouth rounded to amplify the sound. When asked how he learned to do that, he stated, "It's amazing what you can learn in college." Some people thought he was silly, but most were entertained and enjoyed his company. One thing was for sure—Johnny wasn't boring.

They crossed the Ohio River on a ferry boat at Wheeling and he boarded the B&O Railroad. It had been the nation's first common carrier train system since 1837. Little did he know that Abraham Lincoln would travel that same rail route the following year to take reign of the nation as the sixteenth president of the United States. Johnny began to realize Mr. Moneypenny was right about the train being a smoother way to travel. He was glad to be traveling on the train too because this third day of his trip was a cloudy rainy day. It was pouring down when he arrived in Washington DC. He didn't have time to take a tour of the city, although he would have liked to do so, since it was his first time in the nation's capital. He only had time to find a hotel, eat his dinner and get some sleep before the next leg of his journey which would put him back into a coach to take him south through Fredericksburg and on to Richmond, Virginia.

The next morning Johnny boarded a commercial *vis-à-vis*, a French word describing a carriage where the occupants sit face to face, just as they did on the stagecoach. But the vis-à-vis was black and more refined with a longer wheelbase for a more comfortable ride. It was used primarily to transport dignitaries. When it was time to leave, the coachman approached Johnny.

"It looks as though you're our only passenger this morning. Do you mind waiting about a quarter hour to see if more passengers arrive?" Johnny wasn't in such a hurry that fifteen minutes would make much of a difference so he agreed. "I suppose I can wait a few minutes." But the time passed without a single soul arriving to take the coach ride to Richmond and they departed with Johnny as the only passenger. His mind was reeling from the stresses of travel, and having not slept well the night before, he soon nodded off.

About a half hour later the carriage rocked from side-to-side in the ruts of wagon wheels in the road and shook Johnny awake. Much to his surprise, a lovely lady was sitting across from him. She appeared about the age of his mother but had curly golden hair that seemed to shine in the soft light that glowed about her. She wore a shiny white dress made of a satinlike or silklike material. But it wasn't a wedding dress. The lady had a kind face full of love, and she was smiling pleasantly at Johnny as if she knew him somehow, although he had never seen her before. He stared at her momentarily, not certain whether he was awake or dreaming. He glanced out the window and realized the carriage was moving across the countryside and he could feel his weight shifting with the swaying movement, so he reasoned he must be awake. He looked back at the lady in the white dress whose hem flowed down to the floor of the carriage, and he marveled at the mild glowing light that shone 'round about her as she continued to smile, gazing pleasantly into his eyes. He had slid into a slouch while sleeping, so he sat up straight, cleared his throat, and said, "Oh, I'm sorry, ma'am, I must have been asleep when you came aboard. I'm a little tired from traveling." She never ceased her pleasant smile and with a tender, understanding voice said, "Yes, Johnny, I know." He was astounded that she knew his name, and a little embarrassed that he didn't recognize her at all. He thought, *Who is she? Where have I met her before? Is she a distant relative, perhaps who visited us when I was a child?* Before he could speak she leaned forward, ready to impart something confidential, looked him in the eyes, and in a very sweet soft tone, said, "Your mother loves you very much. She prays for you all the time."

Now Johnny's curiosity was really piqued and he wanted to know who this woman was. He decided to go ahead and suffer embarrassment, admitting he didn't remember her to satisfy his puzzled mind. "I'm sorry, I must admit I don't remember you. Are you a friend of my family?" The little lady smiled even more and said, "Yes. You can truthfully say so. For many years, too."

Johnny knew his mother had many friends. Clara Van Worth delighted in helping people who were less fortunate. She was very active in their church, often planning and directing many humanitarian activities.

So Johnny was satisfied this lady must be someone from another Columbus neighborhood his mother had known and helped in some way. But then he thought, *What a coincidence to meet this woman traveling over here in Virginia.* He was sure she would volunteer to tell him her name, but she was more interested in telling him about what lies ahead in his life.

She prophesied, "Before this year ends you will meet the dream of your life. The moment you see this person, you will know."

Johnny was curious, "Know? Know what?" The lady smiled deeply. "Believe me. You will know!" She continued saying, "You will make a lifelong friend by an act of kindness. You will enter a conflict that is not of your own choosing. And you must be aware that danger lurks all around you. Beware, Johnny, beware and prepare! For there are evil forces eager to attack you. Beware, Johnny, and pray often, lest you lose your way." She paused and observed the speechless look of shock on Johnny's face and concluded, "There now, let it sink in . . . and take heed!"

Johnny's mind was taxed with the weight of her words and his eyelids grew heavy with the urge to sleep again, as if she had cast some sort of spell over him. He blinked several times. Within seconds he dozed off once more, and his subconscious dwelled on the things the lady had said.

-0-

Upon arriving in Richmond, the coachman had to wake Johnny for him to depart and catch the train to Charleston. His mind still dwelled on the lady and he was curious about where she had gone. He addressed the coachman, "What happened to the lady? Did she go in the depot?" The coachman was puzzled, asking, "What lady?"

Johnny responded urgently, "The lady you must have picked up along the road. The lady in the white dress, you know." The coachman again looked inquisitively at Johnny, saying, "There was no lady. You were the only passenger I had since we left Washington. You must'a dreamed something." With that, Johnny himself was convinced it may have been just a dream too. He made up his mind he would never mention it to anyone. But he couldn't forget it, especially the things she predicted.

-0-

By the time the train arrived in Charleston, Johnny had grown weary of traveling and was anxious to see his Uncle Fred and Aunt Elsie. His father had sent a telegraph message from Columbus, Ohio, the day Johnny left, letting them know when he would likely arrive.

As the train was pulling into the station, he spotted them in the crowd and waved from the window of his passenger car. There was Aunt Elsie, a frail woman in her fifties, wearing a plain, simple farm dress with a flowered pattern and bonnet to match. She also wore a bright smile, and was waving enthusiastically. And right beside her was Uncle Fred, also a thin person, wearing his everyday work clothes, waving his straw hat at Johnny. He stepped off the train and Aunt Elsie greeted him with a big hug, and stepped back to look at him dressed in dapper clothes, although they were soiled from the trip.

She was all smiles as she said, "Johnny! You look great! It's so good to see someone from home."

Johnny answered, "It's great to see you too, Aunt Elsie."

He turned to his Uncle, who was quick to offer Johnny a hardy handshake, saying, "It's mighty fine of you to do this Johnny!"

Johnny told it like it was. "Well, I have to admit it was mostly Dad's idea. I'm not sure what to do about raising cotton."

Uncle Fred was anxious to assure him, "Don't worry, I'll show you. You'll have help. I have some slaves to help with the plantin' and pickin'."

Johnny hid his concern about Uncle Fred giving in to the use of slave labor, but he was determined that if he could find another way to raise the crop economically he would surely recommend it.

They called the Van Worth farm "Pleasant Acres." At least eighty acres of the one-hundred-acre property was allotted to the growing of cotton. The farmhouse was simple compared to the Victorian Van Worth mansion Johnny had grown up in and was accustomed to in Ohio. But it was cozy and charming with touches of filigree accenting a front porch facing east, so that it began to get shady past noonday. The home had four bedrooms all on the second floor, and every window was equipped with dark green shutters that would be closed and buttoned when storms or hurricanes threatened. The house was surrounded by large trees accented with lilac and snowball bushes, and flower beds spotted beside the house that Aunt Elsie loved to maintain with pansies, petunias, and marigolds. Blue morning glories climbed a trellis on the sides of the porch. Honeysuckle grew wild on the edge of the nearby woods which separated the home from a small swampy area they always referred to as "the pond."

In the spring and summer months, Johnny learned more about the raising of cotton than he ever wanted to know, experiencing firsthand the crude nineteenth-century ways of plowing, planting, cultivating, picking, and baling the crop. He worked side by side with the slaves and asked them and his Uncle Fred many questions to learn as much as he could about it. The process was simple, but the work was hard under the blistering South Carolina sun. The heat intensified with an atmosphere of high humidity, something Johnny was having a hard time getting used to enduring. But he did endure, and he was maturing both mentally and physically, his muscle tone hardening and bulging beneath a skin turning more bronze with each day's exposure to the beaming rays of sunlight.

Occasionally Johnny would go down to the slave shacks at day's end and talked to them like no one ever had. He showed them respect and asked their opinion about farming and their lives as slaves. He taught them to read and write, earned their respect, and they trusted and confided in him.

There were only ten adult males among them; seven had wives and children. The oldest was docile and reluctantly accepted slavery, not knowing anything different. To him it was a way to always have some kind of shelter and food provided. Others had horror stories of beatings and cruelty. One named Jethro welcomed these opportunities to unload his misgivings about these things on a white man who was sympathetic enough to listen to his concerns.

"Yassuh, Mistah Johnny, ah's heared o' many a fambly dat wuz on da ocshun block and ever one of 'em ended up gettin' bought by a diffrunt owner. Dat's whut happen to us. Me an' mah daddy was sold to a plantation owner heah in Do'chestah Coun'y, and mah mama and sistah wuz sold to a man in Berkeley Coun'y. We wuz a cryin' and screamin' and nobody cared 'bout us. Ah ain't never seen mah Mama

or mah sistah since . . . even tuh dis very day. It ain't right ah
tell ya."

Johnny agreed, "Yeah, I reckon there has to be a day of
reckonin' somehow."

"Dat's right," chimed in another of the male slaves named
Charco. He related,

"But dey's been worse t'ings, like da beatin' mah bruthah
took on da Warfi'l' plantation when ah wuz jus' a pup. Massa
Warfi'l' . . . he got da notion one us niggahs wuz messin'
wid da missus afta he come back frum a long trip ovahseas
'cause she wuz in da womanly way, iffen ya know whut ah
mean. Massa Warfi'l' come down to da shacks and he pick
out da one he 'spek it wuz. Mah bruthah Tony wuz a biggen.
So massa Warfi'l' he tuk it out on him. He whupped him
and whupped him and whupped him some mo'e wid' a big
black snake whip. Ovah a 150 lashes! Dey hadda drag 'im
back in da shack. But he bleedin' so much from da beatin'
he wuz dead da next mornin'." Den when da baby come, it
wuz white. So iffen anybody wuz messin' wid da missus, it
wuz some white man."

Johnny was appalled at such stories and he was thankful
Uncle Fred had never done any of those things. Those stories
were from other farms and larger plantations and were
passed down from generation to generation.

Johnny developed a liking for one young slave in
particular. He called himself Jay Brown, assuming the
surname of his former owners on the neighboring Brown
family plantation. Jay took the surname as if he were a freed
slave. Most slaves were just given a first name and had no
surname of their own. Jay was about eighteen years of age
that summer. He had a humble spirit that made him
easygoing and easy to like. The young slave saw that Johnny
was different than most white men he'd known because he
was sympathetic to the yoke of burden upon the slaves.
Johnny learned a lot from Jay. While out in the cotton field
one day, he directed Johnny. "Now watch dis, Mistah Johnny."

He quickly snatched a boll weevil off the stem of a cotton plant with two fingers and crushed it with his thumb. He liked Johnny and showed him everything he knew. "Dose critters 'bout did us in las' year. Ah reckon it's best dat ever time you see one tuh snatch 'im like ah done showed ya and crush 'im dead. Sometimes ya see a bollworm or aphids. Jus' thump 'em to da groun' and stomp 'em, or rub dem aphids off an' bury 'em in da dirt. Den dey become fertilizer."

They had to do that a lot as the cotton plants grew to maturity that year. Since Johnny had gained the respect and confidence of the slaves, they were anxious to please him. They worked extra hard to bring in a healthy crop of cotton that summer of 1860. It was quite a sight to look out over the fields with the cotton bolls popped open exposing the snowy-looking crop ready for harvest. With so few workers attending so many acres of cotton fields that was quite an accomplishment. Johnny had achieved his goal of getting his Uncle Fred back on his financial feet, but he was a bit disappointed that he had no solution for the slave issue.

-0-

Johnny was planning to attend the Harvest Social Ball in Charleston the last Saturday in September, the twenty-ninth, and head home to Ohio before Christmas. The social ball was a big event as growers in the area would celebrate the end of the harvest season with fine cuisine, music, and dance.

It was a time when they would put on their finest clothes and hobnob with the elite society in the area of Charleston. The young debutants would gracefully parade themselves before the eligible bachelors of the day, putting forth their sweetest smiles and most alluring manners. It was a time of romantic charm; a simple time of horses and buggies, bonnets and bustles, hoop skirts, and ladies holding parasols to hide their fair skin from the sun. It was a time of cravats and high hats, and the age of ornate Victorian architecture. The rich would gather in grand mansions and plantation houses, and the social style of the day was one of elegance, charm, and purity. Respectable people were expected to adhere to the proper social conduct and protocol of the times, which required permission from the head of the family for courtship or marriage, and of course, the centuries old custom that all young ladies must be virgins until the wedding night. In order to ensure that no rumors to the contrary could be spread that would cause a scandal, a chaperon was provided throughout the courtship, and was nearby whenever the couple was together. Of course, everyone loved the social events because no personal chaperons were necessary in such a large public gathering, and the young ladies and men could freely engage in private or semiprivate romantic conversation. They spoke to one another in an eloquent and polite manner, regarding themselves ladies and gentlemen, and they proudly displayed their lingual charms at all garden parties and county fairs and balls where they danced waltzes. For the elite, one's dignity and pride was paramount in everything, from their manner of speaking and social standards to their possessions and lifestyle; a time when men would politely contest to the death in a duel, sometimes over the slightest affront to their dignity. Nothing accented that lifestyle more than a superb social gathering. The Charleston Harvest Social was the grandest ball of them all, and everyone looked forward to this very special occasion.

In preparation of the grand event, Aunt Elsie had gently hand-washed and pressed Johnny's frock coat and trousers and was excited to get him to the ball. With enthusiasm she said,

"Johnny, I want you to look your best so I've readied your clothes for the ball. Put them on and let's get ready to go."

Johnny thanked her and took the clothes to his bedroom to get dressed.

Aunt Elsie continued fluttering about, busying herself with getting ready like a hummingbird going after nectar. She barked orders to her husband, who was not as enthused.

"Fred, have you hitched up the carriage?" He was frustrated with her anxious attitude.

"Yes, I'm goin'. I'm goin'. Don't get in a big tizzy now. We've got plenty of time. Why are you in such a hurry to dance? You know I don't like dancin' that much."

"I just don't want to be late and miss out on things," she said, but Fred saw it differently.

"Oh, you just want to get in on the latest gossip, Elsie. I know you."

She denied it. "I do not! Just get the team hitched. Hurry now!"

Uncle Fred just laughed to himself as he went out to the barn to hitch the carriage, content he had her figured out, and getting a bit of a kick out of her excitement.

The ball truly was a time of excitement for all who attended. It was an all-day event with meals served at noon and suppertime. It was to be held at the renowned, luxurious and magnificent Magnolia Plantation along the Ashley River, owned by the affluent Drayton family originally from England. The plantation house, built in 1676, was huge and featured tall, two-story columns, with second-floor veranda-style porches all around. The home covered 15,600 square feet on three floors. The verandas alone covered forty-five hundred square feet. For years the plantation was known for its gardens of azaleas and camellias covering fifty acres, half the size of the entire property of Pleasant Acres. Aunt Elsie was anxious to get going because it was nearly a two-hour ride. Following the supper meal they would all depart to start home at twilight time.

As they were on the road they were joined by many other carriages converging on the lovely Magnolia Plantation. It was one of the most popular, and among the largest of plantations in the entire state. They passed acres and acres of cotton fields that were already harvested, and saw many fields that were still being harvested by the more than three hundred slaves that worked the eighteen-hundred acres of land, now owned by John Grimke Drayton, who inherited the estate due to a sudden death in the family, although he continued to pursue his ambition to become an ordained Episcopal minister. In addition to overseeing the plantation, he was pastor of the nearby St. Andrews Church.

They pulled their carriage into the stable area and were directed to an adjacent grassy field now filling up with carriages and buggies. Walking toward the plantation house, Johnny ignored most of the salutations and friendly conversation as many neighbors greeted one another and speculated on the events of the day. He was focused on the gracious design of the Magnolia Plantation House itself, surrounded by a variety of trees, including huge live oak trees with the very southern-looking Spanish moss lazily draping down from the branches like nature's laundry hung out to dry. It created a timeless, peaceful atmosphere. The home had a third floor primarily consisting of bedrooms above the two stories of columns and verandas, and what appeared to be a gabled square tower rising one story above the rest of the structure that gave it somewhat the look of an enchanting castle or palace.

The gracefully groomed and landscaped grounds were full of people chatting, nibbling appetizers and sipping cider. The broad lawn was dotted with men in their finest black, gray or brown suits and hats. And the women were adorned in a variety of brightly hued or pastel dresses with hoop skirts, all looking as colorful as the beds of flowers tastefully spotted about the grounds. There were cozy rockers, elegant tables, and chairs of hand-carved woods, with soft embroidered cushions aligning the shady verandas, and a ballroom of pure opulence within the plantation house.

Aunt Elsie was on the lawn trying to introduce Johnny to one of her neighboring friends. He was attempting to be polite but was totally obsessed by the appearance of a young lady on the veranda of the plantation house nearby. His head vacillated as he tried to break away gracefully.

"Here now, Johnny, I want you to meet Mrs. Brown. She's one of our neighbors. Emma, this is our nephew, John William Van Worth III."

Mrs. Brown beamed a broad smile, saying, "It's a pleasure to meet you Mr. Van Worth!"

She curtsied, holding her skirt and bowing to him. Johnny took advantage of her looking down to glance back at the veranda. He responded, "Oh, *uh* . . . Pleased to meet you too, ma'am." She was taken with Johnny's looks and complimented him, "My, aren't you a handsome one! It must run in the family, huh?" She and Aunt Elsie giggled since Fred wasn't that handsome.

Johnny looked back at the sight on the porch once more and unconsciously mumbled, "*Uh*, well . . . Thank you. You're mighty handsome yourself, ma'am. *Uh*, could you, ladies, excuse me for a moment?" Mrs. Brown was slightly flustered at his comment and his hasty exit, but when both she and Aunt Elsie quickly saw what had drawn him away, they raised their eyebrows and nodded at each other, sensing love might be in bloom.

Johnny strolled toward the second-floor veranda, his eyes fixed on a sight he'd never forget. For there at the top of the long, wide staircase stood Molly Marie Mitchell in a wine-colored hoop-skirt, the dress flowing out from her small waist like the bell of a blooming flower hanging down. Tapering up from her midriff, over her shapely breasts and shoulders was a pink satin material lined at the v-shaped neckline with a rim of fluffy white ostrich feathers. A black choker with a mother-of-pearl cameo adorned the base of her neck. The feathers fluttered in the gentle breeze highlighting her refined facial features and hazel eyes, big and warm like those of a doe, with long lashes.

Her brunette hair was piled high under a petite matching bonnet with graceful sausage curls dangling down the back of her neck. Tiny ringlets coiled from her temples just below a red rose in her hair. She had soft luscious lips breaking into a captivating smile and her eyes sparkled as she gazed at Johnny gallantly ascending the staircase with an air of confidence and authority as though he owned the place. They couldn't take their eyes off each other as they came closer and Johnny took the last step onto the porch slowly and gracefully to stand before her, staring at her beauty with a pounding in his chest like he had never experienced in all his life. He tipped his hat before removing it, and for a brief moment they were both speechless and just smiled, eyeing each other in anticipation of something new and exciting. Molly was adorable with an air of innocence and charm so casual that it appeared she was unaware of what a gorgeous thing she was for his eyes to behold. The words of the lady in the white dress momentarily echoed in his mind, *Before this year ends you will meet your dream. The moment you see this person you will know.* Yes, Johnny knew this girl truly was someone special. She was feeling the same about him. A great peace came over him and he exuded confidence and charm in his frock coat and shoulder cape.

It was a moment of pure infatuation as Johnny addressed her. "Well! I believe you may be the very person I came here to see."

Molly chuckled with delight. "Oh! And what do you want to see me about, sir?"

Without hesitation and without thinking, he said, "Well, to start with . . . I'd like to . . . see you about this lovely plantation so we can get better acquainted. I'm John William Van Worth III. And you are . . ."

She curtsied, holding her folded parasol, and said, "I'm charmed I'm sure, Mr. Van Worth."

Johnny grinned and rubbed his chin, amused she was playfully flirting with him.

"I . . . *uh* . . . I'm sure I'm charmed, too. Pleased to meet you, Miss . . . *uh* . . ."

She cooed forth, "Since you came here to see me I thought you already knew my name." Her voice was almost musical, soft and sweet with a mild southern accent. She gracefully held out her right hand, her arms clothed in long white gloves up to her elbows, and dropped her wrist for him to take her hand.

She finally admitted, "I'm Molly Mitchell. Most pleased to meet you!"

"The pleasure is mine, Miss Molly."

Johnny's smile widened as he raised her hand, bent over and gently kissed the back of it.

They were compatible and comfortable with each other right from the start. She was ten years younger than Johnny, who had turned thirty about two months before, although she acted more mature than her twenty years of age. She picked up the conversation to take him up on his offer.

"So you want the see me about the plantation? Well, I'm ready to take the tour," she said eagerly.

Johnny realized he may have been a little too bold and became a bit shy, knowing he knew little about the place, and said, "Uh, why don't we just start by walking over here by the railing." He escorted her away from her fellow debutants who were also gathered near a table full of drinks and snacks at the edge of the stairway. He put his hands on the railing and assumed a fake authoritative orator's voice as if he was some sort of expert on the architecture of the building.

"Yes, now, my dear, this is what we call your typical Magnolia Plantation hand rail, obviously made by hand . . . uh . . . for use by many hands . . . hands of the men and women who might stand here and look down upon the crowd gathered here for this grand occasion . . . on the great lawn . . . and throughout the plantation house itself." Molly could see he was just basically faking it in a jesting manner and she broke out laughing then, mocking his "Mr. Expert" tone, said, "I'm so pleased to be so well informed by someone who is so knowledgeable and uh . . ." She chuckled again and took on a more confidential tone, "Tell me the truth, sir . . . you've never been here before have you?"

"Well, to tell you the truth . . . uh . . . No! No I haven't." They lightly chuckled.

She was pleased he was so honest. "I knew you weren't. If you had, I'm sure I would have noticed a gallant gentleman such as you."

"Oh, really now?" He was pleased she seemed to be attracted to him.

She suggested, "Perhaps, I should be the one to give you a tour. But first, tell me, where are you from?"

"I came over here from my uncle's plantation, Pleasant Acres in Dorchester County. I've been more or less helping to oversee the place since last April. But I'm originally from Columbus, Ohio. That's really my home. I'll be heading back there before too long to help my dad run our family business, Van Worth and Son Hardware and Supply. Now, tell me, Molly, where do you live?"

"I live in Charleston. My family owns Mitchell's General Store and Fabric Shop. I mostly tend to the fabric part of the business along with my mama. That's what I like most about it." She stroked her hands over the hips of her hoop skirt, "I made this dress. Do you like it?"

"My dear Miss Molly, I must say . . . you're not only a skilled seamstress, but you have excellent taste as well. I'm very impressed with your work." He wanted to go on and say, "*But I'm mostly impressed with you,*" but thought she might think he was being too forward.

"Thank you, Mr. Van Worth. It's one of my favorite dresses."

Johnny was uncomfortable with formal protocol so he suggested, "Please! Just call me Johnny."

"Johnny!" She paused to consider what it would be like to call him that always and said it again.

"Johnny!" She had laughing eyes that always sparkled when she smiled. "I like that name!"

"I would prefer that you like me more than my name." She just beamed another sparkling smile. He glanced down at the white, yellow, and purple lady's slippers orchid attached above her left breast, gently stroked one of the petals, and said, "Did you make this lovely orchid too?" She softly answered, "No. I have to give God credit for that. And my daddy. He got it for me. My daddy is my escort for today. I was engaged to a man but we ended it about three weeks ago."

Her father noticed her conversing with Johnny and took his wife's arm to lead her over to where they were standing. Molly noticed them approaching and told Johnny,

"Oh! Here's my mother and father now! Daddy, Mama, I'd like to introduce you to Mr. Johnny Van Worth III. He's the overseer of the Pleasant Acres plantation. Johnny, my father, Thomas Mitchell, and my mother, Marion."

Her father was a man with a mustache and beard; had they been gray, he would have resembled a younger, somewhat shorter Robert E. Lee. He was quiet and reserved while Molly's mother was very outgoing and cheerful. Even though Johnny was from the North, there were no great feelings of irreconcilable differences relating to Northerners with the Mitchells, and they accepted Johnny because he seemed to be a respectable gentleman, and they could see both he and Molly were somewhat infatuated for the moment.

And so it went, with many introductions and light conversation as Molly and John wandered about the plantation house and the grounds that day, enjoying each other's company and getting more and more acquainted. Molly liked the fact that Johnny was lighthearted and downright funny at times as they played simple yard games while an organ grinder hired for the occasion cranked out polkas. They were often seen laughing and smiling together in the afternoon. Fred, and especially Elsie, were pleased to see it. But Molly and Johnny had their serious moments of conversing too.

When she was giving him a tour of the plantation house, they got on the subject of the three hundred slaves the Draytons owned and Molly related that the owner, John G. Drayton, had been heard affectionately referring to them as his "Black Roses."

Johnny didn't see how that was an affectionate term and said, "Black Roses? I suppose he realized it's their labors that caused his bankroll to blossom."

Molly pointed out that Mr. Drayton was an Episcopal minister and treated his slaves better than anyone in the South probably did. She added, "Can you keep a secret?" He assured her he could. "Reverend Drayton is defying State law by educating his slaves in a special schoolhouse he built for them. And of course, he teaches them all about the Bible, too."

Johnny was surprised. "I didn't know it was against the law to educate slaves. I've been teaching some of ours how to read and write, add, and subtract. Does that make me a criminal?"

Molly was sympathetic. "Of course not! Not in God's eyes anyway. And certainly not in mine." Molly admired Johnny for wanting to help the slaves, although they both agreed it would be best if there was no such thing as enslaving people of any race. However, she warned Johnny to keep his sentiments quiet because John Drayton's two aunts, Angelena and Sarah, had been officially banished from South Carolina for being notorious abolitionists.

But most of their time spent together was light and happy. They danced waltzes in the plantation ballroom and Johnny loved holding her hands and moving around the ballroom floor even though he really didn't know how to dance when they started. She took him aside to teach him. And even though Johnny's clumsiness led to a few "accidents" on the dance floor, they enjoyed themselves immensely.

Their infatuation was quickly blooming into a dreamy romance. All told, this was the most enjoyable day in Johnny's life. And when he told that to Molly she agreed it was the same with her. It was a beautiful day, mostly sunny with gentle breezes and a high temperature of seventy-four degrees. There was only one cloudy moment, when in the afternoon a small shower sprinkled the grounds for only about five minutes. And even that they enjoyed, letting the light droplets of water momentarily wet their faces, then laughing joyously while scurrying for shelter under the verandas.

But as the day went toward evening a darker moment arose to cloud the atmosphere of the party. Molly's recent partner in courtship, Louis B. Madden, showed up and had been talking with many of the gentlemen, who were of the growing political opinion that, in order to save the Southern lifestyle to which they had become accustomed, it was necessary for South Carolina to secede from the Union.

Billy Bob Walker was one of Madden's closest friends and addressed him. "Louis! Ah was wonderin' when you were gonna get heah. Whut occupied ya suh long?"

"Ah was attendin' a gentleman's meetin' in Charleston," said Louis. "We were speculatin' it's verah likely that the State legislature will vote beforah the year's ovah tuh secede from the Union," he gloated with a proud smirk.

Billy Bob nearly jumped off the ground with excitement, responding, "Oh, ah sure hope so! Ah cain't wait. We don't need no gov'ment in Washin'ton pushin' therah foolhardy ideas off on us." Then he noticed Louis Madden was already holding a glass of cider. "Ah'll drink tuh that!" They clinked their glasses in a toast and laughed. As the laughter died out, Madden turned and noticed Molly walking along with John. He just stared at them and his countenance turned mean as he gritted his teeth. It had only been about three weeks since he and Molly had broken their engagement. Billy Bob saw Madden's concerned face and quickly informed him, "Ah, uh . . . ah suppose you're noticin' your former fiancée didn't waste any time gettin' herse'f another beau."

"Yeah!" said Madden. "Who's that escourtin' her around. Ah've nevah seen that gentleman beforah."

"Ya ain't gonna like whut ah've got tuh tell ya," said Walker.

When Madden was told his former fiancée was seen being escorted about the grounds all afternoon with a man from the North, he became jealous and furious. After two hours of drinking and growing more and more angry, he worked his way to where Molly and Johnny were standing on the lawn.

"Hello, Miss Molly. Ah hope it's not too late fo' us to make amends." Molly was disgusted but unshaken, and she looked at him with disdain, and then at Johnny, took a deep breath, and said, "Mr. Madden, if it's not too impolite of me to do so, I must say this is not the proper time or place to be discussing a matter that I thought I clearly indicated was over. Now if you'll excuse me!"

As she hooked her arm around Johnny's and they turned to walk away, Mr. Madden said, "Oh, so ah'm not good 'nuff fo' ya, huh? But this stinkin' Yankee heah is! Is that wherah it stands?"

They continued walking away to avoid making a scene and Johnny sarcastically whispered to Molly,

"Who is this . . . uh . . . 'gentlemanly' fellow?" Molly was ashamed to admit it and whispered,

"I'm sorry to say he's my former fiancé. I believe he's had too much of the hard cider today." Mr. Madden, who was twenty-four years old, relatively handsome, tall and thin with sandy blond-colored hair and a Van Dyke beard, continued his verbal badgering as his friends gathered around.

"Don't you walk away from me you yella-bellied Yankee coward." Johnny froze in his tracks, gritted his teeth with his eyes winced, took a deep breath and slowly turned around, gently pulled Molly's arm away and with deliberate measured steps walked back to face his false accuser.

"I'm going to assume you've had too much hard cider so you're probably too drunk to realize what you just said, sir. So, as for me, I'm going to excuse your inebriate behavior. But I believe you owe the lady and everyone standing here an apology for ruining a perfectly grand occasion." Johnny's words meant nothing to Mr. Madden who was very jealous and determined to pick a fight.

"How dare you! A filthy Yankee demandin' an apology of a fine Southern gentleman. You have greatly insulted mah honor, suh! Ah demand satisfaction. Ah challenge you to a duel this very day! Choose your weapons, suh!"

Johnny lowered his head and snickered while Molly tugged at his arm. "Don't do it, Johnny! He's delirious. Let's go!" Johnny ignored her to face up to the challenge. "Choose the weapons? All right, in order to duel with you I think . . . uh . . . wet noodles at two paces would do. I'll flog you to death with it." Molly and a few bystanders appreciated Johnny having the courage and wisdom to make light of the situation and they started to laugh. This infuriated Mr. Madden even more. "Choose your weapons like a man, suh, or fo'evah be branded a coward," came his surly reply. Some of Madden's friends started agreeing and egging Johnny on saying, "Yeah. That's right. Let's get some duelin' pistols!" Johnny started to get defensive and pulled a small pistol from his inside coat pocket. Madden ducked a little thinking Johnny was getting ready to use it on him. "That won't be necessary, I have a weapon. Do you have a pistol, Mister . . . *uh* . . ." Johnny suddenly realized he was about to engage in a duel with a man and didn't even know his name. "This is ridiculous, I don't even know your name." Madden snarled back, "It doesn't mattah. Ah know yours . . . Dirty Yankee Coward! And yes, ah have a pistol."

That was enough for Johnny. He was determined to take this fool on just to shut his surly mouth. One of Madden's supporters yelled, "Let's go down behind the carriage house."

As word of a possible duel involving their nephew was quickly spreading across the grounds, Elsie and Fred ran toward the plantation house to get Reverend Drayton. They knew the minister wouldn't stand for having a duel on his property. It took a few minutes to locate him but it seemed like a month. Fred was now getting anxious and left her to go see what he could do to stop a tragedy. But he knew it wouldn't be easy. The popular myth about duels in this age was that a man's honor was on the line and that by submitting to a duel the men were putting their lives in the hands of the spiritual forces of good and evil and they believed the outcome to be the will of Divine Providence. Elsie found the reverend talking to Molly's parents. When she blurted out the news, they quickly ran out of the house to where Master Drayton's buggy and horse were tied up. The two men quickly untied the horse, jumped in, and headed toward the rear of the carriage house, with Molly's mother and Aunt Elsie running out of the house on foot, scurrying after them.

Rounding the carriage house, they were horrified to see that the pacing off had already started and Molly was running out of the crowd and in between the two men, right in the line of fire, yelling, "I won't let this happen. I won't!" Men were yelling and the few women who had joined the crowd out of curiosity were screaming. Molly's father cried out, "Oh my god! Molly! Molly! No!"

Billy Bob Walker could barely be heard continuing the count as Madden and Johnny were reaching the point where they would turn and fire. "Sixteen! Seventeen! Eighteen!"

Reverend Drayton stood up in the buggy and yelled at the top of his lungs, "Stop! I won't have this sin upon my property!" But it was too late, the twentieth count had already been sounded. The two men quickly turned to fire, both of them shocked that Molly was halfway between them defiantly facing Madden with her fists on her hips and was blocking their line of fire.

Johnny yelled, "Molly get down!"

Madden fired a shot over Molly's head and shouted, "This is a disgrace to mah honor!"

Molly's father raced to the side of his daughter.

Molly yelled, "You're the disgrace Louie Madden. I'm glad I'm no longer your betrothed!"

Johnny was coming up behind her.

Reverend Drayton yelled out in a mighty voice, "I won't have this and I mean it! Put your weapons down now!"

Johnny slipped his pistol back in his coat and put his arm around Molly as he and Molly's father escorted her back to the crowd.

Madden continued to rave, "What a disgrace! You've hurt mah honor, woman!" Then he directed his rage at Johnny pointing his finger at him. "And you! You Yankee coward, hidin' behind a woman's skirt! Hold that woman aside. Ah want the count tuh begin all ovah."

Reverend Drayton pulled his buggy closer to Madden, still standing up in it. He looked down, pointed his finger at him, and orated the power of the word with righteous anger, in a loud voice.

"Sir, there is no honor to a duel. Don't be deceived. It's not your honor that is hurting. It's your *pride!* Don't you know it was pride that got Lucifer thrown out of heaven and cast down to earth? Self pride isn't a virtue. It's a *sin!* The very chalice for arrogance, hatred, rebellion, and violence. Just as God swiftly cast Lucifer from heaven, I cast you off my property! Sir, you are not welcome here unless you repent of your iniquitous ways. You are hereby trespassing. Now put that gun away and leave here immediately!"

Madden looked disgruntled and embarrassed by the truth of Reverend Drayton's words, and he reluctantly and cockily holstered his gun and walked away, huffing and puffing, cursing under his breath. Then he turned around and raised his fist, yelling at Johnny, "You haven't seen the last of me! This Southern gentleman will not be disgraced!"

Molly yelled back, "You're no gentleman, Louie Madden!"

He shook his fist at her, saying, "We'll see!"

Molly thrust her arms around Johnny and hugged him with all her might, hoping he would not lose his interest in her over Louis B. Madden. Johnny felt good with them holding each other and he kissed her cheek as she returned the sweet gesture. They stood there cheek to cheek for a long moment, gently rocking from side to side, until Molly's mother, Marion, tapped them to signify they may be seen as too cozy for having just met, not wanting to give people too much reason to gossip.

But gossip they did because it was just too much of an incident to forget, and people were curious as to how it was going to turn out. Johnny was smitten with Molly. He saw her not only as beautiful and charming, but exceptionally brave to assert herself in the middle of a duel the way she had. Johnny thought, *I was of the opinion I was the brave one protecting her, but she showed even more courage than I did.* He further wondered, *Did she do it because she was angry with Louis Madden or infatuated with me, or both?*

One thing for sure, he decided he wasn't going home to Ohio until he knew for certain. So he planned to find ways to be near her and see what her true feelings were, and perhaps to eventually ask her father's permission to formally start a courtship. Earlier that day she had related how her faith in God was very important to her, and told him where the quaint little church that she attended in Charleston was located. Tomorrow was Sunday. Even though Johnny wasn't as deeply religious as Molly, he planned to be there.

❋Chapter 3❋

COURTING DISASTER

"**D**early beloved, avenge not yourselves, but *rather* give place unto wrath; for it is written, vengeance is mine; I will repay, saith the Lord." These words being read from the Bible by Molly's pastor, Matthew Collins, caused Johnny to wonder about this whole triangle involving Molly, Louis Madden, and himself. Was Madden seeking revenge? Johnny thought, *I'm not. I just want Madden out of the picture.* Pastor Collins continued reading from the book of Romans. "Therefore if thine enemy hunger, feed him; if he thirst, give him drink: for in so doing thou shalt heap coals of fire upon his head. Be not overcome of evil, but overcome evil with good."

Johnny was there mostly to see Molly, but he couldn't help but wonder if the sermon was somehow being directed at him. He had gotten there a little late and took a seat where he could see Molly and the rest of her family. Her younger brother Kent was with them. Molly was pleased to see Johnny and they were trying not to be too obvious and disruptive as they constantly exchanged glances and smiles at one another.

After the service, they all met and greeted one another, exiting in the center aisle as they filed out of the quaint little church, with architecture so typical of the times—a pulpit with a stained glass window on the back wall behind it, and an upright piano off to one side. Two sections of pews for seating only about one hundred parishioners were situated on either side of a four-foot-wide center aisle. Three-foot-wide aisles lined the outside walls with large windows arching to a point at the top.

Molly's father was the first to greet Johnny. He shook his hand and said, "It's good to see you in church, Mr. Van Worth, especially after yesterday."

Johnny replied, "It's good to be here, sir." Molly's mother, Marion, chimed in, "Did you enjoy the sermon, Mr. Van Worth?"

"Uh . . . yes. Yes, ma'am, I did. Especially the part about overcoming evil with good. That was something my mother taught me when I was just a young lad." Marion smiled pleasantly as she told him, "Your mother taught you well."

"Yes, ma'am, she's a good lady."

"I'm sure she is," she said as she took her husband's arm, slowly shuffling toward the exit. During the conversation, Johnny kept glancing between Marion and her daughter, as Molly was entering the aisle. He dropped back to walk beside her and they gazed adoringly at one another, but felt awkward, remembering the dueling event of the day before. She spoke first. "Good morning, mister . . . oh! I mean . . . Johnny. And what brings you here?"

"Good morning, Miss Molly. Oh, I think you know." Molly beamed her magical smile that captivated Johnny's heart. Her eyes were radiating sparkles of delight as she held her hand out so he could take it. Then she introduced her twelve-year-old brother Kent who tended the store and missed all of the activity of the previous day.

"Oh! Johnny this is my brother, Kent. Kent, this is Johnny Van Worth." Kent eagerly said, "How do you do, sir. Are you the one who was in the duel yesterday?" Molly put a forefinger to her lips and shushed him.

They walked out through the church's small vestibule, topped with a bell tower and steeple. Johnny escorted Molly a few yards away from the crowd and was inquisitive about her feelings, but didn't quite know how to approach the subject. Then seeing how everyone was noticing them, he realized this was not a good time or place, and was pleased when she began speaking.

"Did you ride all the way here just to go to church?"

"Oh, Miss Molly. I can't lie about church now, can I? I have to admit *you* are the reason I got up at the crack of dawn and made a two-hour trip in Uncle Fred's carriage to be here."

"Oh my goodness! You'll be starved by the time you get home. Won't you eat with us before you head back? I'm sure Mother and Daddy won't mind. I'll ask them."

"Well, I wouldn't want to impose," he said. Molly assured him, "It's no imposition. Come with me." She walked him to where her parents were standing, explained the situation, and they agreed he could join them. Johnny feigned a humble reluctance to the notion, in order to make sure he was welcome, and was pleased at how happy they were to have him as a guest. Molly's father concluded the invitation with a mildly sarcastic jest, "I suppose it's only proper. How could we refuse since you were both willing to die for each other yesterday?" They had mixed feelings and were both a little embarrassed and pleased by his comment.

Molly helped her mother and their maid, Nicole, prepare the meal while Mr. Mitchell talked about business and politics to get better acquainted with Johnny. Following the meal, the Mitchell family chatted with Johnny at the table for a while, telling him more about their family background. Mr. Mitchell was relatively quiet and reserved while his wife Marion was a very spunky, lively, and outgoing personality. She was a well-educated yet down-to-earth lady with a lot of common sense. She wasn't quite as prone to always endorsing the formal social decorum of language of the times as other ladies of the South. She was full of energy and her speech was slightly loud, but emitted a very happy-go-lucky tone. "Tell me now, Mr. Van Worth, would you care for more green beans or mashed potatoes?" "Oh! No, thank you, ma'am. Everything was quite delicious, but I don't think I can eat another bite. I don't want to be too much of a load for the horse to tote back to Pleasant Acres," he said with a dry wit. They all laughed, especially Molly's bother Kent. Mrs. Mitchell howled back, "Now that's the kind of man I like, one with a sense of humor . . . like me." Mr. Mitchell gave her an inquisitive look. "Marion, I didn't know you had a sense of humor."

She quickly retorted, "I would offer Mr. Van Worth some noodles but I'm saving them to sell as dueling weapons." They all laughed again.

In a jesting confidential tone, Mr. Mitchell leaned toward Johnny, and said, "She's not always this funny. I think your humor is rubbing off on her." Marion just ignored him, saying, "Would you care for some desert, Mr. Van Worth? We have some delicious peach cobbler. Molly made it herself." Even though Johnny was full, he couldn't refuse cuisine prepared by his adorable Molly.

"Well, I can't say no to that, can I?" He turned to Molly who was pleasantly smiling at him.

"Did you bake the cobbler?" She was being very quiet and just humbly shook her head, "Yes."

In the course of the conversation that followed, Johnny discovered the Mitchell family was of English descent; however, there was a bit of Cherokee Indian blood on Molly's mother's side. Johnny thought that might be where Molly got those long dark eyelashes. They learned Johnny was of English and Irish descent. Both the Mitchells and the Van Worths were well-off financially through their successful businesses. They weren't hurting for much and could be classed as on the lower side of the upper crust of society. Not "filthy" rich, just a little "soiled" around the edges, as

Johnny once put it when asked. They had most of the necessities and a few of the luxuries that the era provided. Eventually they excused themselves from the table and Marion excused her daughter from helping to clean up after the meal, knowing Molly and Johnny wanted some time together before he had to leave. They had things to talk over that couldn't be mentioned at the dinner table. Molly was quiet after dinner as she was wondering about how to approach Johnny and what he might be thinking about her relationship with Louis B. Madden.

The day before, following the dueling incident, everyone had left rather rapidly and both of them had questions on their minds. His curiosity about her former fiancé was piqued as they entered the cozy living room which was well decorated with elegant draperies, ornate wallpaper, carved wood moldings, and French provincial furniture. It was a romantic setting. They sat on the love seat and Molly brought up the subject first.

"I'm sorry about yesterday. I must apologize for Mr. Madden's behavior. He wasn't always that way or I never would have agreed to him courting me."

"Please, my dear Molly, you surely don't need to apologize for his actions," Johnny replied. "How long were you betrothed to him and why did you break it off?" Molly responded, "He gave me the ring the first of August. He was so nice back then, but it seems that when he thought he had me hooked, he began to change. Or maybe it was because he got involved with politics . . . talking about South Carolina needing to secede from the Union. I don't know. He just became so filled with hatred and a penchant for violence it started to scare me. Then he began to take me for granted and not show as much interest in me . . . not showing up when he said he was going to because some political meeting was more important to him. I just got the feeling it would get worse and worse if we got married. And when I told him I didn't want to marry him, he showed me the kind of anger that made me realize I had made the right decision."

Johnny was satisfied she was sincere but he still wanted to know if she ran in between them during the duel because she hated Madden or had feelings for him. So he said, "You must have loved him at one time. Did your love turn to hate? Is that why you ran between us, because you hate him?" She began to get more emotional, fearing Johnny had the wrong idea about her.

"Oh, Johnny, no! I don't hate him. I pity him. I hated what he was about to do."

"You mean duel with me?" Johnny said hastily.

"I mean wanting to kill you out of jealousy because he thought I was falling in love with you." Johnny replied, "Were you? Were you falling in love with me yesterday?" He hoped with all his heart she was. To encourage it he said, "Because, to tell you the truth . . . I . . . uh . . . I fell in love with you."

"Oh, Johnny. Don't say that. It's too soon. I believe we're definitely infatuated with each other. But love is something that goes beyond physical attractions. Love is very special, something deep in one's soul. It's caring for someone else more than yourself. It's being committed no matter what . . . for better or worse . . . for richer or poorer . . . till death do us part. Is that the way you feel about me?"

"Miss Molly, I want you to know that . . . I believe our meeting yesterday was something very special. And . . . I'm hoping you feel the same way."

She quickly and eagerly responded, "Oh, I do. I most certainly do. You're very special to me. But is it a match made in heaven? Will it last? Will you begin to change on me too?"

"I've courted several ladies and I've never met anyone as heavenly as you, Molly. Ever since I met you I've had a special feeling I can't explain." Tears started to well up in her eyes and she threw her arms around him. "Oh, Johnny, I have the same special feeling about you . . . I've been fighting it because of what I've been through with my previous betrothal. But yes, from the moment I saw you coming up those stairs, I had a special feeling about you . . . like I've known you all my life. Johnny, I feel as though we've been called into each others arms for a reason. Tell me it's real. Tell me I'm not dreaming. Tell me it won't turn sour like my last affair."

"Oh, Molly, may I court you? It's the only way to know for sure. I believe true love will stand the test of time. Don't you?" She quickly responded, "Yes. You're right. It's the only way to know. Go ask my father's permission now . . . before you have to leave."

They arose and embraced each other with enthusiasm before ending it by kissing each other's cheeks. It was an age of conservative manners and passionate kissing was reserved for a time of commitment to marriage. But they were already feeling the urge, for their attraction was like a strong magnet drawing them together. Molly took Johnny by the hand and led him to her father's den, where he was reading. She knocked on the door and scurried toward the kitchen where her mother was cleaning up from the meal. She told her mother, "Johnny's asking Daddy's permission to court me."

"Oh! So Soon?" said Marion. She and her mother embraced.

Meanwhile, Mr. Mitchell answered the knock by opening the door to see Johnny standing there with a dreamy look on his face. He knew what he wanted. "Do you want to see me, Mr. Van Worth?"

"Yes, sir. I know it's a little soon for me to be asking, but my heart won't rest until I do. May I have the honor, sir, of courting your daughter?"

Mr. Mitchell smiled and said, "Come on in, Mr. Van Worth." He continued to talk as they moved past a wall of bookshelves filled with literary classics of the time. "Have a seat, son!" Johnny was pleased to hear Mr. Mitchell call him "son." It was as though Molly's father had already been thinking about having him as a son-in-law someday. They sat down on firm-cushioned high-back chairs as Johnny eagerly and somewhat nervously awaited an answer. Mr. Mitchell was a very reserved and businesslike gentleman who got to the point of conversations quickly. With a mild and dignified southern accent he said, "Mr. Van Worth, I appreciate the fact you're a gentleman from a respectable family, but you and Molly have been acquainted for only two days, and my first inclination is that it's much too early to be considerin' courtship." Johnny's heart sank to his toes. He was afraid Mr. Mitchell may have been persuaded to think less highly of him because of the dueling incident. Johnny's masculine outward appearance was frozen, concealing the emotional seesaw within him.

He was acting cool while hanging intensely on Mr. Mitchell's every word as he said, "I hope you realize this is not a good time to be courtin' Molly. It could be dangerous with that 'Madden the madman' so jealously prowlin' about in a state of wounded respect." Johnny agreed. "Yessir, I know. But I can't let that stop me. I think very highly of Miss Molly. She's worth the risk. And I can't blame Mr. Madden for being jealous. Molly's such a special girl, I'd hate to lose her love, too." Her father responded, "I don't think Mr. Madden loved her. I think he was proud to own her. I must warn you. A man may love her, but he can't own her. Molly isn't like most girls. She's headstrong . . . an independent thinker. She was quite a tomboy growin' up. Didn't get interested in feminine things 'til she started workin' in the fabric shop at the store with her mother." Johnny said, "I think I like her because she *is* different. It's a difference I can appreciate." Mr. Mitchell squinted and leaned forward to say, "I know there's appreciation. I've seen how you look at one another, but just the same I believe we should wait at least a couple more weeks to see if that appreciation is still growing or if it will fade away. In the meantime, you can join us for worship at church and I'm sure Marion won't mind if you join us for Sunday dinner as well." It was Mr. Mitchell's way of allowing them to be together without formal permission so they could put their young love to the test. Johnny was there for the next three Sundays, but the wait through each week was hard and their longing for one another only intensified. The only fault he found with her was that her insanely jealous former fiancé may appear at any moment to spoil the day.

-0-

Johnny's interest in Molly hadn't gone unnoticed, and one morning at the breakfast table his Uncle Fred asked, "You've been seeing a lot of that Mitchell girl haven't you?" Attempting to be casual about it, Johnny at first tried to act as though it was nothing special. "Oh, *uh* . . . you mean Molly?" Uncle Fred grunted, "Uh-huh!" in such a way Johnny knew there was no use in trying to hide his interest in her and he freely relented, "*Uh* . . . Well, yes, sir, Uncle Fred, I have. I've never met anyone like her before." He stared off, his eyes glassed over, daydreaming about her. Elsie winked at Fred and said, "She's a lovely young lady . . . and from a very respectable family, I must say!" She softly inquired, "Are you going to see her again at her church this Sunday?" Johnny wasn't at ease with being too open about his love life. After all, his parents made him too self-conscious about previous romances.

"Well, *uh* . . . yes, Aunt Elsie . . . I'm thinking about it . . . weather permitting. You don't object, do you? Aunt Elsie was quick to respond, "By all means go ahead. You have my permission. And if you start courting her, Fred and I will be your chaperones. Won't we, Fred?" Fred cleared his throat. "*Uh hmm*! Now, don't go rushing things Elsie. There are things for John to do around here yet." He leaned toward Johnny with a man-to-man confidential tone in his voice. "I

have one chore I'd like for you to finish before the cooler
weather sets in. Termites have made too much of a meal of
the outhouse. Tomorrow I'd like for you and that young
slave Jay to rebuild it with new boards from the lumber pile
out back." Johnny answered, "Sure thing, Uncle Fred. I'll
take care of it."

The next morning, after breakfast Johnny struck out to
the slave quarters to get Jay Brown to help with the project.
They began pulling out boards they could use from the wood
pile which was behind the barn, and didn't see Uncle Fred
stroll down the path to the outhouse. While back by the
barn, Johnny suggested they could have a little fun and get
the old shack out of the way by running toward it carrying a
few boards and throwing their weight against it to topple it
over.

So they started running at full speed and took a flying
leap into the old pile of lumber and flipped it over, much to
the chagrin, yelps, and screams of uncle Fred who was inside
unbeknownst to them. Realizing their folly, Johnny kept
running into the nearby woods. But Jay just stood there in
shock, looking at the outhouse lying on it's backside with
Fred on his backside inside. Fred moaned, pushed the door
up and it flapped over with a loud clatter. He climbed out,
attempting to pull his trousers and suspenders up at the
same time. He looked at Jay and shouted at the top of his
lungs causing his voice to crack, "What the hell did you do
that for?"

Poor Jay was so upset to think Uncle Fred thought he
did it on purpose he could hardly talk. He kept trying to
explain but fell feeble before Fred's rage saying, "Ah's sorry!"
He kept repeating,

"Ah's maghty sorry, Massa Fred! Maghty sorry!"

About that time Johnny saw the need to get control of
his laughter and he came walking nonchalantly out of the
woods. Uncle Fred looked over at Johnny and barked out at
him.

"Did you see what this wild savage did to me?" Johnny acted surprised and casually said, "Oh, you mean you were in there just now?" John started to snicker. Uncle Fred stamped his foot and belted out, "It ain't funny by damn, I coulda been hurt real bad! We've gotta teach him a lesson!" Johnny tried to console Uncle Fred, whose face was red with anger. "I'm sure he didn't realize you were in—" Uncle Fred interrupted him in a fit of anger like Johnny had never seen from his uncle.

"I don't care! He needs to be taught a lesson! You take my whip and give him some lashes!"

Johnny was beside himself because he knew this was the first time anything like that had ever been ordered by his Uncle Fred. He thought for a second and came up with a scheme he thought might work. He explained to Uncle Fred that he would take Jay over in the woods so the women folk wouldn't be upset, especially Aunt Elsie. She was a sensitive lady who abhorred violence. Johnny got Jay over in the woods, out of sight behind some brier bushes, and whispered,

"When I whip this tree you scream bloody murder." Each time Johnny smacked the tree Jay yelled such things as, "Oh, Lawsy, Mistah Johnny, don't whup me so hard!" and "Ah won't do it ag'in. Ah promise!" and "Aaah! Hep! Hep!"

His Uncle Fred was never the wiser over the incident. Jay appreciated John's kind scheme, but even more so, Johnny appreciated the fact that Jay never revealed tipping the outhouse was John's idea. From that day on there was a bond of friendship between them.

It was mid-October when Johnny again asked to court Molly. This time Mr. Mitchell said,

"In the light of sound judgment it would not be wise to hold apart two people who seem to be so strongly attracted to one another. I believe Molly needs you at this time. Knowin' how headstrong she is, no tellin' what she'd do if I refused. Therefore, I grant you permission to court my daughter." Johnny's heart started racing. "Oh, thank you,

Mr. Mitchell." He stood up and shook her father's hand vigorously. Mr. Mitchell again warned Johnny. "I'm still uneasy about your safety and hers after the threats Mr. Madden made at Magnolia Plantation."

Johnny suggested for a while perhaps they could spend time together at Pleasant Acres and his Aunt Elsie and Uncle Fred would be their chaperons. So Molly was transported in the family coach to spend the day at the farm for the next few weekends, with her whole family accompanying her on those trips. The Van Worths entertained them as guests, preparing special snacks and treats for the occasion. Everyone in both families enjoyed those early days of the couple's courting. Sometimes they would take short carriage rides on the property or go horseback riding. John and Molly would sit in the swing on the porch and talk of many things and sing songs together. Occasionally Kent delighted in getting a little too close to listen in and tease his older sister.

Molly would often have to shoo him away from their private conversations, but she related to Johnny how much she loved her little brother and had helped her mother raise him, right down to changing his diapers as a baby. She told Johnny how much she loved children in general and longed to have some of her own. Johnny wasn't as interested at first, but Molly planted ideas in his head to bring him around to her way of thinking. She said, "Johnny . . . wouldn't you like to have a little boy that is just like a little you? You could show him things and teach him things and go fishing together. Wouldn't that be fun?"

The more he thought about it the more he liked the idea of having children.

During these early romantic courting days they shared many stories. Johnny told Molly about the lady in the white dress, saying he wasn't sure whether or not she was real or if he had just dreamed her. At any rate, her predictions seemed to be coming true. He did meet the dream of his life and he told Molly he was sure that was her. He entered into a conflict not of his own choosing with Louis Madden. And it seemed Jay was so loyal, his friendship might last a lifetime after Johnny's kind act of not really beating him. Jay enjoyed seeing Johnny and Molly so happy together in courtship.

Of course, Johnny was always doing things to make Molly laugh or smile. But there was one story that Molly told that had Johnny belly laughing for a change. She said, "Promise me you won't repeat this to anyone." Of course, that always gets a man's attention.

"I promise," said John.

"About two years ago, when our preacher, Pastor Collins, first came to the church, he couldn't remember everyone's name correctly. We had a deacon back then named Harold Butts and Pastor Collins kept calling him Harry." Johnny laughed hardily, "Oh no." Molly said, "But . . . there's more. One day Harold came into church with two ladies he invited as guests. We had just finished a song and Pastor Collins noticed Harold and the ladies entering and wanted to welcome them and have Harold introduce them to everyone. He blurted out without thinking, 'Well, what do we have here? Who are these lovely ladies with Harry Butts?'" Johnny doubled over with laughter as she went on laughing herself to tell him, "Everyone was stony quiet for a moment or two, and then someone snickered and the whole congregation erupted with laughter." Johnny continued to laugh. Molly was on a roll, saying, "That was the last time he referred to Harold as Harry." Johnny was holding his belly by then. Even though the story was very risqué for the times, the fact that Molly was willing to confide in him to tell it was an indication to Johnny that she trusted him, and their relationship was moving from formal to a more personal one.

And so it went those few weeks in late October and November, with Johnny and Molly enjoying each other and everyone else having a good time too. In November they paid little attention to Abraham Lincoln of Illinois being elected president of the United States. Johnny had his mind on other things and began to list in his mind many reasons why he loved Molly. She was down to earth, humble, honest, straightforward, devoted, affectionate, and had a good sense of humor. She was fun to be near and had strong faith. Her vivacious personality sparkled through her happy mouth and laughing eyes. Being together created a dreamy atmosphere for both Molly and Johnny, but as the cooler months came, the rains also came and interfered with their courtship. Travel was becoming difficult as the roads turned muddy and the burden of courting fell entirely on Johnny as he had to get through the twelve miles to Molly's place in Charleston. He wasn't able to spend every Sunday with her because of weather and bad road conditions; however, they did have a joyful Christmas in spite of a dark shadow falling on South Carolina just five days earlier. The state legislature had given Louis Madden his Christmas wish. They voted to make South Carolina the first state to secede from the Union, December 20, 1860.

It should have been a time of "peace on earth and good will toward men," but there was a spirit of resentment, hatred, and rebellion in the air. To Molly and Johnny, it was only politics and nothing had really changed—at least not yet. They were determined to keep a feeling of peace in their hearts and enjoy the Christmas holiday. They were at peace in their souls, hoping it would last forever. But when spring arrived in 1861, something happened that changed everything.

-0-

There was an eerie sense of calm on the tiny island in Charleston Bay; the Stars and Stripes gently waving in the cool early morning spring air of the South Carolina night sky. But the peace and silence was suddenly broken by a commanding Southern voice yelling out to the battery of cannons along the Charleston shore. "Fire!" It was the command of Confederate general Pierre G. T. Beauregard, proudly ordering cannon fire on Fort Sumter.

The birds flew from their nests, startled by the sound and flash of firing weapons. The clean fresh air was suddenly filled with the smell of exploding gun powder—fouled with the stench of men at war. It was the morning of April 12, 1861. Three days later, President Abraham Lincoln issued a military call to arms and the American Civil War officially began.

Of course, Louis B. Madden was already a member of the militia and eventually traveled north to become part of Confederate forces on the front lines of battle in Virginia. Johnny and Molly were relieved and thought it might be the last of him interfering with their relationship. Now they could go on courting without any fear of him being a threat to a wonderful romance—or so they thought.

At the outbreak of war, many of the customers that patronized Mitchell's General Store and Fabric Shop were buying up war-related supplies and urging Mr. Mitchell to join the rebels in their fight to keep the Yankees out. He sold out of gunpowder and gray cloth right away. They convinced him it was his duty to join up and that the war would be over in a few weeks. He left his wife, daughter, and young son to manage the store, and joined a group that eventually became part of Gen. "Stonewall" Jackson's command. He would later say giving in to their pressuring him was the biggest mistake of his life because the weeks turned into months and the months turned into years. It was as if a dark and evil cloud hung over the nation.

The war wasn't the only tragedy of the times. It struck again in March of 1862 when Johnny's Uncle Fred died of a sudden heart attack. It was a sad time, especially for Aunt Elsie. She was a weak and frail woman who relied on Fred for everything. Now she would have to rely on Johnny and the slaves. Her nearest neighbors Kathryn and her husband, William Brown, were there for her too. At the funeral, Mrs. Brown was very sincere and meant every word of it when she said, "Dear Elsie, Bill and I will help you in any way we can. You can come and stay with us if things get to be too pressing for you here. We'll share what we have with you, honey. Just don't worry about a thing. Everything will be all right." Elsie leaned her head on Kathryn's shoulders and bawled her eyes out. She was saddened by her husband's death, but she cried tears of joy at seeing how people were so sincerely comforting her in this terrible moment. Molly's mother told her, "We'll try to ride out here and see you as often as we can, Elsie. You know, with Molly and Johnny courting and all. It will be a real pleasure. I'll bring you some of Nicole's dishes. She's our maid, you know, and she's a wonderful cook." Molly did her best to console Elsie as well. "I love you, dear, because you're *my* Aunt Elsie too," she said. "We're all like one family."

"That's right!" said Johnny. "As soon as we can arrange it, I'm going to make Molly a Van Worth. Just as soon as the war's over and her daddy comes home." His Aunt Elsie's face blossomed into a sweet smile upon hearing this and she expressed pleasure in the thought. "You young lovers are like a breath of fresh air to me. I don't know what I'd do without you."

A few weeks after Uncle Fred's death, Johnny approached his Aunt Elsie about giving the young slave Jay Brown his freedom. She had no comprehension of whether or not she should. She just trusted in Johnny's judgment and wasn't in favor of slavery anyway. But Jay didn't want to leave his friend Johnny, and didn't know where to go, afraid others in the South might hold him as a runaway and would simply enslave him again if he fell into the company of the wrong people. So he stayed on at Pleasant Acres, paving the way for the rest of the Van Worth slaves to be freed because Johnny polled them and found most of them would stay on the farm also if freed. However, Jethro and his family left in search of his mother and sister.

-0-

By 1863, Molly wanted her father to be home for her wedding. She kept thinking the war would soon end and he would be coming home, but after nearly two years she was getting impatient. She had Johnny write to her father and ask for his permission for them to marry. They planned to get married in June that year, but those plans went awry when Louis Madden got wind of it through a letter from Billy Bob Walker, who was still stationed at the home front in Charleston. Madden was also under Jackson's command. He and his friend, Billy Bob Walker, who had called the count at the duel, plotted to have Johnny drafted into the Confederacy.

The Confederate draft act was passed in 1862 and had been in effect for about a year. Their sinister plan concluded that if Johnny tried to escape, he could be shot as a deserter. So Billy Bob faked up draft papers and got them in the hands of Confederate recruiters.

On a Saturday in late April of 1863, Johnny brought Jay with him to Charleston to help the Mitchells get some supplies unloaded for the store. They shut the store down early, and late that afternoon Johnny was sitting with Molly on her front porch, conversing with her, while Jay waited in the carriage on the street.

Unaware that what they were doing was part of an iniquitous plot, two Confederate officers were just carrying out orders when they walked up and served draft papers to Johnny. He tried to resist, but one of them pulled a pistol and held it to his chin as they literally dragged him away by the arms, with Molly hanging on to his legs. They even dragged her several feet before they noticed her. One officer said, "*Whoa*, ma'am! We're sorry. The draft only applies to

men. Ladies are exempted." Molly was furious they treated
Johnny that way. He was needed to run the farm and help
out at the store, and of course, she wanted him close to
home for more personal reasons. She was angry with herself,
too, for losing her calm and getting her dress dirty and
tattered, but Johnny admired her all the more, seeing how
much she loved him. Jay also joined in the fray. He couldn't
believe what was happening. Jay knew he was powerless to
stop Johnny from being drafted, but he also knew he couldn't
be separated from the man who had set him free.

He told the Confederate soldiers he was Johnny's slave
and would have to go with him. Johnny insisted Jay was
his valet. The soldiers figured the Confederacy could use
every fighting man they could get and carted them both
away.

By the latter part of June, Molly and Johnny had been
apart about three months and the only communication they
had was the few letters they could exchange. Often, the
letters traveled slowly with the sometimes undependable
wartime mail service. They were discovering that absence
really does make the heart grow fonder. Johnny daydreamed
about her often as he wandered about Smoky Meadows, a
plantation in Southern Virginia near Danville, where he was
stationed two months after being drafted into the
Confederate Army. He never dreamed he'd see such an
odd turn of events—forced into a war he didn't support,
and on a side against his native Ohio.

Johnny's mind was reeling as thoughts of Molly, his
past leading up to where he was now, and the
predicament he was facing, raced through his head. He
was staring off, as if in a trance, hardly noticing his friend
Jay Brown sitting on the log beside him. Jay became a
devoted friend and was extremely loyal to Johnny,
fulfilling another prophecy of the mystery woman in the
white dress when she said, "You will make a lifelong friend
by an act of kindness."

"Penny fo' yo' thoughts, Mistah Johnny!" He spoke softly, sensitive to things that concerned Johnny. "Ah bet you thinking' 'bout Miss Molly, ain't ya?" Johnny snapped out of his trance and glanced over at Jay. "Yeah, Jay . . . I'm thinkin' about Molly." He pulled the piece of straw he was nibbling out of his teeth and threw it on the ground. "I'm thinking about a lot of things." "Yassuh, me too," said Jay with a knowing nod. Johnny began to reflect on what a loyal friend Jay had become and the incident they shared.

Thinking of the outhouse episode, Johnny began to snicker. "What you laughin' 'bout, Mistah Johnny?" He replied, "Remember the time we tipped over Uncle Fred's outhouse?" "Lawd! Do ah evah. He come up out dat thing like a dead man comin' up out a coffin. Scared me half to death." They both broke into a laugh.

When the laughter subsided, Johnny went back to his momentary solitude of mind, looking from left to right, observing the activity and beauty of the Smoky Meadows Plantation. There was a platoon of regular Confederate soldiers stationed at the stately mansion which was owned by Major Michael Wilburn, a Confederate volunteer who was in charge of enforcing the military draft. The plantation was alive with continuous activity as the soldiers, members of the Wilburn family, and a few slaves moseyed about, tending to daily chores with a slow pace as if there were no tomorrow. It was a beautiful late spring day as the sweet aroma of honeysuckle filled the air. It seemed so peaceful here in the south-central region of Virginia that it was hard to believe just a hundred miles or so to the northeast men had already been fighting and dying by the thousands for over two years at such places as Bull Run, Fredericksburg, Sharpsburg, and at a very recent battle at Chancellorsville where the South had been victorious but suffered ten thousand casualties, including Gen. Stonewall Jackson, whose death had just become the latest talk of the day.

Johnny noticed a couple of soldiers moving out of the guesthouse that was out back of the mansion and joined to it only by a brick walkway cutting across the plush, green lawn which was kept trim by the grazing of the horses and a goat. The plantation was a much nicer atmosphere than the makeshift military campsites they had to set up on their two-month journey through the Carolinas. Johnny and Jay were here because they presented an unusual problem. They seemed to be in violation of an unwritten social code in the South regarding the relationship between blacks and whites, master and slave. The unwritten rule was that whites didn't associate with blacks on the same social level. The most acceptable Southern protocol of the times required Jay to join an all-black brigade under the leadership of a white commander. Johnny and Jay were forced to march to the rear of formations. The Confederate officers who arrested Johnny and forced him to join the Confederacy were confused by Jay wanting to fight alongside what they thought was his white master. The confusion was further complicated by Johnny persistently telling them Jay was his personal valet. Rather than insult or embarrass John, whom the Confederates considered to be a wealthy gentleman of some influence, they elected to direct the matter to Major Wilburn.

They had been at the plantation for several days while Major Wilburn pondered what to do, never seeing Johnny. All the while Johnny was being told that the major was busy with other matters and would send for him at the proper time. Actually, Major Wilburn was waiting for a telegraph reply, attempting to find out more about John before addressing him.

During this time Johnny had even thought of deserting because he certainly didn't believe in the "cause." Being from the North, "State's Rights" was never a concern to him and he wasn't even sure what the "cause" really meant to Southerners. But he dismissed the idea of desertion because he knew what it meant to experience dishonor, and he didn't want any more of that. Even though Johnny was physically manhandled to join the Confederacy, he was now being shown a certain degree of respect as a gentleman, and he liked it. Besides, he didn't want to appear cowardly to Molly, or Jay for that matter, whom he admired for his bravery, sticking by him in this troubled time. In fact, he was beginning to enjoy the luxury of leisure time afforded them by the wait. In order to pass the time John looked for ways to entertain himself and others. He began to admire Major Wilburn's youngest son, Michael Jr., who was near five years old. Johnny thought how he would like to have a son like that. So he began to treat the boy as if he were his own. After all, the boy did seem to have Molly's eyes and his own playful disposition. He told him a variety of stories, played catch with him, tossing sticks or stones, and occasionally ran a short footrace with him, always slowing down letting the young lad think he won.

One evening, an hour or so before the sun began to set, Johnny remembered a homemade toy his mother had fashioned when he was young. He asked young Michael Jr. to fetch a large button and some thread or string from his mother, Libby Wilburn. Johnny put the thread through two button holes and tied the thread together forming a loop that hung out about a foot on each side of the button. He slipped his hands into the loops and began to wind the button in a circle about twenty times or more. When he had enough winds on the threads, he pulled his hands outward and the button began to twirl, much to the delight of the little boy. The button would twirl in one direction until the threads had so many winds it would stop, and another outward pull would cause it to unwind in the other direction. All that was necessary was to keep pulling outward each time it stopped and the button would spin one way, then the other, indefinitely.

Suddenly, Johnny closed his hands on the button to stop it, and handed it to Michael Jr.

"Here you are, Michael. Now you try it!" He slipped the loops of thread over the lad's outstretched fingers and the boy chuckled as he began to play with the toy.

"Oh, this is fun. Thank you, Mr. Van worth!"

"You can just call me Johnny, okay?" The lad liked Johnny's response.

"Okay, Mr. Van Wor . . . uh . . . Johnny. You're my friend, huh?"

Johnny smiled broadly.

"That's right, son. We're friends." Johnny put a hand on the boy's shoulders, looking down at him as he continued to play with the homemade toy and didn't notice his mother, Libby, walking toward them, holding the hand of her blind daughter, Rebecca. They walked up behind John and the mother said, "Mr. Van Worth, Major Wilburn would like to see you right away!" "Indeed, Mrs. Wilburn. Nothing serious, is it?" Johnny had not been told why he and Jay were dropped off to see the major while the rest of the troops went on.

"I hope he doesn't mind me befriending your son." Libby smiled and said very softly and charmingly, "Quite the contrary, Mr. Van Worth. Both Major Wilburn and I appreciate the interest you've shown in Michael. It's been most beneficial to all." Johnny nodded his head and turned to look toward the mansion as Libby said, "Major Wilburn is in the study." Johnny conjured up the best of southern manners he had learned. "Thank you, ma'am." He tipped his hat at Libby and her daughter. "And good day, Mrs. Wilburn! Miss Rebecca!" As the ladies curtsied, he turned and walked toward Jay, who was standing nearby. They took a few steps side by side when Johnny said, "Wait here. I'll be right back."

"Yes, suh, Mistah Johnny! "What you think he wants?" Stopping momentarily, Johnny gave Jay a concerned look.

"I don't know. I just hope it's not bad news."

As Johnny walked away, Jay's countenance took on a serious look also, and the voices of the slaves could softly be heard from their shacks beyond the mansion singing an old Negro spiritual as the sun was getting lower in the southern Virginia sky.

"Nobody knows da trouble ah sees. Nobody knows but Jesus. Nobody knows . . ."

Chapter 4

THE ASSIGNMENT

Major Wilburn was a distinguished gray-haired man approaching the age of sixty. He had authority written all over him, from the slow steady way he carried himself when he walked, to his deliberate manly manner of speaking in a clear tone of voice. He was standing in his den, which was now used as his war office, looking out the window of the Victorian mansion. He had no response from the telegraph query concerning Johnny, but since John seemed to be an honest man and Libby extolled how Johnny was influencing their son, he thought it was time to confront John directly to get answers on his background and see if he was the man qualified for a special assignment the major needed to fill. When he saw Johnny approaching, he turned to sit at his desk and began looking through papers and war documents that had accumulated on it, patiently waiting for Johnny to knock on the door. When John timidly knocked, Major Wilburn cordially yelled out, "Come in!"

As Johnny entered the room, Major Wilburn stood and walked around his desk.

"Good to see you, Mr. Van Worth." He extended his arm and they shook hands.

"Good to see you too, sir!"

Johnny was surprised the major knew who he was because they had never been introduced before. He assumed that he must have been pointed out to the Major by someone, but said nothing and thought no more about it as the conversation continued. The major nodded to the chair in front of his desk as he walked around it.

"Have a seat! Make yourself comfortable." Before the major took his seat, he reached into a humidor on his desk.

"Care for a see-gar?" Very awkwardly, Johnny stood up to take the cigar.

"Oh . . . *uh* . . . well, all right . . . *uh* . . ." Major Wilburn noticed Johnny's hesitation.

"What's the matter? Need a light?" He pulled out a match and looked for a place to strike it, then decided to strike it with his fingernail as Johnny somewhat embarrassed, said,

"Oh, well . . . *uh* . . . actually, sir, I . . . *uh* . . . Well, you see, I really don't smoke."

"Don't smoke? Well . . . why didn't you just say so." He blew out the match and smiled at Johnny, and even though Smoky Meadows was primarily a tobacco plantation, the major said,

"Truthfully, Van Worth, I commend you. It's a nasty habit anyway." Relieved, Johnny smiled confidently and muttered, "*Uh*, well, yes, sir . . . I just prefer to breathe fresh air . . . whenever it's available . . . you know." As Johnny backed up to sit down, he missed the chair and fell butt first onto the carpet. Major Wilburn was looking down at papers on his desk and didn't notice Johnny's folly right away.

"Yes, I know what you mean." He looked up surprised when he heard Johnny hit the floor.

"Van Worth? What the—" Nervously, Johnny tried to cover his clumsiness.

"Oh, I was just noticing your carpet, sir." He patted the carpet, got up, and sat in the chair. "Verrrry nice, sir. *Uh* . . . Oriental, isn't it?"

"Why yes! It came from India. By the way, Van Worth, where are you from? That's why I requested to see you. I'd like to know a little more about you." Johnny didn't know whether to be flattered or not and he smiled and said,

"Well, let's see . . . *uh* . . . I was born at a very early age . . . in Columbus, Ohio." Major Wilburn chuckled, "Now, you don't have to go back that far. Did you go to military school?"

Johnny didn't want to reveal he was expelled from Yale, but he wanted to impress him with the fact that he attended the elite private university.

"*Ummm* . . . You might say I had to more or less fight my way through college." Trying to sound a bit Southern, he mispronounced Yale.

"I went to Yell." Major Wilburn looked slightly puzzled. "You went to Yell? You mean . . . you were a cheerleader?" Realizing his error, John quickly responded, "No . . . . *uh* . . . NO! I meant to say Yale . . . Yale University." Then he thought perhaps Major Wilburn wasn't familiar with the world-famous learning Institution, so he said meekly, "It's a little school up east . . . in Yankeeland."

"Certainly, I'm familiar with Yale." Then Wilburn proudly stated,

"I attended West Point myself . . . a few years after Robert E. Lee graduated." Waxing nostalgic, he said, "I still have fond memories of that place. I suppose you have great memories of college too?"

"Oh . . . *uh,* yes, sir! I most certainly do . . . *uh* . . . have memories."

Johnny was choosing his words carefully so as not to reveal the complete truth as his mind raced back to the time he was expelled, and the professor who caught him blatantly cheating had made a sweeping gesture of the arm, pointing toward the door while shouting, "Get out!"

"Why, I'll never forget old professor Hardbore. That kindly old gentleman! Well . . . I guess you could say he definitely 'pointed' me in a new direction in life." Wilburn was pleased with Johnny's answer, "Ah yes! There's no substitute for mentors who strive for excellence." Johnny was pleased that he had fooled the major and said with great confidence,

"I couldn't agree more, Major Wilburn."

The major picked up John's enlistment papers and read Johnny's name aloud,

"John William Van Worth the Third! I can't help but be impressed with you, Van Worth." Then a gleam of inquisitiveness came across his face. "But there's one thing that puzzles me. How does a man from Ohio wind up in the Confederate Army?" Johnny was quick to respond, "You know, sir, you may not believe this, but I've asked that question many times myself. You see, it all started before the war when Uncle Fred, my father's brother, inherited a small farm near Dorchester County, South Carolina, northwest of Charleston. Then they fell on hard times and my father wanted me to go down there and help them run the place. Well, at first I didn't want to go." He thought about his father forcing him out. "But alas, I thought more about it and considered it would be the noble thing to do." With that, Major Wilburn was beginning to see Johnny as a man very dedicated to duty.

Raising an eyebrow, the major smiled and said,

"Very admirable. Very admirable, indeed." Seeing he was doing a good job of pulling the wool over Major Wilburn's eyes, Johnny put up an act of humility. "Yes, sir . . . I suppose so. But what else could I do?"

"Uh-huh," said Major Wilburn as he got up from his chair and walked to the window.

"That explains how you went south. But what about the Confederacy? Did you Volunteer or were you caught up by the newly legislated draft?" At that point, Johnny was getting a little nervous but totally concealed it.

"Well, there again, sir, this was one of those soul-searching experiences." Johnny was again carefully choosing his words, searching for a way to hide his resistance to being drafted, which was difficult since the memory of a gun to his chin and two soldiers dragging him by the arms with Molly hanging on his boots was still vivid in his mind.

"It was hard because I had just met this lovely lass I truly adored, my sweet Molly Marie, the love of my life, when a couple of really nice Confederate officers showed up and well . . . I must say they did present a rather convincing argument, and . . . well, here I am! Need I say more?"

Turning from the window and walking back to his desk, Major Wilburn squinted his eyes at Johnny and nodded, obviously touched to the heart.

"You, a man from the North, left your true love to join the Confederacy?" Playing humble, John sheepishly said, "Yeah, I left. She's still back there. Pretty well sums it up, sir." Smiling with a gleam in his eye, Wilburn looked intently at Johnny.

"Van Worth, I like your attitude. I believe you're just the man I've been looking for." Feeling somewhat like a cornered criminal, Johnny surprisingly said, "Who? Me?" Wilburn said, "How long have you been in this man's army?"

"Oh, almost three months now. *Uh* . . . why do you ask?" came Johnny's nervous reply. Wilburn looked away for a moment and said, "I know this is somewhat irregular But . . ." He then looked Johnny in the eye, grinned broadly at him, and proudly announced,

"Private Van Worth, how would you like to be promoted to lieutenant?" Johnny could hardly believe his ears, but was so elated he jumped to attention and started to salute with his left hand, then quickly corrected it to the right.

"Private . . . *er* . . . *uh* . . . I mean, Lt. John William Van Worth III at your service, sir!" Major Wilburn casually returned the salute and leaned back in his chair.

"Please sit down, Mr. Van Worth. Let me tell you about your command assignment." He rubbed his chin, anticipating just how to impart the facts to Johnny.

"I've been informed by commanders at the front there are a few men who have been drafted who . . . *uh* . . . let's say are not quite ready for battle." He sighed. "They need a little extra training and discipline so they can return to the front lines and not be a disruption to commanders. Do you savvy what I'm talking about?" Johnny didn't have a clue how the major was going to involve him, so he cautiously said,

"*Uh* . . . well . . . I think so." Then the major leaned forward, "Let me be perfectly frank. These men have repeatedly shown signs of being troublemakers of one sort or another."

Johnny arched his eyebrows. His curiosity was piqued as Major Wilburn continued,

"For instance, one man was more or less an outright pirate before the war, but when the war broke out he became a blockade runner for the Confederacy, which proved to be a profitable business for him until Union Navy vessels sunk his ship and took him captive. He managed to escape, and then outraged, he determined to get revenge on the Yankees . . . so he joined the Confederate Army." Attempting to appear wise and experienced, Johnny said, "I see. A thing like that could dampen a man's sense of humor." Ignoring Johnny's attempt at wisdom, the major continued as if John said nothing.

"I understand he's a man of uncontrollable anger. There are other men too . . . some that are a little . . . *uh* . . . shall we say, uneducated, ignorant, immature . . . or perhaps downright stupid. Some are a bit on the wild side, and some with mild mental disorders such as paranoia. Think you could shape these men up, Mr. Van Worth?"

Wanting to appear worthy of his appointment to lieutenant, Johnny confidently said,

"Believe me, sir. I can handle those unsophisticated gentlemen!"

"Uh-huh! Well, if these men could return to their units as useful battle-ready troops, it would be a real feather in your cap, Mr. Van Worth . . . and mine, I might say." With great confidence, Johnny said, "I'll give it my best, sir!"

"Excellent! Then it's all set!" The major reached across his desk and they shook hands.

"The first of these troops should arrive day after tomorrow. Oh, *uh* . . . in the meantime, since you're now a lieutenant, you'll need this." He opened a drawer in his desk and pulled out a Confederate cap with a lieutenant bar on it and handed it to Johnny.

Putting the cap on, Johnny smiled broadly. "Thank you very much, sir! I'll prove myself worthy. You can count on that! They don't call me Van WORTH for nothing you know." With a chuckle in his voice, Major Wilburn said, "I'm sure you'll do just fine." He got up and walked around his desk. Johnny also arose, and they strolled slowly side by side toward the door. The major put his arm around Johnny and reassured him by saying, "But you won't be handling this alone. There's a kindly old preacher down the road. His name is Jeremiah Prather. His prayers back here are much more powerful than his presence would be in battle. I've enlisted his services as a chaplain to assist you in this assignment."

Again Johnny tried to lighten the mood.

"Well then, no one can say I don't have a prayer, huh?' Wilburn didn't pick up on Johnny's little joke. "Yes. I'll introduce you to him tomorrow. And in the meantime, move your belongings and gear to the guesthouse out back. It's now vacant. You can use that as your headquarters. It has a cellar. You can quarter your slave there if you like."

"You are most gracious, sir," said Johnny in his most appreciative tone of voice.

"I thank you once more." As they shook hands again, Johnny decided to tell the major the truth about Jay.

"By the way, he's not a slave. I gave him his freedom. To show his gratitude he enlisted with me. He's very loyal. His name is Jay Brown." The major flashed another broad smile, pleased by Johnny's straightforwardness.

"You are indeed a man of unusual character, Mr. Van Worth. Which reminds me, I want to thank you for the kind attention you've shown my son. The war has taken me away so often. I haven't been able to be the father to him I need to be. It was affecting his attitude—until you came along. Libby tells me the boy has become quite fond of you." He paused, then went on to say, "If you handle these men as well as you've handled my son you'll do us all proud." Johnny was more relaxed and comfortable by now and answered, "It's my pleasure, sir. I hope to have a son as fine as he is, someday myself." Major Wilburn smiled proudly. "Yes, I know what you mean. Are you married?" "I would be, but the war interfered, you know."

"Oh! Yes. Well, I'm sure she's quite the lady who will anxiously await your return."

"Yes she is. She writes me often." With that, Major Wilburn patted Johnny on the back and again shook his hand.

"Well, perhaps you'll have your own son someday. Good day, Lieutenant!" He saluted Johnny.

"Good day, Major Wilburn," he said, returning the salute with the proper hand this time. Johnny turned with confidence and strolled out of the den toward the front door, his footsteps echoing in the high walls of the mansion.

Major Wilburn stared after Johnny, shaking his head in admiration. When Johnny was out of earshot, he whispered to himself, "What a dedicated man!" He then paused thoughtfully, rolled his eyes upward, and whispered, "God help him!"

Outside the mansion, Jay was patiently waiting for Johnny. When he saw him coming, he stood up with an inquisitive look on his face, for it appeared, even from a distance, that Johnny was smiling and wearing a new cap and carrying his old one. As he got within speaking distance, Jay's countenance broke into a smile too. Johnny spoke first.

"Jay! You're not going to believe this. He promoted me to lieutenant!"

"Whut? Ah knew it wuz sumpin' good, Mistah Johnny, when ah saw you smilin'!"

"I told Major Wilburn I freed you. But it might be best if we go on pretending you're my slave. Some of the other men might not be as gracious and understanding as the major." Then they turned to walk toward the guesthouse and Johnny said,

"C'mon I'll tell you all about it."

Sitting by the coal oil lamp in the bedroom of the guesthouse that evening, Johnny was thankful to have a roof over his head for a change. They had spent many nights sleeping on the ground, or at best under makeshift tents. Even though Jay was in quarters in the cellar, it was still more comfortable than what he had been used to since being in the Confederate army.

Johnny was thankful also for his promotion. He laid on the bed, rested his head in his palms behind his head, and stared up at the ceiling while his mind rolled over the course of his meeting with Major Wilburn. He was proud of presenting a better image of himself to the major than what was really true, but at the same time realized how lucky he was not to have goofed up something. He wondered what might have happened if Major Wilburn had had a copy of his school records, or some other information. He vowed to be more truthful in the future and to do what the lady in the white dress told him, "Pray! Lest you lose your way."

He thought it was time to thank his lucky stars, or better yet, thank God for his good fortune. That's what Molly would do. His heart warmed at the very thought of her, and he wondered if that inner peace about her really came from her strong faith. He reminisced about those wonderful moments they spent in church during their courting days and wished he could turn the hands of time back to those simple and innocent times. Being apart was tearing at his heart and without a doubt the greatest agony he had ever known.

Whenever he was alone at night, his mind was constantly focused on every memory of their relationship. Their romantic courting was slow in developing because they lived twelve miles apart. Back then it most often meant considerable travel time on a horse to be together. The days on the farm were often long ones for Johnny, not allowing much leisure evening time. So in the early months of their romance, especially that first winter, letters played an important part in keeping the fires of love burning.

In many of those letters she expressed concern for her father, hoping he would return from what they thought would be a few weeks of fighting, but the weeks had turned into two years already and there wasn't much to indicate that an end was in sight. Johnny knew Molly prayed often for her father. He reasoned that having a father she loved far away at war was a good incentive to turn to a higher power for protection. Of course, now John also knew she prayed often for him. She so much as said so in practically every letter he received from her. He had saved them all. Suddenly, he realized he now had a coal oil lamp to read them by. He got up, shuffled through his pack, and found her latest letter. He hastily unfolded it under the dim light. As he began to read it, he could picture her sweet face, and in his mind hear the sound of her charming, mildly southern voice.

My Dearest Johnny,   *Saturday, June 6, 1863*

> *It's so sad to think we were to be married today. I only live to be in your arms again. I know from your letters that you feel the same. It seems so cruel that two people who love each other so much must be apart. I pray every day that God will bring you back to me soon so we can get married and have the little children we both*

desire. If our first child is a boy I want to name him after you, John William Van Worth IV. I think it sounds impressive, don't you? And if we have a girl, I think it's sweet of you to want to name her after me. But when you suggested calling her Molly Marie Junior in your last letter I had to laugh. It might be considered socially confusing in the South to call a girl Junior. Is that the custom in the North?

Sweetheart, do you have any idea of when you might be able to come home? Many of the women are hoping they'll allow military furloughs in time for Christmas. So please, as soon as you know something, be sure to write me.

There was more to the letter, but John had read it a dozen times over the last week and now he had the urge to correspond back and let her know all about his latest experience before it got too late in the evening. He carefully folded her letter and put it back in his pack. Then he brought the coal oil lamp over to the small desk in the room where there was a pen and ink and began writing.

Dear Molly,

Like you, I yearn to be in your arms, and I can't wait until that wonderful day arrives. I'm not sure about Christmas furlough. It's too far away to know. There's a war going on, and for all we know we could be in the midst of a battle by then, although I certainly hope not.

But something miraculous happened today that may have a bearing on me qualifying for a furlough. I have been promoted to commissioned officer status. Can you believe it, darling? I am now a first lieutenant—and I've never even been to military school or trained as an officer.

Johnny stopped writing, put the pen down, leaned back in the chair, and started reading to himself what he had just written to see how it would read to Molly. When he got to the part about being promoted, he slapped his leg and laughed, saying, "Oh, she ought to like that!" Then he grabbed the pen and continued writing.

There is one drawback, however. My first assignment is to discipline a platoon of troublemakers in a schoolhouse deserted for the summer near the Wilburn Plantation where I'm now stationed. These are undisciplined men they say need extra training. This could be a great opportunity, and of course, you know me—I'll be up to the challenge. I'm certain I'll have these gentlemen under control in no time at all.

❊Chapter 5❊

ROLL CALL

Johnny couldn't believe his eyes. Less than a minute
after entering the room, he was witnessing a full-blown
riot. He was so confident he could handle these military
troublemakers the same way he handled his college
classmates, often feeling he had them eating out of his hand.
Now everything was totally out of hand. Men were fighting
as if in a barroom brawl, punching and sometimes strangling
one another. John's voice could barely be heard yelling for
order, "Order! I said ORDER! Stop!" Suddenly, a knife
whizzed past his head. Johnny had had enough, and he said
to himself, *That does it!*

He ran out of the schoolhouse where the "new arrivals"
were suppose to be getting an orientation, and quickly called
for help from three regulars and Jay Brown, who were waiting
under a shade tree nearby.

Meanwhile inside, the pirate in the group, Harry
Leech, a heavy man with a mangy beard, was choking
another man, Ben Grimm, and saying in a raspy, cockney
English accent,

"*Aarrg!* Nobody calls me a Yahnkee spy! I 'ates Yahnkees!
Ya know what I does to bloddy Yahnkee's, matey? I bloddy's
'em even more!" He bonked his forehead into the smaller

man's face, sending him reeling backward onto the floor with a bloody nose.

As Johnny entered the building again with the regulars and Jay trailing behind, the brawl was at a peak with one man flipping another over his back, while yet another man was trying to tie one poor skinny fellow's legs in a knot. Johnny was toting a pistol in each hand as he ran to the front of the room and jumped up on the teacher's desk. Jay and the rest of the men, carrying long rifles, took positions on each side of Johnny, pointing their guns at the rioting men. Johnny started firing the pistols rapidly in all directions overhead. The men froze and their mouths dropped open as they watched John attempting to fancy-twirl the pistols back into the holsters and out again, fumbling awkwardly in the process. Finally, he just gave up trying to impress anyone with his expert ability to handle firearms, and just pointed the weapons threateningly at the men as one of the regulars said, "Don't move and do what the lieutenant says!"

Immediately, Johnny fell into his nonchalant demeanor and said, "Now that I have your attention, gentlemen, would you kindly sit down?" As the men seated themselves, John stepped down from the desk, stood behind it, and said, "All I was trying to do was take a roll call. Now—" He was instantly interrupted and distracted by a scuffle between a dwarf standing on a school desk and another man. While they were pushing at one another Johnny inquired,

"What's the problem over here?"

The dwarf responded in a falsetto voice, "He keeps trying to sit where I want to sit!"

The man snapped back, "And he keeps trying to—" Johnny quickly interrupted them, "Gentlemen! Gentlemen! Let's not get unruly again. It really doesn't matter where you sit. Just sit down anywhere." Johnny attempted to remain calm and collected as the dwarf sat on the tabletop, crossed his arms, and pouted. The other man sat in the seat attached to the desk, crossed his arms, and pouted as well. Johnny continued to ignore this immature display and went on with the roll call. But the distraction did cause him to get momentarily confused and he inadvertently said something he wished he could rephrase.

"Now, when I call your name just yell, 'Here!" If you're not here, don't say anything! Is that clear?"

The men looked at one another with confused expressions and one scratched his head. Johnny realized he just pulled another one of his verbal slips, but nonchalantly continued as if what he just said made perfect sense, "May we proceed then?" The men all responded at once, "Aye aye, sir! Proceed! Yeah! Sure!" Johnny began baby-talking to the men, "Well den, I'm gwad I have your permission!" When the men began to chuckle, Johnny abruptly changed his tone to severely stern and mean. "For an undetermined length of time I'll be your mama and your papa! You won't get to do much of anything without my permission. I'll tell you when to go to bed and when to rise; when to eat and when to march. Is that understood?" The men answered in unison, "Yes, sir!" However, the motley crew was obviously unhappy, casting disgruntled glances at one another. Johnny picked up papers from the desk, walked around it and sat on one corner of it. He remained serious but friendly and soft spoken. "I'm Lt. John Van Worth. However, when we get to know one another better you may call me Johnny. But for now, just address me as Lieutenant Van Worth or simply as Sir! Now, let's get better acquainted. When I call your name, stand and tell us about yourself." He looked at the papers and called out the first name, "James H. Morgan!"

James jumped up and said, "Heah, simply as suh!" Johnny remained unshaken as the men laughed.

"Drop the 'simply as' and call me sir, Morgan!"

"Yes, Suh Morgan!" Morgan's comment was met with greater laughter from the men. Not certain whether the man is smarting off or just plain stupid, Johnny ignored the comment and laughter and asked, "Are you any relation to Gen. John Hunt Morgan?"

"No, suh! He's respectable!" This evoked snickers from the men but Johnny just went on as if there was no humor in the conversation, like his father often did when Johnny was being a wise guy.

"Oh? And just what did you do before the war?"

"Oh, raise cane mostly!"

"Sugar cane?"

"No, suh!"

With that the men burst into hardy laughter, but Johnny remained cool because he had plenty of experience with the shoe on the other foot. He concluded he had met his match with Morgan and decided to not give him any more fodder for humor.

"Ohhhkay. You may sit down, Mr. Morgan." He looked at the papers to call out the next name on the list. "*Uh . . .* let's see . . . Goober . . . *uh . . .* Askew!" Two men called out simultaneously, "Here!" Johnny replied, "Which one of you is Goober Askew?" A very hicky voice cried out,

"Oh, he's Goobah Askew. Ah'm Goobah Shaw!"

"Well, then I didn't ask you. I asked Askew, right? I think we've got too many Goobers around here." As the men chuckled at Johnny's remark, Goober Shaw nervously replied, "Oh yeah! Ah guess ah'll just sit down."

"Please do. We'll get to you a little later, Mr. Shaw." He turned to the other Goober.

"Tell us about yourself, Mr. Askew!" Wanting to inject some humor Johnny said, "What part of the south are you from? New York?" The room filled with chuckles from the men who knew Goober Askew was as Southern as a man could be.

"Lard Amighty, no! If ah's fum New Yawk, ah'd be dead by now. Ain't no Yankees gonna git this fawr South. Ah'm fum Souff Care-o-lina." Then he proudly stated,

"We started this wawr at Fote Sumtah, ya know!"

"Yeah, I know. But what we need to do now is figure out a way to end it."

"You git me back up to da front and we'll end it soon 'nuff."

The men all chimed in to agree, "That's right!" "Yeah!" "You bet!"

Askew continued, "Ah'd like ta git this wawr over wit' an' git back to mah daddy's fawm on the Savannah Rivah." Then he really got assertive.

"You jus' let me take chawge an' ah'll show you whut to do!" Johnny felt the need to nip this aggressiveness in the bud.

"Well, right now I'm in charge," he said, addressing all of the men. "And if you gentlemen cooperate with me you'll see action soon enough." He looked for the next name on his list. "Which one of you is Buster Bottom? Or do we have two Bottoms here too?" A man in his midthirties, with a mustache, stood up.

"Ah'm Bustah Bottom, but ah'm known by a couple diff'runt names. Some call me Drag Bottom or Bad Bottom, but most of mah frien's call me Bustah."

"You must have some odd friends, Buster," John retorted.

"Some are odd, some are even, some are weird, but mostly they're just good ol' boys."

John quizzed Buster, saying, "Do you have any occupational skills or a trade that might be useful in this army?" Buster paused a moment to think and responded,

"*Uumm* . . . pro'bly not. Ya see, ah'm a professional gambler, mostly. But ah did learn a little 'bout ship-buildin' workin' at a yard in Norfolk. That convinced me to try gambling. It's easier on a man's back."

Suddenly, one of the men, Ben Grimm, interrupted the conversation to interject his paranoia, saying with a very suspicious tone, "*Aw*, he ain't no gambler!" Buster snapped a retort, "Wanna bet? What kinda odds you want?" Dripping with sarcastic suspicion, Ben followed with, "I'll bet he's a

Yankee spy!" Johnny then addressed Ben, "What's your name?"

"Ben Grimm!"

"Well, Ben, let's not talk until I call your name. That goes for everybody here, *understand?*" No one said a word, so John repeated, "I said, understand?" Still no answer. The silence lasted about five seconds with Johnny scowling at the men and finally Goober Shaw felt a need to exclaim, "You said we cuddunt tawk 'til you said owr name." Johnny just closed his eyes in exasperation, while the man sitting next to Ben Grimm, James Woodward, reached down to light a match he had inserted in the edge of the sole of Grimm's shoe to give him a hotfoot.

Meanwhile, Johnny didn't know that just a few miles off help was on the way. Trotting along an old country lane, Major Wilburn spotted a carriage coming in the opposite direction. Riding in the carriage was Pastor Jeremiah Prather. When they drew closer, Major Wilburn addressed the preacher. "Good morning, Pastor Prather!"

"Mornin', Mr. Wilburn! God's blessing to ya!"

"I was on my way to get you. Let's get over to the schoolhouse and see how Mr. Van Worth is handling the troops. From what I hear, they'll need your blessing most!" Pastor Prather suggested, "If there's trouble already, perhaps we should pray about it on the way over there!" Major Wilburn replied,

"Yes, I understand Johnny was having trouble with them. But perhaps that's to be expected. After all, they've been sent here because they're undisciplined men."

"Yep, I reckon we need to pray," said the pastor. Major Wilburn inquisitively looked at the preacher. "We ought to be there in ten minutes, can the Good Lord act that fast?" Pastor Prather laughed, and said, "Sometimes faster than that!"

Back at the schoolhouse, Johnny was continuing with his roll call—and his problems.

"Uh-huh, well, Mr. Grossman, we're grown men here. Surely you can wait 'til we finish the roll call to go to the outhouse!" Johnny glanced over at Jay Brown who gave him an "Oh, brother" sort of look and rolled his eyes up as Grossman sat down frowning. Johnny gave Jay a tongue-in-cheek look and read off the next name on his roster.

"Lester Moore!" Lester was the dwarf. He stood on his desk. In his falsetto voice, he said, "Here, sir! You can just call me Les. Les is short for Lester, ya know."

John responded, "I'll take you as an expert on knowin' what's short." The men laughed.

"So you're Les Moore, huh?" Smiling, Les said, "More or less." And the men chuckled some more.

"My folks started callin' me Les when I was little." The room was abuzz with snickers. Looking down, trying not to laugh, Johnny said, "*Uh* . . . Mr. Moore, how come you got drafted? It seems they could have skipped over you, if you know what I mean."

"It would be easier to skip over me than anyone here." Laughter again filled the room.

"They said I could duck bullets better than most other fellas." Johnny asked, "What did you do for a living before you were drafted?"

"I'm a shoemaker! I dreamed of being a hatmaker but thought it would be too much of a stretch for me." As the men laughed again Johnny reassured Les to ease his self-consciousness.

"You're unique and that makes you special. Remember that Mr . . . . *uh* . . . Les. I'm sure we can find some little job in the army to fit you." John went on with the roll call.

"George . . . *uh* . . . Crummy?" A heavyset man stood up in response.

"Heah! Name is Crumley, suh. Ah'm from Awgusta, Gawgia. Ah ran a bakery there 'til the draft caught me." Then he dejectedly said,

"Now mah daily bread is mighty stale." This comment evoked chuckles from the men because they frequently ate stale hardtack, a brittle biscuit served in the army of that time.

"And so is the hardtack we're eating these days," said Johnny. "If those biscuits were big enough and round, we could use them as cannonballs 'cause they sure are hard enough." The men smiled and shook their heads with a confirming yes, obviously warming up to Johnny who continued talking to Crumley. "We might put your cooking skills to work here. Think you can bake hardtack a little softer than granite?" said John.

Crumley answered, "The secret is eatin' it while it's fresh, suh. Aftah it's a week old ah make no guarantees."

"Uh-huh. Nice to meet you, George." Then Johnny remembered his formal manners. "*Uh,* I mean, Mr. Crumley." He once again called a name from the roster.

"What's this? *Uh, puh . . . puh . . .* Poddymouth?" Practically all of the men yelled out simultaneously, "Here!" "You Bet!" "Yeah!" Rising to his feet, a thin man spoke shyly from the side of his mouth,

"That's Pettymuth, suh! Buford T. Pettymuth!"

Johnny squinted at the man's name on the paper.

"Pettymuth, eh? Might want to work a little bit on that penmanship, Pettymuth!"

"Yes, suh!" Pettymuth whispered to the man beside him, "What's pena ship?" The man beside him just shrugged his shoulders and whispered back,

"I think it was one of Columbus's ships." Johnny heard them and said, "For your information, I'm talking about your handwriting, Mr. Pettymuth. You need to learn to write better."

"*Uh . . .* well, suh . . . Ah nevah went to school much. Mah daddy figgered I should just always hep with the fawm work mostly. An' ah didn't zackly join the ahmy . . . ah wuz shafted . . . *uh,* I mean drafted." The men snickered again.

"Believe it or not Buford, I can sympathize with you being drafted. You can sit down, Mr. Pettymuth." Johnny called out another name, "Ben Grimm!"

The strange acting man stood to his feet and said in a paranoid tone,

"Whadda ya want with me, Mr. Van Worth? How do we know you aren't a Yankee spy? Ya don't sound Suthen!" The men mumbled a groan to themselves.

"Would it help If I said"—John then poured on an exaggerated Southern accent—"bless mah cotton crop . . . if it ain't Bruthah Ben Grimm. How long you been this grim, Ben?" The men laughed as Johnny held out his hand to shake with Ben, who was sitting on the front row. Shying away, Ben said, "See! Ah tole ya he wuz a Yankee spy! Why the nerve . . . makin' fun of us Suthen folk." Johnny ended his charade with an honest admission.

"Well actually, ol' Ben here is very observant. The truth is I'm not originally from the South. I came down here about three years ago to help run my uncle's farm near Charleston . . . and well . . . I was passionately persuaded to join this Confederate cause. I'm sure some of you have relatives in the North—" Johnny was interrupted by James Morgan.

"Mah Aunt Sally has been in prison in Boston fo' years!"

Johnny was surprised, but stayed nonchalant as he turned to Morgan, exclaiming,

"See what I mean? But that doesn't make you a spy, now does it, Morgan?"

"Hail no! I'd much rather rob banks! Or shoot a Yankee!" Johnny decided it was time to move on.

"Ohhhkay! Let's go on with the roll call. Harry Leech!" Rising to his feet, the former swarthy pirate replied in his cockney accent, "'Ere! I was wonderin' when ya'd get to me, sar! And to tell ya the truth, I think ya got to me the minute ya stepped through the door. *Haw haw haw!*" The men laughed also, but Leech abruptly cut off his laugh and reached out his hand to shake with Johnny.

"Please tuh meet ya, mate! But I must let ya know, I outrank ya. I'm *Capt.* Harry S. Leech, former skipper of the *Renegade of the Seas*, the finest ship those damn Yahnkees ever blew outta the water."

John focused a squint at the mangy Leech and boldly stated, "Weren't you a pirate of sorts before the war?"

"Please, sar! I've reformed since those days and became a respectable blockade runner for the Confederacy. Made three trips to Mexico and two to France. Brought back plenty of weapons, powder, and supplies . . . and other treasure before the disaster overtook me. I'll never forget it." Leech's eyes seemed to glaze over as he recalled the incident. "We got off a flurry of cannon fire at the Union Navy. But alas, they outnumbered me . . . and with a lucky shot, they sank the *Renegade*." What Captain Leech didn't reveal was that when his ship was burning, he took a flying swan dive into the sea with the blousy sleeves of his shirt ablaze all the way to the water. "But I will say this. I went down with the ship in a blaze of glory! But I managed to escape from the dairty bawstuds . . . and unable to build another ship because of the war . . ."—at this point he became increasingly enraged—"I joined the Confederacy to get my revenge on those bloddy Yanhkee scallywag scum!" Johnny was a bit shocked to see Leech's rage turn him almost cross-eyed. "And I won't rest! Until I see 'em all to a dark and ugly death." He got louder and louder, his gravely voice reaching a fever pitch. "Death! DEATH to 'em all I tell ya! Dark and ugly DEATH! *Aarrg!*" Johnny didn't realize his eyes were open wide, as he was totally caught up in the intensity of the near-insane anger just displayed. However, he quickly regained his nonchalant composure, and not knowing exactly how to respond, he said, "Oh, well then . . . I . . . *uh* . . . suppose you don't want to *wait* too long to get at the dirty scoundrels, huh?"

Harry Leech came back at Johnny like a roaring lion, "Wait? Wait to kill those scummy Yanhkees? Are you CRAZY? Wait is the nastiest four-letter word I know!" Leech got right in Johnny's face, nose to nose with him, almost bending him backward.

"I 'ave no patience to WAIT AT ALL!" Johnny was shocked but tried to act unshaken.

"Good! Good! *Uh* . . . now, if you'll just have a seat, Private . . . *uh* . . . Captain Leech, we won't have to . . . *uh* . . . WAIT to finish the roll call. Then we can be about the special training that will make you gentlemen the perfectly mad killers we all desire to be, huh?"

Still growling, Leech took his seat. Johnny searched for his place on the papers to read off the next name and didn't notice Major Wilburn with Chaplain Prather enter a side door behind him. They stood quietly watching the proceedings.

"All right, gentlemen! Let's see . . . Next we have Robert Johnson!"

Robert was on the opposite side of the room from Major Wilburn and the chaplain, so Johnny still was unaware of their presence. Shaking from the effects of battle fatigue, Robert Johnson answered weakly, "*Hu* . . . *hu* . . . heah, suh!" Johnny was surprised to see this teenage boy, who had been calm earlier, trembling.

"Are you all right, Johnson?" The boy's response was dead serious.

"Ah can wait, suh! Ah've seen enough killin' to last me fo' the rest of mah life. Not jus' on the battlefield, but every night ah see 'em." He stared into space as if in a trance. "They keep comin' at me. Ghost after ghost . . . all dead soldiers. Yanks and Confederates . . . hundreds of 'em. Thousands of 'em. They keep swoopin' past me whisperin' one word—Gettysburg . . . Gettysburg . . . Gettysburg!" He buried his face in his hands. "Oh god! When will it ever stop?"

Johnny was moved by the sincerity of the boy's words and mood. He tried to delve into his problem looking for a way to help him or console him.

"What do you mean every night? How long has this been going on?"

"For twenty-eight days now, suh."

"How old are you, Robert?"

"Ah'll be nineteen in Novembah."

"It's probably just a figment of your imagination. Maybe the result of battle fatigue. When you were younger, did you ever have scary dreams?"

"Nuthin' like this!" He looked down. "And it's not a dream, suh. It's a nightmare." He looked up at Johnny with concern. "Ah've heard people say sometimes these things have meanin's."

"Are you from a town named Gettysburg?"

"That's what haunts me 'bout it, suh. Ah've never heard of it."

"Neither have I. Any of you men heard of a town called Gettysburg?" As Johnny turned toward the other men, he noticed Major Wilburn and Chaplain Prather.

"Oh, Major! I didn't notice you come in. Men! TENS-HUT!"

"As you were, gentlemen," said the major with soft-spoken authority.

Johnny was anxious to show the major he had things under control.

"Men! I'd like to introduce our commander and owner of Smoky Meadows Plantation, Maj. Michael Wilburn. And the man with him here is Chaplain Jeremiah Prather."

The chaplain nodded toward the men as Major Wilburn said, "Good morning, men!"

Because the major was soft-spoken, the men just mumbled good morning in return. Johnny seized the opportunity to take control and impress the major and chaplain.

"Gentlemen! This is your commander. I think we can respond a little more enthusiastically, don't you?" They shouted in unison, "Good morning, sir!"

"That's more like it!" Johnny smiled, proud of his appearance of control.

"We don't mean to interrupt, Lieutenant," said the major, "but I am interested in Private Johnson's dreams . . . or nightmares, if you prefer." Chaplain Prather immediately followed with, "It might not be a dream or a nightmare. It could be a premonition, a forewarning of something that's going to happen. But God-forbid what your vision is, son. It sounds like another terrible tragedy of this war."

Suddenly, a sense of serious concern swept the room as Johnny looked over at the chaplain and Major Wilburn, the latter looking down reverently, gently biting his lip. As the men exchanged similar concerned glances toward one another, Pastor Prather continued, "Gentlemen! Shall we pray? Heavenly Father, bless these men. Send us angels of protection that your will might be done on this earth. Let hell not prevail. Bring an end to the evil that plagues this land."

Johnny's mind began to wander as Chaplain Prather continued to pray. Johnny was thankful that for these first three months he was not close enough to the fighting to be in real danger. And for the first time, the fact he could soon be injured or killed was becoming a very real possibility, haunting his mind.

❊Chapter 6❊

GHOSTS AND DEATH

That evening, as the sun was setting over the stately Smoky Meadows plantation, painting a heavenly glow of scarlet hues on the horizon, the sound of singing echoed from the slave cabins, as was often the custom at twilight time in this quaint valley in south-central Virginia.

The cabins were crude, some with dirt floors. The slaves would go about their chores of surviving, preparing a meal from whatever food they could scrape together in this countryside not far from war-ravaged battlefields. It was a minimal existence, a mother holding a near-naked child in her arms surrounded by other piccaninnies of various ages; the Negro men gathered around, some with musical instruments—a banjo, a harmonica—all singing their spiritual songs in perfect harmony.

On this evening, one sang the lead vocal and the others joined in on the Glory Hallelujah Choruses. "Ah wanna go where Moses gone."

"Glory Hallelujah!"

"Ah wanna go to da promise land."

"Glory Hallelujah!"

"Sweet milk 'n' honey overflows."

"Glory Hallelujah!"

Johnny and Jay could hear the soulful Negro spiritual, off in the distance from where they were talking on the edge of the mansion lawn, away from the military encampment.

"There's something mournful and sad in the songs of the slaves. Yet there's something ironically peaceful and glad in their voices, too. Does that make sense to you, Jay?" Jay smiled, pleased that Johnny cared enough to make such an observation about the slave's music.

"Sho' 'nuff, Mistah Johnny. Ah unnerstan'." He began to speak in a confidential tone, as if he was letting John in on some kind of secret. "Ya see, dey's sad 'cause da life of a slave is a terr-bul burden on da soul. But dey's glad 'cause dey have faith da Lawd gonna dee-liver 'em from dere mis'ry somehow. Ah knows! Ah've been on bof sides of dat fence, an' ah kin tell ya . . . it feels a might bettah to be free. Ah cain't thank ya 'nuff fo' dat, Mistah Johnny."

Johnny turned to Jay with a smile, and said, "Whadda you talkin' 'bout? You've been more of a slave to me since I freed ya' than you were before."

"*Aww* . . . dat's jus' 'cause ah likes ya . . . an ah'm beholdin' to ya, Mistah Johnny."

"Well, I'd better warn ya' . . . likin' me can get ya in a heap of trouble." They both chuckled to themselves and Jay said, "You mean like dis mornin'?"

"Oh my god! What kind of crew am I in charge of here? Or should I say . . . what kind of 'crude' am I in charge of?" They both laughed again. "I guess it just shows how desperate the South is for military men."

"Yassuh! Ah bleeve you right 'bout dat."

As they turned to walk toward the tented encampment, they were surprised to see a Confederate soldier come staggering out of the woods and onto the grounds. He appeared exhausted and his uniform was dirty and torn.

He held his hand out, waving to Johnny and Jay to get their attention, and gasped for breath as he called out, "Help! Help me!" As he fell to the ground, John and Jay looked at one another in disbelief and then rushed to assist the man. They helped him to his feet with questions in their minds as to who he was and what he was doing here.

"Who are you?" Johnny asked. Jay followed with, "Where'd you come from?"

Still trying to get his breath, the man pleaded, "Water! Water!" Johnny pulled out his canteen and gave the man a drink, after which he tried to answer their questions.

"Ah'm . . . Andrew Payne! First . . . . First Division . . . Army of Northern Virginia. Ah've been sent here to see Major Wilburn."

"Here, sit down. You look exhausted," said Johnny. The man collapsed to a sitting position as Johnny explained, "Major Wilburn has retired for the evening. I'm Lieutenant Van Worth. Could I help you? I might be able to relay a message if—" Interrupting, Payne said, "No! Ah must get to see Major Wilburn right away myself. It's very important!"

Johnny and Jay exchanged concerned glances at one another and Johnny said,

"This is Jay Brown. Stay here with him. I'll see if Major Wilburn can see you!" As Johnny walked toward the mansion, Jay's eyes followed him, and neither of them saw the expression on Andrew Payne's face turn from one of desperation to a sly one.

Later on, at the nearby encampment of Johnny's "motley misfits" the newly arrived troublemakers were gathered around the smoldering remains of their cooking fire, telling ghost stories. All were focused on Goober Shaw whose eyes were opened wide in the dim twilight, a flicker of light from the fading fire occasionally shimmering across his face.

Goober was talking in a low spooky tone of voice. "And there they wuz . . . out on the wilderness road with the moon shinin' down . . . and here comes someone on a gallopin' horse with a black cape flappin' in the wind. An' jus' as he got closer, they could see the horseman had no head." Some of the men groaned, "Ooohh!" Shaw went on with his tale.

"An' then they could see the headless horseman wuz a ghost." The dwarf, Les Moore, was the most spooked by the story, and he jumped up, rubbing chills off his arms, and said,

"Ooohh! Talkin' 'bout ghosts gives me the goosebumps." James Morgan responded, "Huh! Ah thought you wuz a goosebump." The dwarf shook his fist at James and growled in defense of himself while the rest of the crew laughed.

At this point, John and Jay strolled into the camp and Johnny said, "What's going on, men?"

Buster Bottom answered, "Talkin' 'bout Private Johnson's nightmares has got us tellin' ghost stories, Lieutenant! Have you ever seen any ghosts, suh?" Johnny responded, "Believe me, I've had my share of strange experiences, Buster!" as he wondered about the lady in the white dress. Harry Leech, the former pirate, seized the moment and everyone's attention to relate his firsthand encounter with a ghost. His eyes reflected an insane glare.

"Me too, mates! There's nothin' as frightful as seein' a ghost at sea, 'cause there's no place to run from it." His scratchy voice became low and confidential. "Like the time I was captain of the *Scarlet Dragon*. We had just raided a French frigate off the Barbary Coast the day before and the captain of that ship tried to stab me in the back with a dagger. But I caught him comin' outta the corner of me eye, and turned just in time to shoot him right in the heart. He died instantly and fell overboard. Well, we were celebratin' the haul of a great treasure the next evenin'." The men leaned in closer with their eyes widened and mouths agape.

"Most of the crew was gettin' mighty drunk on some of the French wine we took. So I ordered 'em to their quarters, went to my cabin in the forecastle . . . and fell asleep. But somewhere in the night I was awakened by a rustlin' noise and footsteps walking up to my bunk. I looked up and there was the ghost of that French captain I killed, standin' over me with that dagger raised to stab me." A wave of fear rippled across the faces of the men listening in captivated silence as Leech continued his tale of horror. "I instantly reached for my gun . . . but when I turned back to fire at him, he was gone!" This comment evoked another "Ooohh" out of Les. "I searched the ship over, from stem to stern, above and below, and saw nothin'. It had to be a ghost to disappear that fast without a trace. But the eeriest part of all was when I arose in the mornin'. Right there on my desk, in the broad daylight, was that dead Frenchman's dagger. The hair raised up on the back of my neck and all of a sudden, without warnin', the dagger jumped up in the air ready to stab me again and I could see no man a holdin' it." Several gasps could be heard, otherwise all was silence as the spellbound men's widened eyes were trained on Leech, hanging on to his every word. "I fired me pistol but the damned thing came down on me anyhow."

Goober Shaw belted out, "Ya mean it stabbed ya?"

"That's how I got this!" Leech held up his arm and rolled back the sleeve of his shirt to reveal a scar that stretched almost from the wrist to the elbow. Some of the men gasped again as Leech said, "Take my word for it, the worst ghost is the one you can't see. It wasn't long after that I became a blockade runner for the Confederacy."

Robert Johnson started his shell-shocked trembling again, and responded, "Th . . . th . . . then ghosts are real. So what do you make of the ghostly nightmares ah've been havin'?"

Johnny and the rest of the men just exchanged concerned glances and the silence said more than words could have. Some looked frightened. Buster turned his head away and stared off into the night. Les stared down at the ground. James Morgan rubbed his chin, searching his mind for an answer—but nobody had an answer.

About a month later, the answer came drifting into camp from the front lines of battle. Robert E. Lee's Northern Virginia Army suffered its worst defeat with over twenty-two thousand casualties; the Union had over seventeen thousand killed or injured. It was the greatest battle ever fought in the Northern hemisphere, a battle near a town in Pennsylvania that John and the rest of the men had never heard of except in the nightmares of Robert Johnson—a little town called Gettysburg.

It was mid-July of 1863 before word of the Battle of Gettysburg reached the makeshift hospitals in Danville, Virginia, and the Smoky Meadows Plantation, about fifteen miles to the northeast. Finally, Major Wilburn returned from a trip to Richmond and the full impact of the tragedy hit the Wilburn family. It was a sad day when the major announced that his nephew, Daniel Wilburn, was among those killed at Gettysburg.

Johnny had never met Daniel, the son of the major's brother, Samuel. But observing the grieving Wilburn family rested heavily on his heart.

The next evening, he was lying on his bunk in the guesthouse, unable to shut out the sorrowful images of what he had seen over the last two days. The image of the grieving Wilburn family gathered on the front porch of the stately mansion was still vivid to him.

There was Major Wilburn hardly able to utter the words to his sister-in-law that her son was gone. The tears of Sarah flowing endlessly at word her only son was not ever coming home, and she cried out mournfully, "Oh . . . No! No! No! Not my Daniel. My one and only Danny boy!" She nearly collapsed and the major and his wife, Libby, grabbed her to hold her up. Libby, also in tears, tried to console her saying,

"Sarah! Oh, Sarah! Come, come in the house and sit down."

As the women, servants, and children proceeded into the house, Major Wilburn, his father, and Pastor Prather momentarily stayed behind. The major turned to the other two men and said, "I hate to be the bearer of bad news." Grandfather Wilburn whispered, "We all do, son." Pastor Prather added, "This war has brought much sadness."

Grandfather Wilburn looked down sadly, saying, "He was so young. I would rather it had been me." Major Wilburn was touched by these words from his father because he felt the same way, and he closed his eyes, grimacing with grief as he uttered, "Father! I know . . . I know!"

That evening, Johnny recalled how he walked to the family cemetery not far from the mansion with Major Wilburn's son, Michael Jr., and Jay. They stood there momentarily, looking at the makeshift wooden tombstone the family had erected as a temporary memorial. The shaky hand-engraved inscription simply read:

In memory of Daniel L. Wilburn
Born Feb. 26, 1845-Died July 3, 1863.

Johnny remembered how the crying of Sarah could still be heard as he, Jay, and Michael Jr. gazed upon the rustic monument and then slowly walked away.

That evening, Johnny's thoughts turned to Molly as they always did each evening. He got up and began to write her another letter.

My Dear Precious Molly,

More than ever, I long to hold you in my arms and feel the warmth of life inside of you. I need your love so much. The cold death of war is getting closer to me, and it's not a pretty sight. Major Wilburn's nephew was killed in the battles at Gettysburg, Pennsylvania. He was one of over twenty thousand men in Robert E. Lee's Northern Virginia Army who died. They say at least that many Union men died during the three-day battle too.

I never met his nephew, but seeing his mother and the family grieve so much is hard on a man's heart. How many tears are being shed across this land we once called the United States? It makes me realize how fragile life can be and how precious you are to me. I don't know when this war will end, but it can't be soon enough to suit me. Write me soon, my love, and let me know how you're doing and how your mother and Aunt Elsie are getting along.

I want you to know that no matter what happens, even if I die in battle, I will always love you.

All my Love,
Johnny

Due to the slow travel of the times and the limits of the wartime postal service, it was almost a month before Johnny received a return to the letter he wrote that night. When it arrived, he read it several times, and again that evening under the coal oil lamp in the guesthouse. He pictured Molly's charming face surrounded in dark curls dangling as he read her words.

My Darling Johnny,

I'm sorry to hear about the death of Major Wilburn's nephew, and even more sorry to hear how it has grieved you. My heart goes out to you. I want to press your cheek to my breast and comfort you. I hope you will hold this thought in your heart and mind until the day comes when we can hold each other in our arms. It's been over

*five months since we've been together, but it seems like a
century to me. The only way I can get through each day
is to think about the good times we had together.*

Do you remember when we met at the Charleston Social?

Johnny began to recall how bold he was to ask her to
dance even though he couldn't dance very well at all. He
kept getting everyone out of step, bumping into other
couples, knocking a gentleman down and creating chaos,
trying to help the young man to his feet and starting to
lead the fellow for a few steps of the dance, then turning
back to dance with Molly like nothing happened. He
remembered Molly smiling, laughing, and enjoying it as
he continued reading her account of the incident in her
letter.

*You were so funny and cute. You were so anxious to
please me and didn't tell me you couldn't dance. I believe
Charles Hawkins thought you were going to dance with
him. I'll never forget that shocked look on his face. I love
the way you acted so casual about it all. You told me
later you didn't care about anything as long as you could
hold me close. You're so sweet.*

Do you remember our first kiss?

Johnny remembered it vividly. He had invited Molly to
go horseback riding on her first visit to Uncle Fred's farm. It
was when Uncle Fred was ill and Aunt Elsie was chaperoning
them, following along in a small carriage. Johnny galloped
ahead and into a clump of trees as Molly raced her horse to
catch him. Aunt Elsie was shouting, "Slow down. Wait! Wait!"
Johnny and Molly reached the trees way ahead of Aunt Elsie.
Riding sidesaddle, Molly almost fell off of her horse when
she suddenly stopped in the trees beside John. Johnny
reached out to catch her and he pulled her close. They
stared longingly at one another for a brief moment and then

kissed passionately. Picturing this exciting moment, he continued reading Molly's letter.

We went horseback riding with your Aunt Elsie as chaperon. You took off and said, "Catch me if you can!" I tried my best to keep up, and then you stopped in that grove of trees and I started to slip since I was riding sidesaddle. I can still see the desire in your eyes when you grabbed me and kissed me. My heart still skips a beat when I think about that very special passionate moment. That's when I knew we were truly meant for each other.

My dear Johnny, when the hell of war comes too near I want you to think about the heavenly times we've had together. It helps me. And I know it will help you get through the rough times too. I love you, darling. And I want you to know I'll be thinking about you no matter what you're doing. I'll wait for you no matter how long it takes. Tonight, when I go to bed I'll hold my pillow close and dream of the day when we will be together as man and wife. I pray for that wonderful day to be soon.

Affectionately Yours Always,
Molly ♡

P. S. Mother and your Aunt Elsie say hello. Elsie moved in with us for a while and left the darkies to care for the farm because she's been so lonely since Uncle Fred passed away. It's too bad they never had any children. She said she will give us the farm when you return home as long as we care for her in her old days. Isn't that sweet? I haven't had such good news since the day I got that letter from Daddy and knew he was among the survivors at Chancellorsville.

Chapter 7

MARCH TO LEAVE

More than anything in the world, Johnny wanted to be back home, holding Molly in his arms. The idea that he would have his own piece of the world, including inheriting Aunt Elsie's farm, was a cozy thought. He figured the war couldn't last forever, and if he did his job well—and with God's help he could stay alive and healthy—their dream would have to come true.

To make time pass faster, Johnny threw himself into the task at hand, shaping up his crew of misfits. He wanted to impress Major Wilburn, so he had been attempting to get them to drill in regimented military fashion for several weeks, but to little avail. They still marched all out of step, and the dwarf, Les Moore, had to skip rapidly to keep up. They looked like a band of ragtag circus clowns as Johnny called cadence.

"Yo left. Yo left. Yo left, right, left!" Some of them didn't even know their right from their left.

"C'mon, gentlemen, let's get in step! All right, repeat after me. If I can't march right, I've been told . . ." The men repeated each line Johnny chanted.

"If I can't march right, I've been told . . ."

"I won't get home until I'm old."

"I won't get home until I'm old."

"That girl that's waitin' way back home . . ."
"That girl that's waitin' way back home . . ."
"Will get fed up and start to roam."
"Will get fed up and start to roam."
At this point, some of the men sported a disgruntled face.
"Some other man she's bound to meet . . ."
"Some other man she's bound to meet . . ."
"While I march here with two left feet."
"While I march here with two left feet."
Johnny decided to bring his creative spree to a halt because the men didn't seem to be getting the message.
"Company . . . Hawt! At ease, men!" He paused a moment with his mouth twisted in a disgusted smirk. "Of course, I hope you realize that's the problem, men. You've been 'at ease' the whole time we've been marchin'!"
Michael Wilburn Jr. walked up beside Johnny. John looked down and put his hand on the young lad's head and said, "Why, Michael here can march better than that. Right, son?" The boy looked up at Johnny, shook his head yes, and said, "Uh-huh!"
James Morgan felt the need to express his mind, breaking out with,
"Aw come on, Sarge . . . whut diffrunce does it make?" Johnny snapped back at him, "It's lieutenant, Morgan! You're not only ignorant, you're apathetic! You know that?" Morgan lackadaisically said, "I don't know . . . and I don't care."
All this time, Major Wilburn had been looking out his study window observing Johnny and his assigned men. He turned from the window toward his father, who was sitting in the chair in front of the desk, and addressed the elder Wilburn, "You know, Father, Lieutenant Van Worth is trying hard to discipline those men and make them into soldiers but . . . I sometimes wonder if he's ever going to get them ready before we're forced to send them back to the front. Since Gettysburg, General Lee needs every man he can get."

He walked from the window to his desk. The major's father had white hair, was nearing eighty years old, yet he was spry and alert, exuding wisdom and experience when he talked.

"Well, if it were me . . . I'd give Van Worth a little more time to make them into useful soldiers. It won't do any good to send Lee men who are going to cause problems. We can't afford to lose many more battles . . . or any more good men . . . like Daniel."

"Yes, of course. Losing Daniel, my own brother's son, makes me feel guilty for my duty of being in charge of enforcing the draft."

"It's not your fault that Daniel died. That's the result of forces far beyond your control. A man has to do what he has to do, and you're doing a good job, son. You shouldn't feel guilty about those things you can't control."

"I respect your wisdom, Father. I should call upon it more often." He paused a moment, remembering another matter about which he can seek his father's advice.

"In fact, I have a perplexing problem I'd like to discuss with you. I had some important papers that seemed to disappear. The first time it happened, I thought I was getting careless. But when even more papers—showing troop movements—vanished from my desk the very next day, I became convinced someone deliberately took them." Grandfather Wilburn incredulously exclaimed, "Could there be a spy among us?"

"I don't know," said the major, stroking his chin, trying to recall what could have happened. "But if it is so, it's a very serious matter. This mystery must be solved." His father thought a moment and pointed at his son as he said,

"Do you think it could be one of the men under Van Worth's command? Or perhaps Van Worth himself? After all he is from the North. Perhaps that's why he got friendly with Michael Jr., to get closer to you."

Major Wilburn was puzzled, but hesitant to accuse Johnny.

"Maybe! But our family's originally from Philadelphia and we're not spies. I don't know. I hope it's not Van Worth, but I plan to question him and investigate this further just the same."

Later that afternoon, Jay watched as Johnny came walking back from the Wilburn Mansion with a solemn look on his face.

"You don't look so happy this time. Whut'd Majuh Wilburn want?" When Johnny hesitated to answer, Jay said, "Or should Ah ask?"

"I guess I can tell you, Jay, 'cause I know I can trust you. I'm not so sure about the other men." Jay asked, "Whadda you mean?"

"I don't want you to talk to anyone about this. We must keep it a secret—at least for now." Johnny looked from side to side to make sure no one was observing them, then spoke in a very confidential whisper. "It seems some important papers disappeared from Major Wilburn's study." Jay got a worried look because slaves often got blamed for things they didn't do. He blurted out in a whisper, "He don't think you . . . or me . . ."

Johnny quickly reassured Jay, "No! I hope he doesn't suspect us. But he believes it could be someone possibly under my command." Then he suddenly remembered, "Wait a minute! Could it be that Andrew Payne who showed up here demanding to see Major Wilburn a while back?" Jay's response was immediate.

"Yeah! Ah bet he da one. Dere wuz somethin' strange 'bout dat man!"

"He stayed overnight and left the next day to supposedly go back to General Lee's army. That's about the time the papers disappeared. He could be taking information to the Union army . . . such as troop movements . . . who knows?"

"Dat's right, who knows? It's too bad he ain't around to be questioned 'bout it." Johnny agreed, "Yeah, that *is* too bad."

Later that evening, the men were gathered around a freshly dug gravesite. It was the grave prepared for David Dunn, one of the regular soldiers stationed at the plantation. He had died from dysentery, a common plague to the men of Civil War times. Men also died as much from infectious wounds as they did from the wound itself, due to ignorance about sanitary treatment. For those who had been in the army any length of time, they were growing disgustedly used to death. For others, like Johnny and some of his men, it was still a troubling thing to see.

As the last few shovelfuls of dirt were tossed on the grave, some of the men held their hats over their hearts and looked at the wooden tombstone reading "David Dunn." Goober Shaw drawled out, "Poor ol' David Dunn. He really is done now fo' sure."

With disgust, Buster Bottom expressed his sentiments. "Another man dead from dysentery. Ya don't even have to take a rifle ball to die in this army."

Off in the distance, the dinner bell could be heard. George Crumley, the baker, had been pressed into service as the company cook. He called out, "Supper time! Supper time!"

Buster sarcastically commented again, "Well, it looks like we're next. Y'all ready to chow down on some dysentery?" The other men just shrugged their shoulders or shook their heads, obviously never stopping to consider the thought before. Buster concluded,

"That's just somethin' that occurred to me."

The men started toward the mess area with their heads down, leaving Johnny and Jay to bring up the rear. Johnny turned to Jay and said, "You know, Jay, the men are starting to get restless." "Ah think dere a-hankerin' fo' some action, Mistah Johnny." Johnny paused a moment before answering. "That's what bothers me. I know the kind of action they're hankerin' for."

At the campsite, when the men started eating, James Morgan commented, "Is it my Imagination or does this food taste worse every day?" Mr. Grossman, who spent a lot of time running toward the outhouse, added, "I don't know which is worse. The ache you git from bein' hungry or the achin' cramps you git after you eat!"

George Crumley didn't take kindly to the men complaining about the food he had prepared, even though he knew it wasn't the best and definitely not the freshest.

Crumley blasted back a retort to the men. "Are you guys complainin' 'bout the food? Well, it's not mah fault! Most of the food supply is runnin' low 'cause it's bein' shipped out to the troops on General Lee's front lines these days."

Ben Grimm chimed in, "Well, I feel sorry for those guys. It'll be rotten by the time it gets there." Morgan concluded, "That figgers! If it's rotten when it leaves here ah gar-on-tee it'll be rotten when it arrives there." Grossman complained, "All ah know is ah keep havin' to go to the outhouse and—" He stopped in midsentence when he looked down at his food. "Hell! Lookit that! There's a beetle on my bacon!"

Goober Shaw casually looked over at it and said, "What? You don't want it?" He reached over to Grossman's plate, picked up the beetle, and promptly plopped it in his mouth. Almost immediately, he yelled and then spit it out violently.

"Ow! *Sptt! Sptt!* That damn thing bit me!" Johnny casually replied, "Serves ya right for hoggin' all the *fresh* food!" Morgan followed with, "Why does the army call food a 'mess'? That oughta tell ya somethin'!" Buster Bottom added, "They probably do that so's a fella don't get his hopes up too high."

Goober Shaw let go of his tongue to say, "Ah know one thing. Ah sho could use some of Mama's home cookin' 'bout now." This triggered a thought in the mind of the swarthy Harry Leech. "Mama? Now you're talkin', mate! I'm feelin' like I've been at sea for a whole year and I'm buildin' up an appetite for more than food. I could use the charmin' company of a lovely lady . . . if ya know what I mean."

The men broke into a lusty laugh and Johnny knew all too well what he meant, and whispered to Jay, "That's what I was talkin' about." Jay nodded his head yes.

Buster Bottom picked up right away on Leech's desire, "Oh yeah, sounds like you'd like to make a little trip over to Madam Fanny Sellers's place outside of Danville."

Les Moore chimed in with his falsetto voice, "Fanny Sellers? Who is she?" Harry Leech looked at Les like he was from another planet and said, "Where 'ave you Been 'idin', mate? Why, they've even 'eard of Fanny Sellers in Paris, France."

Buster Bottom decided to enlighten Les. "She has a home she turned into a bar downstairs. And the ladies she employs sorta work the upstairs area . . . ya might say."

Johnny thinks the conversation has gone far enough and jumped up to address the men.

"Okay, men, let me have your attention! You can forget about Fanny Sellers's girls until you learn a little more military discipline." The men grumbled at this comment.

"But I'll tell ya what I'm gonna do. If you can learn to march in step to my satisfaction and can demonstrate that you will show your commanding officers the proper respect, I believe I might be able to convince Major Wilburn to give you leave to visit Danville for one evening." With this, the men cheered wildly.

Johnny was proud that he finally figured out an incentive to get the men shaped up. He drilled them for the next week, and when he saw how they were able to march expertly, he began to wonder how in the world he ever had the guts to think he could convince Major Wilburn to give these men a leave when the major hadn't even made the slightest suggestion this was a possibility. That evening John carefully rehearsed his strategy to convince him. Before he fell asleep, he was feeling his old confidence returning. Then his thoughts turned to Molly and how much he loved her and would stay true to her.

The next day, Johnny had been granted permission to see Major Wilburn and found himself being challenged by the commander as he stood at attention before his desk. Major Wilburn sat back in his chair, somewhat shocked by what Johnny was requesting.

"You want to do what? Sit down, Van Worth!" As Johnny sat down, he repeated in a humble low tone, "*Uh* . . . let the men have one night's leave in Danville. But only provided you feel I have shaped them up as useful soldiers, of course . . . as I promised I would do according to your assignment." Major Wilburn pursed his lips, turned his head from side to side, and said, "Well, I don't know, Van Worth . . . *uh* . . . This is highly irregular!" Wilburn paused to think about it and John seized the opportunity to put his "convincing" plan into effect.

"Irregular? Yes, sir. As I recall, that's the word you used when you appointed me lieutenant and gave me this command assignment."

The major didn't exactly remember, but said anyway, "*Uh* . . . Well, perhaps I did."

"Sir, I recall you once told me these men could have been severely punished for their conduct, thrown in the brig, or hanged. But since the Confederacy is short of men you sent a telegram to commanders asking they give unruly draftees a second chance to be turned into useful soldiers."

"Well, yes . . . that was my plan."

"I hope you'll forgive me, sir. But to give the men an incentive to shape up, I promised them I could perhaps convince you to allow them a two-day leave."

"Oh, you did, did you?"

He was a bit shocked that Johnny was bold enough to ask such a favor, but he admired John's courage just the same. Johnny went on with his well-rehearsed dialogue.

"Yes. I hope you don't feel I was out of line or too assuming to do that, sir. But I was desperate, because . . . to be perfectly frank . . . the men were getting a little restless and bored with just dying from dysentery and disease and they want to see a little action, you know."

Major Wilburn cleared his throat and said, "Well! You present a rather compelling argument, Lieutenant." Seeing the major was leaning his way, John went for the close.

"Sir, please! At least give them a review. They've been working very hard."

Breaking into a smile, Major Wilburn relented, "Well . . . I suppose I can at least see how they're coming along. I owe that much to them . . . and to you, Van Worth."

"You won't be sorry, sir. I'm sure of that." As they stood to go outside, Johnny had confidence the major would be surprised to see what he had in store for him.

Johnny had been drilling the men out of sight of the mansion for the past week so that Major Wilburn would have no idea of the unusual performance he had put together. As the major stood watching, Johnny and his men came marching past him in perfect step, even though the commander was a bit amused by Les Moore, the dwarf, leaping at the end of a column in order to stay in step to John calling cadence.

"Yo left. Yo left. Yo left, right, left!" After several minutes of regular close order Drill, Johnny yelled out, "Repeat after me! We're good soldiers, that's our quest." "We're good soldiers, that's our quest."

"Obey commanders, do our best."

"Obey commanders, do our best."

"We can really move our pants."

"We can really move our pants."

"We can even march and dance."

"We can even march and dance."

At this point, Johnny yelled out, "Grab your partner . . . promenade! Yahoo!" The men paired off and did square-dance moves, going in circles, sashaying hand-offs. One man held the dwarf up off the ground to complete a move. They then resumed the march formation, and shortly thereafter

Johnny called an odd cadence that had the men hop-scotching perfectly in step.

"Yo left, left, left! Yo right, right, right! Up, back, up, back, up, up, up, and hawt! Left face!" The men were brought to parade position in front of Major Wilburn! Johnny barked out, "Address commander! Present arms!" John and the men saluted Major Wilburn in unison and held their positions.

Major Wilburn returned the salute and said, "At ease!" Afterward, he dropped his hand as the men dropped theirs to stand at rest. The major smiled as he walked toward Johnny.

"Lieutenant, I must say, I am duly impressed! You and your men may have your leave!"

"Thank you, Major!" The men started cheering, shaking hands, and some jumped up and down. Then Major Wilburn took Johnny slightly aside to talk confidentially.

"Mr. Van Worth! You may go to Danville Friday. But you and your men must be back in camp—and sober—by twenty-hundred hours Saturday. Is that understood?"

"Yes, sir! You can depend on me, Major!"

"Very well! I want you to have the men in formation and meet me here for a formal dismissal at noon Friday." Johnny could hardly hold back his exuberance as he said,

"We'll be here, sir!" He reached out to shake the major's hand and then they saluted each other. The major turned to walk back inside the mansion, took a few steps, and turned back to say, "Oh, there's one more thing. You might want to avoid something. Just this side of Danville is a house with a bar, Fanny Sellers's place. She has a *reputation*, if you know what I mean." Johnny quickly responded, "Oh, well . . . we wouldn't want to ruin a lady's reputation, sir."

"Right!" said Major Wilburn. Then he did a double-take, looking puzzled as he walked away.

For Johnny and his troops it seemed as though Friday would never come. But finally, here they were, with their backpacks and weapons, ready to march up to the mansion where Major Wilburn was to formally dismiss them. Excitement was in the air as they made final preparations.

Meanwhile, on the front porch of the great mansion, Major Wilburn waited with Pastor Prather, whom he had summoned for the occasion. The chaplain was apprehensive about it all, and he said to Major Wilburn, "Are you sure you want to do this? They could get into trouble, you know."

"I know!" said the major, still pondering his decision. "It's against my better judgment, but I feel compelled to let them go. Besides, I've already given my word. Lieutenant Van Worth is very persuasive."

"What if he's the spy you suspect? You're giving him an opportunity to get away."

Major Wilburn assured Prather, "I've thought about that! And if that's the case, I'm giving him plenty of rope to hang himself. I'm going to have some of my regular troops trail them." He looked over Pastor Prather's shoulder and saw John and his men approaching, "Oh, here they come now!"

Johnny and his troops proudly came marching in their "newly found" perfect step to John calling cadence. "Yo left. Yo left. Yo left, right, left!" When they were even with the major and Chaplain Prather, Johnny commanded, "Company, hawt!" Even Pastor Prather was impressed with the apparent improvement the men seemed to have made.

Johnny did a left face, walked up to the major, and they exchanged salutes.

"At ease, men!" Then Major Wilburn addressed Johnny. "I see you're carrying your weapons. I was going to suggest you do. After all, there's still a war going on, and even though you'll be traveling a few miles farther away from the battlefields, you never know what you're going to encounter." Johnny replied, "Yes, sir. We might run up on a mama bear. I hear they're dangerous protecting their young this time of year."

Harry Leech overheard the conversation and whispered to the man beside him, "I'd rather run up on a bare mama." He winked lustily. In response to John's statement, Major Wilburn said, "Yes, that's true. But there are greater dangers than bears. Even though we're far from enemy lines, I still have reports of a gang of deserters and hoodlums who have been robbing people, stealing horses, raping women, and terrorizing people in five counties, including here in Pittsylvania County. That's why I've asked Chaplain Prather here to pray over you men before I dismiss you." Pastor Prather addressed the men in his dramatic theological voice,

"Gentlemen! Let us pray!" He bowed his head and the men respectfully followed likewise. "Lord! We ask your blessing upon these men as they leave these premises. Send angels to walk beside them and protect them from all harm. Let them fall not into temptation." Some of the men, especially Harry Leech, looked out of the corner of their eyes at one another with disturbed glances as Chaplain Prather continued to pray.

"Let no man be deceived. Let no man deceive others. And if there is one who would betray others, let his wickedness be revealed. And let him be brought to justice. Amen!"

Prather looked up to address the men with a personal appeal following the prayer.

"Now, men, I want to warn you to stay away from Fanny Sellers's house. I'm sure it's a sinful place. You wouldn't enjoy that naughty atmosphere. There are many places in Danville where you may enjoy yourselves. Try visiting Berry Hill. It served as a hospital during the Revolutionary War." Harry Leech leaned over to the man beside him and whispered, "I wonder if it's a sin to shoot a preacher?" Pastor Prather continued, "It's being used as a hospital again, today. You can go there and pray for those who have been injured in this war. And God bless you wherever you go." Major Wilburn said, "Thank you, Chaplain!" He then motioned Johnny aside.

"John! Your leave could be a blessing to us if you'll stop by and see Major Sutherlin on Main Street in Danville. He's in charge of Quartermaster. See if he can spare to issue some fresh rations and a few more munitions."

"Major Sutherlin on Main Street. Got it! I'll ask him." Major Wilburn smiled at Johnny's eagerness to help with this chore and said,

"Good! And good luck to you!" He addressed the entire platoon in a loud voice, "Gentlemen! You're dismissed!"

Once again, the men started cheering wildly, shaking hands, and jumping. Yelling above the cheers, Major Wilburn warned, "And remember, no Fanny Sellers!"

Chapter 8

FANNY AND THE GANG

Before the war, Danville, Virginia, was a thriving community of about four thousand residents, located in the midst of the rich tobacco lands close to the border of North Carolina. It was a town proud of its ordinances that levied fines for such violations as throwing wood or dirt on walkways, and further prohibited cow pens or pigsties on the front part of any lot or making any unusual or hideous noise by night.

That's why Madam Fanny Sellers located her restaurant, bar, and brothel on the edge of town north of the Dan River. It was still close enough to town that church bells in Danville could be heard from her front porch, but still far enough away that the ruckus from the bar didn't disturb the townsfolk.

Danville was a growing and prosperous community before the conflict began, but here in the summer of 1863, many refugees from Fredericksburg and other war-torn communities east and north of this town on the southern border of Virginia, found safety in this quaint and quiet village on the shores of the Dan River. Danville was also a primary point for the exchange of prisoners which were housed in large tobacco warehouses. They were shipped in aboard the Richmond and Danville Railroad by the thousands. With other buildings, including some churches, being turned into temporary hospitals, the little town was beginning to feel the hardships of the war. Food, clothing, and many of the necessities of life were growing more and more scarce.

Adding to the pains of the day was anxiety over word that some escaped prisoners and deserters were pillaging the countryside, robbing, raping, and terrorizing the citizenry. This was the gang of which Major Wilburn had warned Johnny and his men before leaving the plantation.

It was late afternoon when Johnny and his crew arrived at Fanny Sellers's place. The sign outside read "Fanny Sellers's Bar and Good Time. It's a business doing pleasure with you." The men were hungry and ready for whatever snacks, drinks, and "Good Time" the girls had for them, regardless of the stern warnings of Major Wilburn and Chaplain Prather. After all, Fanny Sellers was their primary destination all along. They were excited and intrigued about what might lie behind the door to Fanny's, as the loud upright piano could be heard even before they entered the building.

Inside, it was a bawdy barroom scene with men cheering the girls dancing the cancan on the bar. The dwarf, Les Moore, was so excited he began to turn cart- wheels on a table while "waitresses" and the men cheered him on. Other girls were flirting and serving drinks.

However, the center attraction in all of this was the buxom Fanny Sellers herself. She always dressed the part to the max with bright-colored satin dresses, complete with delicate dyed ostrich feathers and makeup, all designed to tease or tickle a man's fancy.

It didn't take long for her to corner one of her former customers, Harry Leech, to see what kind of loot she could garner for herself. She had been getting him warmed up with lots of whiskey, and he smiled like a simpleton at her as she decided it was time to sit down with the seedy varmint to take a little more advantage of his drunken state.

"Why sure, Cap'n Leech, ah remembah little ol' you from the days when ah had mah place ovah in Norfolk. When the war broke out ah had to move mah operation ovah heah to Danville where it's a lot safer. When men start to shootin' their guns all ovah the place it's kinda scary for 'peace' lovin' folks like me and mah girls."

Stoned, smiling, and looking googly-eyed at her bust, Leech drooled out, "Aye, aye to that, ma'am. I must say, Madam Fanny, you're lookin' doubly fine and Dandy . . . as always."

"Oh, aren't you cute." She brushed her hand against his ugly beard and said, "And ah see you still have those charmin' fuzzy whiskah's . . . as always."

Faking a bashful turn of his head, Leech laughed, "*Haw haw* . . . gosh . . . Miss Fanny, you could charm a savage beast!"

"Ah know. All in a day's work, Captain. All in a day's work." She turned her head Gracefully, checking out everything in the room. She did a slight double take when she spotted Johnny and Jay sitting alone at a table.

"Could you excuse me fo' a moment, Cap'n Leech?"

"*Aw* . . . sure! Do what ya hafta do." He grinned.

With charming confidence, she assured him, "Ah always do. Be right back."

As Fanny slowly worked her way through the crowd of men attempting to flirt with her, Johnny and Jay continued their conversation at their table, "Come on, Jay, you mean James Woodward used to work in a shipyard too?"

"Tol' me he worked at the Howard Shipyard on da Ohio Rivah."

"That makes three men in this outfit that know something about shipbuilding. Might come in handy if we ever need to build a boat." They both laughed at the unlikelihood of the idea. Jay noticed Woodward, who was one of the few handsome young men in their outfit, as he was kissing a waitress. Jay pointed with his thumb.

"Looks like he's buildin' up to somethin' right now."

While Johnny and Jay were checking out James Woodward, arching their eyebrows and smirking their lips, Fanny approached their table.

"Well, how ya doin', fellas? Is there anything ah can get ya? Ah'm Fanny Sellers. Ah run the place." She held her hand out to shake and said, "Nice to meet ya!"

Jay just stared quietly, happy that he'd been allowed into this white establishment against the normal custom of the times. While shaking her hand, Johnny said,

"So you're the famous Fanny Sellers!" He wasn't impressed with her but politely said, "Nice to meet you too, ma'am. I'm Lt. John Van Worth, and I'm in charge of part of this mob you have in here." He turned to introduce Jay and started to say Jay was his personal valet, but changed his mind, "And this is my . . . *uh* . . . This is Jay Brown." Surprising both of them, she shook Jay's hand also while saying,

"Nice to meet you too." Jay nodded bashfully and Fanny again extended her hospitality, turning back to address Johnny. "Ah appreciate your business. Like ah say, we're here to please. Just let me know your needs."

She winked, and when Johnny and Jay said nothing but just smiled and nodded their heads in approval of her comment, she decided to let it rest and drop another hint later. Then she gracefully slipped away to work the rest of the men.

As she walked away, Jay leaned toward Johnny and said in a near whisper,

"She's pretty smooth, huh?" Johnny said nothing for a moment and Jay went on to inquire, "Are you gonna tell her 'bout yo' needs?"

John paused and then uttered, "I'm afraid my needs are back in Charleston." Jay smiled and knew exactly what Johnny meant, but he had to verbalize it anyway.

"Miss Molly?"

"Yeah!" He sighed, "I miss her a lot." He paused, bit his lip, and looked down at the empty glass he was nervously rocking back and forth. Finally, he told Jay,

"I don't feel right about this, Jay. I shouldn't be here. Think I'll step outside for a little fresh air." Jay began to chuckle as he got up to go with Johnny.

"What're you laughin' about?"

"Ah's just wonderin'. Could ol' Chaplain Prather's prayer be workin' on you?"

Johnny cast an uncomfortable glance at Jay as they both started to go out, leaving behind all of the noise and lusty men flirting with waitresses. As they walked out on the porch, they heard a desperate-sounding female voice coming from the side of the building. Johnny and Jay looked at one another as if to say, "Did you hear that?" They rushed to the corner of the porch and in the moonlight saw one of Fanny's girls, a lovely blond, with both of her hands being held against the building by a man with a nasty mustache and a scar on his face. He was pushing his body against hers, trying to kiss her as she yelled, "No! No! Get away from me! Leave me alone! Stop it! Help! Help!"

Johnny and Jay rushed to her aid. Johnny grabbed the man from behind, wrestling one of his arms in a hammerlock while holding his right arm under the man's chin.

The man grimaced as Jay took the man's pistol, pointed it at him, and said,

"Mistah, you got some bad manners!" Then a look of shock came over Jay's face.

"Oh mah god! It's him!" Holding the man from behind, John couldn't see the man's face and he asked, "Who?" The man struggled to free himself, but Johnny tightened his grip and Jay fired a shot at the ground.

The man shouted, "Don't shoot! Don't shoot! I'm not hurtin' anything!" Jay snapped back, "Da hail you ain't. You dat spy, Andrew Payne!"

Johnny pushed the man to the ground, pulled out his Colt .44, and jumped around in front of him to get a look at his face. The man froze with his knees and palms on the ground and looked up into the barrels of both guns being held on him as Johnny questioned him.

"All right, Payne! I thought you were going back to General Lee's army at Richmond after your so-called important meeting with Major Wilburn. Just how do you explain being here?"

The blond girl they just freed from the clutches of this man who had been intent on raping her, stood nearby, watching the scuffle. When she heard Johnny refer to her perpetrator as Andrew Payne, she quickly corrected him.

"He ain't no Andrew Payne. He's Rowdy Roberts! He and his men come in here and just take whatever they want— money, our bodies, whatever!"

Johnny and Jay, distracted from Rowdy Roberts when they turned to hear what the girl had to say, were further thrown off guard by approaching men on horses who started firing pistols into the air. It was the rest of Rowdy Roberts's Gang, who had been waiting out of sight and alerted to action by the shot Jay fired a few moments earlier.

The girl, Nellie, yelled out, "That's his gang now!" From his crouched position, Rowdy Roberts took advantage of the distraction and threw a block into Johnny and Jay and they, in turn, fell into Nellie. All three of them fell to the ground. Rowdy ran and jumped on his horse, which his men had brought along. Johnny and Jay bravely lay their bodies over Nellie to protect her from gunfire while they awkwardly fired their weapons over their shoulders hitting none of them. As Rowdy and his gang galloped away Johnny and Jay got up and fired at them. They got off a shot or two and then their guns only clicked against empty chambers. They were out of ammo.

They quickly turned their attention to Nellie. Gently helping her to her feet, Johnny said,

"Are you all right?" Nellie looked at him with adoring eyes and responded, "I'm fine. Thanks to you!"

Aroused by the gunfire and horses, the men inside came running out with Fanny and some of the other girls. Goober Shaw was the first to speak.

"Whut's goin' on? Are the Yankees heah?" Jay and Johnny rolled their eyes and Jay said, "What a goober!"

Fanny called out, "What is it, Nellie?"

"I was coming back from the outhouse when Rowdy Roberts dragged me over here and tried to rape me." Fanny expressed her anger, "That filthy rat!"

"These men pulled him off of me but the whole gang showed up and . . . well . . . we're lucky to be alive!" Fanny Sellers exclaimed, "You sure are! That Rowdy Roberts is ruinin' mah business! Come on, everybody, get back inside before they decide to return."

As they all started to go inside, Nellie was still looking at Johnny with loving eyes. Johnny walked up to Fanny and said, "Sorry we let 'em get away, ma'am, but there were too many of 'em."

"Ah know! Ah just hope they stay away! She paused momentarily, thinking about what must have happened and said, "Thanks for what ya did!" Johnny answered, "Still wish I'd done a more permanent job." As they entered the door, Nellie wrapped her arm around Johnny's, held his bicep, and softly said, "You were wonderful!" He just barely smiled, appreciative of Nellie's admiration but not wanting to encourage her affection.

When they filed back into the barroom they discovered one man who hadn't made it outside. Harry Leech was face down on his table, passed out drunk. Fanny yelled to the piano player, "Sonny! Play somethin' lively! Let's get this party started again."

"Sure thing, Miss Fanny." He scooted onto the piano stool and broke into a hearty rendition of "The Yellow Rose of Texas." Fanny yelled out above the music, "Free round of drinks for everybody!" The men cheered wildly. Les started turning cartwheels in place, one at a time, and the dancing girls took to the bar, doing cancan moves with their skirts. The party went on well into the wee hours of the morning. There was a lot of revelry, mostly done by Johnny's men, while the regular customers kept the girls busy upstairs. Fanny had a strict rule of closing down the bar by 2:00 a.m. but by then it had been a long day for John and company. Some of the men had joined Captain Leech and were in drunken stupors. Some had passed out in their chairs.

Throughout the barroom most of the men were pretty well incapacitated, sprawled on the floor as well as the tables. Only Johnny and a few of his men were still sober. Fanny started blowing out candles and lamps, while some of the girls were wiping tables and stacking chairs on tables.

Johnny and those still sober didn't seem to be aware of Fanny's closing rule, and they continued with conversation as Fanny worked her way toward their table. The handsome James Woodward was expounding upon his experience working at the Howard Shipyards, located on the shores of the Ohio River at Jeffersonville, Indiana.

"Oh yeah, Mr. Howard's known for buildin' the finest boats on the river. All the captains prefer a Howard-built boat 'cause they don't shake as much in the water and they last longer." Buster Bottom, who worked at a shipyard in Norfolk, Virginia, was aware of the integrity of the Howard boats and agreed with Woodward's claim, saying, "Yeah! That's what ah've heard." John injected, "I was just telling Jay earlier this evening, that it's unusual we have so many men in this outfit with boat-building and sailing experience. You never told me you knew so much about buildin' riverboats, Woodward."

"I don't remember you askin', Lieutenant."

"I think we're getting to know one another well enough for you men to start calling me Johnny like I promised, especially when we're on leave in a civilian place like this."

By now, Fanny was approaching their table. "Are you boys gonna stay all night? It's past closin' time for the bar, ya know." Johnny pulled out his pocket watch and noticed it was past 2:00 a.m.

"Sorry, Miss Fanny. We weren't paying too much attention to the clock."

Fanny blew out the candle on their table and became more consoling, saying, "Well, ah've been thinkin', since you ran Rowdy Roberts's bunch off like ya did, ah'd feel safer if you'd go ahead and spend the night. At least, ah want ya to know you're welcome to." She glanced at the men on the floor. "Besides, it might be easier than soberin' up these galoots." Pleased by what she said, Johnny responded, "Well, that's mighty friendly of you, Miss Fanny. I think the boys and I will take you up on that offer. Right, fellas?" They nodded yes to one another and stood up. Fanny qualified her proposal, saying, "Ah can't let ya sleep upstairs with the girls unless ya pay me. This is a business place, ya know. But you're welcome to unpack your bedrolls here in the barroom or over in the dinin' room."

"Much obliged, ma'am." Johnny turned to his men. "Well, let's get our blankets."

Fanny confidentially whispered to Johnny, "Are you boys too tired to go upstairs?"

John replied, "I think we've had enough 'good time' this time. Maybe next time." He winked and Fanny smiled knowingly, satisfied she had made every effort to nurse her business. As Johnny started walking away, Nellie came up beside him and sweetly said,

"You can sleep with me tonight, Johnny!"

"My, my, Nellie. You're mighty pretty." He paused thinking about it. "I must say . . . it's a very tempting offer

but I have a lady back in South Carolina who is faithful. She
writes me often. I'm afraid if I sleep with you I won't be able
to sleep with myself afterward. Savvy?" Admiring his
faithfulness she said, "Uh-huh, sure do! You must love her
an awful lot."

"Yes, I do!"

Nellie was moved by the character Johnny had shown
her and she looked down bashfully. Then she meekly looked
Johnny in eye and said, "She's a lucky woman. I wish I was
her."

"I wish you were too." He respectfully bowed his head to
her and said, "Goodnight, Miss Nellie."

"Goodnight!" She paused and softly whispered his name,
"Johnny!"

Johnny slowly walked away and Nellie stared admiringly
at him with an intense look of melancholy.

✤Chapter 9✤

TRAIL TO TERROR

When Johnny and his men bedded down for the night at Fanny Sellers's place, they were so exhausted from the march to get there, the excitement of confronting the Rowdy Roberts Gang, and just generally partying, that they hardly noticed the lightning and thunder from scattered showers over the area just before dawn. The rain provided just enough moisture as to hold the dust down on the trail that next morning. They overslept their usual hours and didn't rise until 9:30 a.m.

Grateful for them routing away the Rowdy Roberts Gang, the girls prepared a simple breakfast for them before they hit the trail, and of course, invited them to "Come back again when they get a paycheck." After paying for drinks, they had little money left to accomplish the purpose of their mission, namely "communing" with the opposite sex. Part of their military disciplinary action included being deprived of pay until they returned as useful soldiers. However, they were pleased to have, at least, gotten the attention of these charming ladies with an occasional hug or a kiss. As Fanny Sellers let them know, they were "Welcome anytime." They said their goodbyes and headed in to Danville to pick up the supplies Major Wilburn had requested while visions of "charming" ladies still danced in their heads.

Before they started through the more than three-hundred-foot-long covered bridge leading across the Dan River, they encountered a trainload of Union prisoners being brought to the prisons in the Danville area. They watched with a crowd of curious townsfolk as the prisoners filed off the train from Richmond where they had been held at Belle Isle.

The order to transport them away from Richmond came directly from Robert E. Lee himself. Lee reasoned that large numbers of Union prisoners posed many complications since Richmond, being the capitol of the Confederacy, was the focal point of many Union military campaigns.

The prisoners were even more exhausted-looking than Johnny and his men. Their journey of a hundred and forty-five miles took twenty-four hours, because the cattle cars they were packed into were so loaded with prisoners and Confederate guards that it could travel a top speed of only twelve miles per hour, if it traveled at all. The train had frequently spread the track apart and they had to stop and spike it back down before proceeding. On several steep grades, the engine had bogged down, requiring the train to be unloaded of its human cargo of four thousand men, who were walked under guard to the top of the hill and reloaded onto the cattle cars. It was during a previous similar journey that Rowdy Roberts and his mangy crew managed to escape in the night.

Even though the Union prisoners had no sleep at all during their trip, some still hadn't lost their sense of humor. A procession of them, led by a Negro band, started through the covered bridge to the tune of the popular song of the time, "Dixie." A prisoner of Irish decent proclaimed, "Begorra! Ain't that foine now. And ain't it gintleminly in the divils to be after tratin' us to such music and military honor?"[1] Johnny and his men were amused by the man's gumption.

Arriving at Major Sutherlin's, Johnny received a warm welcome from this Danville man of distinction, who was instrumental in the building of the covered bridge across the Dan River. Although supplies were short, Major Sutherlin filled Major Wilburn's requisition for supplies from the Confederate quartermaster as best he could.

Johnny noticed James Woodward questioning Major Sutherlin about some steam-powered equipment he had stored away. He also saw the supply of uniforms, saddles, and other such equipment was running low, and he couldn't help but wonder how long the South could go on with the war. However, there was a good supply of pistols, since a small arms foundry had been established on the banks of the Dan river. They toted a number of bags of flour and cornmeal over their shoulders, and some carried wooden boxes of ammunition and a few of those brand-new pistols.

So off they went, packing their supplies on the journey back to Smoky Meadows, not knowing of the horror that had taken place at the plantation while they slept at Fanny Sellers's place. After Johnny's encounter with Rowdy, the thieving rapist and his gang of cutthroats traveled on horseback to the Wilburn Mansion, arriving after everyone had gone to bed. Rowdy banged on the door, dressed in the Confederate uniform he had taken off a dead soldier months before. Major Wilburn came to the door in his nightgown and nightcap, holding a lantern, recognized Rowdy's face and uniform, and let him and one of his henchmen into the house, thinking he was a legitimate Confederate courier named Andrew Payne. While the rest of the gang waited

---

[1] Recorded as a true quote. Solon Hyde, *A Captive of War* (New York, 1900), p. 100; and *The Virginia Magazine of History and Biography,* July 1961, n.3, Vol. 69, p. 330.

outside, Rowdy pulled a gun on the major and attempted a robbery. Rowdy took the lantern and marched the major to the study where he thought gold or other valuables might be hidden.

Meanwhile, the other henchman proceeded to the Wilburn's bedroom upstairs and startled Libby Wilburn. He demanded her valuables. Libby quickly gave him her jewelry box and he told her to stay in bed or he would kill her. He then rushed downstairs to the study to show the jewelry box to Rowdy, who was holding the major at gunpoint and rummaging through his desk. When the henchman entered the room he held up the jewelry box and said, "Look what I've got, boss!" Rowdy walked around in front of the desk to take it from him, as Major Wilburn backed around the desk on the opposite side. Rowdy let his henchman keep the major at gunpoint as he holstered his pistol to open the jewelry box, handing the lantern to his sidekick. Holding the jewelry box up to the light of the lantern, Rowdy ran his finger among the rings, bracelets, pins, earrings, and necklaces. Major Wilburn told Rowdy, "That's all we have to give you." Greedy for more, Rowdy snarled out at the major in his naturally nasty voice,

"Aw, come on, major. Are you tellin' me these are the only things you've got of value 'round here? Major Wilburn remained silent, determined not to reveal the location of his safe.

"You're bound to have some gold pieces here someplace. Or maybe some military papers. The Yankees pay us some good money for the right information. Now, why don't you just save some time and tell me? 'Cause if I hafta just shoot ya and tear this place apart, that's what I'm gonna do. Do I make myself clear or—"

At that moment, he was interrupted by the major's blind daughter, Rebecca, who ran into the room in her nightgown, crying out, "Daddy! Daddy!" Then she blindly stared.

Major Wilburn nearly panicked as he called out her name, "Rebecca!" When she heard her father's voice she knew he was behind the desk and she darted toward the back corner of it, where Major Wilburn wrapped his arms around his daughter, stepped sideways and gently pushed her to safety under the desk.

"Is this your little girl?" Roberts inquired in a tone indicating he was planning to harm her in some way.

"Leave her alone, Payne! She's blind!"

"Leave her alone?" He looked at the major with a nasty smile, and with an equally nasty tone of voice he snarled, "How would you like it if she wuz dead?"

The major gritted his teeth and leaned forward, "You rotten . . ." Meanwhile, Rebecca persistently kept tapping him on the leg with the barrel of a pistol she had pulled from under her nightgown. He glanced down and saw it. Rowdy Roberts continued his nasty laugh thinking he now had the major in a compromising position.

"Now, are you gonna cooperate or am I gonna have to kill your whole family?"

While Roberts's henchman was looking at Rowdy, admiring the meanness of his gang boss, Major Wilburn grabbed the pistol from Rebecca's hand and shot the thug in his gun hand. He dropped his firearm and the lantern, yelling, "*Aaah!* Damn!" He then grabbed his wound with the other hand and ran out of the study toward the front door of the mansion. With his gun in his holster, Rowdy quickly saw the major had the drop on him and he rushed out following his evil sidekick.

Major Wilburn immediately ran around the desk and began stomping on the burning oil-soaked carpet. Outside, the regulars that were still at the plantation were alerted by the gunshot and came running barefoot from their nearby bunkhouse holding long rifles, wearing only their trousers. When they saw what was happening they fired into the darkness in the direction of the fleeing Roberts Gang, but didn't hit any of them. They rushed inside to help Major Wilburn with the fire, grabbing throw rugs to snuff it out.

A while later, Libby Wilburn came rushing in the door in her nightgown, holding Michael Jr. by the hand. She frantically called out to her husband when she saw him hugging their daughter, not knowing if she was injured on not.

"Michael! Michael!" The major consoled his wife. "She was a brave girl, Libby. A brave girl!" Libby fell on her knees and hugged Rebecca. "My baby! My precious baby!"

Rebecca calmly said, "I was so afraid for you and Daddy and Junior!"

Michael Jr. was also touched by his sister's bravery and concern and said,

"I love you, Becca." The young brother and sister put their arms around each other in a warm embrace.

Major Wilburn looked at his family, thankful they all survived the treacherous ordeal. He realized they were lucky and could have all been easily killed by the ruthless criminals that had the audacity to invade their home and their lives. He stared off into space, gritting his teeth, vowing silently to himself to find this "Andrew Payne" and his gang and bring them to justice.

By noon the next day, Johnny and his men were casually marching back to the emotionally charged Wilburn Plantation, toting supplies and smelling the freshness of the air along the countryside. In order to amuse the men on the walk back, Johnny had gotten a bit creative with the lyrics of another of the popular songs of the time, "The Yellow Rose of Texas," which the piano man at Fanny's played so well. The catchy tune and memories of the occasion were still vivid in their minds as all of the men were singing along with Johnny's new lyrics.

You can talk about your Clementine and sing of
Rosalee but Fanny Sellers's ladies still have virginity.
They got us drunk on whiskey and this here you can
quote, the most we saw of fanny was just a petticoat.
Oh, Fanny Sellers loves us. She said, "Come back again
and sock that Rowdy Roberts a good one on the chin."

Even though they had sung the lyrics a half a dozen times
already, they still broke out with laughter. Johnny turned
around, marched backward, and called cadence.

"Yo left. Yo left. Yo left, right, left. Company, hawt! Here's
a shady spot to rest and chow down, men. Fall out!"

They hastily headed for the cool of the shade, threw
down their supplies, and looked for a place to sit down and
eat their hardtack and jerky. They gathered around more
or less in a circle and faced one another. Tossing down a
thirty-pound bag of flour from his shoulders, Pettymuth said,

"Totin' these supplies is makin' the trip back seem twice
as far." Morgan concluded, "Not gettin' any sleep is whut's
wearin' me down."

Woodward revealed what was on his mind. "That little
Anna Belle sure got my boiler steamin'. I can't get her outta
my mind." Buster Bottom queried him.

"You didn't slip upstairs with her, did ya?" Morgan
answered before Woodward. "Ah heard he was runnin' in
circles in her bedroom. Know why? So he could 'catch up'
on his sleep!" They laughed at his corny joke and Woodward
retorted, "Oh yeah. Very funny! I'll tell ya, after buyin' a few
drinks you can't afford those expensive women on eighteen-
dollar-a-month army pay, especially when you haven't gotten
it in several months. Those girls want a whole month's pay
and then some."

Smiling and pulling out some hardtack to munch on,
Les Moore gave his analysis.

"True. But they wuz some high-class ladies." He pecked
on the hardtack and it sounded like he was pecking on wood.

Johnny responded to Les Moore's statement. "They weren't high class, just high priced." Then he looked down at the dwarf. "They stood higher than you, maybe." Les put up his dukes and swung punches like he was mock fighting Johnny. John jokingly held him off by putting his hand on Les's head, holding him at arm's length while the dwarf's punches just swished in the air. The men laughed to see such a sight. Then Harry Leech lamented about his present state compared to his former experiences at Fanny's.

"Aye, mates. But I could afford 'em when I was captain of me own ship. Had so much treasure I didn't know what to do with it all." He tried to take a bite of hardtack and found it too hard. He then opened his mouth wider to get more leverage and clamped down, grimacing as he bit off a chunk with a loud crunch. Johnny ignored the loud crunching and addressed the men with one of his recent concerns.

"All right, men! Let's forget about the ladies for a minute. I'm concerned about the Rowdy Roberts Gang. They might try to ambush us before we get back to Smoky Meadows." Jay expressed his thoughts about it.

"Ah wonder why dat Rowdy claimed to be Andrew Payne? And where'd he git dat Confederate uniform?" Jay took a bite of hardtack and went through the same sequence as Harry Leech did, making a lot of noise. The crunching noises got more frequent as more and more men attempted to eat the hard biscuit, making it difficult to hear the conversation. Morgan continued the talk following Jay's comment.

"Andrew Payne? Ah knew a man named Andrew Payne when ah was stationed out of Richmond with Lee's first division. We got transferred to Stonewall Jackson's command and he was wounded in the battle of Chancellorsville. Last ah heard, they put him on a train to Richmond along with other wounded, and sent 'em south to hospitals in Danville." The crunching of hardtack got even louder as men leaned in to listen to what was being said. Johnny noted, "It doesn't seem likely Rowdy's gang would hijack a train just to get Confederate uniforms. Of course, for those scum, uniforms would be secondary to robbin' the train." Jay tried to talk above the crunching sounds.

"Or rapin' da wimmen." Johnny missed what Jay said due to the crunching noises.

"What did you say?" Johnny yelled at the other men. "HEY! Can you guys stop eatin' hardtack for a second? I can't hear what Jay is sayin'!" They stopped, but Les Moore took a half-eaten biscuit out of his mouth, threw it on the ground, crossed his arms, and pouted.

"That's more like it." Then Johnny addressed Jay. "Now, what were you saying, Jay?"

"Ah wuz jus' sayin' 'bout dat Rowdy guy . . . robbin' da train would be secondary to rapin' da wimmen fo' him." Johnny shook his head in disgust and stated, "Yeah, when Major Wilburn warned me of deserters and hoodlums raiding a five-county area, I didn't think we'd run into 'em this soon. And I've got a feelin' we haven't seen the last of this bunch."

"Dat's right! You know Rowdy gonna be gunnin' fo' you and me, Mistah Johnny!"

"I know! Too bad we didn't nail him or jail him last night." Johnny's face reflected a deep expression of concern.

When they got back on the trail, Johnny put his concern in the back of his mind, and he had the men marching and again singing his newly created tune.

They got us drunk on whiskey and this here you can quote.
The most we saw of fanny was just a petticoat.
Oh, Fanny Sellers loves us.

Suddenly, Jay noticed something in the distance, elbowed Johnny, and pointed. Johnny stopped singing, held up his hand to the men, and yelled, "Take cover!"

The men crouched down on the side of the trail. Johnny whispered loudly to Jay on the other side of the road, "What is it, Jay?"

"Don't know fo' sure. Looks like somebody lying in da road."

"Could be a trap. Let's flank off through the woods and see if it's some of Rowdy's gang waitin' to ambush us." Johnny then turned to the men behind him and waved to them to come along. "Follow me! Pass it on!" They followed Johnny and Jay into the woods.

They crept along in a crouched posture with their weapons drawn, looking all around for any telltale signs that someone had been through the area, or for any glimpse of someone in the area now. The tension mounted as they crouched slowly forward and Jay whispered to Johnny, "Don't see nothin' at all movin' in here."

Just then, a scared rabbit broke out of a bush and rapidly hopped in a zigzag pattern across the woods. Jay jumped and impulsively fired his pistol.

"Damn! Dat spooked me!" Johnny held quiet for a moment then broke into a snicker. Jay saw the humor in it and began to chuckle too. They took a few more steps, crouched Down, and started to laugh again. Still chuckling, Johnny stood up and said, "Oh, what the heck! If there was anyone around here that shot would have triggered some kind of response." He yelled back to the men. "Let's move back to the road!"

Back on the road they crept cautiously as they approached a gray lump of material ahead. It was the familiar gray of a Confederate uniform. When they saw he wasn't moving, they quickened their pace, and as they got close enough to see the man's face, Jay exclaimed,

"Oh mah god!" Johnny instantly recognized the dead man also.

"It's Charles Adams! One of Major Wilburn's regulars. What's he doing out here?"

Buster Bottom said, "I want to know who shot 'im." Johnny's countenance displayed an expression of anger and concern.

"I don't know! But I've got an idea who did. Give me a hand. We'll have to carry him back to Smoky Meadows." They hoisted the young soldier onto Johnny's shoulders and continued the trip back to the plantation.

An hour later they reached the edge of the plantation and William Knight, one of the regulars that shot at the Rowdy Roberts Gang in the night, was standing guard on the porch of the mansion, rubbing the barrel of his long rifle. Michael Wilburn Jr. was nearby. William looked up and a shocked expression came over his face as he saw the men approaching with Johnny toting a body over his shoulder. Junior ran toward Johnny as William rushed in the front door of the mansion, yelling, "Major Wilburn! Major Wilburn!" The major came running out of the study to meet William in the hallway, who excitedly exclaimed, "Come quick! The lieutenant and his men are back and they're carrying a dead soldier. It might be Charles Adams!"

They rushed out the front door to greet Johnny and his men. Major Wilburn was saddened to see the sight as they met on the lawn of the mansion. "Oh no! Is it Charles?" Johnny nodded and sighed. "I'm afraid so. Where should I take him?" Major Wilburn looked down and sighed, thinking about it for a moment. Then he looked back at John.

"We might as well take him to the cemetery area. His family in South Georgia could never be notified before we'd have to bury the body." As they started walking toward the private cemetery on the property, Major Wilburn asked, "What happened?" John answered, "We found him this afternoon, shot two times, lyin' dead on Danville Road 'bout two miles back." The major's concern intensified as he questioned Johnny.

"What about the other four men who were with him?" Surprised, Johnny said, "What men?"

"The other four regulars!"

Johnny stoically answered, "We only saw Charles!"

Major Wilburn gritted his teeth trying to withhold his anger. They walked silently for a few steps and the major turned to address Jay and the men walking behind.

"Some of you men better run down to the tool shed and get some shovels and spades."

Jay and two other men headed off to the tool shed as Major Wilburn continued to walk alongside Johnny, both men looking grave. Only the sound of their footsteps could be heard as they solemnly shuffled along with many thoughts and questions in their minds. Finally, Major Wilburn quietly murmured to Johnny, "After we bury Charles you and I need to talk." Johnny glanced over at the major, not knowing what to expect.

Chapter 10

LAUNCHING AN ATTACK

Following the burial of Charles Adams, Major Wilburn walked back to the mansion with Johnny, describing the horror with the Rowdy Roberts Gang in the middle of the night. Johnny was surprised that Rowdy Roberts had the audacity to attempt such a crime against the Wilburn family after leaving Fanny Sellers's place. He was concerned for them and proud to hear how Rebecca bravely saved them.

The major finished his story as they reached the front door of the mansion. He opened the door and gestured for Johnny to enter. John can hardly believe what happened, exclaiming, "That's incredible, sir! It's hard to believe all that happened last night."

Libby, holding Rebecca's hand, rushed up to greet Johnny, and said, "Lieutenant Van Worth! Thank God you and your men made it back safely. You must be famished after your ordeal. Won't you join us for supper?"

"Well, I . . . *uh* . . ." Johnny wasn't expecting this gracious show of hospitality, being just in off the dusty trail, and he turned to the major to see if he approved. The major said,

"Please do. Afterward, we can discuss a plan of action. Come on out to the well and we'll wash up." John said, "Thank you." He turned to Libby. "I'd be honored to join you, Mrs. Wilburn." As they started toward the well just outside the backdoor of the kitchen, Major Wilburn expressed his pleasure in Johnny's return.

"You came back early. Some thought you might not return at all."

"After you granted our 'irregular' leave, I wouldn't think of letting you down, Major."

That evening, Johnny enjoyed the company of the entire Wilburn family with all of the formal trappings, and a tasty chicken dinner complete with gravy and dressing. Johnny knew this was a special occasion because chickens were becoming scarce, due to the fact that the demand for food at the battlefront was beginning to exceed supply, and it put a strain on many parts of the South.

Of course, most of the conversation during the meal was centered on the events of the raid on the plantation by the Rowdy Roberts Gang. Libby was right. Johnny truly was famished from the trip to Danville and the rigors that it entailed. He cleaned his plate, and as one of the black house servants was taking it away, John, wiping his mouth with his napkin, proclaimed, "That was excellent, Mrs. Wilburn. That's the best meal I've had since I joined the . . . *uh* . . . the 'Cause.' I am most grateful. My compliments!"

"You're most welcome, Mr. Van Worth," came her gracious reply. "It's a pleasure to have someone with character and manners in the house after last night."

"Yes. That's what I'd like to address," said the major, and he softly asked his wife, "Libby, would you and the children excuse us? I have some important matters to discuss with the lieutenant."

"Of course!" She reached her hand out to her daughter. "Come along, Rebecca. Michael, come with me." Michael Jr. ran out ahead of them, and as her mother led Rebecca, Johnny felt the need to compliment the young girl once more.

"You're a brave girl, Rebecca. We're all very proud of you." Turning in Johnny's direction Rebecca replied, "Thank you, Mr. Van Worth! But I only did what I had to do."

"Yes! And you did it very well!"

Breaking into a smile at Johnny's comment, Major Wilburn said to him, "An angel must have influenced her. We might not even be alive if it wasn't for her inspired quick thinking and bravery. Something has to be done to stop that traitor, Andrew Payne." Johnny bit his lip wondering how to set the major straight.

"Sir, there's something I haven't told you. His real name is Rowdy Roberts."

"What? Rowdy Roberts? How do you know this?"

"Well, Jay and I had an encounter with him last night ourselves."

"And he told you his real name is Rowdy Roberts?" Now Johnny felt he was in a dangerous spot. There was no way he could reveal they went to Fanny Sellers's place after the major and Pastor Prather had been so adamant about staying away. So again, Johnny found himself walking on eggs to explain things while maintaining his discretion.

"Well, no . . . *uh* . . . a lady told us."

"Lady? What lady?" Johnny's nonchalant manner barely covered his nervousness.

"It wasn't Fanny Sellers was it?" Johnny was relieved that he could tell the truth without incriminating himself and he blurted out, "Oh no, of course not! It happened just this side of Fanny's place." He thought he really wasn't lying since it happened on the north side of the building. Just stretching the truth a little. He explained, "We came upon this Rowdy guy trying to molest a lady and we ran him off. We thought he was Andrew Payne too until she set us straight." Wilburn blurted out, "Aha! That explains a lot of things!" Now Johnny thought his goose was cooked for sure, and he nervously said, "Oh! It does?" The major went on to explain, "Don't you see? This Rowdy Roberts coming here under the guise of being Andrew Payne, claiming he had a note from Jefferson Davis—he was out to rob us all along!" The major's eyes lit up with this revelation and Johnny was all too eager to agree with him. Johnny's eyes lit up, too as he realized he wasn't in trouble yet.

"Yes, sir! And I believe he's the one who stole your papers!"

"Of course he is! He so much as admitted it, saying the Yankees would pay good money for the right information. What a ruthless bunch of scumbags this Rowdy Roberts Gang is." Then he looked at Johnny intensely, and insisted, "They must be brought to justice!"

Johnny agreed and thought he had a simple solution.

"Why can't you just send word to General Lee to send down some troops?"

"Impossible! We're so outnumbered on the front lines now, that's why Jefferson Davis put me in charge of enforcing the draft. Besides, they aren't going to call out the military to handle a civilian matter." Johnny was still searching for an answer.

"Looks like we'll have to get the sheriff to round up a posse."

"Are you kidding? There isn't an able-bodied man left in civilian law enforcement around here, let alone enough for a posse. If there was, I wouldn't be doing my job of enforcing the draft." As the major jumped up and paced behind Johnny's chair, John froze and tried to follow the sound of his voice, shifting his eyes from side to side as the major continued.

"I'd take off after 'em myself if I knew where to look. But even so, now I'm so short of regular troops since they killed Charles Adams and they must have kidnapped or killed the other four men who were with him. I can't leave this place defenseless."

Wilburn sat down and stared at Johnny to see if he was getting the message and leaned in to be more intensely

profound saying, "Don't you see the predicament I'm in?"
Feeling the major was leading up to enlisting the services of
Johnny and his men to take on this unholy group, John
nervously cleared his throat and shakily mumbled,

"Huh? *Hummm! Uh,* well . . . yes . . . I think so." Thinking
Johnny is ready, the major unloaded the big bomb of his
intentions on him, saying, "Good! Then you realize you and
your men are the only ones left to go after these thugs!"
Johnny feigned surprise, "We are?" Then he quickly regained
his composure and said with confidence, "Oh yeah . . . we
are! Sure!" He began to have doubts about going after this
ruthless crew with the kind of men in his command and
mumbled almost to himself, "We'll be glad to . . . *uh . . .*"—
his words got slower and softer—"go after the worst criminals,
killers, and rapists around." He paused. "But how? We don't
even know where they are!" Major Wilburn grinned with a
determined expression, and said, "We'll work on that.
They're bound to have a hideout somewhere."

-0-

After meeting with Major Wilburn, Johnny shared
information about this new assignment with Jay and the rest
of his men. Then he retired to his bedroom in the
guesthouse. He thought about how stony-faced the men had
been when he told them they were saddled with the
responsibility of taking on the entire Roberts gang. He didn't
know if they were frightened or just too stupid to realize
the seriousness of the situation.

Then his thoughts again turned to Molly, and he began
to write her. It was almost two weeks before the letter arrived
in Charleston since it traveled by military couriers. Molly
frequently visited the post office to mail a letter or see if
Johnny had written one to her. When Johnny's letter arrived,
she rushed home, hurriedly opened the door, and yelled
out to her mother while running upstairs to her room, "It's

a letter from Johnny, Mama!" Her mother yelled back, "I'll be glad when you marry that boy!" Of course, Johnny was a man, but he seemed young for his age, while Molly seemed more mature for her age, which made them very compatible. Molly sat on her canopy bed and hurriedly opened the letter.

My Darling Molly,

> *I miss you more and more each day. I wish I had you in my arms instead of the burdens I now have on my hands. Major Wilburn has put me and my men in charge of tracking down the most dangerous and ruthless criminals in this part of the country. It's the Rowdy Roberts Gang. They've been killing, robbing, and raping men and women in five counties. They save the raping mostly for women.*
>
> *We're trying to find out where their hideout is, and how many men are in this gang. I just hope they don't have us outnumbered. As soon as we know more about them we have to come up with a plan of attack to wipe them out or put them behind bars.*

That's all of Johnny's letter Molly had to read to start preparing a return letter which she sent by the Southern Express Company and it arrived at the plantation in just ten days.

When Johnny received the letter, he walked away from everyone and opened it under the shade of one of the trees on the plantation. As he leaned against its trunk, he began to read Molly's concerned words.

My Dear Loving Johnny,

> *I know it's not proper and ladylike to say this, but I almost wet my bloomers when I read your letter. I can't believe you're in more danger now than if you were on*

the front lines of battle. Please be sure to say your prayers every night. And I don't mean any, "Lay me down to sleep" stuff either. Pray for the protection of angels over you. I do!

I do! *Those are the words I want to hear from you more than anything in the world. I want us to wrap our arms around each other and never let go. I don't want the honeymoon to ever end. I pray that whatever plan of attack you use it will be clever and efficient, and that there will be little loss of life—especially yours.*

My darling, I love you so very much. Please be careful. I'll be praying for you. And don't forget to pray for yourself. I only live to see you again.

All my love Always,
Molly ♡

XOXOXOXOXOXOXOXOXOXOXOXOXOXOXOXOXOXOXOXOXO

It had been nearly a month since what they were now calling "The Wicked Weekend." Suddenly the quiet calm of the plantation was broken by the sound of galloping hooves as William Knight came riding rapidly up to the front porch of the Smoky Meadows Mansion. He hurriedly dismounted and rushed through the front door as Michael Wilburn Jr. opened it before him. He headed straight for Major Wilburn's study where the major was going over papers on his desk. William knocked on the facing of the open door and spoke at the same time.

"Major Wilburn?" The major quickly responded to the urgency in William's voice.

"Yes. Come in!" William pulled out a map from his coat and unfolded it on the desk.

"We've located them here!" He pointed to the map. "They're dug in and highly fortified. The sheriff at South

Boston says they have a cannon." Major Wilburn looked at the map and glanced up to see Michael Jr. standing in the doorway of the study.

"Son! Go get Lieutenant Van Worth right away!" The youngster excitedly said, "Yes, sir!" He ran down the hall, out the front door, and onto the front lawn where John was talking to his men gathered around him. They thought something was astir since they saw William come riding in so rapidly. Buster Bottom speculated, "Maybe we ought to see what's happening." Johnny urged them to be patient. "It might not be anything at all, but if it is, the major will let us know. So until we find out, we'll just have to—" Just then Michael Jr. came running up to him, shouting, "Mr. Van Worth! Johnny! Johnny! Come quick! My Daddy wants to see you."

Johnny told his men, "This may be it. I'll let you know!" He turned and took off in a jog, keeping pace with the five-year-old boy as they "raced" toward the mansion.

Johnny slowed his pace and let the boy pass him so the lad would think he was beating John in the race to the house. When the boy got there first, Johnny said,

"You're too fast for me!" The lad giggled gleefully. Johnny smiled at him. The race was not only a way to please Michael Jr., it also served as a way for John to expel some nervous energy in anticipation of what Major Wilburn had in store for him. As they entered the mansion, Johnny's countenance began to take on a more serious expression. He stopped in the doorway as William was concluding his report.

"And the sheriff says it's not safe to travel South Boston Road right now. Well, that about sums it up, sir!" Major Wilburn said, "Thank you, Corporal!" They saluted and the corporal exited, leaving the major studying the map. He saw Johnny.

"Come in, Lieutenant. I have a good deal of intelligence to share with you concerning the Rowdy Roberts Gang." Johnny was not surprised. "I thought so." The major pointed to the map as Johnny came around to take a look.

"Their hideout is here, along the Dan River up toward South Boston. Here are the problems we face. First of all . . ." Johnny's mind was spinning as the major outlined the situation, complete with the dangers involved, and strategy on how to attack the Roberts compound. His head filled with the problems they faced, John saluted Major Wilburn and prepared to inform his men.

Johnny went out, squatted down, drawing a map in the dirt with a stick. His men gathered around him to see what kind of fate the near future may hold as Johnny spoke.

"They've stolen the best horses in the five-county area and there's about forty of them. So they have the advantage there. Now, they're hideout is here, at this sharp curve on the Dan river. They're heavily armed and have a cannon. Anyone approaching them from the west, north, or east, they are prepared to pick off like fish in a rain barrel. Major Wilburn believes we need to create a distraction to their south on the Dan river. They know there are no gunboats on the Dan, so they won't be expecting that. Major Wilburn thinks the element of surprise is a big advantage. Any questions?"

Buster Bottom answered, scratching his head while expressing his doubts.

"What are we suppose to do, float in there on a raft?" Harry Leech quickly added, "We'd be sittin' ducks! There's no control with a raft, poles, or maybe oars. You're just adrift without even a sail for power, mate. I'm not a river captain, but I think we need a ship with power to navigate that S curve." James Woodward interjected, "Wait a minute! When we were pickin' up supplies at the quartermaster I saw two small steam engines with boilers. I asked Major Sutherlin what they were for and he said they were used to grind meal. But since there's now plenty of grist mills in the county, no one wants to fuel boilers. They're just sittin' there. They could power a boat maybe thirty feet long with a ten-foot beam. I'll bet Major Wilburn could requisition those babies and we'd have all the power we'd need." John fired a retort. "Oh sure! Steamin' in there on that noisy contraption." He laughingly finished the thought. "That would be the wrong kind of surprise I'm afraid." Morgan said, "If you're gonna go fishin' for sumpthin' you gotta have the right bait tuh catch it." Johnny asked, "Bait? Now what kind of bait do you use to catch a bunch of robbin', raidin', rapin' men?" Les Moore empowered his falsetto voice to answer,

"Ask Fanny Sellers, I'll bet she knows." Everyone broke into laughter.

Suddenly, Johnny stopped laughing abruptly, slowly stood up with a gleam in his eye and a grin on his face, obviously turned on with an idea. The men looked up at him, stopped laughing, rose, and looked at him in wonderment. Johnny spoke as never before.

"Whoa! Yeah! Yeah! That's it!" He paused to think some more as the men just stared in awe. Johnny put his hand on James Woodward's shoulder and called out,

"James! Buster! Leech! Come here a minute!" He pulled them into a huddle.

"Just how much do you men know about boat building? I've got a great idea! We need a boat that doesn't look military . . . something friendly . . . something that will catch them off guard to draw them out of their trenches leaving their weapons behind. Now here's my plan." Johnny went on to explain the details of his plan to see if these three men with ship-building knowledge thought it was feasible. They all agreed it was, and John took the plan to Major Wilburn for his approval. He was pleased to hear Wilburn say,

"Brilliant, Lieutenant, brilliant! That would surely be a surprise. Let's do it!" "Get started on it right away!" Johnny was ecstatic. He knew his plan was a good one. The image of what to do just popped into his mind. Could it have been the answer to Molly's prayer? Didn't she say she was praying for a clever and efficient plan of attack in her letter? Johnny just thought, *Thank God,* and went back to his men to initiate the plan. The men were eager and they organized themselves into various work teams.

By the third day the foundation of the project was starting to take shape. Johnny was checking with each team on the progress they were making and to see if they were having any problems. Woodward and Buster Bottom began with the hull construction. As John approached their work area along the shores of the Dan River, just downstream from Danville, they had already cut down some Carolina pine trees. They had one mounted on saw horses and were shaping the bow end of it to an edge with a two-man saw when Johnny approached them, smiling his approval of their work.

"How's it coming, men? It looks pretty good to me!" Woodward answered, "By mounting the boat on three logs like a raft, we'll save construction time 'cause we won't have to build a keel frame and caulk a planked hull."

Buster added, "With three solid log hulls she'll be darn near unsinkable."

Johnny was pleased with their quick and simple construction plan and said to them,

"And they thought you men were troublemakers. You're geniuses!" Showing their appreciation, Woodard returned the compliment.

"You are too, sir! The whole idea came from you." Johnny humbled himself, saying, "I'm not sure I can take full credit for it. Carry on, men. I'm proud of you." They saluted and Johnny continued his rounds to check on the progress of construction. He headed across South Boston Road to a nearby barn he temporarily secured from a farmer for the building of other parts of the boat. Entering the barn he saw Harry Leech sitting on an upside-down bucket near a crude lathe. He was polishing a small pilot wheel he had assembled. Harry proudly held it up for John's inspection. A broad smile told Leech the lieutenant was pleased and Johnny shook Leech's hand, saying, "Nice work."

Leech was more enthused than Johnny had ever seen him as the old sea captain said,

"We'll have 'er together in no time at all. I'm anxious to get to that Roberts bunch. Those scum are dirty Yahnkees, aren't they?" Johnny assured Leech they probably were just to be sure to sustain Leech's enthusiasm. In another section of the barn young Robert Johnson and Buford Pettymuth were assembling two sections of spindles.

"Lieutenant! This is a piece Woodward designed. Fits on the front of the boat to fancy it up. He says it will add to the disguise . . . and the surprise." Johnny told Buford, "I like surprises." Robert Johnson added, "Yeah! Me too! Do you really think this plan will work, Lieutenant?" Johnny assured him, "It has to work! We'll make it work."

"It's a little scary, don't you think?" "Don't worry Johnson, you'll be on dry land. You'll do just fine." Johnny wanted to console the young man, knowing he still wasn't over his tendency to suffer from shellshock.

In a nearby stall of the barn, several pieces of freshly painted scrollwork were hanging on a line to dry. They were the result of work being done by Jay Brown and Les Moore. Jay was cutting a board into sections, each with a pattern of a scroll on it. He handed them to Les Moore, who was carving out each scroll. Les was enjoying his work. As chips of wood were flying in the air, the dwarf asked Jay, "You know how I carve wood?" Jay said, "How, little man?"

"Whittle by whittle! Get it?" He laughed. Jay decided to play along with him. "Ah can see you jus' a chip off da ol' block!" Les mocked being upset. "Hey! Let's not put down the 'whittle man.'" With that, he laughed. Just then, Johnny walked into the stall. He'd been listening just outside the door. He jokingly dressed them down. "All right, you guys, knock it off! We've got a boat to build." Jay picked up on Johnny's jesting and made a statement relating to work he used to do.

"Great! Sho' beats pickin' cotton." Johnny could relate to that and broke into a chuckle.

"Yeah! Hey, fellas, let's try to think of a name for the boat. We don't want her to sound too military or stately, you know?" Jay promptly responded, "Yeah, we'll work on dat too!" As Johnny was about to exit, he said, "How 'bout callin' 'er Miss Molly?" Johnny smiled as he thought about it, and said, "Naw. The Roberts Gang shootin' at Miss Molly? I wouldn't like that." Jay nodded.

After only two weeks, the thirty-man work crew had the little boat beginning to come together. The engines and boilers were mounted and attached to the side wheels. The wheelhouses were in place. Spindles with scrollwork near the top were applied around the deck which made the boat look lacy and fancy, causing Harry Leech to say,

"Now she's startin' to look like one of those wedding cakes." That was one of the favorite terms used by sea-going captains in those days to make fun of the fancy filigree that encased the riverboats of the era.

James Morgan and George Crumley were putting bull railings on the spindles near the bow of the boat when Johnny approached to inspect the work. Morgan tapped on the thirty-inch-high iron-plated bulkhead behind the spindles and said, "Iron plate! 'At'll stop some bullets!" Johnny shook his head in agreement, saying, "Yeah, I think so." He tapped on the low wall himself and winked his approval.

The next day the smokestacks were hoisted into place, complete with a crowned top and "feathers," to help prevent sparks of charcoal from falling back onto the deck.

The pilot house was hoisted into position and locked down. It was just for appearances, only three feet high, but it was in scale with the rest of the boat so that from a distance the tiny vessel would appear as a larger steamboat approaching. The pilot house was just a shell with no stern-side bulkhead. The boat would be steered by Leech's pilot wheel mounted on a centered helm located between the two paddlewheels. Right behind the false pilot house they mounted a compartment about one foot high, three feet wide, and eight feet long. The compartment was lined on the edge with fancy filigree and looked like a skylight deck, but it would be used for storage of weapons and supplies.

All of this engineering design was primarily directed by James Woodward due to the experience he acquired while working at the Howard Shipyards on the banks of the Ohio River in Jeffersonville, Indiana. He had learned his craft well, working directly with the shipyard's owner and founder, James Howard, who had a reputation for building the finest steamboats in America. Actually, Woodward lived in Louisville, Kentucky, located on the southern shore of the Ohio River, about a mile or so downstream from the shipyard. When the war broke out, he joined the Confederacy because his family was partial to the South. Kentucky was the most split state in the country in terms of sentiment for the North and South. James was the only man with riverboat-building experience and Johnny was impressed with his skills. He was thankful James left Kentucky and traveled to Richmond to be part of Robert E. Lee's legions. James was the most disciplined and educated among the men Johnny had under his control. The only reason he was part of John's motley crew was because he occasionally played practical jokes on people, and a Confederate officer had thought that was his normal demeanor.

Nevertheless, Johnny was glad James was here and could bring John's vision of a fancy boat to fruition. It was getting fancier with each little scroll Jay and Les Moore installed. Johnny and Woodward helped Grossman and Ben Grimm slide the stage booms into sockets and hook up the rigging for them. The booms controlled the raising and lowering of the stage. Riverboat men always called it a "stage." They took offense at the term "gangplank." That was a seaman's term. There was a friendly rivalry between the captains of the rivers and captains of the seas in those days.

-0-

Excitement was in the air as they neared completion of the tiny vessel. Johnny stood back to eye it, admiring the graceful swanlike curve of the deck as he waited for James Woodward and Buster Bottom to approach with the name plate. This was a special occasion and they had sent for Major Wilburn to witness the attachment. The major showed up with his father to view this final preparation before the launching. They had considered many name suggestions such as "Miss Molly," "Miss Fanny," and "Miss Behavin'," "Southern Belle," "Plantation Queen," and "Poop Deck Baby,"—all of which were quickly rejected by Johnny.

They all smiled as James and Buster began to attach the name chosen as the one the Roberts Gang would least expect to be threatening. They named her *Baby Belle*. It was a fitting name. The little boat, with all of its fancy filigree and spindles was like a baby wrapped in a lacy dress. It was most often referred to as "cute."

Major Wilburn was pleased to see Johnny and his men had done such a good job of preparing this unique "Trojan Horse" disguise. He saluted John and headed back to Smoky Meadows to prepare his troops for the next day's launch of the attack.

That evening Johnny was surprised by a visit from Fanny Sellers and Nellie. What John didn't know was that, being so close to Danville, Ol' Captain Leech had fallen to the temptation of sneaking away one evening, several weeks before, to see his old "girlfriend." After a few drinks, he had exposed plans of the boat project to Fanny as a way of gaining her favor, letting her know how they were going to "surprise" the Roberts Gang.

Nellie was holding two paintings of a romanticized steamboat with a beautiful sunset and rainbow behind it on a turquoise river. The paintings were rounded across the top with scalloped edges resembling the letter *D* lying on its flat side. They were the perfect size to fit on the side of the wheelhouses of the *Baby Belle*. John couldn't believe it. "Where did you get these?" Fanny took the initiative to speak. "We heard what you're doin'. Nellie here painted 'em. Like 'em?" Johnny said, "I sure do. It's beautiful! Just beautiful!" Beaming a big proud smile, Nellie responded, "Thank you, Lieutenant Van Worth. A girl needs something to do during the daytime, you know." Johnny smiled and nodded approval, thanking her. They handed him the paintings, revealing something hot pink in Fanny's hand. Johnny took a puzzled glance at the pile of shiny material. Fanny grinned, enjoying Johnny's wonderment.

"We believe in your cause, so ah brought along somethin' else to add to the surprise. Could you use some satin fringe?" Johnny saw a use for the fringe as decoration and said, "Yes, Miss Fanny, I believe so!" He paused a moment, obviously curious. "By the way, how did you know so much about what we're doing?" Fanny retorted, "Aha, Mr. Van Worth. You wouldn't want me to get one of your men in trouble now, would you?" John knowingly smiled and quietly said, "Who was it?" Fanny answered, "I'll tell you only if you promise not to harm the . . . *uh* . . . old pirate."

"I see. No, I won't discipline him. At least not now. I need his skills too much. We're going after them in the morning. I just hope no one else has heard, and word hasn't reached the Roberts Gang. Our lives depend on this being a surprise attack."

"Don't worry, Lieutenant! We want you to be successful. Getting this gang is to our advantage too, you know. I can assure you it was told to me in private, and Nellie is the only other person who knows anything about it. Besides, Rowdy Roberts hasn't been to town in quite awhile. I've heard his gang doesn't go out as much on raids here lately. They've discovered they can rob people or coaches passing near their camp off South Boston road." Johnny was amazed at how much information Fanny had accumulated and was glad she was willing to share it with him, but still he wondered.

"You seem to know quite a few things that I thought were private, Miss Fanny."

"Private things are mah business, Mr. Van Worth!" She winked and said,

"Good evenin', Lieutenant." Johnny mumbled, "Good evenin', ma'am!"

He stood there somewhat in quiet shock and wonderment over the cheap education he just got from this woman of the world. Fanny and Nellie climbed into their carriage and she added, "Don't worry! You can consider me and Nellie here as allies to your cause." All this time, Nellie had been smiling and looking at Johnny with adoring eyes. She said,

"Good evenin', Mr. Van Worth . . . *uh* . . . Johnny!"

"Good evenin', Miss Nellie. You did a wonderful job on these paintings. I didn't know you had so much talent." She smiled, accepting his compliment with a nod. He tipped his hat as they rode away, and then wandered back to the nearby camping area.

The following morning, the *Baby Belle*'s mooring lines were slashed and she slid down the ways (temporary timbers along the shore) and splashed into the murky waters of the Dan River to the cheers of the men who gave her birth. Major Wilburn, who paid for her construction, joined in the cheers, along with his regular Confederate soldiers and a small crowd of supporters from Smoky Meadows, including the Wilburn family, house servants, and Pastor Prather.

Before boarding, Pastor Prather prayed for a blessing on the men and success for their mission. Concluding the ceremony, Major Wilburn said, "There's one final thing!" He reached behind his back and Michael Jr. stepped out with a Confederate hat in his hand. The major took the hat and proclaimed, "Lieutenant! Since you're now taking charge of a ship, I believe it's only fitting that you be promoted to the rank of captain!" Everyone cheered as Johnny took the hat and put it on, handing his lieutenant hat to Michael Jr., who promptly put it on to the chuckles of the crowd.

The plan called for only six men to board the boat: John, James Woodward, Captain Leech, Buster Bottom, Les Moore, and James Morgan. After they generated a head of steam in each boiler, Johnny pulled down on a wooden handle attached to a rope leading to the whistle atop the false pilot house. The whistle howled a melodic toot and Johnny shouted, "Full steam ahead!" Woodward engaged a valve, sending steam to the engines, and the six-inch-wide side paddlewheels of the *Baby Belle* began to churn water. Johnny let Captain Leech take the pilot wheel to steer them downstream to the gentle rhythmic hiss of the steam engines. Those on shore cheered as the tiny steamer sailed along the winding bends of the Dan River.

Meanwhile, on shore, Pastor Prather, the Wilburn family, and servants boarded carriages to return to the plantation as the *Baby Belle* was sailing out of sight. Major Wilburn turned to his troops and said, "All right, men, we know Rowdy Roberts made a raid on Ringgold last night, so they'll be at their camp resting up and counting their plunder. Let's move out!" Major Wilburn and the regulars mounted the horses. The rest of John's men, including Jay, fell into a route-step march behind them. This was the first time Jay was separated from Johnny since they "joined" the military. He didn't like it, but he understood it was necessary. A short way downstream, Fanny Sellers and Nellie were spotted by John and his men along the shore. They waved and the men waved back. Captain Leech nearly lost control of the boat, gawking with a big smile at Fanny.

"Hey! Let's not get out of control," chided Johnny. Johnny gave a short toot on the whistle. It would be the last time they would use it until they reached their destination.

Woodward was pleased that the simple little steamboat was performing so well on this trip, which was serving as a shakedown cruise. She was simple but well built and making about five to six miles an hour.

Four hours later, they were getting close to the South Boston area where the Roberts Gang hideout was located. The compound consisted of several makeshift shacks made from stolen pieces of lumber. Near the shacks was a twenty-five-foot-high wooden tower with a platform on top housing a stolen cannon mounted on a two-wheeled caisson. Two nasty, dirty men were keeping watch on the platform. They were lazily leaning against the blocked wheels of the cannon, chewing tobacco, spitting, and talking.

"Hey, Snake! *Sppptt!*"

"Whut izzut, Jake? *Sppptt!*"

"Ah wuz just a-thinkin' . . ."

"At damn! 'At'll git ya in trouble ever time." He broke into a nasty laugh.

"Naw! Ah reckon as how Rowdy and the boys is all sacked out after last night's raid, this here'd be a good time tuh sneak down and git us a little extry spoil fer oursevs. Savvy?"

"*Aw*, Jake! They shoulda named you Snake 'stead'a me." He broke into his wheezy, nasty laugh. "Let's see if they got any liquor." They started to descend the tower, but getting about halfway down, they heard the faint sound of the calliope on the *Baby Belle* in the distance. Jake froze to listen, saying,

"Hold up, Snake! Do you hear sumthin'?" Snake cupped his hand to his ear.

"*Uh* . . . Yeah! Whut da hail izzat?!" Jake listened some more, then answered Snake. "Sounds like music. Let's go back up an' take a look!"

About three quarters of a mile up the Dan River, Les Moore was playing a small calliope keyboard mounted behind the helm on the *Baby Belle*. His stubby little fingers rolled across the keys, playing a shaky rendition of a Stephen Foster tune "I Dream of Jeannie with the Light Brown Hair." Johnny had taken over piloting duty, while Capt. Harry Leech was looking through a telescope. He turned around and yelled at Les.

"Aye, mate! Quit playin' that thing and come 'ere."

Jake and Snake can't see the *Baby Belle* because of the trees along the shore of the narrow river. Snake had just said, "Sounds like a circus tuh me," when the music quit. Jake said, "Now whut? It stopped." He turned to Snake and said, "Ain't no damn circus. Ah kin tell ya that. Ah bleeve it's comin' from the rivah."

Meanwhile, back on the *Baby Belle*, the reason the music stopped was Captain Leech wanted Les to get a better view of the shore downstream, saying to the little man,

"I want ya to climb up on my shoulders and tell me if ya can see anything." Leech hoisted Les to his shoulders putting Les up through the bottomless pilot house. He handed the telescope to the dwarf, who looked downstream. Leech wobbled a bit and said, "See anything, mate?" Les was looking at the edge of the shore downstream and said, "Nope! Nothin'. Just water and trees. and . . ."—he paused—"two beavers kissin'!" Johnny remarked, "What? Look farther down river!" Under his breath he mumbled, "Beavers have all the fun." Les continued, "He's still kissin' 'er—oh! Oh!"

Startled, Leech called out, "What is it?" Les casually replied, "She slapped him!" Johnny and the rest of the crew groaned at Les's humor. Then he seriously bolted out, "Wait a minute. I see two goons and a cannon!" Johnny reprimanded the little fellow, saying, "Quit horsin' around! This is a serious mission!" Les defended himself insisting, "I'm not foolin'. Here, look for yourself!" He handed the scope down to Leech. "Above the trees off to the left . . . see?" Leech corrected him, "That's off to port!" Leech squinted into the scope. "He's right, mates! Off the port bow. It's gotta be them!" John's eyes lit up and he wasted no time responding coolly and immediately, "Les! Get back on the music! This is it, men! Get into your battle gear!"

At the tower, Jake yelled down to a greasy comrade on the ground, "Hey, Lizard! Did you hear some music?" Just then, the calliope started again.

"There! Hear it?" Lizard is scroungy, with some teeth missing. He yelled back up to Jake, "Yeah! 'At's whut ah come out tuh check on! Sounds like it's comin' fum the rivah."

Jake and Snake began to descend the ladder of the tower once again, jumping to the ground, skipping the last few rungs. Snake spit out tobacco and yelled, "C'mon, boys, let's check this out! They scurried to the river and saw the *Baby Belle* off in the distance steaming around a bend as the whistle blew. They squinted to see what was coming. Most steamboats stopped running during the Civil War unless they were converted into iron-plated gun boats. They hadn't seen a sight like this since before the war. Something colorful could barely be made out on the bow of the deck. Jake, Snake, and Lizard looked puzzled at one another and scratched their heads. Jake said, "Whut da—? Izzat whut ah think it is?" From a distance it appeared that girls in cancan dresses were waving and flirting. Little did they know it was Johnny and his men dressed in women's clothing, complete with wigs and makeup. James Woodward and Buster Bottom were wearing cancan dresses on the bow. Johnny and the other men were wearing hoop skirts and bonnets and they were all yelling in falsetto voices,

"Yoohoo! Hi, boys! Yoohoo!" Lizard was the first to fall for it. He jumped up and down, blurring his vision, saying,

"By damn! It's a party boat! We gonna have us a good time now!" Snake was taken in by Lizard's enthusiasm. He blinked at the approaching "feminine" sight.

"You ain't just a-kiddin'. That's Fanny Sellers's girls! Let's tell Rowdy! Oh, man, is he gonna like this!" As they run to go tell Rowdy, they are met by others from the gang who have left their posts and rifles behind, running up to the terrible trio to see what's happening. One of the newcomers said, "Whut's goin' on!" Snake excitedly told them, "Hail, man! Fanny Sellers and the girls is comin' tuh see us on a party boat!" The horny thugs yelled out, "Yahoo!" and they jumped for joy. But one man had doubts.

The doubter expressed his concern. "How do ya know they're coming to see us?" Lizard replied, "Hell, if they ain't, we'll hijack 'em anyway." That satisfied the man. Then Rowdy Roberts ran out, wearing only his pants and boots, strapping on his guns.

"What's all the fuss about?" Snake told Rowdy, "Fanny Sellers and the girls is comin' tuh see us on a party boat!" Rowdy stared upriver at the slow-moving floating, flirting apparition approaching, with the likes of dance hall girls aboard. With an evil grin he said, "Well, hell far! This calls for a celebration. Break out the whiskey, boys!" His men shouted and yelled wildly as they ran toward one of the shacks and rolled out a barrel. They popped out the bung and rolled the barrel just enough to cause a near-steady stream of whiskey to pour out. They slipped tin cups and mugs into the stream to fill them, throwing down as many straight shots as they could. All the while they cheered and sang as they toasted one another on the "good fortune" floating toward them down the river. Rowdy toasted, "I say . . . here's to Fanny!" He sang, "Fanny . . . Fanny, that's her name. Fanny . . . fanny that's our game!" They all broke into a nasty laugh, clinked mugs, and yelled, "Hip, hip, hooray! Hip, hip, hooray!" Most of the men scurried toward the shore of the river.

The *Baby Belle* was getting closer, but not close enough to show the difference between men and women. Captain Leech couldn't disguise his beard, so he manned the helm as Johnny and the rest continued their "woo talk" in falsetto voices. Johnny warned them, "All right, men! Don't shoot 'til you see the whites of their eyes." He paused and added, "And the pinks of their tongues." On shore, Rowdy's men were getting drunker and goofier by the minute. Lizard was

staring at the "femmes" aboard the *Baby Belle,* looking googly-
eyed. Other men behind him were waving their mugs,
laughing and acting stupid.

Snake, Jake, and Rowdy clinked their mugs in another
drunken toast. Lizard hung his tongue out and started
licking his lips like a hungry dog eyeing a steak being held
just out of its reach. Rowdy went for another toast and
concluded, "Okay, men, bottoms up!" Back on the *Baby Belle,*
Johnny called his command, "Okay, men, bottoms up!"
Woodward and Buster Bottom on the bow of the boat turned
their backs, bent over, and flipped their skirts up to reveal
their petticoated rears. Rowdy and his men cheered wildly.
What they didn't know was that James and Buster were
bending over to pick up long rifles and pistols. Johnny,
Morgan, and Les Moore pulled out their weapons also.
Johnny called out the command to attack. "Fire at will!" They
unleashed a flurry of gunfire at the Roberts Gang. Woodward
and Buster squatted down and waddled through the gate
of the thirty-inch-high front bulkhead and closed it behind
them. Leech stalled the *Baby Belle,* letting her drift slowly
with the current. The flurry of fire had left several of Rowdy's
gang lying on the ground, dead. Snake looked around and
said, "Whut da hail kinda wimmin is they?" The mood on
shore rapidly changed from revelry to panic. The men still
standing closest to shore turned to run, knocking down the
men behind them. John and his men picked up other
preloaded weapons and proceeded to deliver a second
round of fire at the panicky crowd. As Lizard was running
away, he grabbed his buttocks, where he'd just been hit,
and fell down. John and his men ducked down to load
weapons as several shots fired by Rowdy's men ricocheted
off the iron plate of the bulkhead. Snake and Jake took off
running toward the tower where their cannon was facing
the wrong direction. They would have to climb the tower
and roll the caisson around to take a shot at the *Baby Belle.*
Harry Leech spotted them. The seasoned former sea captain

went into action to do his predetermined duty, taking out the tower and cannon. Leech pivoted up a small-caliber cannon they mounted on the top edge of the iron bulkhead. John and the rest of his men had gotten their long rifles loaded and took another shot at the fleeing Roberts crowd. Snake and Jake reached the base of the tower and knocked each other down trying to be the first on the ladder. They got up and ascended a few rungs of the ladder as Captain Leech took aim at the platform and cannon above. He fired! Much to everyone's surprise, he hit the platform where the cannon balls were stored, setting off an explosion that demolished the platform, blew the wheels off the caisson, and sent parts hurling into the air and down to the ground. Everyone aboard the *Baby Belle* cheered then ducked down as Rowdy and a few of his men got off a round of fire that again ricocheted off or missed the structure of the boat—except for one shot. Capt. Harry Leech was enjoying the triumph of hitting his target and didn't duck in time. He grabbed his chest and fell backward onto the deck.

Meanwhile, Major Wilburn, his regulars and the rest of Johnny's men, including Jay Brown, arrived at the scene of battle from shore, blocking the escape of the Roberts Gang. Major Wilburn caught Rowdy off guard from behind as Rowdy was firing toward the *Baby Belle*. Roberts ran out of bullets and tossed away his weapon, grabbing a pistol off one of his dead men nearby. Major Wilburn called out, "Don't anybody move! Throw down your weapons! You're all under arrest by the authority invested in me by the Confederate States of America!" John and the boat crew held their weapons on the Roberts gang, not noticing Leech had fallen.

Rowdy Roberts glanced over his shoulder at Major Wilburn and the rest the men who had the drop on him. Wilburn hadn't taken his eyes off this evil man, who once threatened to kill him and his family. Rowdy froze for a moment, his eyes darting around, trying to think of some way to escape. Suddenly he turned, attempted to fire a shot at Major Wilburn, and was cut down in a hail of bullets. The regulars, Jay, and the rest of the men under John's command started rounding up what was left alive of the gang.

Aboard the *Baby Belle*, James Woodward commented, "Looks like this is the last of the Rowdy Roberts Gang." Choking out the words, Captain Leech groaned out from the deck, "Looks"—he coughed—"looks like it's the last of me too, mates." They turned and looked down at Leech lying mortally wounded on the deck, holding his hand against his bloodied chest. They kneeled down beside him, still wearing the women's clothing, looking silly at this serious moment, except for John who had pulled off his wig when the fighting started and replaced it with his hat. Johnny spoke, "Captain Leech! How bad are you hit?" Straining to talk, Leech moaned a reply in between fits of coughing. "I . . . I'm afraid . . . I know when my ship is sinkin'! I won't see the sun go down this day." Johnny didn't want to believe him and said, "You'll make it, Old Salt. You've got to. Why, don't ya know? You're a hero! You took their cannon out on the first shot. You'll make it!"

"Not this time, mate!" Leech grabbed the lapel of John's coat. "John! There's"—he coughed—"there's somethin' I want you to have. In my coat . . . inside pocket. I have no use for it now." Johnny reached into the pocket, pulled out a piece of folded paper, and as he started to unfold it, he did his best to try to cheer Leech up and take his mind off the wound, saying,

"What is it? A picture of Fanny Sellers?" Leech looked at the men in their drag costumes.

In spite of his pain, Leech broke into a choking laugh and struggled to speak. "*Haw!* Oh! It's not nice to make a dyin' man laugh. *Haw haw!*" His expression turned serious. "It's much more valuable. Much . . . It's my treas—" he broke off coughing. His eyes glazed over and his body went limp as his head dropped to one side, and he wheezed out his last breath. James Woodward softly said, "Captain Leech?" He gently shook the old captain, then looked up at Johnny and said the obvious. "He's gone!" Johnny removed his hat and held it over his heart. James and Buster removed their ladies' wigs and placed them over their hearts. James asked Johnny, "What did he give you?" Johnny finished unfolding the heavy-weight paper. He was shocked. "Oh my god! It's a treasure map!" They looked at one another with surprise and wonderment at what was surely a homemade treasure map, but it was written in some kind of code with capital letters in odd places. Part of it read "Find Total SUM of capital To Enter paRallel. Follow To South Under Mount The Earthen Rise."

Chapter 11

THE GREATEST TREASURE

The plain and simple makeshift wooden tombstone read "Capt. Harry S. Leech Born, God knows when. Died a hero, Sept. 21, 1863." This time it was Major Wilburn who handled the funeral ceremony and eulogy due to Chaplain Prather's being unavailable. Johnny was standing next to the major. They both held their hats over their hearts until the major's final words, "Ashes to ashes, dust to dust. May God have mercy on his soul. Amen!" As some of the men started shoveling dirt into the grave, John and the major put on their hats and turned together to walk away. The major softly said to Johnny, "I understand the ol' sea captain gave you a treasure map." Johnny honestly admitted, "Yes, sir, he did. A last act of kindness. But I can't make heads or tails of it. It seems to be written in coded messages of some kind. Unfortunately, Captain Leech died before he could tell me more about it." Major Wilburn changed the subject. "John! I think we're lucky that only one man was lost on this raid. It could have been much worse. Johnny, I want you to know I'm very proud of you. Not just for the success of the raid but . . . but for the way you've been able to perform your original assignment of shaping up these men." Johnny simply but appreciatively answered, "Thank you, Major!" The major was silent for a moment, reluctant to tell Johnny what he must say next.

"That's why I . . . *uh* . . ." He hesitated, looked off, sighed deeply, and looked down sadly.

"Is something wrong, Major?" queried Johnny.

Wilburn rubbed his chin, not wanting to tell John what he must. He somberly said,

"Well, we lost so many men at Gettysburg the first part of July that Jefferson Davis has been requesting every man available to reinforce Lee's army in Northern Virginia ever since. I was suppose to send you and your men a couple of months ago, but I didn't think they were ready . . . and then this project to stop Rowdy Roberts came up and—" John understandingly interrupted him with a sincere, mature sense of duty. "I understand, sir. We both knew this day would come sooner or later." Somberly and softly, John asked, "When do we leave?" Major Wilburn said, "Tomorrow!" He paused, put his hand on Johnny's shoulder, and continued. "I don't mind telling you. You'll be missed by me and my family. Especially my son." Johnny replied, "Yes, sir, I'll miss all of you folks too."

The following morning, John and his men were assembled for a formal departure. The entire plantation was also gathered to send the heroes off. But it was mostly a sad occasion. No one wanted to see them leave, not to mention they weren't too happy to go. Michael Jr. was the saddest of all. He was losing his best friend. Everyone stood with their heads bowed as Pastor Prather concluded another prayer.

"And once again, Lord, we ask your blessing upon these men as they embark on the uncertainties and dangers of war. Truly put them under the protection of your angels. Amen." Johnny stepped forward to face Major Wilburn. They saluted. In a soft, sincere tone, Major Wilburn told John, "I wish you good luck . . . and may you pass this way again someday . . . soon." Philosophically, Johnny responded, "Perhaps the war will end soon and you'll get your wish, sir."

Johnny looked down at the sad face of Michael Jr. and said, "Oh! Before we leave, there's something I want to give you, Michael." He reached into his pocket and pulled out another button-type spinning toy. This one was larger, three inches in diameter. Johnny had carved it out of a solid piece of oak. It had spokes painted on it, simulating a paddle wheel. The boy smiled as Johnny handed it to him. Libby Wilburn was beside him and told John, "How kind and thoughtful of you." She addressed her son. "Say thank you to Mr. Van Worth, Michael!" The lad was winding the wheel and said, "Gee thanks, Mr. Van Wor . . . *uh* . . . Johnny!" The Wilburns were getting used to Michael Jr. breaking with the normal manners of the day to call him Johnny. They understood the special friendship between the two and approved of it. Michael Jr. pulled out on the strings, and the disc began to spin. Johnny encouragingly said, "Atta boy, Michael! Just pretend this is like a paddlewheel on the *Baby Belle*." The boy laughed and the adults chuckled, enjoying his amusement. John addressed Wilburn.

"Now that things are rolling smoothly here, sir, I suppose it's time for us to leave." They saluted each other. As Johnny turned to take command of his troops, Major Wilburn remarked, "You may leave, but certain memories never will." He glanced down at his son. John glanced down also, smiled, nodded his head, and turned to lead the men away. Michael Jr. turned to his father and said, "Is he comin' back, Pa?" Swallowing before answering, Major Wilburn said, "I hope so, son." He stared at the departing group of shaped-up soldiers Johnny was leading into an unknown future, and repeated, "I certainly hope so." Libby Wilburn and several of the others dabbed handkerchiefs at the moisture gathering in their eyes.

It would take almost a week for Johnny and company to march on foot along country roads to Richmond. He knew the journey would be hard. They would have to forage for food along the way since they only had enough to last a day or so. The late September air was beginning to cool enough that they would not get too hot on the trail, still they walked at a comfortable pace, taking in the beauty of nature. Johnny saw many birds in the wilderness of Virginia and he envied their freedom. He thought how nice it would be to not have to worry with the duties and dangers he and his men were now facing. He was proud of how he had had a positive influence on them. He realized this march would be the perfect opportunity for a man to try deserting. But they had been together through so much the last three months that there was a bond between them and they had a sense of purpose and duty they couldn't shirk. Even though they faced possible danger to life and limb, they felt a boyish excitement at the thought of going into battle and winning. Defeating the Rowdy Roberts Gang had given them confidence, and they were eager for another chance at victory. They were no longer the "Motley Misfits." They had become a band of "Merry Men," except for Ben Grimm who still hadn't quite overcome his paranoia.

One thing they did to pass the boredom of marching was to try to come up with a name for themselves as a fighting unit. They had heard of several outfits that did so using such nomenclatures as "Carolina Crushers" or "Manassas Marauders." John's men made suggestions that were sometimes amusing. They thought of such names as "Johnny's Fighting Jackals" and "Johnny's Jokers." James Morgan wanted them to be called "Morgan's Raiders."

But everyone reminded him that name was already taken by Confederate general John Hunt Morgan, who was famous for his raid into Southern Indiana and Ohio a few months earlier. Of course, James Morgan already knew that. It was reported in *Harper's Weekly*, a popular journal of the period. When they shot his Raiders idea down, he came back with "Morgan's Marauders" just to be contrary. It received the same degree of enthusiasm. George Crumley thought "Crumley's Crushers" would be a good name. "Moore's

Morons" was quickly rejected also. Buster Bottom suggested they call themselves "Fanny's Fighting Force," but that idea was only good for laughs as well. Johnny reminded them that they might as well forget it since they didn't even know if they would be allowed to fight together as a unit. That was a thought they didn't want to consider. The idea that they may not be able to stay together brought silence.

At times when it was quiet, Johnny always thought about Molly. Getting back to her was the thing that was uppermost in his mind. So many things reminded him of her. The wild flowers along the road. A field of goldenrods. The birds, the sunshine, the sky and clouds—anything beautiful or attractive. He thought how he would like to put his arms around her small waist and draw her close, pressing her breasts against his chest and feel the warmth of love between them. He dreamed of what the future would be like with her as his wife and the mother of their children. Nothing in the world was more important to him than getting back to the woman he loved. He thought, *I must survive. I must get home to her outstretched arms. I want to see her dark curls dangling down the back of her neck, hear her sweet voice, touch her soft skin, hold her hand, kiss her lips. Oh, God! This war must end soon.* He began to recall the words of his last letter to her.

My Dear Precious Molly,   *Sept. 22, 1863*

You just don't know how much I love you and miss you. I wish I could be close to you and hold you in my arms once more. But by the time you receive this letter I don't know where I'll be. Major Wilburn has put me in charge of getting the men back to the trenches on the front lines of Lee's Army.

By the way, our mission with the Baby Belle *caught Rowdy Roberts completely by surprise. He was killed, along with almost half of his gang of thugs. The rest we marched to jail in South Boston to stand trial. It was a*

*very successful mission, except that the old pirate, Captain
Leech, was killed. He was kind enough to leave me a
map to his personal fortune. It could be a considerable
amount of silver and gold or precious jewels. When the
war is over, I hope to find it and enrich our lives when
we get married. I just hope I can figure out where the
treasure is. He wrote the directions in some kind of code.
I haven't been able to make sense of it, but hopefully in
time I will.*

*I love you dearly, and dream of our future together.
I'll write you again when we arrive at our destination
and let you know my new address. Keep praying for me.
I need that now more than ever.*

Lovingly Yours,
Johnny

When Molly read Johnny's letter, she prayed, "Lord, I
can do nothing except trust that you will put angels in charge
to watch over them. Grant them guidance and protection.
I'm putting my faith in you to put him back in my arms once
more."

After marching along the dirty, dusty country roads
toward Richmond for four days, the faces of John and his
men were already beginning to look tired and weary. The
sun was fading toward the horizon and Johnny called out,
"Company, hawt! Fall out, men! Let's camp here for the
night. If anybody spots a squirrel, a rabbit, a bird . . . anything,
take aim! We're runnin' low on food. Correct that—we're
out of food."

They shuffled into the wooded area near the road. Some
sat with their backs against a tree. Others just sat on the
ground. Goober Askew expressed everyone's mood,

"Ah'm so hungry ah could eat a rattlesnake." Morgan
taunted Ben Grimm, "Better be careful, Ben. Goober here
wants to eat you for supper."

"He's a dirty Yankee spy!" They chuckled at Ben's absurdity and Woodward said, "What's the matter with you, Ben? You've accused everyone of being a Yankee spy except Rowdy Roberts . . . and he's the only one who was!" Over the laughter, Ben snapped, "You fools! How can you be so jolly? Don't ya know we're bein' marched off tuh git killed like sheep goin' to the slaughter?" Buster Bottom took Ben to task, answering, "Well, you've sure got the right name . . . Ben Grimm! You've been grim evah since ah've known ya. Hell, ah say let's be jolly all we can 'cause we don't know if we're gonna make it 'til Christmas. Anybody heard any good jokes lately?" Ben responded, "You're the only joke I know." Les Moore took Morgan's line as his cue to be funny. "Did ya hear 'bout the two boll weevils that grew up in South Carolina?" Morgan said, "What about 'em?" Les continued, "One of 'em went to the capitol and became a famous politician. And the second one stayed in the cotton fields and never amounted to much. So what did people say about the second one?"

Ben Grimm grumpily said, "That he minded his own cotton-pickin' business." Les Moore and the rest of the men looked disgustedly at Ben and Les Moore retorted, "Naw! Give up?" Before anyone could respond, Les blurted out the punch line of the joke, "They said he was the lesser of two weevils! Get it? Lesser of two weevils!" He held up two fingers. Some of the men snickered; others just groaned.

While all of this was going on, Johnny and Jay separated themselves from the rest of the men and were sitting with their backs against a tree outside the perimeter of the others. They were looking at the treasure map Captain Leech had given John. Jay respectfully said, "Cap'n Leech musta thought a lot of you to leave you dis map." Johnny responded, "I know. But I wish he was here now to show me what it means. I can't make much sense of it." Jay agreed. "Dat's fo' sho! Maybe one of da men might recognize somethin' on it."

Johnny thought about Jay's suggestion a moment and acknowledged, "Yeah. then we'd have to share it. Hopefully there's enough treasure to share. One thing's for sure, it's not gonna do anybody any good if we can't find it. Let's try it!"

They stood up and walked a few steps to join the rest of the troops, who were piling sticks to make a campfire. Johnny and Jay walked into the center of the camp and John proclaimed,

"All right, men! Let me tax your minds a little with a riddle of mine. What did the campfire say that was hot for another campfire?" Morgan responded, "Tax my mind? Ah cain't pay taxes on this cheap army pay!" John retorted, "Wrong answer! He said, 'Hey, ol' flame, why don't we go out together?' Get it? Fires? Go out together." With that, he laughed. The men chuckled, except for Ben Grimm, who said, "'At's stupid. Everybody knows fars cain't talk." Johnny fired back another thought, "All right, men, here's another riddle. Help me with this treasure map. Any man who can figure it out will get a fair share of the treasure." The men responded enthusiastically, getting up to come over and look at the map which Johnny laid on the ground. They kneeled or squatted and looked at it as John continued to explain what he knew.

"Captain Leech was a sailin' man so he knew how to navigate. He mentioned eighty degrees longitude west of Greenwich minus fourteen M. Eighty degrees is clearly marked here." He pointed to the eighty on the map. "But that's about all I can figure out. Woodward! Buster! Do either of you know anything about navigation?" Woodward spoke first. "I know how to build 'em. But I don't know much about sea navigation usin' the stars and a sextant and all that." Buster Bottom knew just a little more about it, saying, "'Bout all ah know is there's somethin' called dead reckonin'." Goober Shaw asked, "Dead reckonin'? How can ya reckon if you're dead?" They all just stared at Goober disgustedly until he said, "I wuz just askin'!" Buster continued his explanation. "It has somethin' to do with plottin' a ship's course and speed on a chart. We need to locate a map that has longitudes and latitudes and see if there's a land mass at eighty degrees longitude that matches the land mass on this map." Woodward interjected, "Maybe if we get in the area on the map it might make more sense." Johnny replied, "Possibly. But where is that? If Captain Leech were only here to tell what it all means." Then Johnny tried to spook the men. "Maybe his ghost will appear and show us!" The men's eyes widened and they looked a little concerned by John's words. Just then, they were startled by a strong but mellow voice crying out of the twilight behind them.

"Seek not treasures upon the earth for such is only temporary!"

The startled men spun and pointed their weapons at the stranger who had come upon them. He was an older man with long white hair and a long full beard, wearing sandals and a white robe, girded about the waist with a very wide leather belt. A large two-edged sword was sheathed through it. He continued speaking boldly, beaming a constant smile.

"Seek treasures in heaven that last forever!" Then his voice became softer and even more mellow. "Have no fear! I come in peace to share the blessing of a meal." He smiled, pulled a string of fish from over his shoulder, and held them up for all to see. They looked at one another in amazement. Then John directed his men with a command. "Put your weapons down!" He turned to address the intruder. "Who are you, stranger?" The man lowered the string of fish to his waist and said, "I am one who is sent." He glanced up briefly. Johnny asked, "Did Major Wilburn send you?" The man replied, "I come on much higher authority. But let us not dwell upon that. Let us give thanks. For I bring you good tidings and good food!" Again he held up the string of fish. Johnny decided it was time to end the questioning and enjoy the blessing this man had brought.

"We are grateful . . . Mister . . . *uh* . . . What's your name?" Johnny held out his hand to shake and the man placed the string of fish in it. Johnny shifted the fish to his left hand and shook the stranger's hand as the man spoke like a wise philosopher orating ageless wisdom.

"For what should it *profit* a man to gain the whole world yet suffer the loss of his soul? You may call me Proffit. Eli Proffit!" Smiling into the man's eyes, Johnny said, "We thank you again, Mr. Proffit." He turned to his men. "C'mon, men, let's get the campfire going and show Mr. Proffit we appreciate his generosity!" The men cheered. Once again Johnny smiled at Eli and Eli smiled back.

John's smile reflected appreciation, thankfulness, and wonderment; while Eli's smile reflected wisdom, knowledge, and pleasure in performing his duty of serving others. Eli walked over to the pile of sticks the men had stacked to make a fire. He held his hand above it and it instantly lit, not starting as a small flicker, but immediately becoming a roaring fire. The men again looked at one another in amazement at this strange man that had come amongst them that seemed to have the powers of a magician.

During the meal, the famished men said little, busying themselves with eating. But they all kept glancing at Eli and he glanced back with a gentle smile. After finishing a small bun of bread, Woodward complimented Eli on its taste.

"This bread is very good." Eli magically made another small loaf appear in his hand.

"The bread of life is always very good. Would you like some more?" He held it out for Woodward to take. Johnny and all of his men stared at this in bewilderment.

"How did you do that?" John asked. "What are you? A magician? A preacher?"

"I am neither. Just one who serves." Johnny momentarily pondered the man, and then said, "*Hmm!* Well, you have served us well and we're most thankful! You're welcome to camp with us tonight, but in the morning we must be on our way to . . ." He realized he shouldn't reveal any military troop movements to a stranger and tried to be covert. "*Uh* . . . well, I can't tell you exactly." Eli shocked them all by showing his knowledge. "Can't tell me that you're headed to Richmond to join up with Lee's forces?" Jay blurted out, "How you know dat?" Johnny, sitting beside Jay, just stared in amazement.

"Do not be amazed for I know much of the past, even some of what is yet to be. But have no fear. I come out of love as the answers to prayers." The men were speechless.

Eli continued smiling pleasantly, knowing he was delivering a profound message.

"Do you not know that love is the essence of life? That we are to love even our enemies?" Johnny was shocked that Eli would say this knowing the nature of their mission.

"Well now, isn't that a helluva thought right here in the middle of a war?" Eli went on smiling, not surprised at all by Johnny's statement as if he had known John would say it. He said, "Love is why life exists. Why you exist. To love your Maker and he to love you. To be a blessing to one another. To love your neighbor as yourself." Ben brashly asked, "Are you a Yankee spy?" Still smiling, Eli compassionately looked at Ben, and said, "Ben! Who gave you a spirit of doubt?" Embarrassed, Morgan interrupted, saying, "Never mind him. He ain't nobody worth worryin' about." Eli turned to Morgan to say, "My friend! There are no unimportant people. For whatsoever you do unto the least of your brethren, that you do unto the Spirit in the Sky." Johnny felt the need to speak. "I know little about you, Mr. Proffit. But I know a wise man when I see one. You said you have seen what is yet to be. What does the future hold for us? How will this war turn out?" The men are intrigued by Johnny's question and lean in to hear the answer.

"There will be great sacrifices on both sides. And one nation will emerge, a land of the free, that will then spread from sea to shining sea." Goober Askew was puzzled and asked, "Whose side are you on?" Eli never lost his gentle understanding smile, and answered, "I side with no man. Only with that which is right." Johnny fumbled his words. "Oh, Wise Guy... *uh*... Wise One! Tell us more of what we can expect in the years ahead! Chaplain Prather once spoke of the latter days. Is this that time of which he spoke?" Eli smiled even more, looked up, then down, as if contemplating how he should answer.

"Look for it beyond a century from now. As time goes on, the pace of life will quicken. In that day man will travel in horseless carriages at high speeds on smoothly paved roads." He held his hands as if he was steering an automobile and made car sounds with his mouth, even imitating a horn honking. Johnny and his men were showing momentary puzzlement, but then were amused by the display of these unfamiliar antics.

"What?" Johnny smiled and scoffed, laughing at Eli's strange depictions, saying, "Naw! Naw! No horse? Impossible!" Johnny's men shook their heads, agreeing. Eli ignored them, saying, "And man will travel through the air on wings like a bird's and will span the earth." He gestured, spreading his hands like the wings of an airplane, and made airplane engine sounds with his mouth. To men who had never heard of such things, it seemed so ridiculous as to totally amuse them. Johnny wondered if Eli was wise or mad, and said, "Oh, no way!" He laughed. Eli, once more, ignored their laughter as if he was being entertained by them as much as they were amused by him, and continued predicting, "Many restaurants will spring forth, and some will serve chicken fingers, others will have buffalo wings on the menu." "Ain't no such thing!" retorted Buster laughingly. Eli said, "There will be many wonders you cannot imagine today. A man in New York will be able to talk to a man in California." At this, Johnny totally cracked up with laughter. "Ohhh! A big man with a big voice, huh?" The men doubled over laughing. Eli seemed to enjoy telling the truth of the future to these men who couldn't even imagine it.

"Also in those days, men will create pictures that move, and idolize the images of those cast upon a large silver screen. They will call them 'stars' and some will talk like this." He began to imitate movie stars of the twentieth century, starting with John Wayne.

"Well, listen up, pilgrim, and listen tight. I'm gonna kiss me a woman and wrestle me a bear. Sure hope I don't get that mixed up again." The men laughed. Then immediately he broke into the actions and voice of Jimmy Stewart, saying, "Now wait a minute, Clarence, you say you're an Angel Second Class?" Then he imitated a Yul Brenner line from Cecil B. DeMille's *Ten Commandments.* "I warn you, Moses, the temple grain belongs to the gods. So let it be written. So let it be done." Instantly he went into an impression of Rodney Dangerfield with a line from *Caddy Shack.* "Hey, that gopher stole my ball. I tell ya, I get no respect." With each star Eli mimicked, the men were amused, yet confused. Laughing, Johnny pointed at Eli. "You are a weird and crazy one, Eli! Are you saying these are people of the future?"

Eli was enjoying their wondering and continued to entertain, mimicking more twentieth-century stars.

"And there will be small screens with many characters in nearly every home." He did impressions of characters from the *Andy Griffith Show,* starting with Gomer Pyle. "Well, gollee! Surprise! Surprise! Surprise!" He instantly broke into Andy Griffith. "Well, looky here, everybody. Look who's home from the marine corps. Whadda ya say, Floyd?" Eli imitated Floyd, the barber. "Oh yeah, Gomer! Do ya want a haircut?" He mimicked Gomer again grabbing a single hair. "You can cut this hair right here." The men laughed. Imitating Floyd he said, "Oh, he's become a funny boy, Andy." The men continued to laugh as Eli switched to Gomer's voice, "The Marines took care of my hair. The main reason I came home was to see my girlfriend, Thelma Lou!" As the men snickered,

Eli jumped into an impersonation of a riled-up Barney Fife. "You know darn good and well Thelma Lou's my girl. Why, I've got half a mind to put you under arrest!" He did Andy briefly. "Now, Barn!" Then broke into an imitation of Goober. "You've got half a mind, all right. That's the dumbest thing I ever heard." Then he went into Andy again. "Now, Goober, you stay outta this!" Eli did a brief Aunt Bee impression. "Oh, Andy!"

Then he instantly went back to Andy. "You too, Aunt Bee. Now everybody just calm down." Eli broke into Barney Fife again. "Calm? I'm plenty calm! Gimme my bullet, Ange! I'll show ya calm!" He did an instant Andy line. "Now, Barn!" Then right into Gomer. "Shazam! If I've gotta duck bullets I might as well git back in the marine corps. It's safer!"

Finishing his *Andy Griffith Show* routine, Eli wore a big grin as he enjoyed the men chuckling to themselves, amused by his sudden change from one strange character to another.

Les Moore was the most amused. "Eli!" he said, laughing. "I . . . I don't . . . know what you're talkin' about, but here I am, a grown man . . . and you're so silly I almost wet my britches!" Les was still laughing when he looked down and saw a wet spot on his pants. Embarrassed, he covered it with his hands and mumbled "Oops!" as the men laughed at him.

Eli took note of it and made a prediction. "And that's another thing. The time will come when a man won't have to leave his house in order to relieve himself. The outhouse will become a relic." Hearing that, James Morgan, who was standing beside Johnny stopped laughing and said to Johnny in a low confidential tone, "Now who's gonna mess in his own house? This guy is as fishy as the food he brought us." Johnny turned to Eli. "Eli! Are you holdin' out on us? You brought us fish. But you're eatin' the loco weed, aren't ya?" He laughed. The others laughed at this, but Eli turned more serious, and for the first time since he arrived, they saw him without his bright smile as he orated,

"All that I have told you is the truth, but I forgive you for you know not what you scorn." He stood and prophesied in an authoritative voice, bringing the men to silence.

"So that you may know what I predict is true, I prophesy that in the near future the president will be assassinated, but before that, you will need protection for yourselves to live. Let's hope prayers reach out in time."

John and his men knew Eli was serious, and were taken aback by his complete change in personality and the sincerity of his message. They exchanged puzzled glances with one another, wondering just how to take him. Eli's stance was firm; his voice, calm and wise. "And when you bear witness to the truth of these prophecies, know that all I tell you is true. In the twelfth year of the next century a great ship will sink and humble the world. Shortly thereafter, nation will rise against nation, and it shall be called a world war. In the twenty-ninth year, the economy of this land will fail and bring a great depression followed by a second world war more terrible than the first. Eventually, the world will desert the values that bring blessings and then the end will come."

All eyes followed him as he paused and sat down. His voice became more mellow and his eyes expressed compassion. "So remember above all that love covers a multitude of wrongs. Treasure love for it is more precious than silver and gold, diamonds and rubies, emeralds and pearls. Because love cares, forgives, is humble, and delights in pleasing others." Johnny and his men silently absorbed his words.

Eli slowly turned, gazing into the eyes of each man as he continued to speak.

"It is love that created you. Love that has saved you. Love that sustains you. Until you truly know love, you will not truly know life. And greater love hath no man than he who lays down his life for another. Remember he who laid down his life for you. Forget not my words for they will sustain you in troubled times." The men seem mesmerized by Eli's message. He rose to leave, saying, "For now, though, I must bid you farewell and be on my way." John hoped they hadn't offended him and said, "But, Mr. Proffit, you're welcome to camp with us for the night!" Eli softly replied, "I appreciate your hospitality but I must go." He shook Johnny's hand and smiled his pleasant smile, looking into John's eyes with compassionate understanding and wisdom. Johnny and his men just stared at him as he slowly shuffled away. He took a few steps, then slowly turned around and called out to them a final farewell message.

"Be not forgetful to entertain strangers, for thereby some have entertained angels unawares!" He raised his palm toward them, adding, "Goodbye and God bless you." Jay was standing beside John as Eli walked away. Johnny said in a near whisper, "Goodbye, Eli." After a brief moment of silence Jay followed suit and softly said, "Goodbye, Mistah Proffit." As all of them stared at Eli walking away, he disappeared in what seemed to be a mellow burst of twilight.

No one said anything. But they thought a lot about everything this stranger did and said that evening. He would be a topic of conversation many times during the next eighteen months they would spend in the trenches defending the Confederate capitol. Most of all, Johnny thought about Eli's message to treasure love.

❊Chapter 12❊

HOME-FRONT CONFRONTATION

They proudly marched off to war, with thoughts of victory
But the life that they endured, was sometimes worse than as slavery.
The Gray and Blue entangled, on what was a common ground
Because the government was split, no compromise was found.
A dark and evil shadow fell, all across the countryside
Like an awesome plague from hell, while families and widows cried.
Oh Lord, why must we suffer so, with cruelty to our fellow man?
Why in this world can't we have, peace and love throughout the land?
—Claude Wayne, "Marching to War"

The year 1863 was a year to mark memories for Johnny. Unforgettable memories. He got engaged to the woman of his dreams. He was drafted into the Confederacy. He was sent to Southern Virginia, promoted to the rank of lieutenant, and assigned to rehabilitate a band of unruly men. He shaped them up and earned a leave to go to Danville. He met Fanny Sellers and Nellie and Rowdy Roberts. He oversaw the building of the *Baby Belle*, was promoted to captain, and led the attack to defeat Rowdy and his terrorizing mob. He had to say goodbye to newfound friends and a young boy he adored as his own. He had met a stranger on the road who talked of the value of love. And he expressed love often in letters to the woman he only lived to see again, to cling to again.

He now thought of all of these things in the trenches, as he and his men became a small link in Robert E. Lee's defense of the Confederacy's capital, Richmond, Virginia.

Eighteen sixty-three was also a crucial year in this war between the States. In early May, outnumbered Confederate forces defeated the Union troops at the battle of Chancellorsville. But one of Stonewall Jackson's men accidentally shot the general in the left arm. The rifles used in those days shattered bones so badly it almost always necessitated amputation. Upon hearing of Jackson's wound, Robert E. Lee commented, "He lost his left arm. But I have lost my right." Lee had great confidence in Jackson's abilities as a determined leader and had looked upon him as his right hand man. Two weeks after the amputation, Stonewall Jackson died from infection and pneumonia. It was a time in history that even simple sanitary medicine was not a common practice.

This was the year of the turning point in the battles to determine America's future. Would it be two nations, or one? The tide began to turn in favor of one nation when the North defeated the Southern forces in their most daring offensive drive at Gettysburg. Never again would Robert E. Lee have the manpower to launch an offensive maneuver against the North. The next day after the battles of Gettysburg, on July fourth, the Confederacy was cut in two when Union general Ulysses S. Grant gave total control of the Mississippi River to the North with a victory at the last stronghold on the great river at Vicksburg, Mississippi. Five days later, Port Hudson, Louisiana, was taken by Union Forces, prompting Abraham Lincoln to say, "The Father of Waters again goes unvexed to the sea." The heart of the South was surrounded by the waters of the Mississippi and Ohio rivers, and the Atlantic Ocean from Virginia around to the Gulf of Mexico and New Orleans. Unable to resupply itself, the South was running low on everything from food, clothing, and basic necessities, to fighting men.

The battle of Chancellorsville cost them ten thousand casualties; Gettysburg, more than twenty-two thousand; Vicksburg, another ten thousand; an additional seventeen thousand Confederates were killed or wounded in the two-day battle of Chickamauga in September of 1863. One day after the battle of Chickamauga was fought in Georgia, John and his men defeated the Rowdy Roberts Gang and proceeded to Richmond. By Christmas of 1863, Johnny and his men were often in the trenches surrounding the city and the only thing they looked forward to was a few gifts from home, maybe some hand-knitted socks or a scarf. But what Johnny enjoyed most was just a word from Molly as he read her latest precious letter that gave him hope.

My Dear Darling Johnny,   *Sunday, Dec. 6, 1863*

How I wish you were here. How I wish we could both run away to a place where there is no fighting and war and hold each other close like we did the first day we met at the Magnolia Plantation. It was so nice to be so close and feeling love for each other.

Every day since last August when the Union troops started bombarding Charleston with cannons, it's been awful to live here. The constant threat weighs heavy on my heart, but no one has been seriously hurt. They've evacuated just about everything south of Broad Street. They say that part of the city has been greatly damaged. I haven't been down there but I can hear the horrible bombs exploding all the way up here on Ashley Avenue. My brother Kent ventured down there, even though we told him to stay away. You know how young boys are, always curious and anxious to get into something, even if it is too dangerous.

I hope you enjoy the knitting I'm sending you. The socks and sweater should help to keep you warm with winter coming on. I'm working on a scarf for you but I doubt you'll have it in time for Christmas.

Oh, Johnny, if only we could have "Peace on earth, goodwill toward men" by then, like the bible says. But I know it won't end that soon. When I read those words from the story of the birth of Jesus, I want to cry because I know we're so far from that in these terrible days. I pray to God it will end soon so we can be together again. I pray for you all the time. Keep me in you prayers until we can be in each other's arms again. I look forward to that day with great anticipation.

Dreaming of you Always,
Your Loving Bride,
Molly ♡

XOXOXOXOXOXOXOXOXOXOXOXOXOXOXOXOXOXO

While the Confederate men were trying to survive on the battlefields, their women were trying to survive on the home front. It wasn't easy. The women were pressed into a life like they had never known. It was a life of hardship and heartbreak. They not only suffered from a lack of all the things they needed to survive, including food, but emotional tragedy as well. The news of so many of the men wounded, maimed, or dead was tearing their hearts apart. But still they persevered and did all they could to help the wounded men at home while trying to provide for those at the front.

One of the primary ways they attempted to be useful to the cause was sewing clothing together to ship to the front lines, where men's clothes were put to the test in the grimy conditions. It literally caused the clothing to rot and fall apart. The ladies formed knitting circles where they knitted socks, underwear, and other garments while they consoled each other with conversational gossip to pass the time and try not to fall into lonely mental depression.

Since the Mitchells owned a fabric shop, it was a natural center for sewing circles and communication of every thought that the ladies could imagine. They busied themselves knitting with such repeated practice that the stitches were almost automatic, and they could talk and knit at the same time for hours on end. Some ladies stitched together shirts and trousers. Others cut out the patterns for them. They had rigid daily routines and worked as steadily as honey bees. The Mitchells owned a spinning mule, a machine invented by Samuel Compton in 1779, just three years after the United States became a nation. The spinning mule had forty-eight spindles and produced unusually fine and uniform yarn. The machine was also called the muslin wheel because it was excellent for producing that cotton material. Molly frequently operated the muslin wheel, using its foot pedal while engaging in the talk of the day. Marion and Molly would break and take turns serving customers who came into the general store and fabric shop, but customers were far and few between because people's earnings were down and the Confederate dollars were becoming more and more inflated. Before the war, a spool of thread could be bought for only five cents. But by the end of 1863, it was already ten times that much and still climbing. A pair of slippers that could be bought for five dollars before was more than ninety dollars, with no end to rising prices in sight. The demand for goods was high and the supply was becoming more limited because it was getting more difficult for the blockade runners to slip past the Union blockade.

Union ships and artillery had Charleston harbor bottled up. In fact, a Union ironclad named *Catskill* attacked batteries and forts protecting Charleston from the sea, patrolling constantly against blockade runners. So when one was able to sneak through with a supply of clothing or sugar or other needed items, there was a mad rush to the docks. Such was the case in May of 1864 when Molly's brother Kent rushed into the store one morning, yelling,

"Hurry, Mom! Molly! I just got word a runner got through with clothes and supplies last night. I'll hitch up the wagon. We better hurry before it's all gone." Molly exclaimed, "Good for you, Kent. It pays to keep your ears open." She immediately stopped the muslin wheel. Marion coolly kept on knitting with the rest of the circle of women and said, "Do you think they have any bolts of material?" Rushing back out the door Kent said, "Don't know! Better hurry to find out." Marion then suggested, "I'll stay here. You go with Kent, Molly. And be careful. Whatever you do, don't go south of Broad Street." Molly replied, "Don't worry, Mother. I know better than that!"

They had to go south on Ashley Avenue to Calhoun Street and east to the maritime center on the east coast of the city, at the mouth of the Cooper River; a distance of about two miles. When they arrived, the blockade runners were almost finished auctioning off the items. The only things left were a few jars of pickles and a bolt of broadcloth. Molly immediately spied the gray cloth. No one in the city could make better use of it than they could. She yelled out, "How many yards are in the bolt of cloth?" The runner who was auctioning the pickles said, "Hold on lady! We're dealin' with the pickles right now!" Molly impatiently waited while he called for higher prices for the pickles. "Come on now. Ah have ten dollahs. Who'll give me 'leben?" Someone yelled out "'Leven!" Another hollered, "'Leven fifty!"

Molly, anxious to end the bidding instinctively yelled, "Twelve Dollars!"

"Ah have twelve. Do Ah heah thirteen? Twelve. Do Ah heah thirteen?" He was met with silence. "Twelve once. Twelve twice! Sode to the little lady fo' twelve dollahs!" As

Molly handed him the money, once again she asked, "How many yards of cloth?"

"How would Ah know 'less we unroll it. Heah! Hode on to it." She could see it had a lot of wraps just as someone from the crowd yelled, "Mah wife could make me a nice new uniform with that. Ah'll give ya fifty dollahs fo' it!" Molly immediately yelled, "Fifty one." She turned to the other bidder only to discover it was Billy Bob Walker, the man who had called the paces at the duel between Johnny and Louis B. Madden at the Magnolia Plantation. She was determined to outbid him, but she only had a hundred and twenty Confederate dollars with her. Billy Bob stood there in his dirty gray Confederate uniform and continued to bid.

"Sixty Confed'rite dollars, suh!" Molly retorted, "Sixty-one." Before the blockade runner could repeat it, Billy Bob said, "Sebendy dollahs!" Molly yelled, "Seventy-one!" Billy Bob hesitated a moment. The runner repeated, "Seven'y-one. Ah have seven'y-one dollars. Do ah hear—" "Eighty dollahs!" interrupted Walker. Molly immediately returned, "Eighty-one dollars!" "We have eighty one. Do ah—" Again Billy Bob quickly responded, "Niney on tha nose!" "Ninety-one!" yelled Molly. Billy Bob hesitated, whispering to some the men with him.

"Ninety-one dollars from tha little lady. Do Ah heah a hun'ert?" said the runner with zeal.

"Ah'll go a hun'ert, suh. One hun'ert good as gode Confed'rite dollahs!" Now it was Molly who hesitated. Walker and his men began to smile and chuckled to themselves, thinking they had outbid her. The runner repeated, "One hun'ert dollahs. Do ah heah mo'?"

Then Molly smiled and said, "A hundred and one dollars . . . plus a big hug and a kiss on the cheek for the auctioneer!" Upon hearing this, the proper ladies of the era emitted an embarrassed gasp, as this was considered a breach of respectable conduct for a lady. But the blockade runner was all smiles as he said, "Sode to tha little lady fo' a

hun'ert and one dollahs and a big hug and a kiss from one
of the purdiest ladies mah eyes evah did behode!" With a
rush of anger, Billy Bob Walker responded, "Hey, suh! You
nevah give me a chance tuh top her bid!" As the blockade
runner moved toward Molly to give her the cloth, he looked
at Walker with disdain and said, "Ah ain't gonna accept no
hug and kiss from you, podnuh!" Walker retorted, "Suh,
you are dang fool. Ah wuz gonna pay as much as a hundert
an' thurdy dollahs fo' it." The blockade runner said, "Ah'll
be the judge o' whut ah'll accept fo' riskin' mah life tuh
bring goods in heah, Suh! An' a hug and a kiss from this
heah lovely lady is worth mo' than any mo' monah you got."

Walker slammed his right fist into the palm of his left
hand with such force the smack from it could be heard
throughout the crowd, and everyone knew it must have hurt
because he walked away shaking his left hand. While the
blockade runner was giving Molly her bolt of material and
collecting his reward, Billy Bob stopped at the rear of Molly's
wagon to expound a few choice words to some of the men
with him. He spoke in a low and angry tone, but Kent could
hear every word even though he was facing the other way
sitting in the wagon seat up front. Walker snarled, "She's
Louie's old girl frien', ain't she? The one who jilted him for
that Yankee, Johnny. Well, ah shore am glad we arranged
fo' that fool to git drafted. Ah hope that suckah tries to run
back heah 'cause then ah'll shoot 'im for being a deserter
jus' like me and Louie figgered all along."

"Yeah, 'at's whut's gonna happen too. 'Cause thur ain't
no Yankee gonna be true tuh the Confed'racy. It'll suve 'im
right too!" said one of the other men in an equally nasty
voice.

Kent made a quick glance over his shoulder and Billy
Bob noticed it. He shushed the man and walked farther
away, whispering so Kent couldn't hear what they were saying.
Then they took off running up Calhoun Street. By then
Molly was approaching with the items. Kent jumped down

off the wagon to help her. He put the cloth in the wagon. Molly held the pickles in her lap.

As they turned the wagon around to head back along Calhoun Street, Kent confided to her,

"Molly, I just heard somethin' I've gotta tell ya." His tone of voice was such that Molly thought he was going to relate some uppity comment one of the high-society ladies made. She was prepared to defend herself against it when she said, "Oh? And what old biddy said what?"

"It wasn't some old lady. It was that man who was biddin' against you." She said, "Billy Bob Walker? Who cares what he says! We need that cloth. I made up my mind I was gonna outbid him and I think it was pretty fast thinkin' on my part to—" Kent interrupted, "Molly! It didn't have anything to do with that. He said he and Louie were the ones who got Johnny drafted and they're hopin' he tries to run away so they can shoot 'im as a deserter." Molly was shocked but now things were beginning to make sense. She had always thought it was odd that a man from the North would be drafted into the Confederacy. She turned to Kent and said, "What? This is outrageous! Now I understand why they dragged Johnny off to war the way they did. Oh, that awful Louis B. Madden. I can't believe how he changed into such a nasty, evil man. And to think I almost married him. Thank God I saw his evil ways in time." Kent went on to inform her, "Well, they all must be bad. One of those men said no Yankee would be true to the Confederacy and they think sooner or later Johnny will try to escape from the army and they'll shoot him for desertin'. He said that's what Johnny deserves."

"Oh, I can't listen to this. I must write Johnny tonight and warn him of this terrible thing."

"I'm sorry, sis'. I couldn't believe my ears when I heard 'em talking. They didn't think I heard 'em but—" Just then, one of Billy Bob Walker's men came running out from behind a tree. He rushed into the street to grab the reins of the horses while Billy Bob raced out to steal the cloth Molly purchased. Kent saw them, quickly snapped the reins, and yelled, "*Giddyap! Heeaaah!*" Molly screamed as the horses broke into a gallop and the men kept running alongside. The man in front kept trying to grab the reins from the side but Kent stood up, swatting the horse on the rear so that he pulled to the wrong side of the street away from the men. Then he swatted both horses on the rump and they picked up speed. The man in front soon couldn't keep up and was running out of breath after this hundred-yard dash, but Billy Bob had managed to grab the back board of the wagon and he slung his legs into the air and over it to land in the bed of the wagon. He wobbled forward, pulled a gun, pointed it at Kent, and yelled, "Stop the wagon or I'll shoot!"

Kent was so frightened he just kept on going, whipping the horses even more. As Walker reached down to pick up the bolt of material, Molly turned around and threw the jar of pickles at his face, bloodying his nose and disorienting him. He stumbled and fell, momentarily dropping the gun to catch his balance. Molly jumped into the bed of the wagon and fell on the gun a split second before Billy Bob regained his balance in the unstable bouncing wagon rolling at full speed. She got a grip on it and slipped her finger around the trigger. She rolled over on her back to see Billy Bob's bloody face. He stood over her shakily, still trying to maintain his balance. He threw the bolt of cloth down to put his hands out to maintain his balance, and seeing that he was about to lunge toward her, in a surge of fear she pulled the trigger without taking time to aim directly at him. The bullet fired into the back of the seat, splitting the wood where she had been sitting moments before.

Seeing she knew how to use the weapon, Billy Bob jumped over the side and went sprawling, rolling end over end in the street. Kent kept darting glances over his shoulder at the action behind him. When he saw Billy Bob bouncing and rolling in the street, he let out a whoop, "*Yeeaaah ha!*" Then as they were nearing Ashley Avenue, he slowed the horses down to make a right turn to head north on their way back to the store, when a one-hundred-pound cannon ball exploded northeast of South Battery Street just a few blocks away.

Molly screamed and said, "Oh dear Lord! What was that?" Kent said, "Just another shelling from those cannons on Morris Island, I reckon. Or it could be from that stinkin' ironclad, *Catskill*."

"When will there ever be peace again? I miss the good old quiet days," she noted. Kent said, "Yeah, but this is more fun and exciting." Molly responded, "Fun? Are you crazy?"

As the horses slowed to a walk, Molly got up and dusted herself off. Kent brought the horses to a halt to allow Molly to get back in the front seat of the wagon. He said, "Maybe Daddy was right to make you a tomboy. Sure came in handy today." Molly wasn't pleased and was trembling from the ordeal. But she still was perfectly in control of herself. She was holding Walker's gun and said, "Daddy didn't make me a tomboy." She looked at the gun. "Well! Now what am I going to do with this?" Kent quipped, "You could start a gun collection!" Molly defensively responded, "Oh sure. That's something every girl should have, huh?" "Hah," said Kent, "So Daddy didn't make you a tomboy? I reckon you just did it all by yourself then, huh?" Molly's adrenaline was giving her the shakes, but they both chuckled to themselves as they continued back to the store.

The ladies in the sewing circle were about to get some news that would touch off a round of gossip that would bring the knitting to a halt. The ladies were all sitting around in everyday work dresses that had no hoops for reasons of comfort. The bell on the door jangled as Molly rushed in. She was toting Walker's pistol and carrying the cloth and wearing a worried look. Her mother also noticed how messed up her hair was and how dirty her dress was from rolling in the wagon. She exclaimed, "Molly! What happened? Where'd you get that gun?"

"Oh, Mother! The most unbelievable thing. I don't know where to start!" She was somewhat in a state of shock and Marion immediately noticed that Molly was not her usual cool, calm self. Her mother quickly suggested, "Come here, child, and sit down. Tell me, what is it?"

"We were attacked!" she exclaimed, out of breath from the tight staves in her bodice.

"Attacked? Oh my! By whom? Where's Kent?" said Marion, about to go into shock herself.

"He's okay. He's putting the team in the carriage house." The other ladies in the sewing circle laid their knitting aside to gather around Molly as she went on with her account of what happened.

"I started bidding on this bolt of broadcloth and . . . you know Billy Bob Walker?

"Yes," said Marion. "He attacked you?" The other ladies were as anxious as Marion to get the facts about Molly's traumatic situation, but they just stared with their mouths agape as she went on.

"No . . . I mean . . . yes. I'm getting to that part. He started bidding against me, mentioning that his wife could make him a new uniform with the material."

"Yes! Yes!" said her mother, apprehensive to know everything.

"When the bid got up to a hundred dollars, I knew I had to do something because I didn't want the bidding to go any higher and I saw the way the runner was eyeing me. Well, I got desperate." One of the ladies, Carlotta Gabbert, who was a big gossip by nature, couldn't wait.

"And then what happened?" she said. Molly took a deep breath knowing how some of the ladies would feel. "Well, I made a bid of a hundred and one dollars and . . ." She hesitated, glanced at Mrs. Gabbert, and then looked down to finish the statement, "Well, like I said I was desperate. So I . . ." She paused. "So I said I'd also give the auctioneer . . . a big hug and a kiss on the cheek." Mrs. Gabbert sucked in a huge volume of air in a loud gasp and plopped her hand against her mouth, saying,

"Oh, my, my!" Marion quickly sensed Mrs. Gabbert's social embarrassment but restrained a retort, waiting to hear more about what happened before being judgmental.

"Go on, Molly. What happened then?" said Marion. Mrs. Gabbert interrupted, saying, "That wasn't very proper, but surely Mr. Walker didn't attack you for that. Did he?"

"No!" said Molly." Her mother addressed Mrs. Gabbert. "For heaven's sake! Don't get your bloomers in a wad, Carlotta! Let the girl tell the story! These are desperate times and sometimes it calls for desperate measures! Go on, Molly." Mrs. Gabbert again put her hand to her mouth and whimpered a timid "Oh dear!" as Molly continued with her story a bit more relieved, relaxed, and confident since her mother so boldly came to her defense. Just then, Kent walked in the door.

"Well, when the runner jumped at the chance for a hug and a kiss from me and said, 'Sold to the little lady,' Billy Bob got angry because he didn't get a chance to raise the bid." Kent joined in. "Yeah, Billy Bob said the runner was a fool 'cause he was willin' to pay up to a hundred and thirty dollars for it." "Let me tell it, Kent." said Molly. Kent responded with frustration, "Go ahead, you big tomboy!" With that, Molly's face flushed red, embarrassed to have such an unladylike thing thrust at her in front of these ladies who still clung to the old social standards.

"I am not!" said Molly. Marion corrected her son. "Now, Kent, that's no way for a gentleman to talk to his sister. Molly is a lady now. Just remember that!" Kent lowered his head and murmured, "Yes, ma'am!" The boy was now fifteen and had been anxious to get involved in the action of the war. He loved his sister and family but felt left out and wanted to show he was nearing manhood. But he obeyed his mother and quietly let Molly go on with her report of their dangerous encounter.

"Well, to make a long story short, Mr. Walker must have gotten pretty angry at me getting the cloth 'cause he and his friend attacked our wagon on the way back to steal the cloth. It was awful!"

"I know he was mad 'cause I heard 'im talkin' to his friend," said Kent. Molly added, "Now go ahead, Kent, tell mother about what you heard." The lad was happy to be in the spotlight and anxious to tell this confidential part of what happened that only he had heard. He talked rapidly. "That Billy Bob was talkin' mean about Johnny. He said he and Louis Madden were the ones that got Johnny drafted and they were hopin' Johnny would take off and run away so he could be shot for bein' a deserter." With that, Marion put both of her hands to her mouth and closed her eyes momentarily. She opened them and looked upward to prayerfully say, "Oh dear God! What evil has befallen us? Isn't it bad enough that we're fighting a civil war? Must we have to endure such a hellish attack among our own ranks as well?" The ladies gathered around to hug and pat Marion and Molly on the back to comfort them. Kent continued, saying, "You should be proud of the way Molly took on Billy Bob, Mama. When he jumped up in the Wagon, she fought back like a wildcat. I was on the reins an' racin' the horses as fast as they could go down Calhoun Street. People were rushin' to get out of the way and pullin' up to a halt on the side streets. He put a pistol to my back and said, 'Stop or I'll shoot.' Molly threw the jar of pickles at 'im and hit 'im in the nose. He dropped the gun and Molly jumped on top of it. The next thing I know, a gunshot split the back of the seat. Then I saw 'im jump off the wagon and go sprawlin' all over the street. That's why I called Molly a tomboy. She might be a lady, but I was glad she was a tomboy today." Molly was still sitting in the chair and her mother put her arms around her daughter's head to pull her close to her side, patting Molly's hair with gentle sympathetic taps of her fingers while softly saying, "Poor child. What have you been through? If only your father was here." The ladies were murmuring low such things as to join in sympathy for Molly. Polly Pairrett, who was a very sensitive little lady seldom seen without a bonnet even indoors, repeatedly uttered, "Oh my goodness!"

"Did you ever hear of such a thing?" exclaimed Mrs. Gabbert.

"Lord help us!" said Hallie Wolf, another lady still stuck in Charleston's peaceful past society.

Molly was uncomfortable with all the commiseration she was receiving. She gently pushed away from her mother, stood up, and said, "It's okay! I'll be all right. I only did what I had to do. We all have to. It's like the whole world is in turmoil. Oh, how I wish Johnny and Daddy were here. But they're not. And somehow we have to make do as best we can." Marion looked at Molly with compassion, responding, "Yes. Of course we do. And we're doing it. We can't let anything stop us from our duties. Let's get back to our knitting, ladies. The men need us. They're desperate for the clothes we make."

As the ladies took up their knitting chores in chairs ringed about a round table, Kent was feeling left out and needed attention and recognition for his part in thwarting Mr. Walker.

"Yeah, Mom. I wish you could have seen how fast I had the horses runnin'. It was funny the way that Billy Bob went tumblin' in the street. He musta got the tar knocked out of 'im." He laughed.

"Kent, I'm sure that in spite of it all you both apparently handled the situation very well. I'm thankful neither one of you got injured in any way," said Marion. This set Molly thinking. "Oh good heavens," she exclaimed. "I hope Billy Bob wasn't injured too bad. He doesn't have the character of a gentleman. He seems like someone who might be the revengeful type." A groan went up among the ladies and Marion protectively said, "Let's not think such things. We'll just have to trust the Good Lord to protect us until these terrible times are over."

Kent shocked the ladies even more by revealing feelings he had previously suppressed. Feelings that were the result of coming into the age of puberty and being left out of the manly action that was taking place in distant places around the country and nearby in Charleston.

"Mom, I think I should do my part to help end the war and join the militia." Marion shouted, "You will not! What are you thinking? You're only fifteen! How could you even consider such a thing? We need you around here, Kent. You're the man of the family now, I won't let you desert us." She walked closer to him. "Why, who will take care of the garden and hitch up the team or help stock things here in the store? We need an extra hand to wait on customers too. No! I won't let you go. Don't ever talk like that again." She put her arms around him and gave him a big hug, and Molly did the same. That was enough to stroke his young ego and he almost apologetically said, "Okay, Mom. I didn't know you needed me that much." Molly chimed in with her thoughts. "Kent, mother is right. You've got to be the man of the house with Daddy gone. And besides, we love you and need you. We'd miss you too much." Kent smiled, content to feel loved, needed, appreciated, and manly. Marion set Kent to work in the storage area in the rear of the store, and the ladies began again tending to their knitting duties with the Walker episode the prime topic of conversation.

The knitting circle was near the front window of the store so they could get as much natural light during the day as possible by which to do their tedious needlework. It also allowed them to observe the activity outside on the street. After about a half hour, the conversation was still in heated gossip when they noticed an old customer pull his wagon up and tie his mule to the hitching post. The front door of the store flung open with the attached bell jangling loudly, and in stepped a little seventy-five-year-old man with a white beard and plaid hat. His clothes consisted of various shades of greens and tans. He wore a beige vest under his dusty, soiled olive-colored coat. He puffed on a pipe that twisted down from his smiling mouth—a grin with such mischievous regard as to say this was a spunky man who still hadn't outgrown his youthful prankishness. With great energy for his age, the man wobbled in. If the shillelagh wasn't a dead giveaway of his heritage, his accent immediately identified him as an Irishman.

"Top o' the moirnin' tu ya, liadies. Mizz Mitchell! Mizz Moilly!" It was Patrick McLaughlin, a regular customer who hadn't been in the store for a couple of weeks.

"Good morning to you, Mr. McLaughlin!" said Marion. "And how may we serve you today?"

"Wail, oi wuz a wanderin' if perhaps ye still 'ave stock o' some flar or carnmeal?"

"We only have cornmeal in two-pound bags. Everything is in short supply these days, you know."

"Yas, oi know. Oi'll 'ave a bag of the meal, if ya please." He gave Marion a pitiful glance with his intense squinty eyes, pleading, "And oi shure cud use a tin or bag o' pipe tobaccy."

"I'm sorry," said Marion with a tone of voice matching his pitiful state. "We haven't had any in stock since the last time you were here. But we're expecting some might arrive overland, or perhaps if another blockade runner gets through. One got through last night but we couldn't get there in time to see if they had any tobacco. We know how you gentlemen seem to thrive on it."

"Now ain't that the truth though. Oi wuz aimin' to catch that load mahsef but got wind of it too late. Everything was sold by the time oi got there. After this war is over oi'm gonna open me mah very own tobaccy shop. Oi'll do it too, ar me niame ain't Patty McLaughlin!" As soon as he said that, he spotted Billy Bob's pistol laying on the table on top of the bolt of cloth.

"Faith an' Begorrah! An' when did you liadies take tu packin' a pistol? Or is this foine weapon an item fer sale?"

"*Uh*, no," said Marion. "This is one Molly somewhat accidentally got her hands on this morning."

"Wail, glary be! Oi bet oi know a Confederite gintlemen who's in the market for such. Hitched a ride on me wagon on the way over here. He wuz limpin' with a bad ankle. Said somethin' 'bout losin' his peestol and fallin' off the wagon. Oi warned 'im he'd batter stay off the alcohol. Told 'im that stuff will git a-hold a man and tike 'im straight to the pits o' hell iffen ya ain't keereful."

The ladies all looked at one another, wondering if Mr. McLaughlin had given a ride to the main subject of the morning. Marion attempted to confirm their suspicions.

"Patty, you say you gave a man a ride this morning, who said he had fallen off a wagon?

"Yas! An incorrigible drunkard, oi assume."

"And he was limping?"

"Uh-huh! Sure wuz. Looked like he'd been in a barroom brawl. His uniform was torn up."

"Are you sure he had been drinking?"

"Wail, yas, Mizz Marion! Oi could smell whiskey on his breath." Then McLaughlin continued to affirm his belief that the man had been referring to drinking when he talked of "falling off the wagon."

"Oi told 'im if you're goin' to drink, ya ought at least drink a little wine for your belly's sake." Molly interrupted, "Mr. McLaughlin! Did the man tell you his name?"

"You know . . . yes, he did!" The ladies froze in anticipation as he paused, scratching his head.

"Oi can't remember it though." The ladies groaned with the frustration of wanting to know. Molly said, "Was it Billy Bob Walker?" The little Irishman's eyes squinted and he raised his right forefinger. "Wail, Oi'm not so shure 'bout Walker, he never mentioned that, but oi believe Billy is carrect."

"Where did you pick him up?" said Molly.

"On Calhoun just as oi was ready to turn on to Ashley."
This revelation raised some eyebrows. "Did he ask you to
take him to the military battery?" Patrick eyed the ladies
suspiciously.

"Aye now! And jist what's yer intrist in this fella? Is he
perhaps the apple o' somebody's eye in this room?" The
ladies groaned again, only with more of an expression of
disapproval.

"Good heavens, NO!" exclaimed Molly.

"Now, Mr. McLaughlin you must promise not to breathe
a word of this to anyone," said Marion.

"Wail, of carse, of carse! Word of what?"

"Molly and Kent were attacked by a man who fits the
description of the one who hitched a ride with you. Here's
what happened . . ." She went on to inform the Irishman of
the details and asked,

"Now, where did you take this man?"

"For heaven's sake! He asked to be dropped off a half
block down the street." With this, the ladies again groaned
with deep concern. After considering the situation, Marion
deduced,

"Mr. Walker may be waiting for you to leave, Patty, to
come in here looking for his gun. Here, let's hide it." She
hid it under the bolt of cloth. The Irishman quickly
responded, "That bein' the case, oi'll fake leavin' and go
'round the block to come back and mike sure he does ya no
harm, ma'am." He paid for his cornmeal and left.

Sure enough, as soon as the Irishman's wagon
rounded the corner, the bell on the door jangled loudly
and in hobbled Walker. Molly had walked to the rear of
the store.

"May I help you, sir?" said Marion politely. Walker glared
at her and flashed his eyes around the store, surveying who
was present and hoping to see his gun. After a long pause,
finally he spoke. "Did Miss Molly come in heah a little while
ago?" Marion felt her heart pounding, thinking of what this

man had done to her daughter and son, but she did her best to stay calm and controlled.

"Are you referring to my daughter, sir?" The ladies nervously kept knitting as if they couldn't hear.

"Is your dottah the one that was betrothed to Louie Madden at one time, ma'am?"

"Yes. At one time, Mr. Walker," said Marion.

"Oh, so you know mah name? Ah suppose ah'm famous 'round heah these days, huh?"

"I would say 'infamous' would be more appropriate, Mr. Walker. Why do you want to see my daughter?" Walker snarled a nasty grin and hurled a prejudiced viewpoint at her.

"Ah hate tuh be the one to bear bad news, but ah'm afraid your dottah and son are guilty of some rathuh unladylike and ungentlemanly conduct regardin' yours truly this morning. Your son not only refused to obey a military ordah from a Confed'rite offisuh, but your dottah could also be accused of assault and battery, and worse, attempted murder." At that point even Mrs. Gabbert couldn't control herself, yelling, "How dare you!" Marion quickly and calmly took control. "I'll handle this, Carlotta!" Surprising everyone, Molly coolly walked into the sewing circle and pulled Walker's gun out from under the broadcloth as Marion continued the conversation.

"Well, isn't it interesting to get both sides of the story," Molly said as Kent came up to the front. Molly turned and pointed the gun at Walker, and gritting her teeth, she fired forth her words. "If anybody deserves to be murdered, I would say you certainly qualify, Mr. Walker."

"See! See what your dottah is capable of! Now you listen to me, Miss Mitchell, just because you're a lady don't mean you cain't be accused of the crimes you committed this mornin'." Now ah've got witnesses. You bettah put that gun down and hand it ovah right now. This is not the way a lady should act." Molly couldn't believe this man had such deceiving gall as she said, "I was going to give this gun back because it is your property, not mine. Lawful ownership you didn't seem to understand this morning when you tried to steal a bolt of material from us. But now you've changed my mind. I'm not so sure you deserve to get it back. Let me tell you something, Mr. Walker. What my brother and I did this morning was purely out of self defense. No jury, military or civilian, could see it any different. And as far as witnesses go, these are *my* witnesses to verify what a snake you are."

With that, the ladies jumped up and Hallie proclaimed, "That's right! You need to be put in jail for what you did, young man." Mrs. Gabbert said, "We'll never be witnesses for a low-life, selfish worm like you." Polly Pairrett blurted out, "You ought to be ashamed of yourself. You'd bettah stop drinkin' and repent of your evil ways before it's too late."

Walker realized he couldn't fool them with legal jargon, so he boldly demanded, "All right! Just give me mah pistol back and we'll call it even. It's military property." Kent insisted, "Don't give it to 'im, Molly, unless he promises never to bother us again. Look, Walker, you were the one attemptin' murder when you stuck that gun in my back this mornin'!" Walker retorted, "Therah wuz no way ah was gonna shoot ya ovah a lousy bolt o' cloth. Ah just was tryin' to scare ya into stoppin' so ah could jump off the wagon, that's all." Molly was still steaming. "Yeah! Jump off the wagon stealing the goods I just paid a hundred and one dollars for."

"Plus a little somethin' extry, remembah?" said Walker with a snide smirk.

"I don't want your filthy gun," said Molly. "Here!" Before Walker could step up to take it, Kent grabbed the pistol and emptied the chambers of bullets.

Just after Kent handed the empty gun to Walker, Mr. McLaughlin came rushing through the door with a loud jangling of the bell, wielding his shillelagh. He saw Walker holding the gun and assumed he was attempting to rob the place. As Walker turned to see what all the noise was, the Irishman's ire was already brewing and he raised the shillelagh high over his head and cracked it down on Walker's wrist with a wallop that sent the gun flipping in the air, and Walker writhing in pain, jumping up and down. The Irishman shouted, "Lit that be a lisson tuh ya, ya dairty scallywag! Nobody's gonna go theivin' 'round ol' Patty McLaughlin!" In later days, that moment would become a cause for repeated laughter in the circle of gossip around the knitting table at Mitchell's General Store and Fabric Shop.

That evening, Marion prepared to write to her husband and tell him of the day's events, but before she did she opened his latest letter, which had also arrived that day, to make sure she didn't miss answering any of his concerns.

My Marvelous Marion,   *Sunday, May 1, 1864*

Dear loving wife, I regret so much that I was coerced into entering this terrible conflict. What a fool I was to think it would only last a few weeks or months. It has been three years now, and I can truthfully say it was the worst mistake of my life. I miss you, Molly, and Kent so much there are times it feels as though my chest will cave in to the vacuum in my heart. Instead of seeing your lovely faces during these years, I have been forced to see the faces of dying men and endless heaps of men already dead. I have seen things so terrible I cannot bear to tell you about them because I cannot bear to think about them myself.

So I must dwell on the things that please me most. Your face. Your voice. Your smile. Your cooking. I long to be home and enjoy the aroma of the meals you so lovingly prepared with your caring hands. Oh, to enjoy the company of my family at the supper table on a Sunday afternoon. How sweet the fragrance of life in those days.

What a fool I was to take the good life we had so for granted. If and when I shall ever return, I will cherish every moment with you and our precious children.

They are so close to being of the age to leave home. I hope the war ends soon so we can enjoy their sweet presence again. Kent is nearing sixteen and our lovely Molly will be getting married if this horror will end soon enough to let Johnny come home. Please tell Molly I saw him when my unit camped in Richmond a week ago. He's still alive and healthy, although we've all grown thin due to limited rations. He said to tell you all hello for him if I should get home before he does. In the meantime, all we can do is dream of our loved ones to keep us going. Remember, my darling, that I dream always of you. Every day as well as every night. Pray for us. I love you with all my heart.

Your One and Only Forever,
Thomas

Marion had much to tell her husband of this eventful day, but she hesitated to start writing, dwelling on the love of her life being so far away, so lonely, so tormented, so in need of her love. Before she could write him, she fell to her knees beside her bed and prayed for her husband, for Johnny and Molly and Kent, and all those men and families separated and suffering through the awful tragedy of a whole nation engaged in Civil War. She wondered how they could even call it "civil" when to her mind there was nothing civil about it. Nothing civilized about it.

Down the hall from her mother's bedroom, Molly was thinking similar things as she finished her letter to Johnny, warning him of the plot Louis B. Madden concocted to keep them apart. What a horrible thing that kind of jealousy was, she thought. She pictured Johnny in the trenches around Richmond and her heart ached for him. But even more so, her heart ached to be with him in a cozy, safe place where they could feel the warmth of love they had for each other.

Like her mother, Molly fell to her knees at her bedside to reach out to the God in heaven that she trusted. "My God! My Lord! Our Father who art in heaven! I thank you for all of your blessings. I praise your hallowed name for keeping my Johnny and my father safe in these troubled times. God, I know your will must be done. But in my ignorance I cannot understand why this war could be your will. Maybe someday I'll understand, but in the meantime please forgive me for not understanding. Please forgive me of my trespasses, my shortcomings, my sins. Please forgive me if I was the source of Mr. Walker's fall from grace today. I thank you, Lord, for providing our daily bread, even if on this day our daily bread was a jar of pickles. I thank you that the jar didn't break when it hit his face and fell on the cloth in the wagon. Lord, forgive my violence. I pray that Mr. Walker and Louie Madden will not be my enemies . . . or Johnny's. Sweet Jesus, lead me not into that kind of temptation again. Touch them with your spirit to change them and take the evil out of their hearts." She paused a moment to gather her thoughts and concluded, "But most of all, Lord, bless my family and my family to be. Please bring my precious Johnny and my daddy home to me soon. Surely, Lord, you must feel the pain of my heart. Surely, Lord, you will answer my prayer and let us live in peace and love. Amen."

❋Chapter 13❋

LAID TO REST

I propose to fight it out on
this line if it takes all summer!

—Ulysses S. Grant

All signs pointed to victory for the Union in 1864. Lincoln promoted Ulysses S. Grant to the rank of lieutenant general and gave him command of all Union forces. Grant was a strategist, and the first Northern military leader that earned the respect of Southern general Robert E. Lee as a formidable opponent. Grant coordinated his armies and said they would, "Move like a team pulling together." The noose was tightening on the Confederacy.

Grant put Gen. George G. Meade's Army of the Potomac in charge of defeating Lee in Northern Virginia, with the goal of taking Richmond. On May 5 and 6 of 1864, the Army of the Potomac forged its way into a desolate region of Northern Virginia they called "The Wilderness." It was a huge area of underbrush and wild forests located just west of Chancellorsville. Union forces outnumbered the Confederates by almost five to three when Robert E. Lee marched to meet them. Soldiers on both sides groped blindly through the overgrown forest. The thicket made the cavalry useless and artillery batteries operated blindly. Eventually, the dry underbrush caught fire and created a living hell as wounded men died screaming in the flames with no way to be rescued.

Lee suffered eleven thousand casualties. Even though Grant lost seventeen thousand men in the two-day battle, he failed to halt Grant's move to the south. He forged on like a madman flanking toward Richmond. But Lee again marched to meet him clashing at Spotsylvania Court House in a five-day battle that left nine thousand more Confederates dead or wounded. There were ten thousand Union casualties. Still Grant pushed to his left toward Richmond. Once more Lee followed. On May 31, Grant ordered Maj. Gen. Philip Sheridan's cavalry to move south to capture the crossroads at an intersection called Cold Harbor, about ten miles to the northeast of the Confederate capital. There they were confronted by the cavalry of Robert E. Lee's son, Gen. William H. Fitzhugh Lee. Sheridan's Union cavalry drove them a half-mile southwest from the crossroads to a barricade, where the Confederates started digging in and fortifying with breastworks consisting of rails, logs and earth.

Meanwhile, Robert E. Lee realized he couldn't let Cold Harbor be a breaking point in the nearly seven-mile front his outnumbered forces were holding to protect the Confederate capitol against Grant's advances. Desiring to retake Cold Harbor, Lee sent Maj. Gen. Joseph Kershaw's division to join Maj. Robert Hoke's division for a morning assault on June 1. The attempt was uncoordinated. Hoke failed to press the attack and Sheridan's men, armed with Spencer repeating carbines, repulsed the assault with ease.

When word of this reached General Grant, he was encouraged and immediately ordered reinforcements, planning a major attack that afternoon. He reasoned that if a frontal attack could break through the Confederate defenses at this point it would place the Union Army between Robert E. Lee and the rebel capital of Richmond. Maj. Gen. Horatio Wright, commanding the Union's Sixth Corps, arrived and replaced Sheridan's cavalry. But Grant was forced to delay the attack because outdated orders had Maj. Gen. William Smith's Eighteenth Corps marching in the wrong direction. By the time they retraced their route, they arrived late in the afternoon. The Union attack finally began at 5:00 p.m. They observed a weak spot in the line. Wright's veterans rushed through a fifty-yard gap between Hoke's and Kershaw's divisions, capturing part of the Confederate lines. But the victory was short lived because a Southern counterattack sealed off the break and ended the fighting for that day. However, reports of the action prompted Robert E. Lee to realize the significance of the proposed assault. His extraordinary ability to position his outnumbered army in such a way as to overwhelm his opponent was uncanny. He rounded up all straggling men and units in the Richmond theater of battle to ready them for the action.

Up to now, Johnny's men were regarded as less capable soldiers who may or may not be rehabilitated troublemakers, who were less experienced in the field. As a result, they were left behind and saw little action. Johnny knew that was about to change as a cavalry officer rode into their encampment, yelling, "All men report immediately!" He saluted Johnny's insignia.

"Are you in charge here, Cap'n?"

"Yes, sir!" said Johnny, returning the salute.

"On ordahs from Gen'rul Lee, all men in this area must repo't fo' duty immediately, ready tuh march as soon as poss'ble. Have your men battle ready with weapons, ammunition, entrenchin' tools, and rations. Assemble, ready to march up Creighton Road. Hurry it up now!"

"May I ask where we're going, sir?" questioned Johnny.

"Cold Harbor!" was his cold reply.

The horseman turned his mount and trotted along the trench encampments, shouting the same message to all soldiers. Johnny already knew Cold Harbor was nothing more than a white-framed tavern in a triangular grove where Old Church Road crossed Cold Harbor Road and Bethesda Church Road, about a ten-mile march from Richmond. Johnny didn't have to say anything to his men. They all heard the news and started packing equipment. James Morgan exclaimed, "Ah reckon we might see some action aftah all." Ben Grimm responded with, "It's about time fer us tuh git killed ah 'spose." Then Morgan retorted, "Cheer up, Ben, once yer dead it'll end yer complainin'." They had all heard of the thousands that died recently in the Wilderness and Spotsylvania. Jay sensed the seriousness of what they might be facing and turned with concern to Johnny.

"Mistah Johnny! Ah don't feel so good 'bout dis. Ah bleeve we best be prayin' while we Marchin'. Doncha think?"

"Yes, Jay. I think that would be a very good thing to do," said Johnny solemnly.

Moving out Creighton Road, all the units of men joined together to form a force of several thousand, marching at dusk toward the distant rumbling of artillery fire, sounding more like a thunderstorm approaching rather than men trying to blow each other to kingdom come. Johnny and his men knew this was the first real action they were going to see since their encounter with the Rowdy Roberts Gang.

After their two-hour march, they were all put to work digging trenches before they could go to sleep. The noise of the battle that started at five o'clock had died away, and the only sounds to be heard were the chopping of limbs to help make breastworks, the constant shoveling of the entrenching tools, and the occasional mumbling of men trying to act brave on the outside, while inside, nervously fearing and wondering if they may be facing their last day alive on earth. After digging for hours into the night, Johnny and his men were very tired and ready to sleep.

"Some o' da men been talkin' 'bout pinnin' dere name an' home address on dere unifawms, Mistah Johnny, so's dey can be i-denna-fied iffen dey git killed. Should we do dat?" said Jay.

"I hate to think about it, but I reckon so, Jay. Otherwise the folks back home may never know whatever happened to us. But let's pray it won't be necessary. I'm not ready to go just yet." Jay's eyes widened and he shook his head in agreement, saying, "Ah shore 'nuff feel da same way."

They both closed their eyes and silently prayed to themselves, their lips moving silently as they occasionally almost mumbled a word or two out loud. Johnny was thinking he couldn't stand it if he and Molly couldn't be together someday. He thought about how she and her family and Aunt Elsie would react if they thought he was never coming back. He thought about his mother and father and his brother back in Ohio and how disappointed they would be. No, he couldn't let that happen. He pleaded that God would spare him and protect him and his men, and even the men on the Union side. He thought, *How awful it is to be forced into a position to have to fight and kill, or be killed. I have nothing against any of the men those around me are calling "the enemy." I could be shooting at someone from my own hometown. It could be my brother, Jeremy.* He had compassion for them and began to understand what Eli Proffit meant when he said, "We are to love our enemies." Like Molly, he didn't understand how this war could be the will of God, saying to himself, *Surely, God, you will put an end to this horror before too long.*

Ever since he was a child, Johnny enjoyed seeing the light of a new day. Early on the morning of June 2, 1864, the rising sun shined in brilliant hues of red, orange, and gold against the clouds on the eastern horizon like a light from heaven, as if it were a signal that all is under control in spite of the tribulations of man. There was a quiet anticipation of trouble beginning to rumble amongst the men because dawn was traditionally a time for a military attack.

But the attack never came. One had actually been planned by General Grant for 5:00 a.m., but he had been disappointed by the failed effort of the previous day's battle and decided to change his battle plans to strengthen areas where he felt more troops were needed. He ordered Maj. Gen. Winfield Hancock's Second Corps to march to the left of the sixth corps. When the second corps didn't arrive until 6:30 a.m., Grant postponed the attack to 5:00 p.m. that afternoon. And then seeing how exhausted the second corps troops were from a brutal night march over narrow, dusty roads, he postponed it again. The attack was then planned for 4:30 a.m. the next morning, the third of June.

Here at daybreak on the second of June, the Confederate forces were able only to build shallow trenches and makeshift barricades. General Lee took advantage of these extra hours caused by the Union delays to personally supervise the expansion of the breastworks and trenches. By nightfall his troops had constructed a series of trenches with overlapping fields of fire. Lee also brought in reinforcements under the command of Maj. Gen. John Breckenridge and Lt. Gen. Ambrose Hill to fortify his right flank against Grant's reinforced left flank.

During that day there were a number of Confederate officers coordinating the effort. Johnny was a bit shocked to recognize one such infantryman who was assigned to walk the course of the breastworks and trenches and report on the progress of the work. It was his old rival, 1st Lt. Louis B. Madden. Madden strutted along the line, making suggestions or complimenting various troops on their preparation. He looked at Johnny and didn't recognize him at first because Johnny had let his beard grow for the convenience of not having to shave in the rugged military conditions.

"Hey, you! Nice work on your section. Good protection and slots to fire from." Johnny said, "Thank you, Lieutenant

Madden. But is 'Hey, you' the proper way to address a senior officer?" Madden was taken aback and apologized for not noticing the captain's insignia on Johnny's Confederate cap. He awkwardly stuttered, "Oh . . . *uh* . . . ah . . . ah . . . ah'm sorry, suh! Ah didn't notice." He immediately saluted Johnny. Johnny returned the military salutation and went on to state, "I believe you failed to notice something else, Lieutenant." Madden's mouth dropped open as he then recognized Johnny's voice. "Oh my god," he said. "Are you . . ." He couldn't say it.

"That's right, I'm your old dueling buddy, John William Van Worth III." Madden replied, "Well, isn't this somethin'? Ah thought you woulda deserted a long time ago! How in the world did you git promoted to cap'n?" Johnny was still feeling his overnight conviction to be compassionate to his fellow man, but it wasn't easy at this moment, because seeing Madden brought back the unpleasant memories of their first meeting. At this time, Johnny had *not* received Molly's letter revealing Madden's plot to have him drafted. He smiled and stepped up out of the trench to shake Louis's hand, to let him know he had no animosity toward him, and said, "Lieutenant Madden, I've discovered that life can take some rather unexpected turns. No hard feelings! Okay?" Madden was somewhere between disillusioned and shocked, but he had to admire Johnny just the same. He welcomed the chance to make amends on the eve of what was shaping up as another major battle that could be fatal for either or both of them, saying, "Sure! No hard feelin's." He paused to look Johnny up and down, noticing he had gotten his clothes dirty from digging trenches and was not being just an officer barking orders. He had extreme mixed feelings, but a feeling of admiration began to overwhelm him. He smiled and expressed it. "Ah . . . *uh* . . . ah nevah woulda believed it if ah hadn't seen this with mah own eyes. Ah must say, you are more of a man than ah realized, Mr. Van Worth. Ah apologize fo' mah past conduct wherah you are concerned." Johnny grinned back. "No need to. I forgive you."

"Thank you, suh," said Madden very quietly and humbly.

"It's good to put it all in the forgotten past," responded Johnny, also very soft spoken. Madden was pleased to bury the hatchet, but too embarrassed to tell Johnny the whole truth about his evil plot. He thought Johnny would never find out, so he quickly departed, saying,

"It's nice to know a man from the North can be a gentleman too. Ah wish you luck in the comin' battle. Good day, suh!" They saluted as Johnny responded, "Good day and good luck to you too, sir!" Madden turned and walked on down the line, silently observing things and occasionally glancing back at Johnny, dwelling on this unusual and unexpected circumstance. Jay was standing nearby and overheard the entire conversation. He had been told of Madden's dueling episode and was glad to observe what had just taken place.

"Dat wuz maghty fine whut you jus' done, Mistah Johnny! It's good to put dem t'ings to rest, ain't it?" Johnny grinned at Jay and exhaled heavily, "*Ahh!* Yeah, Jay . . . feels good. Real good!"

"You might just turn out to be a regular Southern gentleman one of these days, Captain," said James Woodward who had also observed what happened. They all chuckled a bit before the reality of their war-ready situation settled in to dominate their minds. Nightfall came and still there was no battle, only a few skirmishes and an occasional explosion of Union artillery trying to attract return fire to get the Confederates to give away their positions. Most of the exhausted men dropped off to sleep while a few rotated guard duty all along the entrenched and fortified lines.

Just before the crack of dawn at 4:30 a.m., all hell broke loose as almost fifty thousand Union troops of the Second, Sixth, and Eighteenth Corps launched a massive attack. General Grant had ordered a full frontal attack on some fifteen thousand well dug-in Confederates in the rolling fields southwest of Cold Harbor. They came in continuous waves of men in lines and columns. Dawn's early light barely lit the area as artillery support also rained down, exploding before and behind Confederate lines.

The men in gray returned artillery rounds from their cannons. Officers in the trenches yelled directions at the top of their lungs to their men to keeping firing at the onslaught of Union troops charging forward. Johnny was no exception. He didn't know he had it in him. John was no military man. He wasn't really even properly trained, but so were many of the Confederates—just citizen volunteers who had taken up arms to fight, with not much more experience than squirrel hunting or home target practice. Johnny copied what he saw other more battle-experienced officers doing around him. "Ready! Aim! Fire!" he said repeatedly, as he and his men and all the entrenched rebel troops fired volley after volley of firepower upon the vast sea of navy blue uniforms in the wide fields beyond their breastworks. After each volley of fire, they had to reload their single-shot Springfield rifles using a long rod to first stuff a load of powder, packing it down the barrel, and then the ball. Les Moore, the dwarf, was most useful in the loading process. His short size came in handy because he could constantly load for Johnny and Jay as they alternated volleys of fire. In between the rifle fire, pistol shots could be heard ringing out a round of fire. Clouds of exploding gunpowder filled the air with so much smoke it was difficult to see at times, especially in the dim early morning light. The men in the fields appeared as dark silhouettes, if they could be seen at all. Many men cursed from stress and fear. Others prayed silently to themselves as they fired to slow the advance of the attackers. After several volleys, John's men were getting all out of time with the call to fire because some could load faster than others. Johnny could see what was happening, and in a fit of frustration he quit calling "ready, aim, fire" and just said,

"Oh, the hell with it. Fire at will, men! Fire when ready!" They kept doing their best to get off rounds quickly, but the irregularity of it added to the confusion of constant firing and the splatter of wood in the breastworks from Union fire.

Each time the artillery battery behind Johnny fired a round, the noise from it was deafening as Johnny could hear the shell whoosh above his head on it's trajectory toward Union troops. Beads of sweat continually rolled down Johnny's brow and his mouth became as dry as cotton, but he didn't even notice or think about these things, except when sweat rolled into his eyes, which were already irritated somewhat from the clouds of smoke drifting over his position from the artillery battery right behind him. He instinctively batted his forearm sleeve against his eyes to brush the perspiration away. All of the men were doing the same, overheated from the intense stress of the battle and the humid early morning air. Johnny batted sweat away again and blinked his eyelids a couple of times, trying to focus while waiting a few seconds for Les Moore to finish loading his rifle. During that brief moment, just fifteen feet away, he saw George Crumley standing to reload. Crumley suddenly fell back, fatally wounded in the head from enemy fire. John ran down the trench and crouched over to see how badly Crumley was injured. James Morgan said, "It's too late, Cap'n. He's gotta be dead. Took it straight through the fo'head." Johnny yelled, "Keep firing, men! It's kill or be killed." Then under his breath he whispered, "Unfortunately!"

As he was hurrying back to his position, he had a sickening feeling in the pit of his stomach. Down the line he saw young Robert Johnson regurgitating on the back side of the trench. Johnny knew how the young lad felt. Les Moore was holding up Johnny's rifle to hand it back.

"It's loaded, sir," said the little man. Just as Johnny grabbed his rifle from Les, a Union artillery round exploded thirty yards in front of the breastworks. The men in the area fell to the floor of the trench as metal fragments whistled through the air, some pounding hard against the logs of the breastworks, while chunks of earth and dust rained down upon them. Jay hollered, "Sweet Jesus! Is we still alive?"

As soon as the air cleared, the men immediately resumed firing back. Johnny's face was a mixture of sweat and mud, black gunpowder smoke, and blood. A piece of debris had lacerated his cheek. He paid no attention to it, thinking only, *Gotta keep firing. Gotta keep firing!*

They had only been in the thick of battle ten minutes but it seemed like an hour to John. When an hour had actually passed, they were still continuing the steady pace of loading, firing, ducking debris from artillery fire, and loading and firing again. Kill or be killed! Kill or be killed! The thought kept echoing in his mind. They fought like machines rushing as fast as they could to load and fire. Load, and fire again. Some of the men didn't know how to load properly so rapidly, which often caused rifles to malfunction. Those men were pulling the trigger unaware and so inexperienced, they didn't even know that no rounds were coming out of the barrel. There was such a volume of the continuous noise of firing, they mistakenly thought their gun had gone off. Some of the Confederates were issued the new Sharp's carbines manufactured in Richmond and didn't know how to keep the weapon clean while in heavy use, letting excessive powder accumulate in the breechblock, causing the rifle to jam or occasionally explode the stock, injuring the soldier firing it.

Just the same, the unrelenting volume of Confederate infantry and overlapping fields of fire had the Union forces pinned down where they could neither advance nor retreat. But Union artillery was still bearing down on positions along the trenches. One aimed for the nearby Confederate battery.

"Look out!" yelled Buster Bottom, who spotted a cannon round approaching and dove for cover. A massive explosion forty feet away hurled particles of metal and dirt high into the air with several bodies of men flung aside like rag dolls. Buster and James Woodward rushed to see how badly they were injured. One of them was the young Robert Johnson. His right shoulder and arm had been blown away, exposing bones of his ribcage. Blood was gushing out of the gaping hole. The boy was able only to pitifully call for help a few times, muttering his last frightful words, "Mama! Mama, help me! Oh god! Ah'm dyin'. Mama, help me!"

The sudden loss of a great volume of blood caused him to fall into unconsciousness, and a quick and merciful death. It was a horrifying sight that tortured the mind of those who saw it. Others who were injured suffered long, agonizing hours before they were laid to rest. Some finally died with agonized expressions of intense suffering still etched on their faces.

But none suffered and died that day more than the Union troops who fell one after the other, on top of one another, in huge masses. At the peak of the frontal assault, over six thousand Union troops fell in a single hour. There were 1,500 Confederate casualties. In addition to Robert Johnson and Crumley, Pettymuth and Grossman were also casualties from Johnny's ranks.

Several ambulance wagons attended to the wounded, which often meant grotesque amputations of arms and legs that were shattered beyond repair. The amputated parts were piled like scrap from a butcher's shop, grossly stacked until they could be tossed into shallow graves along with the dead.

In writing a report to the Confederate secretary of war, James A. Seddon, Robert E. Lee made no mention of the number of dead soldiers during this day. This excerpt from his report was the most significant reference to the battle:

General Finegan of Mahone's Division, and the
Maryland Battalion of Breckenridge's command,
immediately drove the enemy out with severe loss.

Gen. Ulysses S. Grant's report to his secretary of war, E. M. Stanton, stated,

> *On the third of June, we again assaulted the enemy's works in hope of driving him from his position. In this attempt, our loss was heavy, while that of the enemy, I have reason to believe, was comparatively light. It was the only general attack made from the Rapidan to the James* [Rivers] *which did not inflict upon the enemy losses to compensate for our own losses.*

Making matters worse, hundreds of wounded Union soldiers were pinned down on the battlefield for four days as generals Grant and Lee attempted to negotiate a ceasefire. Few of them survived. During this time and through the twelfth of June both armies fortified their positions and settled into siege warfare. These days consisted primarily of skirmish attacks here and there, as well as artillery duels and some sniping. When evening came and the fighting slowed to a halt they might attempt to nibble some hardtack or some other meager rations before attending to the awesome duty of burying the dead in shallow graves due to a lack of time and energy.

In these quieter siege days that followed some men traded places along the trenches and got acquainted with men from other units. There were periods of quiet time, particularly at sunset. The men would then either rest and relax or engage in conversation from foolish to thoughtful.

It was during this time, on the third day after the great battle, that a man came along the trenches to talk to any men who would listen to his philosophical teachings. He found a good listener in Johnny, who had many questions on his mind. The man said he was Frank Christianson from the Richmond area. He regarded himself as a self-appointed chaplain. The day after the battle, he had told Johnny, "Fear of death on the battlefield has brought many a man to have faith in God, hoping there really is a hereafter." Johnny recalled that, at one point during the Union's frontal assault, when so many soldiers in blue were dropping like water over Niagara Falls, a group of Confederates actually stood and applauded their bravery in facing certain death. After that, Johnny couldn't bring himself to raise his rifle and fire at them.

Looking out over the fields, with the stench of death in the air, Johnny remarked to Frank,

"What manner of man am I? I'm very sorry that I've contributed to so much grief, suffering and death as I see on this battlefield. We call these men the enemy. But they're still men with families and friends who will never see them again. For all I know, I may have shot my brother, Jeremy. He could be out there in that field. He's of the right age to be drafted by the federal government."

It was easy for Johnny to open up his deepest feelings to this man who seemed so deep himself, as well as wise and mature. Christianson paused, stroking his long dark beard speckled with lots of gray. He looked at Johnny with discerning eyes of warmth, understanding, and compassion.

"My friend, I've heard that Stonewall Jackson once looked out over a battlefield lined with bodies of dead soldiers from the North and the South and said, 'He who does not see the hand of God in this is blind.' Do you see the hand of God in all of this?" Johnny was confused and quietly replied, "I've been pondering these thoughts for several days. No, I can't see the will of God in this! They say this is a great victory for us, but all I see is horrible suffering. One of my men was only nineteen years old and now he's dead. I even have pity on the Union troops. I'm from the north. I was drafted into the Confederacy. I've been thrown into this war against my will. I don't even understand why I'm here at this place at this terrible time." Christianson nodded and spoke. "Don't take lightly what I'm about to say. You may have to dwell on it for a while until you get what might be described as the

'Big Picture.' Right now, we're seeing a small portion of the portrait. In time, we'll be able to see a much larger picture that shapes the future of men's attitudes. Think on this. The Good Book says we will have tribulation in this life. Why? Most times we don't know. Only God knows. But consider this thought. If a man is born into a life of luxury does he appreciate it as much as a man who grew up in abject poverty and suddenly finds a great treasure? Perhaps it takes bad times to make us appreciate the good times. If we go through hell, won't we appreciate heaven that much more? Sometimes I believe this short life we're living, serves mostly to condition us to appreciate the longer life of eternity. This mortal life we're now living is less than the twinkling of an eye compared to a forevermore glorious life without end."

"Those are some profound thoughts, Mr. Christianson!" said Johnny. He pondered Christianson's words while staring out over the field of mangled navy blue. Then he again was inspired to ask Frank Christianson a question to clarify his observations.

"So, are you saying that it doesn't matter how long or how short our lives are, because we just don't realize how long eternal life really is?"

Christianson responded, "I believe you're getting well-focused already. It's so easy to get wrapped up in the things of this world. But these things are temporary and we can't take them with us, can we?"

"No. Of course, not! You remind me of a man I met on the march to Richmond. A man named Eli Proffit. He said about the same thing. He indicated love was the most important thing in life."

"A wise man, this Mr. Proffit," said Christianson. "He apparently understood what we *can* take with us to the by and by. Love is the key to unlocking the heart of the Creator; perhaps the key to the whole mystery of life eternal. You seem to have it in you, Captain Van Worth, otherwise you wouldn't be concerned about the men in this field. As for them, remember what the Good Book says, 'To be absent from the body is to be present with the Lord.' He is the author and finisher of our lives. He created us for himself. We will not be completely fulfilled until we return to him to experience his grace, forgiveness, mercy, and love." Johnny paused momentarily to reflect on it and said, "I'm not so sure I'm ready to return to him just yet. There is one I feel I must return to in Charleston, South Carolina, first, my dearly beloved, Molly. We were two months away from being wedded when I was drafted." Christianson smiled with a gleam in his eye, and said, "Ah yes, you are still young, my friend, and your desire for living and loving is strong for a holy purpose. There is nothing on this earth like a woman to warm a man's heart. Women are marvelous gifts from God. They are like the good earth that brings forth fruitful life from the seed. And they were created in such a way as to nurture life, and enjoy the fruits of their labors. I will pray that you will be united for this glorious purpose. The world is in need of good people for the sake of a renewed progeny. I can tell you're a good man, Van Worth. That may be your purpose in all of this."

"So is that my part in the big picture? To help breed a generation of people who will have a fresh attitude to prevent the recurrence of more civil wars?"

"Who knows, my son? Sometimes that's how God changes things. He did it with the Israelites. Caused a whole generation to wander in the desert for forty years—until they died—and not enter the promise land, because they feared the giants, having no faith to trust God to make them victorious, even after all of the miracles he performed, including the parting of the Red Sea. Only the two who had faith of that generation were allowed to go in, Caleb and Joshua." Johnny paused, then asked, "Do you think that's why so many have died in this war? To kill off people with bad attitudes who won't have faith in God's will . . . perhaps regarding slavery?" Christianson responded, "Ah, my good man, perhaps. I believe it's certainly a possibility. Again, only God knows."

"But why do you think so many innocent, righteous men have died? I'm sure many of the men lying dead in this field were good men. Probably many of them better men than I. How do you explain that?" Christianson bowed his head and closed his eyes before answering Johnny. "Has there ever been a man more innocent, more good than Jesus Christ? Sometimes the innocent die to save the lost, to change things for the better." Johnny thoughtfully replied, "Do you think each generation will get better then?"

"Probably. At least until the time of the tribulation. We will know those days are coming when we see people turning away from the things of God."

"You're a good Christian man I can see," said Johnny. Christianson broke into a light laugh.

"I must say, when you spend much time in prayer and meditation it will change you, and much is revealed. After seven years of monastery life I felt the Lord wanted me to take the revelations I received to a troubled world. Can there be a more troubled world than we're facing here today? I believe many men will benefit from a deeper understanding of the spiritual puzzle of which they are a single part. We must never forget that in spite of death the spirit goes on into eternity. And there are only two options for where we will dwell forever. And that, my friend, is why it's so important to know we are the product of a Master Designer who created all things according to a master plan.. a plan so magnificent our tiny minds can't even conceive of its glorious scope and magnitude. We must make the right choice now, the choice to live forever according to God's plan, or to be short-sighted and live for this small worldly life we will surely leave behind, and risk forever being apart from God's peace and glory. Jesus died to save all men of all races and creeds who will but accept his free gift of eternal life by faith."

"I will remember these things you've told me and dwell on them until it all sinks in," said Johnny. Christianson shook his hand and said, "I'm sure it will. May you have many offspring to replenish the earth with more creatures in the image of God." Smiling, Johnny bade him a farewell saying, "Thank you, Mr. Christianson. I've enjoyed our brief chats over these past two days."

"I've enjoyed them, too. Cling to those thoughts of love. That will help in bad times."

"I surely will! Good day, and God bless you, Mr. Christianson."

Johnny was inspired by men of deep, gentle character and faith such as the likes of A. Frank Christianson. He matured, dwelling on what he had been exposed to by Christianson and Eli Proffit. In the still of evening time he thought about these things and the prophecies of the lady in the white dress.

The following day a driver from the Southern Express Company arrived in the camp with supplies, mail packages, and letters. At the outbreak of the Civil War, the Southern Express was a company formed by Henry Plant of Louisville, Kentucky who purchased the Southern routes, equipment, and contracts of the nation's largest express company, Adams Express, which was founded in 1835 by Alvin Adams of New England. It was widely believed the Confederacy wouldn't tolerate a New Englander operating a mail-and-freight service in the South. Many people suspected the Southern Express was a dummy company, with Adams secretly in control of it because, for one thing, the two companies worked quite well together. It was about the only way for mail and supplies to be passed from North to South or vice versa, although the service was so pressed with orders from time to time they could be months behind on deliveries. Nevertheless, it worked out well for Johnny. For on this day, he received two pieces of mail.

The express driver set up shop, placing a plank across two barrels, and men came running one unit at a time, as they were released from the trenches to get word from back home. Mail time was a very special moment because anything from home sparked their morale. When Johnny's name was called, he went forward and received a letter from his mother. He walked away and hurriedly opened it.

My Dear Son,   *May 7, 1864*

> *You don't know how much I miss you, how much I pray for you, and wish you were here with me and your father. He has regretted sending you down there ever since we got word of what happened to you. We both regret it. If it wasn't for you finding the girl of your dreams, our grief would be unbearable with you trapped in the South in such an unexplainable way. We still can't figure out how you were drafted by the Confederates. I know it has broken your father's heart to think you are fighting to save slavery.*
>
> *Jeremy has been wanting to join the Union army to counter you being on the side of the South, but your father and I won't let him. We couldn't stand the thought of the two of you fighting against each other in some battle someplace.*
>
> *We love you both so very much. Please write us. I know it's been near impossible for regular mail to go between North and South. Take care, my beloved son. And take comfort in knowing we are constantly praying for you.*
>
> *By the way, the lady you described in the white dress fits the description of my grandmother, Lydia Mattingly. Could her ghost have visited you?*

That was as much of his mother's letter that John read when his name was called a second time. He was intrigued by what his mother had written about the lady in the white dress as he ran back to the express driver to find that this time it was a package and letter from Molly. He opened the package to discover several pairs of needed hand-made socks and her letter. He unfolded it and carefully absorbed her words, while walking back to the trench.

My Dear Loving Johnny,   *Friday, May 13, 1864*

First of all, I want you to know how much I love you, and miss you, and want to hug you and kiss you like never before. I'll be so glad when you and Daddy return. Oh, how we could have used your protection today. This is Friday the 13th. I'm not superstitious but this was a bad-luck day for us.

She went on to explain what happened, and how Louis B. Madden and Billy Bob Walker had plotted to get Johnny drafted. As he read her letter his temperature rose and his cheeks flushed. His natural tendency was to be angry. But then he remembered how good it felt to forgive and forget just four days earlier. Then he thought about all the times he had wanted to desert but didn't. He wanted now more than ever to escape from this insane world of warfare and return to his loving Molly. He resisted the temptation to desert as a matter of honor. He couldn't live with himself if Molly or Jay or any of his men or anyone in his family or just anyone at all would look upon him with disrespect. Now he realized how doing the honorable thing had possibly saved his life. As he considered these things, his anger toward Madden began to dissipate, and a great peace settled over him, knowing he could overcome his animosity which burned as a hot coal in his heart. He made up his mind to seek Madden in the trenches. He thought, *How will it affect him when I tell him I know about the plot, yet I'm willing to forgive him anyway?* He let some of the men know he was looking for Madden, and the next day word came back that Louis B. Madden was on the list of the more than 1,500 Confederate casualties. Johnny was then truly glad he had forgiven the man and laid his anger to rest.

On the night of June twelfth, General Grant withdrew from the area and marched south toward the James River, intent on targeting Petersburg and the railroads that provided needed supplies to the Confederate Army. During the two-week period from May 31 to June 12, Grant had lost twelve thousand men that were either killed, wounded, captured, or missing in action. During the same period, General Lee had lost almost four thousand. Robert E. Lee had now earned Grant's respect with his defensive skills.

Grant learned the hard way that great numbers of men, no matter how many, were no match for well-entrenched soldiers. The Civil War was the first war fought with extensive trench warfare. Since taking command as lieutenant general, Grant had lost up to fifty-five thousand men and he decided that making another flanking assault would send Lee into the Richmond trenches, where the Confederates were well dug in and could withstand a siege.

The great attack at Cold Harbor was over, but for Johnny and his men and all the rest who survived, it would never be forgotten.

Chapter 14

DESPERATE DAYS

War is hell!
It is well that war is so terrible—
we would grow too fond of it.

—Robert E. Lee

Cold Harbor is, I think, the only battle
I ever fought that I would not fight over again
under the circumstances.

—Ulysses S. Grant

This nation, under God,
shall have a new birth of freedom.

—Abraham Lincoln

When the Union troops left Cold Harbor, Johnny and his men and the several thousand infantry troops that had been guarding Richmond in the trenches closer to the city were released to return to their former positions. Marching back, Johnny was a different man. He now knew for sure he was more of a lover than a fighter and longed for the nearness of Molly. It was quieter now, and the calls of the birds sounded more peaceful than he had

235

ever noticed before. Or was it just that he appreciated the beauty of their chirping sounds more, now that the roar of cannons and rifle fire was no longer thundering in his ears, he thought. It was a sunny day with little humidity, and the butterflies fluttered their rapidly jagged flights from one colorful black-eyed Susan to another, and on to other colorful wildflowers and white yarrow in the gently rolling fields and tree lines beside the dusty roadway, while the bees and wasps peacefully hummed amongst the clover.

By contrast, Johnny noticed the men, all of them dirty and exhausted. Some barefoot, clothes torn and ragged. Others were wounded, hanging onto the shoulders of other more fortunate infantrymen. There were many who had to have crude amputations of a foot or an entire arm or leg.

Some suffered with dysentery. Others had died from it in the field beside a soldier who had died from his wounds. Throughout the war there were as many, or sometimes more troops, who perished from disease than from battle wounds. As Johnny observed the sorrowful condition of his comrades, the conversations he had with Frank Christianson reflected on his mind. The men were pitiful to him, from those who bragged about what a great victory they scored at Cold Harbor, to those who were too weak to think, let alone talk. The bragging was disgusting to John.

"Ah guess we showed them Yanks a thing er two!"

"Yeah, boy! They'll think twice 'bout takin' on ol' Robert E. Lee an' cumpnee frum now on, ah betcha!" they would say, laughing. Johnny reasoned to himself, *How foolish they were to think it was a great victory when hundreds of their own men just died. What kind of victory is that?* Then he tried to concentrate on Christianson's idea of the big picture and how somehow the world would come out of it a better place in the long run. Some of the starving men spotted an apple tree.

"Looky yonder!" one exclaimed, as many of them descended on the plant which looked to them like a mother holding out her arms with a load of goodies for her children.

They eagerly popped the fruit from the low limbs, grabbed apples from off the ground, and desperately shook limbs in an attempt to dislodge those they couldn't reach. They munched them rapidly, worrying little about whether or not a piece of the fruit might have worms in it.

As they came upon a creek, the men dashed to its edge, cupped their hands, and drank rapidly before they began to splash the water upon their dirty faces. Some men fell into the shallow stream and rolled over until they were thoroughly soaked, and soon the water turned a muddy brown. Small fish or crawdads were scooped up or splashed ashore with a mighty swat. Some saved the fish in a pocket or pack to fry later. Other less particular men were so hungry they took a knife and skinned them, eating them raw on the spot.

They would soon be back in the trenches of Richmond where they would resume the battles of swatting the hundreds of flies and mosquitoes that attacked especially in the evenings on humid nights. It was a long hot summer they endured that June, July, August, and September of 1864.

After the Battle of Cold Harbor, Grant managed to conceal his next movement from Lee for a time, long enough to order Meade to march the Army of the Potomac south, where they crossed the James River on a pontoon bridge more than two thousand feet long. It was the longest continuous pontoon bridge ever constructed in warfare. Grant's strategy was to advance on Petersburg which was a center supplying all railroad service to Richmond. By closing the railroads Grant could force Lee to come out of the trenches and fight in a less protected arena. Grant's plan came close to being successful, except for a small Confederate force under the command of Gen. G. T. Beauregard, the same officer who directed the first shots of the war by firing on Fort Sumter. Beauregard held Grant's forces at bay until Lee's troops arrived to stop the advance on Petersburg. Grant ordered his men to dig in and prepare for a siege of the city. Lee ordered his men to dig in to withstand it. The siege of Petersburg started in June 1864 and dragged on for nine long months. Grant's men unsuccessfully tried to break Lee's line many times.

In a spectacular attempt to penetrate the Confederate entrenchments, Northern engineers burrowed a tunnel over five hundred feet long under the Confederate lines. On July 30, at the end of the tunnel they set off a powder charge weighing over four tons. The enormous explosion blew open a huge crater that measured over 170 feet long. But when Union soldiers rushed through the tunnel they were trapped behind enemy lines in a deep crater they couldn't scale, and the Confederates picked them off like fish in a rain barrel. Ulysses S. Grant himself called it a "stupendous failure."

Johnny and his men had heard tales about the Battle of the Crater and all of the activity of the war for the year and a half that they had been quartered in the trenches around Richmond. They had remained as backup troops to guard the Confederate capital and were never sent on to defend Petersburg.

During this time the men were suffering more from depression, malnutrition, dysentery, boredom, loneliness, and being away from their loved ones back home. To pass the time and take their minds off the awful tragedies and miseries of the war, many of them played various card games, gambled, made up riddles, smoked or chewed tobacco—if they could get their hands on some—and told stories of all kinds. Some stories were nothing more than outlandish tongue-in-cheek lies, so obviously a tall tale it would evoke laughter. Johnny was good at that.

"Did I ever tell you fellas about the time I was a lumberjack in the Mojave Forest?"

"Naw! Tell us 'bout that," prodded Buster.

"Well, I'd get up at the crack of dawn and chop down big oak trees all day . . . and . . . Well, I'll tell ya, my throat would be hoarse by day's end, yellin' 'Timmmber' a *thousand* times or more.

"Aw, bull! Nobody kin cut down a thousand trees a day," said Goober Shaw.

"I ain't bullin' ya." said Johnny. "I was the greatest lumberjack of all time. Set the record for choppin' down the most trees in the Mojave Forest!"

"Wait a minute," said Ben Grimm. "There ain't no Mojave Forest. The Mojave is a desert!"

"It is now!" quipped John as the men broke into uproarious laughter.

Of course, all the laughter was just a coverup to offset how miserable the men really were deep down in their souls. To combat loneliness, their favorite pastime was reading and re-reading mail from home, or writing their loved ones. John's return letter to his mother consisted of the following:

My Dear Sweet Mother,   *June 14, 1864*

> *It was so good to hear from you. I received your letter while we were engaged in the battle of Cold Harbor near Richmond. I love you and Dad and Jeremy dearly, but I want you to know I'm not fighting to save slavery. As you know, I managed to get all of Uncle Fred's slaves freed, and one of them, Jay Brown, has been so loyal he's been by my side the whole time I've been in the Confederate Army.*
>
> *At last, I finally got word from Molly that my being drafted was an evil plot cooked up by her jealous former fiancé, Louie Madden. He was one of the casualties of this most recent battle. But I'm glad to say, I managed to forgive him due to your teaching me the golden rule, and some excellent advice I received from a former monk I met after the battle of Cold Harbor.*
>
> *Mother, it's a terrible thing to be put in the position of kill or be killed. I was thinking how awful it would have been, for all of us, if Jeremy was among the troops I was firing on. It's a comfort to know you and Dad are*

keeping him from joining the military. Tell him it's not a pleasant duty in life, especially when you have loved ones you want to see again. I'll be glad when this war is over and we can see each other once more. Won't it be nice to all be together when Molly and I get married? I look forward to that more than anything in this world. Tell Dad his wish came true when he sent me off, saying I might meet a Southern girl I like. All I can say is she's wonderful, and truly is the girl of my dreams. Give my regards to Dad and Jeremy and I thank you for your prayers.

Your Loving Son, Always,
Johnny

P.S. It could be your grandmother was the lady in the white dress. All of her predictions came true.

Survival was often as difficult on the Southern home front as it was on the Confederate battle front. By August of 1864 the shelves at Mitchell's General Store were nearly empty. As soon as practically anything arrived to stock them, the demand for it was so high it would disappear quickly. The blockade runners were having more difficulty getting past Union forces guarding Charleston Bay. Even needles—something vital to the ladies' sewing circles—were hard to come by.

"Thank goodness we have a garden behind the house," exclaimed Molly. It had literally been a lifesaver since food was getting more and more scarce. To make matters worse, in mid-August they received a letter from John's Aunt Elsie. She was ill and wanted Molly and Marion to visit her as she was not only sick but also lonely. She didn't know what was wrong and she didn't know if she was going to survive her illness. Marion asked Kent to hitch up the carriage and they headed out toward the farm. It was dangerous to travel since many desperate uncouth stragglers along the roadways might try to stop them to steal the horses, if nothing else. They managed to get their doctor to go with them and packed several guns to ward off ruthless would-be attackers. But the only thing to thwart their journey was a brief thunderstorm that struck just before they arrived. They were glad they had taken the carriage as it provided better shelter from the rain. However, as the coach driver, Kent was soaking wet when they arrived.

The few former slaves who were still at the farm let them in. Aunt Elsie shed tears of joy.

"Thank God you came," she said weakly. "I'm afraid Pleasant Acres isn't as pleasant a place as it used to be." She looked pale, but she tried to smile when she saw Molly.

"You look lovely, child," she said as her eyes barely brightened, then slowly fell shut as if she had nearly expelled her last ounce of energy. Elsie choked as she whispered, "I love you." Molly choked up at Elsie's words, and in a sweet sympathetic voice, gently said, "I love you, too Aunt Elsie." Marion sympathetically informed her, "Elsie, we brought our family doctor here to see you. This is Dr. Orville Mayfield." She tried to sit up but fell back on the bed.

"Now, now, Mrs. Van Worth, just relax and save your energy," said the doctor. "Tell me how you're ailing. Are you in pain?" He put his hand on her forehead to see if she had a fever. As Elsie tried to answer, she broke into a hacking cough. "I'm . . . sick to my stomach. Burning up one minute, then getting the chills the next."

"How long have you had that cough?" asked the doctor.

"Oh . . . I 'spose 'bout a week," she moaned.

"You seem to have a bit of a fever." For reasons of modesty, he whispered to others in the room,

"Could you all wait outside? I'll have to examine her." And he reached for his stethoscope.

Marion, Molly, and Kent stepped out of the bedroom, shutting the door behind them. Out in the upstairs hallway they whispered among themselves their concern for Johnny's frail little aunt. She looked so ill, with circles under her eyes, and sunken cheeks like she hadn't been eating for a while. Molly was thinking, *Oh, dear Lord, please don't let anything happen to Johnny's sweet Aunt Elsie. I don't know how we could bear another tragedy right now. Johnny would be brokenhearted. He doesn't need any more grief. None of us do. I don't know how he's holding up. She just can't die. There's been way too much death and destruction. I don't see how the South will ever be as it was. So many men have left home never to return. We just can't lose Aunt Elsie too. Please, Lord, I will have faith you won't take her home just yet. Let her live to see Johnny come home.* In a few minutes Dr. Mayfield stepped out in the hall to inform them of Elsie's condition. "She has a fever and the peculiar reddish spots typical of a case of typhus. She's very weak and in need of someone to look after her for several days. She'll need some nourishment, but the infection and fever will rob her of her appetite. I suggest a diet of chicken soup. I see plenty of them out in the yard and about the place. And here's a tonic that ought to help fight the infection." He handed it to Molly. She told her mother, "You all can go on back. I'll stay with her until she's feeling better. How long do you think it will take, Doctor?" Fastening his bag, the doctor said, "It's hard to say exactly. Perhaps as much as a week, give or take a few days."

Marion suggested, "We'll come back next Saturday to check on how she's doing, Molly." Then she addressed Dr. Mayfield. "How much do we owe you, Doctor?"

"Well, I don't know." he said rather hesitantly. "Those doggone Confederate dollars these days are so inflated they don't go very far. Do you think you could arrange to let me have one or two of those chickens?" Marion was relieved and pleased at his generosity. She replied, "I'll ask Aunt Elsie. I'm sure she'll agree. Thank you, Dr. Mayfield."

"You're quite welcome, ma'am. Glad to help. We all need to assist one another these days."

It was a very equitable arrangement since they had an abundance of chickens on the farm. That's one thing Aunt Elsie oversaw, insisting to the darkies to not kill the roosters for food and let certain hens roost to keep new chicks coming to produce plenty of chicken dinners and eggs. This minor detail she and Fred had learned the hard way as earlier it had contributed to their financial disaster.

Over the course of the next week, Molly constantly nursed Aunt Elsie, cooking and feeding her chicken soup and giving her doses of the tonic Dr. Mayfield had left with her. As Elsie gradually regained her strength, Molly read the Bible to her, concentrating on healing scriptures. And she prayed often for Elsie to get well. During this week, Molly got better acquainted with the freed slaves who had stayed on the farm, particularly Charco and Bo and their wives Liza and Serena.

"You've done a wonderful job of helping Aunt Elsie keep Pleasant Acres up, Charco," she said.

"Dat's all we knowed tuh do, Miz Molly. We's just doin' what we's always done."

"Just the same, I'm sure Johnny will be proud of you when he returns home."

"Oh! Does ya think he be comin' back soon? 'Cause we sho' does miss 'im," said Bo.

"I know what it is to miss him. My heart feels like it has an aching lump in it," replied Molly with a lump in her throat as well, that caused her to choke up while getting the words out.

"Aw, dere now, Miz Molly," said Liza sympathetically, patting Molly on the back.

"It's gonna be all right. Da wah cain't las' fo' evah." Molly closed her eyes and bit her lip.

"It seems like an eternity already," she said. Serena joined in to console Molly, saying, "Don't you trouble yer soul none, Miz Molly. Why, ah bet Mistah Johnny be coming through dat do' befo' you knows it. Cain't you jes picture dat?"

Molly went out on the front porch and sat in the swing and thought of Johnny each day, wishing what Serena said would come true any second. As the week passed, Molly got more and more melancholy while Elsie got better and better. When Marion and Kent returned the following Saturday, Elsie was sitting in her rocking chair with a pleasant smile on her face. She gently held Molly's hand, looked her in the eye, and repeated her previous offer to will the property to her nephew and Molly as a wedding gift.

"Thank you so much, Molly, for staying with me. I meant it when I said I'm willing this place to you and Johnny if you'll care for me when Johnny comes back and you two get married." The offer was a comfort to Molly's soul. Yes, she imagined, *When Johnny comes back. When we're finally married. I now pronounce you man and wife! You may kiss the bride. What wonderful thoughts. When Johnny comes back. Oh, how I wish he could be here this very minute. I'll hold him and kiss him and never let him go.* She kissed Elsie's cheek and gave her a hug as she said goodbye.

"I love you, Aunt Elsie. I'll be very pleased to help care for you. I hope Johnny gets word today that the war has ended, that the madness is over, and we can live normal lives again. Yes, Aunt Elsie I'll be here for you and for my precious Johnny." "God bless you, child. I'll pray for you and Johnny like you've prayed for me this past week. I believe that's what really healed me," Elsie declared.

Marion was pleased and assured her, "Bless your heart, Elsie. We'll be back before too long to see you again."

Having said their goodbyes, they headed back to Charleston, but Molly was feeling extremely sentimental and insisted they drop by the Magnolia Plantation one more time on the way home. She wanted to stand on the Veranda where she first laid eyes on Johnny. After all, clinging to memories was all she could do until the man she loved returned.

-0-

Back in Virginia, Johnny thought how ironic it was that the *hot* summer months seemed to be pouring forth like *cold* molasses. He started calculating in his mind how much longer the war would continue. He wondered how many men must die before they realize they can't win. The South was shut off from the rest of the world by the Union naval blockade. *If we can't get resupplied with adequate food, clothing, ammunition, and arms, the Confederacy is bound to lose the war. We're down to eating only two skimpy meals a day, sometimes having only two hardtack biscuits a day to sustain us. The men are weak and weary yet there seems to be no end of the conflict in sight. There aren't enough Southern fighting men to hold off the well-supplied Union Army. It has to end somehow someday. How bad will it be if the South loses the war? Isn't it worse to lose so many men? Already, how many homes have no fathers to be the breadwinners of the family?* he thought.

Then he remembered what Frank Christianson said about wars changing attitudes. He wondered what evil attitude possessed men so strongly they could never find a way to change. Never even compromise to work things out. *Why can't men see the light? Why must we be so blind, so deceived, so hardheaded about our ways, and so hardhearted with one another.*

The solitude of his thoughts was broken by a Confederate officer on a horse, shouting, "The colonel wants all men to assemble in the Chickahominy area immediately!"

"Oh no! Here we go ag'in, Mistah Johnny," said Jay. James Woodward commented, "They're probably gonna march us off to Petersburg." Johnny responded, "Probably so."

It turned out that the colonel wanted as many men as possible to witness three young draftees going before a firing squad for deserting, making an example to keep other men from doing the same. It was a pitiful thing to watch. Two of the boys were crying as they put the blindfold over their eyes. They were standing in front of their own graves that they had been forced to dig, so that when they were shot they would fall backward into the holes.

"Ready!" There was one last wailing whimper from one of the deserters.

"Aim! Fire!" The momentum of the rifle fire leaned them backward, and their bodies fell into the graves with a thud.

The troops were then released, and they solemnly returned to their positions to think about the consequences of deserting.

This was especially upsetting for Johnny. He had thought of deserting many times. The disgusting sight he just witnessed could have been him. Then he thought how wasteful war was, using the fear of death to force other men to face the possibility of death. Robert E. Lee was right. War really is hell. A flock of wild geese flew in their familiar *V* formation overhead. Johnny looked up at them and wished he had their wings so he could fly away from this hell, fly home to a place of love with Molly. When he returned to the trench, he got out her latest letter to read again and transfer his mind to a more pleasant atmosphere.

Dear Johnny, My Beloved,   *August 30, 1864*

> *I'm sure you just don't know how much you're missed back here in the Low Country of South Carolina. Even the freed slaves, and of course your Aunt Elsie, said they miss you. We got word she was ill and took our family doctor out to see her. He said she had typhus fever, and I stayed with her for a week to nurse her back to health. I fed her and gave her doses of the medicine the doctor left, but she said she thought it was my reading the Bible to her and my prayers that really healed her. She again told me she'll will the property to us as a wedding gift if we stay to care for her. I love Aunt Elsie. She's so sweet.*
>
> *But, Johnny, there's no one on earth I love more or miss more than you. I sat in the front porch swing where we talked together so many times during courtship. I pictured you sitting there beside me and I whispered to you as if you were there. It was pleasant remembering all of the things we used to talk about and laugh about, and the dreams we shared. Dreams of always being close and happy and having little children to love and share*

that happiness. Remember how we strolled around the house hand in hand and enjoyed the smell of the flowers and the heavenly scent of the honeysuckle on the edge of the woods? I walked in our former footsteps and dreamed of when we'll walk there again. I also imagined our first kiss when we went horseback riding. Oh, my love, if only we could go back to those happier days.

I insisted on going out of our way to visit Magnolia Plantation on the way back. I just had to stand on the veranda where we first met. I could see you walking up that grand staircase like a prince gazing at me as if I was the woman you wanted to be your princess. We couldn't take our eyes off each other. Remember, my love? I do. I'll always remember how charming you are. I'll always desire to be near you. I wanted that moment to go on forever. God knows how I pray that you, my Prince, will someday be here to rescue me from this terrible war. It's only when I fully realize that you aren't here near me that I start to cry my eyes out. When the realities of life become unbearable, it's a comfort to dream that things are better for the moment, and for the future. I must have faith you will return. I must dream that tomorrow a better day is coming or I'll never make it through today. Johnny, before you go to sleep tonight pretend that I'm there with you, and I'll pretend you're here holding me close. It will make us feel near each other, even though we're not, and help the time to pass more quickly until we really are together again at last. Pleasant dreams, my love! My beloved, precious love.

Affectionately Yours Always,
Your Wife to be;

Molly ♡

OXOXOXOXOXOXOXOXOXOXOXOXOXOXOXOXOXOXOXO

P.S. Just think, if I had married Louis Madden, I'd be a widow now. I admire your ability to forgive him in your heart before he died. I'm finding it difficult to be as noble and good about it as you are. It was because of his evil actions that we're apart right now. But I'm working on it. In many ways I pity him. It's not right to feel bad toward someone who has passed on. I know I must forgive him. And I will as soon as you return. I'll have no reason to be resentful then. I pray God will protect you and bring you home to me soon.

In November 1864, Union general William T. Sherman burned Atlanta and began his devastating march through Georgia toward Savannah and back into the Carolinas. Sherman's army swept across the countryside in a path as much as sixty miles wide, stripping houses and elegant mansions, then burning the homes, barns, and fields, destroying everything they couldn't take. Stragglers, who became known as "Bummers," were responsible for much of the destruction. They pried up railroad tracks, piled the ties, and set them afire, then they heated the rails red hot and wound them around trees. These became known as "Sherman's hairpins" or "neckties." Sherman hoped this awesome destruction of civilian property would break the South's will to continue fighting.

But out of the ashes rose a bitter resentment and hatred that would last for many generations. Out of the ashes rose a desire for revenge and a determination to suffer through with a blind hope for victory. So still, the war dragged on. And for many of those who survived, the destitute life they endured was often worse than slavery. Many never recovered from the hell wrought upon them by the Civil War, living out their lives maimed and destitute, with little hope of ever recovering to enjoy the gracious lifestyle they had once known.

❧Chapter 15❧

PANIC IN THE CITY

Word of the destruction wrought in the wake of Sherman's march brought fear and panic to the citizens of Charleston. The sixty-thousand-man army under Sherman's command was resupplied by the U.S. Navy when they reached Savannah, Georgia, on December 21, 1864. Sherman telegraphed a bold message to Abraham Lincoln that read in part,

> *General Sherman makes the American people a Christmas present of the city of Savannah with one hundred fifty heavy guns and twenty-five thousand bales of cotton.*

On Christmas day that year, Johnny had already received his needed presents from Molly, more knitted gloves, socks, and a blanket. He cherished her letter that came with them, again expressing her undying love for him and fear of the devastation-wreaking Yankee Army so near and approaching from the southwest. The telegraph lines were hot with news of Sherman's march. Johnny had great concern as he took up a pen to write her.

My Dear Darling Molly,   *Christmas Day, 1864*

On this cool Christmas Day my heart aches to be near you, especially since Sherman's treacherous army is now a possible threat to Charleston. I want to hold you in my arms and shut out the fears and concerns of these most awful days we're living in. I've been praying for you and your family and Aunt Elsie, and somehow I have peace in my heart that you will not be harmed. You must have faith that everyone will be protected as God looks down on us this special day.

Here in our meager bivouac area the light of his sun dimly shines through the gray skies of Virginia, giving me hope that he is still there in heaven watching over us. Breezes gently whisper your name to me through the swaying needles of the lofty pines overhead. Yes, as you said, we must keep positive thoughts about one another, dream of one another until the time when this war is over and we'll be together for real once more. I pray our generals will realize we can't win this war, and surrender their pride before too many more die or suffer injury for some pitiful cause. I believe God is now bringing pressure to bear on us to change the course of history, to change the way men think and act. How many mothers and fathers, brothers and sisters, sons and daughters must mourn before hearts and minds are brought to a higher level of living together as a more civilized society? I pray that peace will soon rest upon this nation, and we will all strive together for the common good of humanity.

But most of all I pray that you and I will be together in blessed matrimony to love like a man and woman were meant to love. When that day finally comes we will have a greater appreciation of the sweetness of our union. I feel I must live to serve that purpose, to love you and love you and love you evermore. Keep praying for me and dreaming of me, and I will do the same for you.

*Before you retire to bed each night look at the moon
and think of me, and know that I'm looking at the same
moon from an angle a little farther north of you. That
way we won't seem so far apart. Until we meet again, I
remain faithfully your one True Love Forever and Ever.*

Pleasant Dreams to You, My Love,
Johnny

With Sherman's army knocking on the southern door of
the Carolinas, on January 4, 1865, Robert E. Lee released a
brigade of South Carolina regiments from the defense of
Petersburg, Virginia, to head to their home state to try to
prevent the same kind of destructive onslaught of disaster
that was thrust upon Georgia. These veteran troops were
known as "Kershaw's Brigade" and were sent to join some
twelve thousand less-experienced Confederate artillerymen
and garrison troops under the command of Gen. William J.
Hardee who was referred to as "Old Reliable," a nickname
he acquired while previously serving in the Confederate
Army of Tennessee. The region was back under the overall
command of Gen. G. T. Beauregard.

General Hardee assigned Maj. Gen. Lafayette McLaws
to take the new brigade to halt Sherman's army which had
crossed the Savannah River on February 2, 1865. The two
armies met on February 8 near the Salkehatchie River and
the outnumbered troops of Kershaw's Brigade were driven
back, returning to Charleston on the Charleston and
Savannah railroad. At this time it was greatly feared by
Charlestonians that Sherman's army would follow them into
the city with the intent of burning it down too, since it was
the starting point of the war with the first shots fired on Fort
Sumter. It was widely known that many northerners wanted
revenge on Charleston which was the focus of a long siege that
began at the start of the war with a Union blockade and attacks
on batteries at Fort Sumter and Morris Island. It became uglier

in August of 1863 with a barrage of firings on the civilian population in the southern part of the peninsula city.

By February 11, 1865, the Yankees had driven Confederate pickets inland from James Island, located southeast of Charleston. Over thirty Union ships were patrolling the seas near Charleston. The siege on the historic town was getting tighter as federal forces were closing in from land and sea. The next day was Sunday, February 12, and as concerned Confederate officers debated whether Sherman's army would go to Columbia or Charleston, Molly and her family went to church.

It was a good time to seek the protection of God, with danger so near. The Mitchell family, somber like the rest of the congregation, listened as Pastor Collins began his sermon by reading verses from the bible. His voice echoed off the hard surfaces of the interior of the small wooden church as he read from the fourth chapter of Matthew.

"God is love; and he that dwelleth in love dwelleth in God, and God in him." Molly was glad to hear he was talking of love. It was always uppermost in her heart and soul since she met Johnny. To think that "God is love" was a thought most pleasing to her. It made her feel that God was with her. That he was her ally and understood her deepest desire in these troubled times. The clean-shaven—except for the long sideburns—minister continued reading.

"There is no fear in love; but perfect love casteth out fear; because fear hath torment." Then he closed the bible, paused a moment to reflect on his next words and addressed the congregation.

"I know it has been difficult for most of you to keep love uppermost in your minds as we go about our daily chore of trying to survive in a city that has been under siege for nearly four years. It's difficult for me to keep love in my heart when I know there's an enemy out there, just five miles away on Morris Island, that has had the audacity to use church steeples in this city to aim their cannons on us. As you know, that's why they painted the steeple of St. Michael's church black, to make it more difficult to sight from a distance. It has been hit two times. But, in spite of this and many barrages on the point of town, I want to compliment you on bearing up to these attacks without fear and panic. Or is it that you've just become calloused and hardened to it after so long? In which case, I'll retract my compliment a bit." The congregation chuckled at this comment. Losing his smile and regaining his more serious countenance, Pastor Collins continued,

"And now with the latest rumors that danger and even greater devastation might be thrust upon us, we must be spiritually prepared for the worst. We must have deep understandings to survive. The Bible tells us 'Perfect love casteth out fear.' Just what is perfect love? God has made it clear that the greatest commandment is to love him with all our heart and strength and mind. And if we do that, for what shall we fear? For if we seek first the Kingdom of Heaven, even if we die shall we yet live." "Amen, brother!" shouted one of the deacons in the rear of the church.

Molly's mind began to wander with great shocking acceleration as she thought, *He's referring to the rumors Sherman's army may destroy Charleston! He's preparing us to die! I don't want to die, not now. I love God. I want to go to heaven. How can we not love Jesus? His sacrifice on the cross was the perfect expression of love. But I'm only twenty-four years old now. I want to help fulfill that part of the bible that says, 'Be fruitful and multiply and replenish the earth.' I love you, God, but I love Johnny, too. Surely this can work out. Please Jesus! Let us survive this war. Let us live and love! God please, protect us from all harm.* She paused, thinking and feeling, these thoughts permeating throughout her entire being. She sat for a while in a near-frozen state, staring forward, so engrossed in her own thoughts she could scarcely pay attention to Pastor Collins's sermon until he again caught her attention as he said, "I want all of you to pray the Ninety-first Psalm. It's the Psalm of protection. Did you know George Washington had his men memorize it? The Continental Army was beaten back by British General Cornwallis until Washington ordered his men to memorize and recite out loud the Ninety-first Psalm. That's when the victory came. Turn with me now to the Ninety-first Psalm. It says, 'He that dwelleth in the secret place of the Most High shall abide under the shadow of the Almighty. I will say of the Lord, he is my refuge and my fortress; my God; in him will I trust. Surely he shall deliver thee from the snare of the fowler, and from the noisome pestilence.'"

Molly was encouraged by these words from the Bible, and she purposely memorized them. As she began to study the scriptures, a great peace came over her and she felt deep down she would be protected from all harm as Johnny had said in one of his letters.

On that same day, Confederate general W. J. Hardee returned to Charleston after spotting Sherman's army clustered near Orangeburg, South Carolina. He reported that it wasn't clear whether they would proceed toward Columbia or Charleston. Then on February 15, General Beauregard feared Sherman's mighty army was about to cut the Northeastern Railroad which ran from Charleston due north to Cheraw, near the North Carolina border, and he ordered the evacuation of Charleston which began on the evening of February 17 and went on through the next morning.

As the Confederate Army pulled out, chaos and calamity befell the civilian population. Many of them had packed, hoping to stay with relatives or friends in other parts of the state. But they feared they might run upon the dreadful Yankee army and be slaughtered or robbed and the women raped by what they considered to be a bunch of lusty, savage soldiers.

Kent Mitchell was the first in their family to hear that the army was pulling out. He came running in the house on that Friday evening, yelling out the news, "Mom! Molly! I just heard the army is evacuating the city tonight! Tomorrow we won't have any defense against the Yankees. They could come marchin' in here from Morris Island even before General Sherman could arrive. That's what the men down the street said." Marion Mitchell panicked and called out, "Nicole! Hurry! The soldiers are leaving. We must pack up what we can and go to Mother and Dad's place in Mount Holly."

Her panic was quickly transferred into the eyes of Nicole, their live-in maid, a lady of French descent in her forties. She threw her hands into the air, then slapped her palms against her cheeks while turning from left to right, wondering what to do.

"Oh, gracious, Miss Marion! What will we do if the Yankees burn the town down?"

"She's right, Mother," Molly interjected. "If we leave, we're inviting the Yankees to burn it down. Or the lower-class riffraff will come in and loot the place. Everyone is so desperate these days."

"Oh my. What would be best?" said Marion, covering her eyes as she sat down to think. Molly said, "If we leave they'll loot the store, too. We don't have much in stock, but at least it's something, and certainly more than we could ever carry to Grandma and Grandpa's. Where will they put us up? It would be awfully crowded. We'd be better off going to Pleasant Acres with Johnny's Aunt Elsie."

"Yes, but the Yankees are more likely to take the road past Elsie's place if they're coming here to Charleston. Oh, Molly, let me think. We have to do something. Dear God, help us to do something." Marion rocked back and forth in the chair in desperation, to think of what they should do. There wasn't a logical clear-cut way out. She heard voices and confusion in the street. Finally, she said,

"Let's go out and see what the neighbors are doing." Kent eagerly volunteered his knowledge, "The neighbors don't know what they're doin' either. They're runnin' all over the place."

As they stepped out onto the front porch, they could see the panic Kent was describing. Some of their neighbors were stacking as many household belongings as they could on wagons, carts, and carriages. Others were running to spread news of the evacuation, not knowing what to do, showing the same confusion as the Mitchells were experiencing. Mrs. Gabbert, who lived three doors down Ashley avenue from the Mitchells' home, came waddling toward Marion, toting her hefty body as rapidly as she could with a wild-eyed expression on her face, frantically babbling as she barged along.

"Oh, Marion! Marion! What shall we do? Where shall we go? When are the Yankees coming?

How much time do we have? Will they burn the city down like they did with Atlanta?"

"For heaven's sake, Carlotta, one question at a time. My head is in a spin. I'm not sure what to do."

"Mother, you know if they burned Atlanta they're sure to burn Charleston," said Molly.

"Oh, dear," replied Mrs. Gabbert. "I have nowhere to go. Whatever shall I do with my silver and china, and all of our possessions? Everything we own is about to go up in smoke." Molly asked her, "What does your husband think? Does he have plans to stay or go?" Mrs. Gabbert responded, "Oh my, he's practically an invalid with crippling arthritis in his feet and hands, and a bad case of the gout to add to the poor man's misery at that. No matter what we do, we're doomed it seems."

Another neighbor, Wally Steadman, was standing nearby, the nearly seventy-year-old man tapped the butt of his rifle on the ground, holding it by the barrel. He spit out a shot of chewing tobacco and squinted his eyes at Mrs. Gabbert. "Tell ya what we ought do, ma'am," he said with determination.

"We ought stay put and fight for our homes and ever thin' we own. That's whut this whole confounded war is all about. We don't need no federals tellin' us whut tuh do. If any o' them Yanks try tuh set mah house afire he's gonna take a ball to do it. Why, iffen you ladies don't have a stock of weaponry fit tuh hold them Yanks at bay, jes' throw a lighted kerosene lamp on 'im afore he can git close 'nuff tuh torch yer place. He'll be so busy tryin' tuh put himse'f out he won't have time tuh set yer house ablaze." Marion stared at the feeble, daring old gentleman a moment before retorting, "With all due respect, Mr. Steadman, that's not a very pretty picture to envision." Kent explained, "But, sir, there's so many Yankees comin'. The paper said several weeks ago Sherman has more than sixty thousand troops that stormed Atlanta. We don't have that many kerosene lamps around here. And besides, they would shoot us before we could throw one on 'em." The old man hadn't thought it out this far and looked pitiful as he pouted and defended his attitude in a somewhat weakened tone of voice. "Just the same, young fella, ah'm staying here tuh protect mah property, and if ah die doin' it, well they can put as mah epitaph that Wally Steadman stuck to his guns." He turned to Mrs. Gabbert and said, "As fer your valuables, ma'am, better bury 'em somewhere quick."

As Mrs. Gabbert rapidly waddled back toward her house, Marion instructed her family, "We'd better go inside, I think I know what to do now." Walking back inside Nicole questioned, "Do I need to pack anything, Miss Marion?" Marion paused before answering. "Yes, I think so. I'll make a list. Kent, I'm glad you reminded me of how many Yankees are coming. We'll be overwhelmed if we stay. I'm afraid Charleston is going to encounter the same fate as Atlanta. Dear God, how can this be? If only Thomas was here. I don't know if I could bear it if he comes home to discover . . ." Her voice began to crack as she broke into tears to finish the statement. "To discover . . . we have no home." Molly was moved with compassion for her mother. "Oh, Mama. Please don't cry. We don't know for sure the Yankees are even coming, let alone that they'll burn the house if they do. We must hope for the best." Marion took the handkerchief

Nicole was holding out for her. She dried her eyes and regained her composure as Kent consoled her.

"It'll be all right, Mama," he said. "After all, I'm here to protect you." She smiled knowing there was little he could do, but wanting to encourage him to try to be the man of the house. Molly asked, "What do you want to do, Mama? Go to Grandma's or Pleasant Acres?" Marion responded, "I feel we should go to Elsie's place. You're right, Molly. There is more room there, and Elsie could use any help we can give her. We'll be less of an imposition there. We'll take only what we need most. Just what the carriage will hold. Unfortunately, we'll have to leave all of our household items, but we can take what little valuables we have left. Kent! Look for a place to bury the china out back. It would just get broken on the wagon, I'm afraid. Bury it deep. And remember the location in case we're able to come back some day." Again, tears began to well up in Marion's eyes at the thought of leaving their beautiful home with no assurance of when they will ever return. Nicole asked, "Miss Marion, could you drop me off at my parents' home on Mary Street when we get loaded?"

"Well, I suppose so, Nicole. You don't want to go with us?" said Marion. Nicole replied, "I mean no disrespect, ma'am, but if Charleston is going to go down, I feel I must be with my family at such a time. I hope you understand, ma'am." Marion was touched by her desire. "Oh, certainly! I understand. But I think it will be first thing tomorrow. I don't like traveling in the dark, even though I know many people are already leaving the city. Will that be to your satisfaction?" "Oh, yes, ma'am, Miss Marion. I'll help you pack now."

Even though they were all tired and worn out from anxiety, Molly had a hard time sleeping that night. Many thoughts raced through her head, like fence posts rushing by while galloping on a horse at full speed. She was saddened to have to leave the home where she had grown up and felt so comfortable. Everything about the place was homey to her. The bedroom where she had slept since childhood and spent many sleepless nights staring at the floral patterns in the wallpaper. It was warm and cozy. The colors and shapes so familiar they were like a part of her. The kitchen where she enjoyed dining on so many delicious meals with her family—something that had already become a fading memory these last years of the war due to the shortage of food. Her mind was filled with memories of fonder times, like when her daddy would play "horsey" with her, or let her ride on his shoulders in the house or on the front porch. She remembered the times he took her fishing with him and how he loved to tell her stories on those trips, or most often in his den full of manly things like his gun collection and the bookcase that reached to the ceiling in the walnut-paneled room. She had loved to sit on his lap as a little girl when he read fairy tales and Bible stories to her. *Dear Daddy, how I miss those good old secure days. No wonder Mama is so upset. She must be torn apart with all of the memories of her life with Daddy now threatened. Oh, Daddy, where are you now? Off in some shabby bivouac area in Virginia just like Johnny. Yes, Johnny! Sweet loving man of mine. I need you. I want you here with me now.*

She thought of their first romantic moments in the living room. Oh yes, the lovely living room with its high ceiling accented by a large, ornate molding all around, and a sparkling crystal chandelier. She loved the romantic elegance of the French provincial furniture and the hand-carved wooden fireplace mantel. And there was the loveseat that had a special feel because it was the place where Johnny had first said, "I love you!" *Oh, Johnny. My precious Johnny. If only you could be here now. The trip to Aunt Elsie's place would be so much more exciting.* She had mixed emotions about going. She didn't want to leave the home she loved. The thought of it being looted or burned down was such a trauma to her mind it made her sick to her stomach. She associated her home so much with her mother and father and brother it would be as if someone directly attacked their very persons, their bodies, souls, and spirits. *And what's to become of the family business,* she thought. Mitchell's General Store and Fabric Shop was such a service to the community. All of her life's most sentimental feelings were now being threatened. In complete desperation her spirit cried out within her, *Oh, God, help me! Help us! Please help us!*

She lay still for a moment, frozen by the horror of being so uprooted. *Johnny! Johnny! If only you weren't so far away.* Eventually Johnny's face came into her mind's view and she remembered what he said in one of his letters about looking at the moon and knowing he's doing the same thing from a different angle a little farther north. It would make them feel closer. She had done it every night since she received that letter, but in all the stress and confusion she had forgotten it this night. She threw back the covers and scurried to the window. Sure enough, there it was, glowing like a silver ball with a few shadows on it reflecting the faint image of a man's face. She thought about Johnny looking at it this very moment, and somehow he did seem closer. She whispered, "I love you, Johnny! I love you, John William Van Worth III. Do you hear me? I love you and I miss you, and I pray the day you come back home to me will be soon." Tears trickled down her cheeks as she stared at the moon.

She tarried there a long time, with moonlight gently caressing her concerned countenance. Then she again fell to her knees to pray. After which she fell asleep, totally emotionally exhausted.

The next morning, Molly was awakened by the clattering sounds of breakfast being prepared as Marion worked with Nicole to get it ready. It was a simple meal since food of any kind was growing scarce. They would have a little oatmeal and grits, which they washed down with acorn coffee. Real coffee had become impossible to obtain because of the Union blockade. At the breakfast table, Molly was having second thoughts about leaving and expressed her mixed feelings.

"Mama, I'm not so sure about leaving the house and the store. I was tossing and turning all night. I just don't have a good feeling about it." Marion revealed similar emotions. "Yes, Molly, I know. I feel the same way. It's so hard to leave our home and not know if we'll ever be able to return and see it as we've always known it." Kent boldly exclaimed, "I ain't afraid of no stinkin' Yankees! Let's stay here and hold 'em off like Mr. Steadman and some of the other neighbors!" He was being brave even though there was a quiver of fear to be heard in his voice. Marion saw through his juvenile attitude and excused what she saw as Kent's not realizing what was possibly coming upon them. She bit her lip and put her arms around him.

"Kent, my son! My brave, brave son! I know you will protect us to the death, but I don't want death. We must avoid confrontation with men who are trained to be ruthless killers and destroyers. I want us to live. I want your father to have something to come home to. I want us to outlive this awful war, not be victims of it. Now, go hitch up the carriage. We have to take Nicole back to her family, before we leave." She hugged him and kissed him on the cheek. Kent gently said, "Yes, ma'am! I'll do whatever you want, Mother."

After breakfast, they stepped out of the house to lock it up. The street was filled with chaos. The last remnants of Confederate troops were still marching route step out of the city in a last-ditch effort to head off any advance of General Sherman's army heading toward Charleston. As Kent prepared to bring the loaded carriage around, Nicole observed the activity and exclaimed,

"I don't see how the Daltons can get another thing on that wagon, but they're sure trying." The Daltons were neighbors across the street that had packed everything they could and were still tying bundles to the wagon that hung precariously over the sides. Molly noticed that more than half of the neighbors were staying, some holding whatever weapons they could muster, including picks and shovels. Mr. Steadman was sitting on his front porch, still holding his long rifle.

"Still plannin' tuh leave are ya?' he said to Marion.

"Yes, Mr. Steadman, I'm afraid we must. I don't feel we're equipped to hold off an army."

"Well, don't you worry none, Mrs. Mitchell. I'll take down any soldier that thinks he's gonna torch any home along here, yours especially." Marion was comforted but very concerned. "Mr. Steadman, that's very brave and gentlemanly of you, but I'm concerned for your safety."

"No need tuh be. Let's face it, ah oughta be marchin' with them troops yonder. But ah'm an old man with bum knees. Any way ya look at it, ah don't have that many years left. Ah've lived mah life. Might as well die defendin' somethin' and doin' what's decent. Like ah said, 'Here lies Wally Steadman. He stuck to his guns!' Makes a pretty good epitaph, don't ya think?" Molly was moved by the elderly man's pitiful attempt at immortality and she sweetly responded,

"That might be a noble thing, sir, but we're praying you'll still be here when we get back."

"Much obliged, Miss Molly. Have a nice trip now! Ya hear?"

It was disturbing to witness the air of panic that seemed to grip the population as they traveled through the city to drop off Nicole before heading north on East Bay Street and out to Pleasant Acres. As the carriage pulled up in front of Nicole's home on Mary Street her eyes filled with tears.

"Miss Marion, I hope you don't think poorly of me for not leaving with you. You know I love you and your family as if you were my own." Marion was touched by her show of love. "Now there, Nicole! We all feel the same about you. But you have to do what you have to do. There are no easy solutions to the horrors of war. None of it makes any sense to me." They embraced with tears in their eyes as Kent climbed down from the drivers seat and opened the door.

"We'll miss you, Miss Nicole." he said. "But don't worry. We'll be back before too long." Nicole hugged Kent and Molly and Marion one last time before she turned and ran into the waiting arms of her mother standing at the front door of their home. The carriage drove away.

Nearing the intersection of Mary Street and East Bay, suddenly the carriage rocked backward and an enormous roar rumbled through their bodies as Molly and Marion were knocked out of their seats and Kent rolled back onto the carriage roof. The horses reared and whinnied while pawing the air with their front hooves. Before them he could see pieces of debris from the roof of the Northeastern Railroad Depot raining down upon a large area. He could have sworn he saw several bodies flying through the air also. Molly and her mother got up off the floor of the carriage and poked their heads out of the doors to question Kent with great alarm in their voices.

"Kent! What is it!" said Molly. Marion screamed, "Is Sherman here now!?" Kent exclaimed, "I'm not sure. But the train station just blew sky high! I never heard any cannon fire. I don't know what happened, but that's the biggest explosion I've ever seen." Climbing back into the driver's seat, he continued, "Maybe our soldiers blew it up so the Yankeess couldn't use it. I don't know."

A man on a wagon which was headed in the opposite direction overheard Kent and said, "That's not so, ah just helped the Fifteenth South Carolina Infantry load the Northeastern Railroad cars. They didn't do it. Somebody musta accidentally set off a charge. Ah'm goin' back to see!" Kent was curious about the huge glow and pillar of smoke billowing into the sky. Kent followed the man after he turned his horse and wagon around and rolled off toward the commotion ahead. Molly and Marion were still confused. Marion yelled out the door, "Where are you going, Kent?" He yelled back, "I just want to see what happened."

"Good heavens, son, be careful!" She was somewhat curious herself, but was prepared to give him more direct orders to leave if more danger lurked ahead. As they got nearer they could see an enormous fire raging out of control engulfing the brick train station, its large arched windows blown away by the blast. Apparently, a train of the Northeastern Railroad loaded, with Confederate soldiers and supplies, was just pulling out of the station when the explosion occurred. The caboose was only a half block away. The train had stopped and troops were rushing back to help the civilians who were victims of the blast and fire. They consisted mostly of women and children and some Negroes, people from the most destitute families of Charleston who had entered the depot for the purpose of pillaging what they could from the storehouse of supplies left behind. Unfortunately, one of the things left behind was a quantity of damaged powder boxes. A young boy set fire to some spilled powder, which burned into the stacks of boxes, causing the disastrous explosion and fire.

The Mitchells were horrified to see nearly 250 women and children, who had either been killed or horribly wounded, as they were carried out with their clothes burned off and their bodies badly charred and mutilated. Molly and Marion couldn't bear to look upon the sight. Knowing there was nothing they could do to help, Marion ordered Kent to drive on toward Aunt Elsie's place.

They began to pray for the families of those who were casualties of the fire. Suddenly Molly felt a spiritual revelation and told Marion, "Mother, I feel now more than ever that we shouldn't leave Charleston. Remember what Pastor Collins said about praying the Ninety-first Psalm? It's the Psalm of protection. I strongly feel we need to have faith, stay here, and pray it over ourselves."

Marion felt the same. She just couldn't leave, seeing how people were so desperate to loot property. She reasoned that the store could serve the community. Perhaps they could get more of the basic supplies the people of the city needed. She felt deep in her spirit that's what she should do.

"Yes Molly, I believe you're right, we must have faith in God to protect us. We can't do this alone. We can't make it without him. We can do nothing without him. But we can do all things through Christ who strengthens us. That's what the Bible says. We have to believe it and trust him to deliver us, just as he delivered the Israelites from their plight." Molly was pleased and further exclaimed,

"That's right, Mama, God is the same yesterday, today, and tomorrow! If he worked miracles then, he could work miracles now." She popped her head out the window of the carriage and yelled to her brother, "Kent! Turn the horses back toward Ashley Avenue. Mother has decided to stay here in Charleston and we're going to trust God to protect us." Kent yelled, "Whoa! "Whoa! He pulled the horses to a stop. "What did you say?" He heard her, he just couldn't believe it and wanted Molly to verify it. She repeated, "Mama has decided we're going to trust God to protect us and stay right here in Charleston. Let's go back home!" "Are you kiddin' me?" he said. Emphatically Molly said, "No, I'm not! We're going home!" Kent yelled, "Yeeaah!" and snapped the reins, and the horses galloped away as the Mitchell family headed home, charged with a renewed faith to survive.

Mr. Steadman was surprised to see them coming back and he said, "What's this? Have the Mitchells decided to take up arms against the Yankees?" Marion smiled pleasantly and with confidence said, "We've decided to take up arms against the devil!" Mr. Steadman widened his eyes and professed, "Well, yeah! That's what ah said." He laughed.

Once in the house, Marion got out the family Bible and turned to the Ninety-first Psalm. They recited it over and over and received a great deal of comfort from the words of its verses. Words such as,

> *I will say of the Lord, he is my refuge and my fortress:*
> *My God; in him shall I trust.*
> *Thou shalt not be afraid for the terror by night; nor*
> *for the arrow that flieth by day; nor for the pestilence*
> *that walketh in darkness; nor for the destruction*
> *that wasteth at noonday.*

A thousand shall fall at thy side, and ten thousand
at thy right hand; but it shall not come nigh thee.
There shall no evil befall thee, neither shall any
plague come nigh thy dwelling.

The Mitchells saw it as a test of their faith when word finally reached them that other civilians in Charleston lit more fires in certain parts of the city that morning, including burning the Savannah bridge over the Ashley River. Then at noon that Saturday, February 18, 1865, the evacuated town was occupied by some five hundred Yankee soldiers who landed in small boats from the forces that had held it in siege for so long. They burned some six thousand bales of cotton and the shipping was destroyed. They drove spikes into the touch holes of Confederate guns to render them useless. Yes, Yankees occupied the city, but at least they weren't Sherman's troops and they didn't burn the town down. A few days later, Molly wrote a letter to Johnny, telling him all about these latest events.

-0-

In the following weeks, these occupying forces proved to be a blessing because they actually protected the city and prevented looting. One Yankee soldier took a liking to Molly, and even put up some U.S. currency for the Mitchells to resupply their store—to a small degree—from Union ships in Charleston Harbor, and only took a ten percent profit until he was repaid. Of course, most of their customers were Yankee soldiers by then. Compared to several other Southern cities, Charleston's destruction was mild, and limited to just a few blocks on the southern tip of the peninsula. The occupation prevented further destruction and the Mitchells saw that as an answer to their prayers.

Chapter 16

DISARMING TRAGEDY

The world will little note, nor long remember what we say here,
but it can never forget what they did here.
—Abraham Lincoln's Gettysburg Address

I t was now late March 1865. Johnny and what was left of his men had seen a nasty and boring year and a half in the trenches—two cold winters and a long summer in 1864. They were dirty, unshaven, tattered, and weary. Their clothes were muddy from the melting snow and rains falling into the trenches. Most of them were barefoot. Food supplies were now so low, practically all of the men under Lee's command were barely surviving on rations of just two biscuits a day. When news of Sherman's march through Georgia reached the trenches around Richmond and Petersburg, thousands of Southerners deserted to go home and try to find a way for their families to survive. But Johnny and his men were not among them, although they had often entertained the thought.

They figured, now that spring was here, it meant that the trenches and roads may dry out after the showers of April, and then the fighting may become intense once more and surely put an end to the war. They all wondered how long they could hold out against the Union forces that were well supplied.

Somehow, Johnny just knew the war couldn't last much longer. The official coming of spring was turning the grass and brush greener each day. Buds were beginning to appear on the trees, and the birds were chirping their cheerful calls, unaware of the hell the highest creatures on earth were enduring. Johnny slowly pulled the last letter he had received from Molly out of his pocket and began reading it to himself. He pictured her beautiful face with her long dark curls as he did each time he thought of her. As he read her words he could imagine the soft sweet tone of her voice once more.

My Beloved Johnny,   *Feb. 24, 1864*

It was so good to receive a letter from you today. I thank God you're still alive and well. You'll be shocked to know Charleston is now occupied by Yankee soldiers, but thank God it's not Sherman's troops, and they haven't shown any signs of burning the city. Surely this war can't go on much longer. We've heard rumors they're trying to come to terms to end it, something called the Hampton Roads Conference. But so far they haven't been able to agree on anything, or so we're told.

The entire Confederate Army deserted Charleston to try to stop General Sherman from coming this way, and much of the civilian population left too. Mother planned to take us all to your Aunt Elsie's and we packed to leave, but changed our minds. We decided to put our lives in the hands of God and have been praying the Ninety-first Psalm. It's the Psalm of protection. Pastor Collins said when George Washington made his men memorize it and recite it that they became victorious. You should read it like a prayer to protect you and your men.

Our maid, Nicole wanted us to take her to her parents' home on Mary Street. Shortly after we dropped her off we encountered a terrible tragedy. We were shocked by a huge explosion at the railroad depot. They told us it was triggered by a young boy lighting a spill of some powder which burned to a storage of many powder boxes that ignited. It was the most horrible thing I've ever seen, mostly women and children of the poorest class in town. I'm crying as I write this. The visions of about 250 women and children's charred bodies are more than I can bear. This is another result of the threat of Union general Sherman's attack on the South. There isn't a more hated man on the face of the earth. The stories of how they burned Atlanta and so many homes are horrible. I'm thankful they didn't reach Charleston. Our homes are safe, at least for now, since we're told Sherman isn't coming this way. Aunt Elsie's farm and the Brown farm weren't harmed either. But we heard they burned Columbia. General Sherman's army has done terrible destruction to the South. So many homes have been burned, and they've taken everything, even much of the food. I don't know how an army can be so cruel to civilians, women and children. So many are brokenhearted and bitter.

Last Saturday, when our troops left Charleston, was when Yankee soldiers came from the islands and occupied the city. Everyone is tense and worrying about what they're going to do. They burned some cotton bales and took over some ships, but that's about all. They've also taken control of the Charleston Courier. But who knows. Maybe it's the answer to our prayers. We're thankful these soldiers haven't burned down any homes like Sherman did in Atlanta. Perhaps this is a sign of the end of this war.

Oh, Johnny, how I wish you were here. I pray this war will end soon, and you'll come home and we'll be together once more. Until then, I want you to know I will hold you in my heart until I can hold you in my arms.

All My Love, Always
Molly ♡

XOXOXOXOXOXOXOXOXOXOXOXOXOXOXOXOXOXOXO

What Johnny didn't know was that the last words of Molly's letter were part of a song she had composed at the family's upright piano to fight her despair of being away from him for two years. She sang it often to herself to strengthen her faith that God would bring them back together.

When lovers are apart, it puts a longing in the heart
To be together some sweet day. For that I know I want to pray.
The angels up above know all about the need for love
I must have faith he will return, to live the life for which we
yearn.

(Refrain)
You were the one right from the start. You won my love with
many charms
That's why I'll hold you in my heart, 'til I can hold you in my
arms.
Inside you feel a tug. The thing you love you want to hug.
So warm and close just like a glove. Cradled in the arms of
love.

Then she would repeat the refrain.

When Molly sang her song, it brought her a great deal of comfort. It was a positive reiteration of the dream for her future life. An edification of faith. A hope. A reason to live. A way to endure the pain of being away from the man she loved.

Johnny thought about the events Molly described in her letter, especially how destructive Sherman's march was to the South. He thought of how prideful and arrogant the South had been in starting the war right there in Charleston. How ironic that fellow Americans have proved to be our own worst enemies. If only they had known of the hell these four years would bring to a land once united against all foreign foes. If only they had known how many lives would be destroyed, and bodies maimed by amputations. If only they had known how many homes would be destroyed, eradicating the grandeur of rich antebellum plantations that had once been so prevalent in the rural South. If they had known how their lives would be so drastically altered, would they have been so proud to fire the shots that started America's worst war? Only God knows, he thought. And only God knew how America would more truly become the land of the free.

John slowly folded Molly's letter, kissed it, and put it back in his pocket. Jay was in the trench next to him, quietly letting Johnny finish reading the letter before he spoke.

"So how are things back home, Mistah Johnny?"

"Terrible! Sherman's wrecked a lot of Georgia and the Carolinas, but it could have been worse. Yankees are occupying Charleston but they're not Sherman's destructive bunch. At least, they didn't burn Charleston, and missed our farm."

"Thank heaven fo' dat!" Johnny nodded in agreement and slowly pulled out the map Captain Leech had given him. He realized the importance of finding the treasure and uttered, "Jay, we've got to find this treasure. We're gonna need it to survive when we get back home. Get Woodward and Buster for me." Jay's eyes widened and he exclaimed, "Ah'll try! If dey ain't deserted. Dey's been thousands desertin', ya know."

"I know," said John not looking up, studying the map. "Can't blame 'em, though, when they get letters saying their family has been burned out of house and home."

What Johnny and his men didn't know was that an advance platoon of Union scouts were sneaking through a nearby wooded area. The Yankee captain in charge was talking to his men.

"Hold up, men! Here comes the scout!" The scout saluted and addressed the captain. "Sir, they seem to be thinned out. Not near as many men as they had last month."

"Good!" The Union captain smiled confidently. "With our extra reinforcements we should be able to overrun their position."

Back in the trenches, Jay had found Woodward and Buster and they were going over the details of the treasure map. Buster sheepishly revealed something to Johnny.

"Ah've been meanin' to tell ya, ah found out where 80 degrees west longitude is. Ah saw it on a map of the east coast Major Fawbush had out a couple days ago."

Johnny was a little taken aback that Buster has concealed this important information.

"A couple of days ago? What took ya so long to tell me?" Buster weakly responded, "Ah reckon livin' on a diet of two biscuits a day is dullin' muh mind." Johnny agreed. "I can believe that!" He paused waiting for Buster's answer. "Well, where is it?"

Buster hesitated as if in a drunken stupor. All of them had a low energy level due to the lack of food. Johnny understood, and again patiently awaited Buster's response. The former boat builder was still in a somewhat transfixed state of mind and finally responded,

"Huh? Oh! *Uh*, yeah! Well, as near as ah can remembah it runs north and south, of course, just west of Roanoke, to just west of Charleston, South Carolina."

"Charleston, huh?" Johnny was surprised to hear that. He looked at the map, exclaiming,

"Whoa! Could this be a map of Charleston Harbor? Why didn't I notice this before?"

Jay offered John an excuse, saying, "You prob'ly had yer mind on Miss Molly!" Johnny appreciated Jay's observance of his habits. He looked at Jay, smiled, and softly said,

"You know me a little too well, Jay." He looked back at the map and suddenly was overwhelmed with excitement as he was convinced it could be a map of the Charleston area.

"*Yeehaa*! Captain Leech operated out of Charleston Harbor as a blockade runner. It only makes sense that's where he would hide his treasure." He let out another whoop of excitement. "*Wahoo*! Good golly, Miss Molly, we're gonna find your treasure!" He looked back at the map and realized that he had only figured out part of the puzzle. Then he rubbed his bearded chin, and with less enthusiasm, said, "*Uh*... if we can figure out the rest of this mess." There were two *X*s on the map. Johnny pointed at them and said,

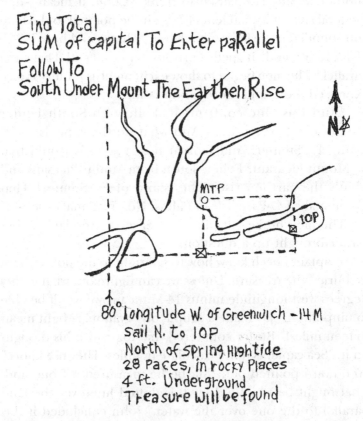

Find Total
SUM of capital To Enter paRallel
Follow To
South Under Mount The Earthen Rise

N↑

80° longitude W. of Greenwich -14 M
sail N. to IOP
North of spring Hightide
28 paces, in rocky Places
4 ft. Underground
Treasure will be found

"Is the treasure buried at this *X* or this *X*?" James Woodward noticed something else. "Yeah! And what does 'Find Total SUM of capital To Enter paRallel' mean? And this M-T-P here and I-O-P over here?" Jay recalled the capital of his home state. "Is he talkin' 'bout da capital of South

Carolina?" Woodward looked puzzled and said, "What's that? Columbia? Doesn't make sense. Too far away." John then spoke up, "The word 'capital' spelled with an *A* means money or value. I wonder, do we need to know the sum of the treasure to figure out the exact location?" Buster answered. "Don't know. But doesn't it strike you odd that he uses capital letters in odd places? Why would you capitalize the R in the middle of the word 'parallel'?" John agreed. "Yeah! And why put 'Find Total' on one line and the rest of the sentence on another? Wait!" He paused to think. "Could it mean—find the total sum of capital letters?" Again he pointed to the map and sounded out each capital letter. "That would be F-T S-U-M-T-E-R. My god! It spells Fort Sumter. That's it! That's the parallel." The men began to show excitement as Johnny's voice expressed more and more enthusiasm.

"And this clue confirms it. Follow To South Under Mount The Earthen Rise. And what do the capitals spell? Again, Ft. Sumter! And look at this . . . M-T-P. Could that be Mount Pleasant? Follow south from Mount Pleasant and what's the earthen rise? The island of Ft. Sumter! That would make I-O-P the Isle of Palms! Now it all makes sense!"

The men broke out with a cheer at the revelations, but Buster brought up a question.

"Captain Leech knew how to sail right to the point where he buried the treasure. Unless we can figure out what eighty degrees west longitude minus 14-M means we won't be able to pinpoint it." Jay made a simple observation. "Might mean fo'teen miles!" Buster countered that logic with his thought on it. "Sea captains don't calculate in miles. They use knots." Woodward pointed out, "Maybe he measured it from land. That might be why he drew this dotted line over the land parallel to the one over the water." John concluded it this way, "Well, men, all I've got to say is, what difference does it make?"

The men looked at Johnny slightly startled. He went on to say, "We know it's buried somewhere on the Atlantic shore of the Isle of Palms. That island can't be more than five or six miles long. We'll find it if we have to search every inch of it. Men, when this war is over we're going on a—" Suddenly he was interrupted by Les Moore running toward their trench from the latrine area, yelling at the top of his falsetto voice. "Captain Van Worth! It's the Yankees! They've got us surrounded!"

Les had noticed a platoon of Yankee scouts crossing the trenches about a hundred yards from their position, at a place where the trench was unmanned due to the shortage of Confederate troops left to defend Richmond. Most were at Petersburg.

Upon hearing Les call out, revealing their intrusion, the Union captain in charge gave the command to "Fire!" A flurry of shots rang out and Les Moore fell to the ground, wounded on the hip. The little man cried out, "Oh! Help me! Help me, I'm hit!"

In the trench the men ducked down. John stuffed the map in his pocket and pulled out his pistol. The others grabbed their rifles as another short flurry of Yankee gunfire burst forth. Johnny couldn't believe what he just heard and asked for confirmation from Buster Bottom.

"Did he say we're surrounded?" Buster snapped, "That's right!" John replied, "Damn! How'd that happen?" Jay said, "Dey's been so many deserters, dey caught us nappin'. Johnny quipped, "No. They caught us mappin'. How could we be surrounded?"

Thinking themselves surrounded, they didn't know which way to turn to defend their position. Just then, Les Moore again cried out in total desperation, "Help me! Captain! Johnny! Anybody! Help me! I can't walk!"

Johnny couldn't bear to hear Les so helpless. He instinctively and unselfishly responded,

"I can't leave him out there like that!" James Morgan, Ben Grimm, Goober Askew, and Goober Shaw came running along the trench to join them. Johnny yelled, "Cover me!

I'm going after Les!" Jay panicked, knowing the danger Johnny was facing.

"You cain't go out dere Mistah Johnny! You be killed too!" John simply replied, "Just cover me!" They all jumped up and started firing out of both sides of the trench.

Not knowing exactly where the enemy was, Johnny jumped up out of the trench and ran in a crouched posture toward Les while firing his Colt .44. Reaching Les, he holstered the pistol, having fired all of its rounds. Les was reaching out to John with one hand, holding his wounded hip with the other. Les was glad Johnny had come to him but was concerned.

"Be careful, Johnny, be careful!" John said nothing, saving his energy. He was suffering from near malnutrition due to their limited diet and was running on pure adrenaline. Johnny picked Les up, took a few steps, stumbled, and fell, but immediately got back up and continued to carry Les. Shots rang out from the Union troops. Suddenly Johnny dropped Les and grabbed his own left arm and fell. Shots blasted out from the trenches to try to cover John. He reached back with his right arm and grabbed one of Les's hands and dragged him into the trench, where Johnny's men were reloading their rifles, stuffing the ball down the barrels with rods. Woodward gave Johnny a paradoxical compliment. "That was a foolish but mighty brave thing you did, Johnny!" He noticed Johnny's wound. Oh! Your arm! You got hit, too!" Johnny stoically ignored his own wound. "I'm, okay! How are you, Les?" Les said, "Don't know! But I can't walk. It'll be a miracle if we get out of here alive. They've got us surrounded." Johnny was growing weak, holding his left arm, not realizing how badly he was wounded. He lowered his head, closed his eyes, and desperately whispered a hasty prayer. "God! Help us! God, Please! Help us!" Just then a horse whinnied. The men looked up to see a rider on a white horse jump the trench. The gunfire, which had momentarily slowed as Union forces reloaded, now began to get heavier. Johnny was concentrating on his short prayer but still heard the horse's whinny and galloping hooves.

He opened his eyes and asked the others, "Who was that?" Jay and the others were peering out of the trench. Jay exclaimed, "Ah don't believe it. It looks like Mistah Proffit." James Woodward followed with, "Eli Proffit? Sure looks like him. We haven't seen him in over a year! He's goin' after 'em with just a sword."

Eli Proffit galloped on the white horse, whirling his two-edged sword over his head riding right into the Union gunfire. Upon hearing Eli was at their rescue Johnny yelled, "Let's cover him!" They opened fire in the direction of the Union troops ahead of Eli. Johnny tried to pull himself up on the mound of dirt edging the trench, and realized for the first time the severity of his wounded left arm. He cried out in great pain. "Oh! My arm! I can't raise it!"

Trying to reload his Springfield rifle, Jay glanced at Johnny's left sleeve, which was almost saturated with blood from the bicep area to the wrist. Shocked, Jay yelled out, "Mistah Johnny! You losin' too much blood! Bettah make us a turn'kut!"

He pulled out a knife and ripped Johnny's shirt sleeve at the point where the ball had entered his arm, revealing a terrible mangled hole exposing the shattered bone. He twisted the blood-soaked sleeve, causing blood to drip out, and tied it above the wound.

But Johnny's concern was with the battle out of the trenches. He inquired of Jay,

"What's happening with Eli? He can't take on a whole army with just a sword!" Buster was beside John, taking aim carefully to make the most of every shot. He said, "Ah don't know what's keepin' him from getting' killed. There's heavy fire all around 'im. He needs a miracle." Buster spotted a hint of navy blue about a hundred yards off, pulled a bead on it, and fired. Meanwhile, Les Moore was lying on his good side in the trench, with his hands folded, his lips moving in silent prayer.

Outside the trenches, Eli was still whirling his sword above his head as he charged again toward the Union troops, but now he appeared ghostly transparent, riding over a Union position as gunfire pointed directly at him had no effect. Suddenly a chill came over the Union captain and his countenance expressed wide-eyed fright as he realized something supernatural was happening. His voice quivered as he talked out loud to himself.

"My god! It's a ghost and he doesn't want us here!" He yelled out to his troops, "Hell, we can't fight this! Move back to camp! Retreat to previous positions! Move back! Retreat! Let's get outta here!" The Union troops retreated hurriedly with a ghostly Eli hot on their trail, waving his sword. They kept turning to shoot at him with no avail. Finally they just ran frantically as a chill of fright encompassed them. Eli halted his horse and the white stallion reared up triumphantly. Then the image of horse and man slowly disappeared as John's men watched from the trenches. They slowly turned to one another as an eerie sense of the supernatural engulfed them also. Then all was silent except for the rushing footsteps of the retreating Yankee soldiers. Only the injured, Johnny and Les, didn't see it, slumped in pain and shock in the bottom of the trench.

When Eli disappeared, the rest of John's men turned and slumped down in the trench also. They stared wide-eyed at one another as a shiver went up their spines. Johnny inquired, "Buster! What's goin' on! Is Eli dead?" Buster continued his entranced stare saying, "Ah could see right through 'im." James Woodward said with astonishment, "The Yankees are retreating!" Buster continued staring straight ahead, mumbling, "Ah could see right through 'im. And then he just vamoosed right before mah eyes."

Johnny closed his eyes in disbelief, saying, "Don't tell me he's a ghost, Buster." Buster turned to Johnny with his eyes frozen wide, and blurted out in an eerie tone of voice,

"Ah'm tellin' ya! Ah'm tellin' ya! Ah ain't nevah seen nothin' like that!" Realizing the significance of what he was hearing, Les Moore looked up at the sky to say,

"Eli didn't need a miracle. He IS a miracle!"

Johnny leaned forward to look at Les. His head was beginning to spin, getting dizzy from a loss of blood. The thought of Eli being a ghost was more than he had energy to comprehend. He was shaking, going into shock from all that had happened in the last few minutes. He fell back against the wall of the trench, fighting to stay conscious. He shook his head a couple of times trying to ward off the oncoming unconsciousness, then collapsed.

Jay rushed to him, kneeled beside him, tried to sit him up, and panicked, saying, "Mistah Johnny! Are you okay? Mistah Johnny! Mistah Johnny!"

Johnny didn't move. James put his hand near his nostrils to see if he was still breathing. Jay put his ear to Johnny's chest to see if his heart was beating. Buster held his wrist to see if he had a pulse. Jay said, "Ah don't know if his heart is beatin' or not." None of them wanted to believe it, but the thought that Johnny could die loomed as a shocking reality.

None of them was more concerned about it than Jay. His whole life revolved around Johnny, this man who had had the heart to free him when such acts were rare. A dark cloud hung over Jay as he, in shock, pondered what was going to happen to Johnny. If Johnny died, he wondered, he feared what might happen to him. *Would they think I'm a slave and treat me as one?* he thought. Jay hardly had time to think about it as he and the rest of the men rushed Johnny and Les to the triage area with other wounded men. He witnessed sickening amputations and the piling of various human limbs, thrown away and discarded like trash.

That evening Jay was brokenhearted as he continuously stared at Johnny, unconscious and lying on a makeshift stretcher on the ground near the railroad station. Jay was so consumed by worry for Johnny that he hardly heard the

Confederate medical officer, with a bloody apron, waving a hack saw as he barked orders out to the wounded around him.

"Let's get the wounded on the train to Danville!" Jay didn't respond.

"Hey you! Did you hear what I said? Get the wounded on the train!"

Jay started patting Johnny on the cheek trying to bring him to consciousness.

"Wake up! Wake up, Mistah Johnny!" The medical officer instructed Jay, "He's not asleep! He's in a coma! Lost too much blood, I reckon. Probably made the amputation easier for him, though. Poor soul! It'll be a miracle if he makes it." He yelled orders to all in the area again. "All you wounded get on the train." A man helping another wounded soldier to get on board turned to the medical officer and questioned,

"Why do they have to get on the train? Can't they stay at a hospital here?" The medical officer explained, "We're overcrowded. They have new facilities in Danville."

James Woodward and Buster moved to each end of Johnny's stretcher to carry him onto the train, but were hesitating because Jay was getting emotional. He was kneeling prayerfully beside Johnny, with his hands on John's shoulders, looking pitifully at him while fighting back tears, his voice cracking as he shakily muttered,

"Please don't die, Mistah Johnny. Oh god! Please! Doncha know? Ah needs ya!" Buster and Woodward bowed their heads respectfully in prayer also. The medical officer was getting exasperated and barked orders at Jay. "Get that man on the train!"

Jay slowly rose to his feet, wiping tears away. As Woodward and Buster lifted Johnny's limp body on the stretcher, the rest of John's men solemnly watched.

Even Ben Grimm looked grim as a tear rolled down his cheek. Les Moore was nearby on another stretcher. He didn't require an amputation as his wound only penetrated the flesh in the upper thigh and the buttocks area. Les was most disturbed because Johnny's more serious injury was due to saving him. The little dwarf put his hands over his face to hide his grief.

Later, as the steam engine puffed its way through the Southern Virginia countryside, far off to the south, Molly was awakened by a nightmare that had touched her soul. She threw the covers back and scurried out of her bedroom, down the hall to her mother's room, and tapped on the door. Even with her long dark sausage curls crushed and messed from sleeping, she looked beautiful. But she felt awful from the fright of her nightmare.

She was shaking from the experience. It seemed so real. She frantically called her mother.

"Mama! Mama! Are you awake?" Marion answered from behind the closed door, "Just a minute, Molly. What is it?" She listened as Molly talked through the door.

"I just know Johnny's in trouble! I had a nightmare that he got shot!"

Marion tried to console her daughter, thinking it's wasn't as serious as Molly thought.

"Oh, honey, it's just a dream. Just your imagination." Molly insisted otherwise. "No! It's not, Mama! Believe me, I know! Please pray for him!"

"I will, child. I will!" Marion sensed by the tone of Molly's voice that it was a very real and serious matter to her daughter, and she got up to go pray with her. But Molly began rushing to her bedroom, to the familiar place where she had prayed throughout the war years. She called out to her mother as she scurried back to her bedroom.

"Thank you, Mama. Thank you!" Then to herself she said, "Oh god, I've got to pray." Molly fell on her knees beside her bed and began to pour her heart out to God, just as she was taught to do since her childhood, especially in times of trouble or need.

"Dear God! Can it be true? Can my Johnny be injured, or . . ." She can't bear to say what she felt in the dream—that Johnny was dead or near death. "Dear Lord, please don't let him die. If he does, it will mean both of us will die. I can't bear to live without him. Please, God, send angels to watch over him and keep him alive and safe. Bring him home to my arms once more. Let us live together. Love together. Have children together."

Molly's mother entered her room as she uttered those last words and kneeled beside her daughter. And they prayed together.

-0-

But another test of their faith came two days later when Marion received a letter from the command of Robert E. Lee, informing her that her beloved husband, Thomas J. Mitchell was reported "Missing in Action." He had been assigned picket duty with two other men to scout the positions of Union forces around Petersburg, and all three had never returned.

Marion, Molly, and Kent were devastated with grief. Marion crying woefully, declared, "Oh, my dear God! Why didn't we think to pray the Ninety-first Psalm over him?"

❋Chapter 17❋

WONDERS AND MIRACLES

During these terrible times, many prayed. Many prayers were answered. Many were not. On the train ride from Richmond to Danville, Jay prayed that his best friend Johnny would survive. But it appeared he would not, his body lying still on the floor of a boxcar, moving only to the swaying and jostling of the squeaky metal wheels clacking and rolling slowly around the winding curves, up and over the inclines of the tracks. The mournful whistle seemed to cry out in the night of the misery of the wounded passengers that the iron horse carried to the constant tune of the steam engine's pounding, puffing heartbeat.

Only Jay had been allowed to travel with Johnny. And only then because John was helpless. As far as the Confederacy was concerned Jay was just a slave to John, or as he told them, his "personal valet." The rest of the men were ordered back to the trenches to ward off what appeared to be imminent future attempts to breach them.

Upon reaching Danville, Johnny and Les Moore, along with other wounded, were taken by wagon to a familiar location. The sign outside Fanny Sellers's place that once read Fanny Sellers's Bar and Good Time, now read, Fanny Sellers's Hospital: Still serving the needs of men.

In the late afternoon of a day in the following week, Johnny was still in a coma. He was still miraculously alive but barely. He was lying on a bed in a room on the second floor of Fanny's place with the stony look of death upon his face. It was a miracle he had no infection.

He had been cleaned up except for his shabby beard. There was a fresh dressing on his left arm, amputated at the elbow. It was a makeshift dressing made from ripping an old gingham dress into strips. Sitting on the edge of the bed was Nellie. Her face wearing an expression of concern. She slowly folded a wet rag and laid it gently across Johnny's forehead, gazing at him compassionately.

As she folded her hands, bowed her head, and closed her eyes to pray, she couldn't see that the prayers of Molly and her mother, Reverend Prather, and others were about to be answered also. The spirit of Eli Proffit was present at the foot of the bed. He reached out and touched the tip of his sword to John's chest. Nellie could not see the cross-shaped starburst that momentarily glowed at the tip of the sword. Instantly, Eli's image faded away.

Nellie continued to softly pray and was pleasantly startled as Johnny opened his eyes and weakly uttered, "Where am I?" Nellie's heart pounded heavily as she heard his voice and she opened her eyes in disbelief of the miracle that had just happened. She excitedly exclaimed,

"Oh my! Johnny! I can't believe it! How do you feel?" Johnny was confused, muttering, "Nel . . . Nellie? Is that you?" Blinking his eyes, he looked at her again as though dreaming. Nellie was ecstatic, but nearly broke into tears trying to hold back her emotions and not shock Johnny too much. She knew he would be shocked enough by knowing where he was.

"Yes! It's me! How do you feel? You've been in a coma for over a week. We've been so afraid for you." Johnny's mind was spinning. He still couldn't comprehend it all. "I feel fine. Where am I?" Nellie tried to break the news to him gently, explaining, "You're at Fanny Sellers.' So many men have been sick and injured she was inspired to turn the place into a hospital."

Johnny was taken aback and didn't know what to say, but appreciated what he heard.

"What? Fanny Sellers turned her place into a hospital?" Nellie said, "That's right!"

"Well, she *is* a real woman of compassion, huh?" They both smiled and Nellie told him, "You won't believe how she's turned her life around. We all have." Johnny looked at her intensely and wondered about it all. He was still weak from his ordeal, but the thought of Fanny and her girls reforming intrigued him. With a most inquisitive tone he said, "Really? Fanny Sellers and the rest of you? How did that happen?" Engrossed in their conversation, they didn't notice Fanny quietly slipping into the room. She said,

"It's pretty miraculous! And it's all Nellie's fault, ah might add! And if ya ask me, ah'd say it's mighty miraculous you're awake and kickin'! You looked pretty hopeless when they brought ya in here." Johnny was pleased to see this new Fanny Sellers. He drawled, "Howdy, Miss Fanny! I want to hear about your turning your life around. But first, I want to know why I'm here. What happened?" Nellie and Fanny looked at one another.

"You don't remember?" Nellie cautiously paused before continuing to say, "You know . . . being shot?" Johnny looked confused again, closed his eyes and winced, trying to remember. He was unaware of his amputation. "No! *Uh* . . . oh!" His memory was beginning to vaguely come back. "I'm not sure." Nellie reluctantly glanced at his amputated left arm. "Your . . . *uh* . . . your arm."

"Arm? What arm?" John looked down at the missing forearm for the first time. He reached across his chest with his right arm to feel the stub and blurted out,

"Oh! What happened to my arm!?" Nellie tried to inform him of his injury. "Johnny . . . they had to . . ."

Seeing the shock on Johnny's face, she couldn't talk and tears welled up.

Fanny then began to finish what Nellie couldn't bring herself to say. "Johnny! The bone was so shattered they had no choice but to amputate." He closed his eyes at the shock of hearing it, and the reality of it hit him full force. He cried out, "Oh no! No!" He put his right hand to his head and felt the damp rag on his forehead, slammed it down on the bed near his thigh, and turned his head away, still wincing at the thought of losing his left forearm. A dozen thoughts of what it meant began to race through his mind as he grimaced with his eyes closed. He first wondered how he would do normal, simple chores. He felt cheated. Unfortunate. Helpless. Violated. Angry. Then he wondered how others would see him. And most important of all, how Molly would see him. He began to feel unworthy to be her husband. He thought she deserved better than what he had become. Now the dream that had driven him, kept him going through two years of hell, was gone. He would never hold her in his arms. He got a sickening feeling in the pit of his empty stomach as a cloud of depression began to set in.

Fanny and Nellie looked at one another, sensing his despair. Fanny softly said, "Johnny, you need some nourishment. How about some chicken soup?" Johnny couldn't say anything or open his eyes, and just continued to grimace at the thought of losing Molly. Seeing it was obvious that he was struggling with his loss, Fanny turned to Nellie, instructing her, "Nellie! Go get him some soup!" Still about to cry, Nellie said softly, her voice cracking, "Yes, ma'am!" As she started to walk away, Fanny addressed her again.

"And, Nellie! Tell the others Johnny is conscious and doing much better." Nellie answered, "Yes'm!" When Nellie left, Fanny turned back to Johnny and tried to console him. She paused, put her head down, and decided to fill him with positive thoughts.

"Johnny! From what they tell me, you're a hero. Little Les Moore was wounded and you braved enemy fire to go get him and carry him to safety."

John slowly opened his eyes as his memory of the incident began to become more vivid. He stared ahead, picturing the scene. Les's cries for help. The decision to go after him. The attempt to reach him. The sharp pain in his arm. The struggle to pull him to safety.

"Oh yeah, I remember now." He turned to Fanny and looked her in the eyes. "But what else could I do? I couldn't leave him out there to die like that." Fanny smiled, put her hands over Johnny's right hand, and said something that proved her new character.

"The Lord will bless you somehow for it. Ah just feel it." Johnny didn't share her faith but appreciated her concern and wondered how she could have changed so much.

"I never thought I'd hear you talk like that!" Fanny smiled again and revealed more. "Like ah said, it's all Nellie Prather's fault. Now that ah look back on it, ah believe it must have been part of *His* plan all along, sendin' a preacher's daughter here."

Johnny was treated to another shock as he tried to confirm this unbelievable revelation. "What? Prather is Nellie's last name?" Fanny quickly confirmed, "That's right."

"Any relation to Reverend Prather, the preacher Major Wilburn asked to serve as my chaplain?" Again Fanny was amused by this pleasant surprise for John. She knew she was keeping him out of depression by diverting his attention off of his arm.

"She's his daughter," said Fanny. Johnny stared, his mouth open. He shook his head and said, "No! I can't believe . . . a preacher's daughter? Nellie?" Fanny smiled, nodding yes.

"How did she become a . . . *uh* . . . well . . . a lady of the evening?" Fanny simply answered, "Maybe you should ask her." They were suddenly interrupted by a familiar falsetto voice.

It was Les Moore hobbling into the room on crutches. He was excited from hearing the news about Johnny being conscious from Nellie, who had gone to get the chicken soup.

"Captain Van Worth! Johnny! I'm so glad to see you're doin' better." He held out his right hand to shake with Johnny, who smiled at seeing his little friend standing up.

"Hey, little buddy," he said, shaking hands with Les. "I'm glad to see you're doin' better too." Les explained, "It was only a flesh wound. But it kinda messed up my sittin' down pad, if ya know what I mean." He lightly patted his bottom where he was wounded while John and Fanny chuckled. Then he went on to elaborate, "They say I'll be able to walk and sit down maybe in a couple more weeks." He paused and looked down sorrowfully, pouting his lips slightly, and continued, "I wish yours was just a flesh wound. I feel mighty, mighty bad that I caused your injury." He sadly lowered his head farther and pouted even more.

Johnny appreciated Les's concern but didn't want him to feel hurt about the situation.

"*Aw*, Les! Don't feel bad. It wasn't your fault I got shot. It's a miracle we weren't all killed." Les remembered the account of the man on the white horse who saved them.

"I think Eli was the miracle. Buster swears it was his ghost that rode in on a white horse and spooked the Yankees outta there." Johnny still only had a vague recollection of it, saying, "How could it be his ghost? Is he dead?" Les's eyes widened as he went on to say, "Who knows? Maybe he was an angel. Jay thinks so. Right, Jay?" He looked around, surprised Jay wasn't in the room, and said, "Where is he? He's been by your side since we got here." Fanny picked up the conversation and told Les, "Jay went into Danville to check on the rumor that Robert E. Lee has surrendered his Army of Northern Virginia." Les confirmed, "Yeah, that's the rumor that's been goin' around." Fanny explained further. "The Yankee's took Richmond and Jefferson Davis set up

Confederate headquarters at Major Sutherlin's on Main street. Lee was supposed to head this way too but got cut off by Union troops. Then we heard Lee surrendered." Johnny exclaimed, "This is unbelievable!" Nellie returned with a bowl of soup on a tray, asking, "What's unbelievable?" John replied, "Everything I've heard. I feel like I'm dreaming." He slapped his cheek and they all laughed. Nellie held the tray, saying, "Here! This soup will make you feel better." Fanny assisted, saying, "Here, Johnny, let me help you sit up." John jokingly said, "Yeah, after all this I wouldn't want to drown in a bowl of soup." They laughed again.

As Nellie placed the tray on his lap, a female dwarf nurse entered the room. She smiled and blinked her eyelids at Les, saying, "Oh, Lessie! Isn't it time to change your dressing?" Les was a little embarrassed but was anxious to introduce this little lady to Johnny. "Lola! Come here, darlin'. I want you to meet Captain Van Worth." He turned to John. "Johnny, this is Lola Hightower!" Walking over to John she dipped her head in a curtsy. "Oh, pleased to meet you, Captain. I've heard a lot about you." Johnny smiled and said, "Pleased to meet you too, Miss Lola." Les was quick to announce to Johnny, "She's my favorite nurse." It was obvious Les and Lola were infatuated with each other. Johnny eyed the short couple, smiled, and jokingly said, "Well, I can't imagine why." Everyone in the room chuckled. Giggling shyly, Lola took the hand of Les, and said, "Come along now, Lessie. Let's tend to that wound. *Teehee!*" Les hesitated. "But . . . but . . . I . . . *uh* . . ." John interjected, "Better do as the little woman says, Les. You don't want to be a pain in the . . . well . . . you know what I mean." Everyone laughed.

Les answered, "Yeah, I know all about that." And as he started to leave, he softly said, "I'm in the room at the end of the hall." Les paused and his tone of voice became serious and humble. "Thanks, Johnny. You saved my life. I'll never forget ya!" He walked to the bedside and shook John's hand again. Johnny said, "Thanks, little buddy."

As Les exited the room, Fanny decided she had better tend to other patients, saying, "Well, Johnny, ah think ah'll let ya eat your soup and get some rest." John replied, "I'm mighty hungry. Much obliged." He took a spoonful of soup as she started to leave. Then he thought about the hospitality she had shown him and wanted to question her.

"Oh! Wait a minute, Miss Fanny. Aren't you gonna tell me why you turned this place into a hospital?" She turned around, smiled, and said, "I think Nellie here can tell it better."

"Well, I just want to say . . . thanks for everything," said Johnny.

"You're welcome." She stopped in the doorway and turned to say, "But it comes natural, ya know. Pleasin' men seems to be mah callin'." Johnny shook his head and turned to Nellie. "I can't believe how much she's changed." He took another sip of soup and told Nellie, "And you too. So you're Reverend Prather's daughter?" She was momentarily surprised. "Oh! So Fanny told you, huh?" He nodded and went on eating the soup as Nellie explained, "I know that it must have come as a shock to you." She sat on the edge of the bed and looked down for a second, wondering where to start the story, then looked at Johnny, and said, "It's hard to be a preacher's kid. You're expected to be a perfect angel, and of course, nobody is. When I became sixteen I was with a man without a chaperon and . . ." Johnny glanced at her with his eyebrows raised. She went on to say, "Nothing happened. We only kissed. But I was socially ruined. I rebelled and ran away. That's how I ended up here."

Johnny stopped eating his soup and had great empathy for her, yet he asked her,

"Why here?" She looked ashamed and paused before answering him, saying humbly, "I was desperate. It was a way to survive. I was too rebellious, I guess." Johnny said, "I'm glad you girls turned away from that life. How did that happen, Nellie?" She smiled, pleased that Johnny didn't have a self-righteous attitude toward her, and she was pleased to tell him a true story that she was convinced would cheer him up.

"You had a lot to do with that!" John was surprised. His curiosity piqued. "Me? I don't understand." She looked away, then looked him in the eyes, and explained, "Do you remember the night you and Jay saved me from Rowdy Roberts?"

"Yeah, how could I forget?"

"Right then and there you became my hero. And later, when I made you an offer to sleep with me you turned me down because you had to be faithful to another woman. It's rare to see that kind of virtue in a man. I respected you for that. But I had little respect for myself. It made me feel cheap . . . guilty about the kind of life I was living. That night I couldn't sleep. I knew I had to change." Johnny beamed at her, a sincere smile of admiration. "Nellie! That's wonderful! I never knew—" She interrupted him to express her view of it. "Sometimes we never know how one small act of virtue may influence someone else."

"I never gave it much thought before. Then what happened?" said Johnny.

"Well, then I prayed for the first time in years . . . asked for forgiveness. And I wanted to go to church—my Daddy's church. But I wasn't brave enough to go by myself, so I asked Fanny to go with me. At first she laughed at me. But when she saw I was serious she agreed to come along. She said, 'What the heck! We might pick up some new customers!'"

With that, Johnny spewed out a mouthful of soup and broke into a hardy laugh. "Fanny Sellers in church! I get it! That caused so many heart attacks she had to open a hospital, huh?" Nellie saw the humor in it and chuckled too. "No! But I thought I was going to have one." She turned serious again, to say, "Fanny only went along out of concern for me." She paused, then said, "Well, we got there early and I walked straight up to Daddy. He didn't recognize me at first. I'm sure I looked more mature and glamorous than the little girl he remembered leaving home. But when I told him, 'I'm your daughter, Nellie' he broke down and cried. He hugged me saying, 'I have prayed for this day.' Mama was there and recognized me right away. Both her and Fanny cried tears of joy for me." Johnny's eyes were getting a bit moist now too.

"Daddy tore up the sermon he had prepared and introduced me to the congregation as his prodigal daughter who had returned. He just spoke straight out of his heart, a powerful sermon on forgiveness and love. He told the story of the adulterous woman where Jesus said, 'Let he who is without sin cast the first stone.' Everyone was greatly moved, especially me and Fanny. Shortly after that, Fanny was inspired to turn this place into a hospital . . . and she insisted all of the girls start going to church with us." Johnny inquired, "But making such an abrupt change in your lives like that. I'm curious. How did you make ends meet?" He saw humor in what he just said and attempted to correct himself. "Well, I know Fanny was a long-time expert at making *ends meet* but . . ." Nellie snickered.

"I mean . . . what did you girls do for money? How do you survive?" Nellie responded, "We just give our services to those in need and people give to us food, money—things we need. We don't know how we make it from one day to the next. We just have faith."

She noticed Johnny's soup bowl was empty,. and said, "Well, you finished your soup in a hurry. Looks like you spilled most of it. I'll take that." She picked up his tray.

For a moment Johnny stared off into space, thinking about what Nellie just said about surviving.

"I wish I had faith like that. But I don't see how I'm gonna make it with just one arm." He reached over and felt the amputated arm, then dropped his chin to his chest in despair.

"How am I going to go home to Molly like this? How can I plow the fields, or do simple chores . . ." Overwhelmed with the thought of being crippled, he ceased to talk. Nellie looked at him with understanding eyes, and in a soft sympathetic voice, she said, "Johnny! I've seen so many amputations over the past two years. There's always a period of depression that follows such a loss. That's only natural. There will be a period of adjustment, but with faith . . . you'll make it! I'm certain of it!" Johnny couldn't't see it though. "I wish I could be certain about it but right now I'm not certain of anything." He turned his head away from her and didn't see any way he would be able to cope with the loss of Molly, even if he could adjust to the loss of his arm. He loved her so much and believed she deserved a man that is whole, and able to provide her with all that she wants. Then he remembered how much she wanted children, how much he wanted a son. The thought that he wouldn't be the one to give her children was more than he could bear. With his head turned aside and eyes tightly shut, he was silently crushed inside. Only a slight shaking revealed outwardly how much pain he was suffering. More pain of the soul than of the body.

Nellie was still sitting on the edge of the bed, holding the soup bowl on the tray. She had great compassion for Johnny as she lightly bit her lower lip looking at him with those sympathetic eyes. She kissed his cheek and left the room. But Johnny's hurt lingered on.

✿Chapter 18✿

CHANGING TIMES

Oh, I wish I was in the land of cotton.
Folks back there are not forgotten.
Look away. Look away.
Look away Dixie Land.

—"Dixie"

I t was difficult for Johnny to look away from the Southern belle he adored back in her Dixie homeland. She would never be forgotten. But he knew he had to try to forget. It was forget or die. But even death at times seemed more desirable than living without his precious Molly. He loved her so deeply.

When Johnny was still in a coma on the Sunday morning following his amputation, Jefferson Davis, president of the Confederacy, was given a note as he sat in church in Richmond. It was a message from Robert E. Lee, telling him to leave the Confederate capitol because U.S. Grant had finally turned Lee's right flank, and all Confederate troops were being overrun at Petersburg. Richmond would be next. Davis packed up what he could. He and other Confederate officials boarded the train bound for Danville, Virginia, where he would set up what would be called the second

Confederate capital. Meanwhile, Lee led his ragged forces west, retreating from the advancing Union Army. What a contrast it was as the dignified Robert E. Lee rode tall on his steed, Traveler, leading a starving, weary group of men away, many of whom were barefoot.

With them went what was left of Johnny's platoon. They were all being pursued by a stocky, rugged cigar-puffing General Grant and his men who were well supplied and well fed. It was apparent to Lee that fighting would now be nothing more than a useless loss of life. Out of compassion for his faithful men, whom he knew would fight to the death for him, Lee wrote Grant, asking for a meeting to arrange surrender terms.

On Sunday, April 9, 1865, the two great generals met in a farmhouse used as the court house in the small country settlement of Appomattox, Virginia, located north of Danville. It was a dramatic meeting. Lee arrived in a fresh clean uniform, complete with a sword dangling at his waist, while Grant was dressed in a muddy private's jacket. The only thing revealing his rank was his shoulder strap. The two conversed as if there had not been a war, talking of previous times in their careers. Lee finally reminded Grant of the purpose of their meeting and they got down to the details of surrender. Lee was pleased to accept what was considered generous terms, which included each Confederate man being released on parole while receiving a full day's rations. Officers were also allowed to retain their horses and side arms. Perhaps Grant's conciliatory attitude came from a recent meeting he had had with Abraham Lincoln, who suggested that he wanted the rebels welcomed back into the nation as full citizens if they would just take an oath of loyalty.

Rumors of Lee's surrender were beginning to filter into Danville and Jay had gone to town to confirm whether it was true or not, looking for some clue from someone, anyone, who had it on good authority. He planned to hang around places near the courthouse or Major Sutherlin's to see what conversations he could overhear. But he didn't need to. Evidence was everywhere as weary, ragged, barefoot Confederate troops staggered into town.

Suddenly, Jay's eyes lit up as he spotted familiar faces. He smiled and cried out, "Mistah Woodward! Mistah Bustah!" They turned, pleased to see Jay running up to them. They quickened their limping pace, shuffling toward Jay. Woodward spoke first. "Jay! Are we glad to see you!" They shook hands. Jay excitedly asked them,

"Is da war ovah?" Buster answered, "Robert E. Lee surrendered at the courthouse in Appomattox three days ago." Woodward was eager to announce witnessing the event. "We were there and saw him. Lee's such a stately gentleman. If ya didn't know better you woulda sworn Grant was surrenderin' to him. I'll never forget it." Jay nodded his head. "Yeah, dere's somethin' ah wish ah could fo'get. Po' Mistah Johnny!" Buster said, "We've been lookin' for 'im. How is he?" Jay relented, "Ain't woke up yet. Dey say it's a miracle he's still alive." Buster and Woodward showed concern. Buster cautiously said, Which hospital is he in?" Jay dropped his voice into a confidential tone and said, "You ain't gonna believe it. He's at Fanny Sellers's place!" They were shocked, saying in unison, "Fanny Sellers's place?" Jay smiled and related, "Ah tol' ya you ain't gonna believe it!" He gestured with his hand. "C'mon, ah'll tell ya all about it as we head dat way." They crossed the covered bridge leading them back across the Dan River.

Fanny Sellers was conversing with a few Confederate stragglers as Jay and the boys approached. She was being as hospitable as she could, politely telling the stragglers, "Ah wish ah had more to give ya but we're 'bout out of everything. The war has ruined the South, ya know." Like James and Buster these men were weary and shoeless.

"We're thankful for anything at all to eat, ma'am!" said one of the hollow-eyed men.

"Glad to serve ya. And y'all be careful—" She was interrupted by Jay yelling to her, Miss Fanny! Miss Fanny! It's true! Lee surrendered! The war is ovah, sho 'nuff. Mistah Woodward and Mistah Bustah, dey wuz dere when it happened." He held his arm out to welcome them toward Fanny.

She stared at them and didn't immediately recognize them because they were so shaggy, dirty, and tattered. Jay noticed and asked, "You remembah dem, doncha?" Fanny stared at them again and questioned, "Are you some of Captain Van Worth's men?" Buster said, "Yes, ma'am! We are!"

"Well, ah've got good news for ya. He's come out of his coma. Go on up! I'm sure he'll be glad to see ya." Jay exclaimed, "Oh, happy day!" He ran into the house with James and Buster trailing along right behind him.

Johnny was in the room alone. He was still depressed, sitting on the side of the bed with his head bent down, cradling his forehead in his right hand. Jay rushed into the room ahead of James and Buster. He was ecstatic to see Johnny conscious and sitting up and blurted out, "Mistah Johnny! Thank goodness you done come to!" He put his arm on John's left shoulder. John laid his hand over Jay's and replied, "Jay! It's good to see you." Then he noticed Woodward and Buster. "Hey! James! Buster! How're ya doin'?" While they exchanged salutations, Les Moore came hobbling into the room on crutches, saying, "I thought I heard some familiar voices." They turned to greet Les as Lola came in behind him. Buster addressed Les first. "Whadda ya up to, Les?" John quipped, "He's up to three foot ten. Same as always." They all laughed. Les told them, "Oh! This is my nurse, Lola." He emphasized her name with unashamed affectionate tones. She curtsied as Les completed the introduction. "Lola! This is James and Buster."

Buster drawled out, "Howdy, ma'am!" Lola replied, "Please to meet ya, Mr. Buster!"

Woodward in turn nodded his head and said, "Please to meet you too, ma'am." Lola said, "Charmed, I'm sure." She giggled her usual "*Tee hee hee.*" Then they all turned their attention to Johnny.

James said, "How are you doin', Johnny?" John held out his wound. "I think I've come up a little short too, ya know?" Buster offered his observation. "Reckon we're all comin' up a little short these days. Short on food. Short of clothes. Short of money. Nobody wants these inflated Confederate dollars." Then he leaned in a little closer to Johnny to say, "Maybe we ought to go after that treasure. Whadda ya say, Cap'n?" Johnny welcomed the idea. In his grief he had almost forgotten about it. John said, "Yeah! It's about the only thing that makes sense to me right now. But I'm too weak to start walkin' to Charleston. Maybe in a few more days." Woodward then revealed, "We really don't have to walk. We stopped off at Smokey Meadows on the way down here. By the way, Major Wilburn said to give you his regards if we could locate ya." Johnny said, "He's a good man. But what's this about not walking? Is he gonna loan us a wagon?"

"Better than that. He still has the *Baby Belle*, been usin' it as a ferry boat on the Dan River downstream. He said we could use it to go after the treasure." Johnny can't quite see how they can get to Charleston on the little boat, but before he could question it Buster suggested, "Of course, my guess is he'd probably like a cut of the loot. It only figgers." John stated, "That's no problem. But what puzzles me is how can we get there on the *Baby Belle*." Jay was puzzled by that too, wondering like John. "Yeah. Dere's no rivah from heah to dere."

Buster smiled confidently and related, "No. Not directly! But there is a navigable water route. We take the Dan down to where it joins the Roanoke Rivah which empties out into Batchelor Bay. From there we go out around Cape Hatteras and down the Atlantic Coast."

John was not certain about this and asked, "Are you sure?" James was confident too. "We're pretty darn sure. We borrowed Major Fawbush's map and studied it." Buster related, "Don't forget. Ah'm a gamblin' man. Ah know a sure bet when ah see one. The hardest part will be gettin' past a section of rapids on the Roanoke. But the *Baby Belle* is pretty tough with those log hulls. If she can run the rapids she can make it on the ocean. We'll stay close to shore just beyond the breakers. Whadda ya say?"

John thought about it. He reasoned that if they found the treasure and he got rich, he might be able to provide for Molly and she might be able to tolerate his amputation. Then he dismissed the thought as quickly as it came because he felt inadequate to hold her in his arms. He told himself he must forget about Molly altogether. He glanced around, noticing that Woodward, Buster, and all in the room were waiting for his answer. Then he told Buster, "I like it. It gives me something to hope for. Can ya give me a couple of days to get my strength back?" Woodward assured him, "Of course, sir! It'll take that long or longer to secure the boat, check it out, make some fishing poles, and stock supplies. Major Wilburn said he would help us with that part of it." John said, "Great!" He reminded Woodward, "And what's this 'sir' stuff? It's still 'Johnny,' okay?" Woodward replied, "Okay. It's just that I have a lot of respect for you. You'll still be our captain." John responded, "Oh no. I'm just a passenger now I'm afraid." Woodward said, "I think you can handle the helm sometimes." Johnny smiled at the suggestion and told him, "I'll do my best."

By now everyone in the room was smiling, except Jay who was nervously biting his lip. Johnny noticed it and addressed him. "What about it Jay. Are you in?" Jay instantly said, "I'm wit ya Mistah Johnny. You know dat." John turned to Les. "What about you, Les?"

Les looked sheepishly over at Lola to get her reaction and she just glanced down in a shy little pout. He told Johnny,

"I don't know. Let me think about it." Johnny said, "Well, we've got a few days before we sail so make sure it's what you want to do."

"I will Johnny." He shook John's hand again, showing his gratitude for Johnny's bravery. "Thanks again for everything, Johnny."

"You're welcome." Buster decided it was time to leave since there was a lot to do to get ready. He suggested, "Well, we'd bettah get started." Turning to John he said, "And let you get some rest." He shook Johnny's hand, saying, "It's great to be under your command again, Captain!" John strongly emphasized, "It's good to have something to live for again." The comment didn't go unnoticed by Jay, who looked at Johnny inquisitively. James shook John's hand.

"See ya in a few days when we're ready, Cap'n!" Johnny was smiling pleasantly and said, "I'm looking forward to it James." Johnny watched as they left the room. Les and Lola waved to exit also. Only Jay was left in the room with Johnny. He shyly approached John. "*Uh* . . . Mistah Johnny? Fo' two years now you been tellin' me seein' Miss Molly again was all you lived for. You ain't give up on dat, have ya? 'Cause ah was hopin' to go back to da farm and . . . well, dere's dis gal Gloretha ah had mah eye on ovah at da Brown farm. She oughtta be 'bout marryin' age by now." This distressed John. He explained, "Oh, Jay! You don't understand. After we find the treasure you can go back if you want. But as for me . . . well, Molly talked about wantin' me to hold her in my arms in every letter she wrote. I went to sleep every night dreamin' about holding her like that. But I can't go back now. Don't ya see? I'm not the man she used to know. Look at me!"

Jay stared at Johnny, almost frozen to see him talking about himself this way. John said, "I can't go back to her as . . ." He winced and closed his eyes. "*As half a man!*"

Jay was speechless, shocked, and saddened by knowing how Johnny felt. He looked at Johnny, tightly holding his eyes shut, attempting to hold back the tears, and agonized over John's heartbreak. Jay closed his eyes and dropped his chin to his chest in despair, wondering how Molly would feel if she could see Johnny in this condition.

That evening as the moon shone down over Molly's home in South Carolina, the crickets were chirping outside, but Molly was choking inside, down on her knees, brokenhearted also, concerned heavily about Johnny as she passionately prayed for him and her father.

"Oh, Lord, please bring Johnny and Daddy home to me. I haven't heard anything from Johnny since that horrible dream. I can't accept the thought that he's dead. I must have faith that somehow you'll bring him and Daddy back. But even if he is dead . . ." Her voice began to crack as she couldn't hold back the tears. "Then just bring his ghost back to me and I'll hold him close that way. I love him so much." She realized her words were of weak faith and sounded pitiful and helpless. She began to sob. She glanced up at a photograph of her and Johnny on her dresser. They had their arms around each other in a loving embrace, with their heads turned toward the camera, smiling joyously. She gazed at the picture, not realizing why she hadn't heard from Johnny since her terrible nightmare. She knew something was wrong. She could feel it in her spirit and soul. She buried her face in her hands and sobbed relentlessly.

"Oh, God! Strengthen me. Strengthen my faith. And bring them home to me." She thought, *Surely God can hear my cries. Surely somewhere an angel can hear me. Surely my prayer will be answered.* She prayed until she fell asleep, exhausted.

The next three days passed slowly for Johnny as his body continued to heal. But the struggle to heal his soul was taking much longer as he continued to wrestle with a dark state of depression due to the loss of his greatest dream, Molly. Nellie, Fanny, Les, and Jay had done all they could to console Johnny. On the surface, he tried to hide the ache in his heart, but it was still eating at his soul. The only thing that kept him going now was the thought of finding the treasure. He delighted himself by talking about it to Jay and the others, giving the outward appearance of being happy while his heart was in agony.

In midmorning of the third day since James and Buster departed, the familiar sound of horses' hooves clopping along was heard outside Fanny's place. It was the carriage of Reverend Prather, who was holding the reins. Major Wilburn was also on the front seat, with Michael Jr. between them. Nellie Prather heard them coming and was at the front door, holding it open while yelling back inside to Fanny, "They're here!" Reverend Prather called out to his horse, "*Whoa! Whoa*, Nellie! *Whoa!*" As the horse drew to a halt, Nellie ran out to greet them, rushing up to her father first. "Daddy!" They embraced with a warm hug and she kissed her father on the cheek and he kissed her, after which she curiously asked him, "Why did you name your horse Nellie? Do I remind you of a horse? Besides, he's a boy horse!" Her father smiled and told her, "I've named all my horses Nellie after you ran away. You see, that way every time I called their name I felt a little closer to you."

Nellie was touched by the endearing thoughtfulness of her father and she smiled, saying,

"Oh, Daddy! You're so sweet!" She noticed Major Wilburn smiling at the love between them and turned to greet him and Michael Jr., as well as James and Buster who were passengers in the carriage. Major Wilburn tipped his hat, "Mornin', Miss Nellie!"

"Mornin', Major Wilburn. I see you brought Michael with you. My, isn't he getting to be a handsome boy? Just like his father!" Michael Jr. immediately asked, "Where's Johnny?"

Before anyone could answer him, Fanny greeted them while holding open the door.

"Good mornin', gentlemen! Come on in! John and Jay are in the kitchen!"

Sitting at the kitchen table, Johnny and Jay were looking at the treasure map. Johnny was well groomed and shaven, looking more like his old self on the surface. He told Jay, "Here's the part I like, Jay. Where he wrote, 'North of Spring high tide. Twenty-eight paces, in rocky places. Four feet underground treasure will be found.' When we find that place we'll shout." He laughed. Jay delightedly laughed, also. "You right 'bout dat, Mistah Johnny!" Just then the guests entered the kitchen, and Jay said, "Hey! Look who's heah!"

Buster was the first to enter the room, followed by James, and he addressed John.

"Mornin', Cap'n. We've got a surprise for you." John brightened up as the others entered. "Major Wilburn! And Reverend Prather!" He stood up and extended his arm to shake hands all around. As they exchanged salutations, Woodward pointed to Michael Jr., saying, "There's somebody else!" The boy, now about seven years old, ran over to Johnny and threw his arms around his waist.

Johnny embraced the lad with his right arm and said, "Hey, Michael! You've grown a little since I last saw you. Do you still have that spin-yo I gave ya!" Reaching into his pocket, the boy pulled out the toy with a big smile. "Got it right here!" Johnny said, "You took good care of it. I'm proud of ya!" The lad began to wind it up and start it spinning, as Johnny said, "'Atta boy, Michael."

Major Wilburn directed his son, "Now, Michael, why don't you play with the toy while we talk business." He answered, "Yes, sir!" Johnny pointed toward the table, saying, "Have a seat, gentlemen!" As they sat down, Johnny addressed the major. "I think I know what you want to talk about. Major Wilburn, I have a great deal of respect for you. And I want you to know I'd be more than happy to give you a fair share of the treasure when we find it." He turned to the others. "Right, boys?" They all responded with a flurry of positive remarks. Johnny smiled confidently, but was surprised when the Major said, "And I want you to know that I really don't care about it unless, of course, you have so much treasure you don't know what to do with it all." They all laughed at that remark and the Major became more sincere. "The Lord has blessed me over the years, and now that the war is over, I'll be able to market crops I need to keep Smoky Meadows afloat. The reason I came down here today is, I want to keep *you* afloat with this expedition. I'm going to give you the deed to the *Baby Belle.* I had one drawn up at the courthouse." He reached in his pocket and pulled out the deed.

"That way, if you wind up shipwrecked you won't feel like you owe me anything."

He chuckled at his own suggestion along with the others. Johnny took the deed and placed it over the map, still laid out on the table, and was pleased at the major's kindness, saying, "Well, that's mighty generous of you, Major."

"We're close enough friends. You can just call me Mike." As they shook hands, Johnny said, "You'll always be 'major' to me!"

Les Moore's voice could be heard calling from the next room. "Johnny! Is Johnny still here?" He hobbled into the room with Lola trailing along behind him. He spotted Johnny.

"Oh, thank goodness! I was afraid you were gonna get away before I had a chance to say goodbye." Johnny shook the little man's hand and said, "How could I forget you, Les? Are you sure you don't want to go with us?"

"I'm sure. I've thought it over and well . . ." He smiled and looked lovingly at Lola. "Like Eli said, some things are more precious than silver and gold." Lola giggled and laid her head on his shoulder. Everyone chuckled at the cute little couple. Johnny said, "I see! Well, I hope you two get married and—and have lots of little ones." Everyone laughed even harder and Johnny remarked, "Well . . . you know what I mean."

When the laughter subsided, Buster picked up the conversation and told Johnny, "The *Baby Belle* is loaded and ready." Woodward quickly reassured him, "All we have to do is get up a head of steam and leave." They began to stand up to leave, as Woodward continued, "Of course, the head of steam is just to blow the whistle for our departure. Once we get going we can sail along with the current. It's all downstream to the sea. We need to save our fuel for the ocean. That's where the power will come in handy, Johnny."

"Sounds like you've thought this out pretty well, James." Johnny turned to Jay and said,

"Well, come on, Jay. Let's go on a treasure hunt!" Jay said, "Ah'm ready fo' dat!" Johnny related, "I hope we get so rich we can give back to others. I'd sure like to be able to compensate Major Wilburn here, and Fanny and the girls for all they've given us."

Major Wilburn suggested, "Just give to Fanny and the girls. Oh! One last thing! I've asked Reverend Prather to come here to ask God's blessing on your trip. Let's get the ladies. Somebody ask Miss Fanny if we can go up front where there's more room for everybody."

Lola excitedly responded, "I'll go ask her!"

They all proceeded to the large living room that had once been a bar. The bar was gone, torn down by volunteers from the church. In its place was a false mantle. Fanny had placed a cross on it that was reflected in the mirror on the wall above it. Some of the tables and chairs remained, along with a sofa and some cushioned sitting chairs. The room was now used as a combination dining area and lounge for Fanny's patients. But for the moment it had become a chapel as Reverend Prather prayed to bless John and his men, concluding with, "And so, Lord, we ask that Johnny and these men will truly find treasure that will be a blessing to them and others. Amen." Johnny walked up to Reverend Prather to shake his hand.

"I appreciate your prayers, Reverend Prather, and I want to compliment you. You have a daughter that is lovely in many ways." Johnny didn't see that Nellie had walked up behind him, and didn't realize she had overheard what he just said. She stepped up beside him.

"I heard that!" She said, placing her hand on Johnny's right forearm. "Johnny. I want you to remember that God can bless us to compensate us for anything we suffer." Her father said, "That's right, Johnny!" John assured them, "I'll try to remember that!" Reverend Prather turned to Nellie, smiling, "You've been listening to my sermons again, huh?" Nellie smiled and held her father's arm.

Outside, the ringing of church bells could be heard off in the distance. Major Wilburn asked Buster and James, "Are you sure the *Baby Belle* will be safe on the high seas?" James said, "We won't be on the high seas much. We plan to stay close enough to the shore, just beyond the breakers." Buster added, "There's a whole series of islands and rivahs along the eastern seaboard to protect us from the big waves." The church bells continued to ring.

Everyone was greeting them and wishing them well as they walked out on the front porch where the ringing bells from Danville couldn't be ignored. At first, Johnny thought it might be a wedding, but there were too many bells. They were ringing as they had when it was confirmed the war was over. He decided to joke about it relating to their mission.

"What are all the church bells? Is the whole town sending us off with a *clang*?" Everyone chuckled at Johnny's remark. Reverend Prather was anxious to leave and said, "Well, gentlemen, are you ready to go to the river? Let's get in my carriage." A stranger was coming along the road up from Danville and Major Wilburn yelled to him, "Sir! Why are the bells ringing? Are they officially hailing the end of the war again?"

The man stopped and yelled back, "No, suh! Haven't you heard? We just got word somebody assassinated President Lincoln!" They looked at one another in stunned silence for a moment. Finally Reverend Prather said, "God help us!"

Jay recalled, "Eli's prophecy done come true!" They all looked solemnly at one another as the church bells continued to ring. Johnny said, "I hope this isn't a bad omen for us."

By the time they reached the Dan River where the *Baby Belle* was docked, the church bells had stopped ringing. The silence seemed to echo the silent heart of the great leader for whom the bells tolled. To John and all those who had borne witness to it, it was a signal of the end of an age, the end of the war, the end of a divided nation, the end of times as they were four years ago, the beginning of a new age. Evidence of changing times.

❊Chapter 19❊

SEARCH FOR SILVER AND GOLD

Mine eyes have seen the glory of the coming of the Lord;
He is trampling out the vintage where the grapes of wrath are stored;
He hath loosed the fateful lighting of his terrible swift sword;
His truth is marching on. Glory! Glory, hallelujah!
Glory! Glory hallelujah! Glory! Glory, hallelujah!
His truth is marching on.
—Julia W. Howe, "Battle Hymn of the Republic"

As they boarded the *Baby Belle*, Johnny walked to the helm and took hold of the familiar pilot wheel that he had manned over a year and a half ago. He looked at the familiar faces of James and Buster and reminisced of the time they departed on the Dan to chase down the Rowdy Roberts Gang. He glanced over on the shore at some of the same familiar faces that saw them off before. There stood Major Wilburn with Michael Jr. and Reverend Prather, Les Moore now with Lola, and Fanny and Nellie, all grouped together with a small crowd of curious onlookers from Danville. Johnny thought how much things had changed since then, how much some of them had changed. There was Fanny and Nellie, now draped in modest dresses with genteel flowered patterns and pleats billowing out gracefully from the waist down to the ground, stopping just short of revealing their high-button shoes. He gazed at Nellie with the morning sun shining through her lovely blond hair, while a gentle gust of spring breeze occasionally fluffed it. He thought how much she looked like an angel.

He pondered the miracle it must have been for Nellie to be so touched by his act of virtue that her life and Fanny's, and the lives of all of those attractive young women, had been positively improved. He felt good about that.

Then he looked upon the most familiar face of all, Jay Brown, as Jay helped James and Buster fire up one of the boilers. Jay was the most unchanged, the most loyal of all. He had been at John's side during all that had been forced upon them over the past two years. Johnny knew Jay genuinely cared about him and he appreciated the fact that Jay was a very humble and honest young man. It made him very likable, and John was glad he had freed Jay before the war had done so. Johnny was hoping they would find the treasure and Jay would be able to go home and fulfill his dream of marrying Gloretha. Even if the dream of marrying Molly was now impossible for him, he thought, at least he could feel good about Jay and Gloretha.

But it was a short-lived moment of good feelings as his thoughts turned to his own personal life which seemed to be shipwrecked. What a terrible thing it was to be forever separated from the woman he adored, to be unworthy to be her husband, her lover. He began to despise his crippled condition, and began to wonder if he would ever be any good for anything at all. He began to wonder if he would be able to handle piloting the *Baby Belle* on this trip as he looked at the strong current that had risen from heavy rains the night before.

James broke his train of thought and the depression that was beginning to close in like a dark cloud upon him. James called him up to the bow. "Johnny! Can you come here a minute? We want to show you what we've packed." John worked his way forward. Buster then chimed in to say, "Yeah, we wanna see if you think we've fo'gotten anything." Jay remarked, "Where'd y'all git all dis stuff?" Jay knew their new clothing came from Fanny and the girls. It was clothing donated to her hospital by widows of soldiers who would never be coming home. James explained to Jay, "Major Wilburn gave us most of it." Jay said, "Ah shoulda knowed." James told Johnny, "We've got some fishing poles and this jar of worms." Buster held up the jar of earth and worms, adding, "Ah dug 'em up mahself. Probably 'nough to last us two or three days. 'Course we can always dig more. We've got plenty of shovels." James exclaimed, "Yeah! We'll need them to dig up the treasure."

John quipped, "That's all we need, shovels! Looks like you've thought of everything." They broke into a chuckle and James continued, "We'll have to tie 'er down once in a while, and if we can't catch any fish, we've got our guns to go after game." Buster said, "Major Wilburn gave us some jerky. We'll eat that 'fore we start huntin' anything." And he gave us blankets to sleep under. It can get cool at night in April, ya know."

"Here's somethin' that might come in handy too," said James. "Spare buckets for the paddlewheels. When we hit a snag in the river or a rock goin' through the rapids it could damage a bucket.[2] Then we just replace it. Six bolts is all that holds them in place. And of course, we've got a couple cords of wood to fuel the boilers. I think we ought to save that for when we get to the ocean. That's where we're going to need the power." Buster concluded, "We've got a tool box so we can repair damage and a supply of spare bolts, screws, and nails." Johnny eyed cooking utensils and other supplies and said, "Well, I think you've done a good job of preparation. Let's go get that treasure!"

---

[2] Rivermen referred to each paddle blade in a paddlewheel as a "bucket."

They all broke into a cheer. The crowd on shore heard them and started cheering as well, standing back on the higher ground away from the muddy shore. Johnny walked back toward the helm, located between the paddlewheels, and pulled on the cord that sounded the whistle. The weak head of steam gave the *Baby Belle* a lower tone to its tiny whistle and she sounded as if she was mourning the departure. But the crowd gave her an enthusiastic send off just the same, as James and Buster loosened the lines to let her back into the rushing current of the Dan River. The current was strong enough that it pushed the little boat downstream even with the paddlewheels churning backward. James quickly threw the valve to turn the wheels forward as Johnny one-armed the pilot wheel to guide her into midstream. They looked back and waved to the crowd that was gingerly waving goodbye to them. Younger children ran along the shore, gleefully laughing and waving also. Reverend Prather was standing beside his wife Alma, who joined them late, arriving in a separate buggy. Nellie was on his other side. The pastor held their hands and looked skyward, offering one last prayer as they departed.

The *Baby Belle* drifted with the current alongside various snags. Buster and James stood on the port and starboard sides of the bow with poles pushing the floating logs and limbs far enough away to miss the paddlewheels, and Jay stood by to help Johnny with piloting duty as the tiny boat gradually drifted out of sight of the well-wishers on shore.

They let the two-log fire under the starboard boiler burn out. The fast current drifted the *Baby Belle* downstream without power almost as fast as it did when they went after the Roberts gang. Memories drifted back as they passed familiar points along the Dan. They spotted beavers constructing a dam on a small tributary flowing into the river and remembered Les.

Johnny recalled the little man standing on Captain Leech's shoulders, with a telescope, joking he saw two beavers kissing and saying the female beaver slapped the male one.

He appreciated Les's humor now more than the first time they passed the area and shared the memory with the others who broke into a smile and chuckled. Later they got serious as the *Baby Belle* approached the former sight of the Roberts Raid. Only a few pieces of the crumpled tower were still there, along with the dilapidated cabins. They held their hands over their hearts in memory of Captain Leech, and as they drifted past the site, Johnny paused and gratefully whispered,

"God bless ya, Captain Leech. Thanks for the map. We're on our way to find the treasure."

In the excitement of being on a treasure hunt they didn't even stop to eat, just chewed on jerky while drifting toward the Roanoke River. As they got near Clarksville, Virginia, the western sky behind them grew ominous with approaching dark clouds. Jay said, "Looks like we gonna git some mo' rain!" "Doesn't look good!" said Johnny.

James and Buster took a break from their snag-watching duties and held their poles upright, looking back at the powerful clouds now darkening the midafternoon sky, making it look more like dusk. Flashes of lightning could be seen flickering down out of the heavens like threatening tongues of fire. Johnny worried he couldn't handle piloting in a storm.

"Woodward! Buster! What do you think? Should we tie her down 'til the storm passes?"

"I don't know!" said James. Buster added, "Don't think we can! The current's already almost too swift to stop now!" They kept drifting for a while longer, often glancing back at the rapidly approaching clouds that were getting blacker and blacker. The lightning and rumbling thunder were getting more and more threatening. They knew they needed to make a decision soon. Should they risk riding the storm out on the narrow shallow river?

Or should they try to pull over and let it pass? The adrenaline rush they were getting added to the suspense and the excitement, until a huge snapping bolt of lightning split a large section off the top of a tall Carolina pine about a hundred feet south of them. The crack of thunder rattled the *Baby Belle's* entire deck and everything and everyone aboard. Johnny took it as a divine sign not to challenge the storm in his crippled condition. But if they got too close to shore, the overhanging tree limbs could damage the smokestacks or knock them off completely. That would severely affect the draft they needed to keep the boilers roaring when they'll need them on the ocean. He spotted a clearing on the starboard shore and decided he wanted to play it safe, yelling to Buster and Woodward,

"I'm gonna try to pull her to shore. See if you can get a line on something or drop the anchor!"

The anchor was simply a rock tied to a hemp rope, not heavy enough to hold the boat against a strong current. Johnny pulled down on the pilot wheel on the right side. Jay pushed up on the left side. They repeated the process several times and the *Baby Belle* began to drift toward the starboard shore. But the current was so strong it began to pull the stern around forward and back out into the main current, and they were now drifting backward downstream. At this point, John realized he couldn't do this with one arm, and yelled out,

"Jay! Take it!" Jay grabbed the pilot wheel like a child grabbing a bull by the horns.

"Whut you want me to do? We goin' backward, Mistah Johnny!" James and Buster came running from the bow. James yelled, "Let me try it, Jay!" He turned the wheel hard to port and the *Baby Belle's* bow slowly swung to the left. It did a 180-degree turn and faced forward again. Suddenly, the darkened clouds were nearly overhead.

The sky turned dark as if it were already night. A few large raindrops started pelting down on the deck and the canopy roof above them. A fifty-mile-an-hour wind blew against the wheelhouses from a northwest angle, making them act as sails, pushing the boat downstream even faster. All at once, a torrential downpour engulfed them. The wind blew the rain sideways in constant sheets of water. They were quickly drenched to the bone, helplessly being pushed along by the roaring wind and rain for nearly an hour.

It seemed like an eternity before the rains began to subside. Then almost as suddenly as it came, the storm ended, and eventually the sun came back out. But the river was now rising as rainwater constantly rolled down the hillsides and poured into every tributary, feeding the Roanoke River they had now reached. They were worried how the *Baby Belle* would perform on dangerous rocks and low falls of the Roanoke Rapids, but she was rushing over them on the flooding waters from the thunderstorm, moving at speeds over twenty miles an hour. Johnny wondered about what had just happened. What they thought was a curse had turned into a blessing, rushing them past the treacherous fall line and rapids toward their destination—buried treasure.

They were so occupied with controlling the boat in the storm, and for the next hour afterward, they hardly noticed that the sun had dried out their clothes. They hadn't paid much attention to their meals either, not realizing they hadn't eaten anything except a little jerky since about noon. But they were used to not eating much from the last year of the war.

It would soon be getting dark. Johnny knew they couldn't pilot the boat through the night on unfamiliar waters so he suggested they had better tie it off this time for sure. He knew it wouldn't be easy with the flooding river moving at a rapid pace.

He began to steer the boat again toward the starboard shore, and much to his surprise, he floated her onto what felt like a sandbar. It was a portion of the higher shore flooded over. The boat hung there with the starboard log-hull immersed in mud. Woodward yelled out, "She's run aground!" They all rushed to look over the starboard side. "Yep! Ah reckon we're stuck here fo' a while!" said Buster. Johnny felt guilty for grounding the boat. "A cripple shouldn't pilot a boat," he said. James responded, "Now don't go blaming yourself, Johnny. Nobody can tell what's under muddy water, especially waters you've never traveled before. We might as well bed down here for the night and tackle getting free in the morning!" Johnny agreed and meekly said, "Yeah! I reckon so."

They were all tired from standing up all day pushing logs, limbs, and debris out of the way, or weary from fighting the pilot wheel. James sauntered over to the supply chest and opened it up, pulling out blankets and some more jerky which he passed out to the others. They sat chewing jerky and talking until the sun went down about how they might try to free the boat, then retired under the covers to go to sleep.

Before dozing off, Johnny stared up at the stars. Looking at the immensity of space, he began to feel small and insignificant. His crippled condition made him feel awkward and vulnerable. His mind started searching for some sense of belonging, reaching out for a measure of security. He thought of the treasure and wondered if it would be mostly gold or silver coins, or valuable jewelry and gems. Or would it be a variety of all of that?

Then he couldn't help but think of Molly as he had done every night since they had been forced apart. He longed for the comfort thoughts of her had brought him over the last two years. It was a habit that was ingrained in his soul. Her spirit seemed to be with him.

Each evening he would imagine she was lying beside him and he pretended to put his arms around her and hold her close, even before she had suggested it in a letter. It was a warm, cozy feeling that would help him to doze off into peaceful sleep. "*Old habits are hard to break,*" he thought, as he wrestled with his need to forget her. He knew he couldn't completely hold her that way ever. He then reasoned he could perhaps go on pretending, just to get some restful sleep, until the time he might find a woman who would have him. But what kind of woman would he have to settle for? What kind of woman would want him? He thought, *Maybe I'll get lucky and find an attractive blind woman who likes the way I "feel" to her.* But he finally concluded to himself, *Might as well forget it. She would eventually feel the arm.* The depression that began to shadow his mind was darker than the night sky and he closed his eyes and soon began to snooze out of sheer exhaustion. The others onboard were quickly snoozing also, while the sound of the constantly swirling flood waters roared in gurgling melodies that were louder than the mating calls of the crickets.

While they dozed, the waters of the Roanoke continued to rise. In a few hours, the *Baby Belle* began to float out of the mud she was mired in, and slowly drift out into the rushing current, but her exhausted passengers dreamed on, unaware of what was happening.

After several hours, Jay was awakened by a washed-out dead tree trunk thumping against the port side of the boat. He opened his eyes and wondered why the stars seemed to be drifting across the sky. Then he looked over the side of the boat and got his bearings, realizing it was the boat that was drifting—and without a pilot. He nearly panicked.

"Mistah Johnny! Mistah Johnny! Wake up! A ghost musta took ovah da wheel! Dis t'ing is pilotin' itself!" John, James, and Buster all woke up shocked and confused.

"What's goin' on!" yelled James as they all rushed toward the helm. "How did she get free from the ground?" Buster responded, "Looks like the water came up and lifted her free!" Johnny said, "I wonder how long we've been free-floating down the river?" Jay remarked, "Ah wundah where we is!" Johnny said, "Somewhere on the Roanoke River, I hope!" James yelled, "Buster! Get out that map Major Fawbush gave us. Maybe we can spot something that will help us pinpoint our location." Buster answered, "Might as well wait 'til daybreak. Can't read that map in the dark!" Johnny agreed, "Yeah we can take turns on the helm to get us through the night. I'll take the first shift while you men get some rest." "You need the rest, Captain Johnny! Your arm still has some healin' to do. I'll take it for now!" John's amputated forearm left him sore from frequently bumping the stump of the elbow on the pilot wheel, so it didn't take much persuasion on the part of James to convince him. "You're probably right about that. I'll take over at daybreak. But who's going to push the snags away from the paddlewheels?" James said, "I don't think we'll need to worry about that. The river is wider here and all of the snags are floatin' at the same speed we are. If one gets too close, I'll just push it away. The boat is practically piloting itself on the swiftness of the current. That's what it was doing while we slept." Buster pulled his watch out and held it up to the moonlight. "Yeah, that's right! Ah'd say we been driftin' fo' more than two . . . maybe three hours."

The time passed quickly that first day, and the little raftlike steamboat passed quickly along on rushing flood waters down the Roanoke River Valley, winding its way on a jagged course though the northeastern region of North Carolina.

By the end of the second day, they reached the Eastern Seaboard. They had covered the first two hundred miles of their six-hundred-mile trip to the Isle of Palms. But it would be much slower going from there, as they depended on the steam power and paddlewheels to move them along the Atlantic Intracoastal Waterway at a cruising speed of only seven miles an hour. They had to stop often to fish for food, or go ashore to hunt for it. It was also a slow process using their axes and saws to cut fresh wood to keep the boilers fired. However, they were pleased to find that the salt waters were not as rough as they expected due to the natural formation of narrow islands and sandbars that rim the Eastern Seaboard, helping to form the Intracoastal Waterway. It consisted of a series of rivers, estuaries, and inland bays that made it easier for the small boat to navigate avoiding high waves.

After nearly two weeks, they finally arrived at the Isle of Palms, and even though they were weary, ragged, and fuzzy from not shaving, their hearts were pounding fast at the prospect of finding great treasure and wealth. They anchored the *Baby Belle*, with two anchors this time, and waded ashore from water a little over knee high. They landed as close as they could determine to the place Captain Leech had marked an *X* on his map, then combed the beach for hours, searching for something that resembled the clues on the map. They were stepping off twenty-eight paces from the high-tide mark on the shore, and were excited like children at play as Johnny and Woodward were counting together.

"Eighteen, nineteen, twenty!" Woodward stopped counting and said, "I see some rocks."

"Twenty-three, twenty-four." They came upon five moss-covered stones buried at the edge of the beach forming an *X*. Johnny shouted, "Look at that! A perfect *X*!" Grass was growing up between the rocks and it appeared they were undisturbed and natural.

But the rocks formed an unmistakable *X*, obviously man made. Johnny stomped his boot on the rocks and gleefully shouted, "This has to be it! It has to be! *Yeeeaaahooo!*" John had matured greatly over the past two years, but now he reverted to a personality prior to his college schoolboy days. He started dancing around in a circle, holding hands with the others, like a child playing ring around the rosy. Woodward held the empty left sleeve of Johnny's shirt. Suddenly John realized how silly they looked. He stopped and got a serious expression on his face, and said, "What the hell are we doin'?" He pointed to the *X*-shaped rock formation and remarked, "Four feet underground there's treasure to be found! Let's start diggin'. Where are the shovels?" Jay excitedly responded, "We lef' 'em on da boat!" Johnny broke into his old company commander attitude, shouting with a big grin, "Company, march!" He pointed toward the boat which was more than a hundred yards up the beach and they all started running frantically toward the *Baby Belle* anchored slightly off shore. In their excitement, as they ran they tripped all over themselves, got back up, and continued on their task with great elation.

Half an hour later they had opened a good-sized hole in the beach, which was difficult because the elusive sand kept falling back into the hole. Suddenly Buster's shovel hit something with a thud. "Hear that!" he said. "Ah think we hit pay dirt." They all cheered, then carefully took out another shovelful or two. Part of the chest was exposed and they started scooping sand up with their hands to get a closer look. They frantically shoveled away more sand to get a grip on it. Uncovering the ends of the chest, they now had handles to grip and pull it out of its gravelike entombment to set it on the beach. It had a lock on it. They smacked at it with the shovels to no avail. Finally, Johnny pulled out his pistol.

He motioned the others to stand clear of possible ricochets as he attempted to shoot the lock apart. "Stand back. I'll take care of it!" he said. Shaking with excitement, he fired at the lock from a standing position and missed it, hitting the chest near the lock. He fired again, and once more missed the lock, striking the chest near it. He held the gun trained on the lock again, and before firing, said, "Who did he buy that lock from? The devil?" He angrily emptied the revolver, firing four more shots in rapid succession. All of them missed the lock but formed a circle in the wood around it. Buster swung a shovel and the entire section of wood to which the latch was attached fell off with the lock. They frantically opened the chest. It was filled with paper money. Buster reached in and grabbed a pack of the bills, ripped off the paper band around it, and flipped the end of it as if he was going to deal a deck of cards. He threw it down and grabbed another pack as the others watched, too excited to say anything. Buster reached his hand down to pull up a bigger pile of bills as Woodward picked up one of the packs Buster first discarded. Buster howled, "Oh no! Oh no!" He started tossing packs to Johnny and Jay and said, "It's all Confederate money!" Woodward grabbed one end of the chest, gesturing with his head for Buster to grab the other. They tipped it over to empty it out and nothing but Confederate paper money fell out. Johnny stood there in shocked silence as Woodward exclaimed, "It's worthless! There's no silver. No gold. Nothin' but Confederate money!" Jay immediately reiterated, "Da whole chest is full of it." Johnny exclaimed, "This whole deal is full of it!" He put his hand on his forehead, closed his eyes, and groaned with frustration. "*Aaaaaahhh*! I shoulda known! Captain Leech was a blockade runner for the South! They paid him in Confederate money, of course!" With great despair, Johnny turned and staggered up the beach.

Buster, Woodward, and Jay momentarily stared at the pile of Confederate money also in disbelief and despair. They couldn't believe they have worked so hard to get here and it had all been in vain. Finally, Buster spoke in his usual laid back dry wit,

"Later on, remind me to shoot mahself. Ah'm too depressed to do it now." He put his hands on each side of his head, started moaning and walking in circles in the sand, saying,

"Oh me! Oh my! And ah thought this was a sure bet." He looked upward and shouted loudly, as if someone in heaven could surely hear him, "Ah ain't nevah gonna gamble again! I promise! Hear me? Nevah gonna gamble again!" Woodward sarcastically responded, "You'll never keep that promise!" Buster instantly snapped back, "Wanna bet?!" Then he realized what he just said and grimaced, saying only an agonized, "Oooh!" Woodward threw his hands in the air and said, "See what I mean!"

All this time Jay had kept his cool, taking in everything going on around him. He turned his attention to Johnny who had staggered far down the beach beyond voice range from the others. Jay started after him, noticing that Johnny was running as fast as he could in his exhausted state, flailing his right arm wildly, trying to maintain his balance while the empty part of his left sleeve was dangling all around. He continued to stumble along with his eyes mostly closed, moaning in deep unbearable pain. He occasionally held his stomach as if he was about to regurgitate. Finally, he dropped to his knees in the sand, uttering a prayer of desperation.

"Ooh God! How could this happen to me? I've lost everything . . . left here crippled and poor. God! Hear me! Help me! What can I do?" Jay was coming up the beach behind Johnny looking very concerned, even from a distance. Johnny was moaning and trembling as he made a last-ditch effort to find a reason to go on living.

He took a deep breath, held it, and regained his composure, waiting for an answer. Without trying to remember, in his mind, he heard the first words Eli Proffit said to him.

"Seek not treasures upon the earth for such are only temporary. Seek treasures in heaven that last forever." Johnny continued to meditate, thinking about the love he had lost—Molly.

Jay stepped up quietly behind him, sensing the severity of Johnny's ordeal. He softly said,

"Mistah Johnny, dere ain't nothin' lef' to do now 'cept go home. We almos' dere, Only 'bout a day away from da farm." Without turning around to look at Jay, Johnny opened his eyes, staring off with a brokenhearted look on his face. He sighed deeply and said, "Jay, you're a free man. Why don't ya just go up North . . . Chicago . . . Detroit . . .

anywhere they'll give you a job." Jay hesitated and again said in a heartfelt whisper, "Ah don't know nobody up dere. But ah knows you. Ah wanna be wit' you. Ah can hep ya wit' da plowin'and da chores." Johnny dropped his head down, sighed, and said, "Go on back then. I don't care. But like I told you, I can't go back there and let Molly see me like this . . . just . . . half a man! It would break her heart. She deserves better than that. If you go back just tell her I died. The way I feel, you might as well bury me in that hole back there. We'd all be better off."

Jay stepped closer. In a tearful whisper he said, "Mistah Johnny, you ain't no ha'f a man. A man is mo' dan jus' a body. We's body an' *soul.* Take Miss Molly yo' heart and soul. Dat's what she really loves. Dat's da best part of a man. Ah know, 'cause dat's da thing ah likes most 'bout ya mahsef. Why you think ah put up wit' all da misery we been through durin' da war? Ah don't think no less of ya 'cause dere's a little less of yer body dan befo'. Jus' reminds me what a hero you is. An' Miss Molly, she loves you so much. She bounda feel da same way. Come on now."

Jay froze because he saw John trembling, trying to hold back tears. He just stood there, wondering if hehad said too much, waiting for some response from Johnny. Again the words of Eli Proffit echoed through John's mind as he was still on his knees in the sand.

> *Treasure love for it is more precious than silver and gold, diamonds and rubies, emeralds and pearls. Because love cares, forgives, is humble and delights in pleasing others. It is love that created you, love that has saved you, love that sustains you. Until you truly know love, you will not truly know life.*

Johnny slowly rose to his feet, turned around to Jay, and put his right hand on Jay's shoulder. He looked Jay in the eyes and softly said, "Jay! Forgive me! You have been more

faithful to me than I have to you. You are a true friend!"
They embraced. Jay said, "Does dat mean we're goin' home?"
Johnny leaned back, smiled broadly, and told him, "If love is
greater than silver and gold, then let's go get some. Yes!
We're going home!"

Jay gleefully yelled, "Good golly, Miss Molly! And let's
get somethin' goin', Miss Gloretha!"

As they turned to walk back toward James and Buster,
Johnny put his right arm around Jay's shoulders, happy that
Jay had opened his eyes to the power of love, pleased at the
thought that maybe, just maybe, Molly may love him enough
to want him in spite of his handicap. Jay put his left arm
across Johnny's back and they skipped along with bright
smiles on their faces.

Johnny made a deal with James and Buster that if they
would transport him and Jay south, along the coast and into
Charleston Harbor to the mouth of the Ashley River, he
would give them the deed to the *Baby Belle*. After all, Johnny
figured he would no longer need the craft and James and
Buster were the ones who perfected her design. They
certainly deserved to have it as a means of transportation
back home for themselves.

James and Buster were delighted with the arrangement.
Johnny was, too. He remembered Nellie telling him that if you
give, it shall be given unto you. She said it was one of God's
laws, and it must have been how the girls had survived at Fanny's
hospital. Johnny figured it was worth a try, thinking maybe if he
gave the *Baby Belle* to them, somehow Molly would be given to
him and overlook his inadequacy in being half a man.

They sailed down the coast from the Isle of Palms, passing
Sullivan's Island on the west side and into Charleston Harbor
where they paused at the site of Fort Sumter, with Old Glory
once again fluttering in the wind above it. They reflected
on the horrors of the great American Civil War they had
been forced to be a part of, and got an eerie feeling, realizing
that it had all started at this place.

As they pulled into the mouth of the Ashley River, they noticed the Savannah Bridge was burned. James and Buster dropped John and Jay off so Johnny could go to Molly's house in Charleston. They agreed to wait until John could see her and return to the boat for a short trip up the Ashley River toward the farm. Then Buster and James would be free to return toward their destinations. Jay accompanied Johnny on the short trip by foot to Molly's home in Charleston. John's mind was reeling. It was exciting to think about the joy of seeing Molly again, but he had a strange mix of emotions as they strolled along these familiar streets. He wondered once more if she would be repulsed by his amputated arm. All kinds of thoughts of how she might react began to fill his head. The worst thought was that she might first appear not to let it matter, but gradually drift away from him in favor of some man who was still normal, and more able to hold her and provide for her. Maybe she would just pity him but never marry him. These thoughts gave him a sickening feeling in his stomach. He tried to dismiss them, distracting himself by looking at the hubbub of activity on the streets of Charleston. Jay was silent, sensing the tension as Johnny nervously bit his lower lip.

The *clippity-clop* of horses hooves echoed off the cobblestoned streets as people went about their business, moving along in horse-drawn buggies and wagons. It was now the month of May and word of Lee's surrender had finally reached Charleston. There were mixed emotions everywhere. Some southerners were downtrodden that they had lost the war, while others, primarily women, were glad the conflict was over.

It was a sunny day, and the air was fresh and clean with an occasional whiff of seawater breezes mixed with the fragrance of flowers in bloom, and the mildly pungent odor of horses. A crowd of onlookers gathered around a group of ladies who were singing.

The song was written in 1863 by Patrick Gilmore, a man of Irish descent who was bandmaster for the U.S. Army in

New Orleans. The tune had become popular in both the North and South, however Johnny and Jay had never heard it. They both marveled that the lyrics seemed to be written about Johnny as the ladies belted out a hearty rendition of the melody.

> *When Johnny comes marching home again, Hurrah! Hurrah!*
> *We'll give him a hearty welcome then, Hurrah! Hurrah!*
> *The men will cheer, the boys will shout,*
> *The ladies, they will all turn out,*
> *And we'll all be there, when Johnny comes marching home.*

Jay remarked, "Hear dat? Dey done up and wrote dat song 'bout you, Mistah Johnny!" Johnny appreciated Jay's observation but told him, "It couldn't be about me. They don't even know me." But the lively tune made Johnny feel welcome just the same. It helped him to turn his thoughts more positive.

An elderly man was standing nearby and heard Jay refer to "Mistah Johnny." The kindly old gentleman looked at John's amputated arm and said, "Is your name Johnny?" John replied, "Yes, sir!" The man grinned broadly saying, "Ah bet you're one of our rebel heroes returnin' Home, ain't ya?" Johnny said, "Well, I'm not much of a hero, but yes we just got back from fighting in Virginia." Jay quickly responded, "He is a hero, too. Lost his arm savin' one of his men from attackin' Yankees!" Delighted, the man turned to the crowd still being entertained by the ladies and now singing the second verse of the song. He yelled out, "This heah man is a true Johnny Reb who's sho' 'nuff come home!" The crowd broke into a cheer and applauded Johnny as the elderly gentleman further said,

"His name really is Johnny! Ain't that right, son?" Embarrassed, Johnny shyly said, "*Uh* . . . yeah. That's right!" The man put his arm on Johnny's shoulder, squinted, and said, "How 'bout me buyin' you a drink, son? There's a tavern just up the street!" John said, "I thank ya very kindly, sir, but I hope you'll understand if I refuse the offer. You see, I'm in kind of a hurry to get over to my fianceé's place. Haven't seen her in two years."

"Fianceé? Where does she live? Ah'll carry ya there in mah wagon heah."

As the white-haired old man untied the reins of his horse, Johnny said, "That's mighty kind of ya, sir. She lives on Ashley Avenue!"

"Why, shucks! That ain't no piece atall from heah. Jump in!" John introduced Jay, "*Uh* . . . by the way, this is Jay. My . . . *uh* . . . My valet!" The elderly man asked Jay, "Wuz you up in Virginia too?" Johnny answered for him. "Yep! Fought them Yankees right alongside me." The old man was amazed saying, "Well, ain't that sumpthin'!"

As the horse trotted out a rhythmic pattern with his hooves, Johnny's heart was pounding out a faster rhythm at the thought of seeing Molly again. He tried to quell any negative thoughts as they drew nearer her house and he saw familiar sights, like the church she attended. He thought about how he would strike up conversations with her and her family after church when they had been courting just a few years ago. He thought about their first kiss while riding horseback, and how he had held her close. He wondered if he would really be able to hold her to her satisfaction again. Jay remained silent and patient as he glanced over at Johnny's solemn face and knew what must be going on inside his head. The melody of the song they just heard echoed in Johnny's mind, but he now imagined lyrics that reflected some of his concerns at this moment:

> *When Johnny comes marching home again, Hurrah! Hurrah!*
> *Will she give him a hearty welcome then? Hurrah! Hurrah!*
> *Will she hold him tight with all her might?*
> *Or turn away, get out of sight.*
> *Will there be despair when Johnny comes marching home?*

Approaching Molly's home, Johnny called out, "There! That's it! The one with the picket fence!" The old man drew his horse to a halt and smiled, holding his hand out to shake with John. Johnny said, "Much obliged!" As they climbed down off the wagon, the kindly gentleman said, "Always glad to help those who gave so much. Good luck!" He saluted them, flapped the reins, and trotted his horse and wagon off, leaving Johnny and Jay standing outside the picket fence in front of Molly's house. Johnny tucked the loose part of his left sleeve between button holes down the front of his shirt.

"I sure hope Molly can live with." He held the elbow of his left arm. "You know . . . with this!" Jay coolly said, "All depends on how much she loves ya!" Johnny just nodded while gritting his teeth. Johnny looked at Jay as if to say, "Should I?" Jay nodded, gesturing with his head for Johnny to go on up to the door. Jay waited outside the gate.

Johnny turned his left side away from the house to hide the amputated arm. As he began to open the gate, Molly glanced out the front window and saw him. Her face brightened, and she ran toward the front door, swung it open, and rushed across the front porch to greet him with her arms open wide, calling out his name.

"Johnny! Johnny! My precious Johnny! I knew you'd come back to me! Thank God!" She threw her arms around him and embraced him passionately with many kisses and continuous hugs, not even noticing his missing forearm as tears of joy ran down her cheeks. He put his good arm around her, whispering, "Molly! Molly! My lovely Molly girl!" They began to twirl. Jay beamed with a big smile at seeing the sight. Molly held her arms around Johnny, leaned back, continuing to twirl, and pulled Johnny off his feet, up in the air for a moment before they tumbled onto the ground in a loving embrace, laughing uncontrollably. They realized how undignified they must look and sat up. For the first time she noticed his amputated arm. Shock covered her face as she wondered if the fall had somehow injured him or what. She reached for the arm and said, "Oh! Johnny! What happened?" Johnny was afraid it was all over, that she was going to be disappointed with him and he pulled away saying, "I . . . *uh* . . . I took a hit and lost it. I'm sorry! I'm afraid I'm not the man I used to be."

He stood up, covering his amputation with his good arm. Molly stood up with him and gently touched his left elbow, "Oh, Johnny! My poor Johnny. I'm so sorry!"

He shied away from her thinking she wouldn't like him as much now. He told her,

"I won't blame you if you don't want half a man." She put her arms around him again in a loving embrace and passionately said, "Oh my darling! Don't you know? I feared I might have lost *all* of you. I'll be happy to hang on to what I have of you now. I love what I'm holding in my arms. Kiss me! Hold me! Love me . . . like I've been dreaming you would these past two years!" He put his right arm around her and stared for a moment at her gorgeous face, framed in dark curls with her moist eyes closed and her mouth puckered, awaiting his kiss. It was a beautiful expression of pure love. It was a look he would never forget, a commitment he would always remember. He paused momentarily, making a mental photograph of her face and tenderly whispered,

"Oh, Molly! My darling Molly! I'll love you forever!"

Their lips pressed together in a long and passionate kiss, and for the first time in a long time Johnny felt whole, more whole than he had ever felt in his life. They both were feeling love like they had never felt it in their lives, and they knew it was a love that would last a lifetime.

❦Chapter 20❦

THROUGH THE YEARS

It was too difficult for Molly to let Johnny leave on the afternoon he had arrived in Charleston, even though she knew he had to get back to James and Buster waiting on the *Baby Belle* to take them to the farm. So she and her brother rode Johnny and Jay in the family carriage, over to where they were docked near the mouth of the Ashley River, and offered James and Buster a meal and a chance to stay the night in the Mitchell home. It was an offer they eagerly accepted. Besides, it was getting near dusk and they would have to sail up the Ashley River in the dark. It would be much safer to travel in the morning daylight.

It was also difficult for everyone to get to bed that evening. They stayed up until nearly 2:00 a.m. talking, sharing tales of all that had happened over the past two years. They laughed at many things, like the story of John and his men dressing in women's clothing to surprise the Rowdy Roberts Gang. And they fought back tears over the sad stories, especially news of Mr. Mitchell reported missing in action and Johnny's injury. All the while, Molly sat very close to Johnny with her arm around him, rubbing his left shoulder often, to assure him it made no difference to her.

Finally, Marion was getting sleepy and suggested they all get to bed so they could get a fresh start in the morning. Johnny and Molly again embraced one another with a warm kiss and a long hug. As James, Buster, and Jay were leaving the room with Marion, Johnny said, "Molly! I can't believe I'm here in your arms."

"Believe it, my darling, believe it!" she said with gleeful enthusiasm.

Once again, he stared into her dreamy eyes, and she into his. In unison they whispered, "I love you!" They kissed again.

Marion reentered the room and took Molly gently by the arm, knowing that they would never part if she didn't urge them. As they left the room, Molly kept staring back at Johnny with eyes that penetrated his very soul. He couldn't take his eyes off of her either. She silently lipped the words again, "I love you." Johnny smiled, and lipped the same love message back to her as she disappeared to go to her bedroom upstairs.

Suddenly, Johnny's heart skipped a beat as he realized that in a few weeks he would be going to bed with her, and cuddling up close to her warm, curvaceous feminine body. His dream of holding her close at bedtime was now close to coming true. He thanked God for her, and he drifted off to sleep that night, feeling the aura of Molly's spirit holding him. While upstairs, Molly prayed, feeling the same way about Johnny. Their hearts were swollen with love for one another. Never again would he search for a reason to live.

The following morning James and Buster reached a drop off point along the Ashley River south of Summerville. They were saying their goodbyes and Jay commented,

"Yeah, comin' up da Ashley Rivah was a good idea. We don't have so far to walk now."

Shaking hands with Johnny as he departed the boat, Woodward gratifyingly told him,

"Thanks for giving us the *Baby Belle*, Johnny!"

"Give and it shall be given unto you! That's something I learned from Miss Nellie."

Buster said, "Well then, if the ferry boat business doesn't work out, we'll give 'er to somebody else!" James said, "I'd just go back to the Howard Shipyards."

They all waved goodbye as the *Baby Belle* slowly turned around and tooted out a whistle salute. Johnny and Jay stood on the shore, and for the last time, looked upon the little boat that was basically a very fancy, steam-powered raft.

Johnny had a special love for the beautiful little vessel, and it was difficult for him to part with it because of memories that went with it. But on the other hand, he looked forward to a greater beauty in his life, his lovely Molly. They waved one last time to Buster and James, and turned away toward their new future life on the farm. On the way, they planned to stop off at the Brown farm because Jay was excited at the prospect of seeing his cherished dream, Gloretha. When they arrived at Pleasant Acres, Aunt Elsie was pleased to see Johnny when he arrived, but brokenhearted to learn of his amputation. She wondered how he would be able to handle the chores that are so necessary on the farm. John wondered about it too.

But Molly had great hopes for their future. Molly gleefully sang her song many times over the next few weeks.

> *When lovers are apart, it puts a longing in the heart*
> *To be together some sweet day. For that I know I want to pray.*
> *The angels up above, know all about the need for love.*
> *I must have faith he will return, to live the life for which we yearn.*
> *You were the one right from the start.*
> *You won my love with many charms.*
> *That's why I'll hold you in my heart*
> *'Til I can hold you in my arms.*

Singing her song was a delightful way for her to lift her spirits while busying herself with the task of preparing for her wedding in late June. It would take that long to get the word out, allow travel time for John's family in Ohio and her family, and distant friends she wanted to attend. She couldn't plan a lavish wedding; the war had left them and most of the South in ruins both socially and economically.

Until crops could be harvested, it was still difficult enough just to find food to eat. It would have to be a simple wedding, but she didn't care. The wedding wasn't important to her. It was the marriage that mattered. It was the dream of children, the dream of family coming true that delighted her heart.

She was also delighted when three days after Johnny came home, there was a knock at the front door. Nicole had come back to her old job and she opened the door and screamed with joy.

"Got any room for a weary soldier here, ma'am!" It was Thomas Mitchell, finally arriving home thin and ragged from the ordeal of war and the difficult travel with many rail lines destroyed.

"Miss Marion! Come quick, Mr. Tom is home," Nicole shouted as she gave him a big hug!

Marion, Molly, and Kent were at the dining room table, nibbling on cornmeal muffins, the only food they had at the moment. Upon hearing Nicole's exciting announcement, they jumped up from the table so rapidly they tipped over two of the chairs and rushed to the door. Marion couldn't believe her eyes. She had been afraid he might be dead, but never admitted her worst fear and kept on praying. Now her prayers and those of the entire family had been answered, she thought as she ran to him.

"Thomas! Thomas!" she said with great emotion as they embraced one another.

"Marion! Oh god! It's so good to be home at last," he said holding her tight with his eyes shut, trying to hold back his tears. When he finally opened his eyes, he looked into Molly's big eyes that were raining tears of joy down her cheeks. He exclaimed, "Molly! My lovely daughter."

"Oh, Daddy! I'm so happy to see you!" she choked on the words as they embraced. Then he looked at Kent who was smiling brightly through dampened eyes. Mr. Mitchell put his arms around his son. "Daddy!" That was all Kent could say before they hugged. Then Mr. Mitchell put his hands on Kent's shoulders and said, "You've grown into quite a man since I last saw ya, son!"

"He's had to be the man of the house since you've been gone," exclaimed Marion. Kent beamed a somewhat shy but proud smile as his father said, "That's my boy!" Marion inquired, "Oh, Tom, we've been beside ourselves with grief since we got correspondence saying you were missing in action. Come sit down and tell us what happened?" They all started moving into the living room with Molly hugging her father on one side, and Marion on the other. Kent and Nicole tagged along as Mr. Mitchell began to tell his story.

"Well, I never knew they sent a letter. I'm glad to know the army missed us. They sent me and two others out on picket. And—" Before he could say any more Kent quickly inquired, "What's a picket?" Mr. Mitchell replied, "It's a patrolling party to spy on the enemy. They wanted us to see how close the Yankees were around Petersburg. Well, to make a long story short, we just accidentally walked up on a bigger patrol of Union pickets. They ambushed us and took us prisoner." "Oh, how awful!" exclaimed Molly. Thomas responded, "It wasn't that bad, darlin'. They fed us better than we were getting at our camp. There at the end, us Confederates had poor rations. Only two pieces of hardtack a day." Marion proclaimed, "Oh, Thomas. It's not much better here. All we had tonight were some cornmeal biscuits. Are you hungry? Want some?"

"Yeah, I'm starved. Had to walk all the way home. I couldn't take the train. I've never seen railroads torn up so bad. Don't know how they were able to wrap rails around trees. Somebody said they heated 'em red hot by stackin' the ties and settin' 'em on fire. We should never have started this war. The Yankees had us outnumbered and outgunned all along. But our boys had a lot of fightin' spirit in 'em. I guess that's why the war lasted so long. The south fought like wildcats." He paused as everyone listened intently, then he said, "Oh, by the way have you heard from Johnny?"

"Yes, Daddy!" said Molly excitedly. "He came home three days ago. He's out at his Aunt Elsie's. Now that you're home it will make the wedding perfect."

Tom Mitchell was pleased that his daughter was so happy, preparing to marry Johnny. He had already given his permission for Johnny to marry his daughter, even though John was from the North, because he saw something in Johnny he liked. Now he admired him even more, knowing that Johnny had fought on the side of the South, and especially when he was told Johnny had been severely wounded. As far as Tom Mitchell was concerned, that made Johnny a Southerner and a hero. He knew how much Molly loved John from letters his daughter had sent him, and was looking forward to having grandchildren.

He observed the zeal of his wife, Marion, as she helped with the wedding preparations. She planned to give Molly her wedding gown, and thus the garment would become a family heirloom. In spite of hard times, there was much excitement in the Mitchell household in anticipation of the joyous occasion they awaited.

In the meantime, Johnny and Jay were busy getting the family farm cleaned up and ready for the new bride. Johnny and Molly had accepted Aunt Elsie's offer to give them the farm if they would take care of her. She was getting along in years and her arthritis made simple chores difficult.

The next week, the Mitchells traveled to Pleasant Acres with friends to help get the farm shaped up and ready for occupation. It had gotten run down and neglected during the last year. And once the war was over, most of the freed slaves left to seek a life of their own. Some moved to the city and some were stowaways on ships heading north out of Charleston Harbor.

The women helped clean up the farmhouse, while Johnny tried to plow the fields with the old horse-drawn, hand-guided plow. He was fumbling all over himself, trying to control the plow with just his right hand. At one point, he tripped over a furrow, flipped, and went sprawling on the ground. Molly and Jay were watching, and she just shook her head, wondering how he was going to manage. Jay went to the barn and began working to make a leather loop attached to a belt. By the next day he had it ready, and John put it on. Much to everyone's delight, the loop held the left handle of the plow, making John's plowing chore much easier.

Johnny was grateful that over the years Jay had proven to be a blessing many times. He reflected on his good fortune to have a friend like Jay, so humble and caring. It was indeed rare for a white man to have such a bond with a black man. But that was Johnny's way. He was totally an independent-thinking nonconformist at heart. Johnny wasn't influenced by popular trends of the times. He had never believed slavery was right, ever! In fact, he had a special appreciation and fascination for people of different cultures. He particularly had enjoyed the singing of the slaves, and the depth of their soul. He wondered if that was a gift from God, given to those who suffer.

He was glad that Jay and Gloretha had hit it off so well. It appeared they would be getting married soon also. Johnny told Molly all that Jay had said to get him to come home to her. She was so appreciative, she insisted they both be provided for on the farm. John, Jay, Molly, her parents, and friends all pitched in to clean up the former nearby slave shanty, and added an extra room and a porch for Jay and Gloretha to live there.

Finally, the day of Molly and Johnny's wedding arrived, and even though it was a simple ceremony at Molly's church

in Charleston, it was nevertheless a joyous occasion. All eyes
were trained on Molly as she came down the aisle in her
mother's wedding dress, holding her father's arm. Her father
proudly, but emotionally gave his daughter away. She was
anything but a blushing bride. She could not contain her
happiness, and beamed a beautiful smile all the way down
the aisle. They walked slowly to a mellow rendition of the
"The Wedding March" played on the church piano. Her
sparkling eyes were fixed on Johnny, and his on her. He
couldn't help but smile in return, thinking she never looked
more beautiful.

Johnny's parents thought she was beautiful too, as they
smiled, inspired by Molly's intense joy. She lit up any room
she was in with her sincere charm, beauty, and magnetic
personality. But today she was truly captivating. It was a small
crowd of family and close friends, but everyone sensed it
was a very special moment. Molly's mother dabbed a
handkerchief to her eyes, while it was all her father could
do to hold back tears of joy for his daughter, knowing how
happy she was as they walked arm over arm together down
the aisle to give her away.

Johnny stood at the alter with his kid brother, Jeremy,
who was the best man. John wore a suit of clothes given to
him for the occasion by Molly's father. He looked handsome
and dignified, and the sleeve of his left arm hung straight
down, nearly all but hiding his missing forearm. It was not
an issue with him now that he knew Molly accepted him.
What he really didn't know was how other people saw it.
Johnny's father was a good provider, but he was very stern
and businesslike, and had never been a warm, loving father,
especially after Johnny was expelled from Yale. But now, he
had changed. Knowing all that his son had been through,
he was moved to great compassion for Johnny, and looked
upon his handicap as a badge of honor. Johnny's personality
was influenced more by his mother, Clara, than his father.
She was an affectionate woman who spoiled Johnny in some

ways, but showed him the importance of love early in life, and taught him to live by the golden rule. "Do unto others as you would have them do unto you," she told him. Her lessons of love showed through as the wedding ceremony was concluded and Pastor Collins said, "I now pronounce you man and wife. You may kiss the bride."

Johnny compassionately placed his arm around Molly as she lifted her veil, and they gently pressed their lips together in a warm, affectionate embrace that produced sighs from all who bore witness to it.

Of course, Marion could hardly see for her tears of joy. She lapped her arm around her husband's as they watched their daughter walk back down the aisle. The reaction was much the same from John's parents. Johnny's Aunt Elsie was beside herself with emotion for the "Young lovers." The wedding was a good sight for all, following the grief and horror the war years had wrought. It gave everyone hope for the future. Molly's kid brother, Kent, who was now nearing his sixteenth birthday, was smiling broadly and couldn't wait for the couple to get outside the church so he could, as he said earlier, "Chuck rice at them." The rest of the wedding guests consisted of Molly's grandparents on her mother's side of the family, who came in from Mount Holly, South Carolina, and a few out-of-town friends and neighbors, including Carlotta Gabbert and the rest of the ladies from their sewing circle. Mr. Steadman and Patrick McLaughlin were there too.

Missing from the gathering was Jay and Gloretha, who were enjoying their honeymoon at the farm, having gotten married in a simple ceremony on the property earlier in the week. Aunt Elsie planned to move back to the farm after the honeymoons, allowing the lovers privacy.

After the "rice chucking," they all proceeded to parade the few blocks to the Mitchell home for the reception, where a merry time was had by all, wishing the newlyweds a happy and prosperous future. Johnny's father took his son and Molly aside to present them with a special gift. He said,

"Johnny! Molly! I've got something here to help you get started on your new life together." He handed them a satchel with a white ribbon wrapped around it, tied in a big bow.

They opened it to discover it contained a considerable amount of gold and U.S. currency. Johnny and Molly were very grateful for this wonderful nest egg to launch their married life.

"Oh, thank you, Mr. Van Worth," said Molly as she flung her arms around him and kissed his cheek. Mr. Van Worth smiled and winked at Johnny while reaching out to shake his hand.

"Well, Johnny, I believe you've done very well in acquiring yourself a lovely wife. I'm proud of you, son." Johnny was all smiles as he replied, "Thanks, Dad. This is great. I recently found a whole chest full of Confederate money. It's nice to have some currency that's worth something."

As Mrs. Van Worth approached, Johnny's father turned to Molly and said, "I'm very proud to have you as a daughter-in-law." Clara responded, "We both are. You're the kind of woman I've always prayed Johnny would marry."

There was much love and laughter as the parents of the bride and groom got acquainted that late afternoon, and many hugs and kisses for them when they finally climbed onto the borrowed family carriage that would take them to their honeymoon at the newly renovated Pleasant Acres Plantation. Everyone was waving, wiping away tears of sentiment, or yelling well-wishing salutations as the new man-and-wife team smiled and waved back, riding away while dragging a couple of pairs of old baby shoes along the street that Kent had attached to the carriage.

A few hours later, Jay and Gloretha discreetly stayed in their quarters, and only peeped out the window, as they heard Molly and Johnny arrive at the farm. A beautiful sunset flooded the sky with magnificent hues of orange, pink, and

purple. They took the carriage to the barn. Johnny
unhitched the horse, put it in a stall, and gave it feed, then
turned to Molly who was still in her wedding gown. She stared
at him with dreamy, passionate eyes. His heart roared with
love for her. He stepped close to her and gently caressed
her dangling curls. He placed his hand softly against her
cheek and rolled his index finger along her chin, tilting her
face up to his.

As their lips met, he placed his arm around her, and she
embraced his body as well. They kissed so long they got dizzy
and fell into a pile of straw. They were both aroused with
excitement knowing they were now free to consummate
the marriage. Johnny slowly ran his hand along her side from
her hip to the hour-glass curve of her waist, up to her left
breast.

She closed her eyes, threw her head back, sat up, and
shook her head, causing her curls to jiggle enticingly. She
whispered, "Not here, darling. You haven't carried me across
the threshold yet." Johnny was bursting with desire for her
and he thought she was teasing him to increase his intensity,
but felt helpless because of his handicap. He whispered,

"Molly, please don't tease me, honey. You know I can't
carry you . . . *uh* . . . you know." He glanced at his amputated
arm. She just smiled sweetly and closed her eyes as she rose
to a standing position, then softly said in a very positive tone,
"We'll see!" He was still sitting on the straw pile looking up
at her. She held out her hand to help him to his feet. She
put an arm around his back and started to skip along toward
the front door of the farmhouse, while Johnny awkwardly
tried to keep pace with her. As they neared the front porch,
she ceased her skipping and slowly walked up to the door.
Johnny unlocked it and stood back, wondering how he was
going to carry her over the threshold. Molly stepped in front
of him with her back to the door, placed her arms over his
shoulders, jumped up, and clamped her legs around his
waist.

"Now, darling. Carry me over the threshold." She began kissing him on his neck. Johnny smiled, took two steps into the living room and tripped over her long gown, sending them sprawling onto the floor. At this point, Johnny's libido was at a fever pitch and he felt as though his trousers were going to catch on fire. He was still holding Molly by the waist, but she rolled over, got on her knees and stood up. She reached out for his hand to pull him up again.

She let out a gleeful giggle and led him by the hand as they dashed up the stairs to the bedroom. They sat on the edge of the four-poster bed and he began to unbutton the back of her gown. He tossed his jacket and cravat on a boudoir chair and turned to remove Molly's gown from over her shoulders. She modestly resisted for a moment, looked down, and blushed.

Johnny gently kissed her again and continued to pull apart the upper part of her gown in back. Molly then started to unbutton Johnny's shirt. Their hearts were pounding, their temperatures rising. Johnny raised the window and saw only a hint of the beautiful sunset dissipating into moonlight. The fragrance of lilacs and honeysuckles drifted into the room on a gentle spring breeze. They turned away from one another and removed the rest of their clothing. Somewhat embarrassed by her nakedness, Molly scurried to get under the covers. Johnny put his arm out to embrace her and rolled her over on her back, and for the first time he saw what a beautiful thing a woman is, just as God designed her—especially his Molly. Suddenly, he was filled with the desire God gave man for a woman. She was filled with the love God gave a woman for a man. They adored each other with tender caresses and kisses. They were in no hurry. Slowly and longingly kissing time and time again, experiencing for the first time the dreamy ecstasy of matrimonial togetherness, and their two bodies cleaved together as one, totally engulfed in the warm and intimate, exciting and heavenly sweetness of true love.

Conceived in love, nine months from that honeymoon week, the first child Molly gave birth to was a girl. She was a brunette like Molly and Johnny joked again about naming her Molly Jr. But they named her Marion after Molly's mother, and called her Mari for short. Twenty months later, Johnny finally got a son, John William Van Worth IV. In 1874, they would eventually have another daughter, Clara Elsie, named in honor of Johnny's mother and his Aunt Elsie, who had given them the farm.

Jay and Gloretha gave birth to four children, Glory Bee, Jay Lee Jr., Johnny James, and Jubilee Ann, born in 1876. All of the children, black and white, played together inside and outside of the houses. Gloretha, whom they now referred to more often as Glo, spent much of her time at the Van Worth farmhouse helping to prepare meals and do housework. Glo was a shy young girl with a sweet smile who was a joy to have around the house.

She would often respectfully look down when someone addressed her, making only a flash of eye contact, then looking down instantly again with a childlike charming blink. Jay helped Johnny with farming and the chores. It was Jay and Glo's way of helping to compensate for a free place to live. They shared the meals they prepared and enjoyed the fellowship of one another's company. When money for the crops came in, Johnny gave Jay and Glo a fair share so they would have money for things they needed. They lived and loved as one happy family. Johnny learned to play the harmonica and Jay played the banjo. They would often play and sing songs in the evening, many of them gospel songs.

As time passed, they all became more spiritual, read the Bible often, and attended church on Sundays. Molly and Johnny started going to a small church in Summerville because it was closer than having to go all the way to Charleston. But on special occasions, and at least once a month, they made it a tradition to travel to Charleston and attend church with Molly's family and visit with them afterward.

Molly's father would talk about the small textile mill he had opened, Mitchell Mills. Prior to the war most textile mills were in the North. He felt fortunate to have secured a loan to build the mill, using the store as collateral, and was pleased with how well the business was doing. The price of cotton rose after the war since there was a heavy demand for it.

There was much to talk about and think about. Of course, they respected the Sabbath to be mindful of heavenly things and would frequently get into heavy discussions about religion on these Sunday afternoons. Occasionally, Jay and Glo would come along on these visits, and Jay would remind them of the angel that visited them on the way to Richmond.

Normally, Jay and Gloretha would attend a small black church near Summerville, and one time Jay invited Johnny to tell his congregation about their experience with Eli Proffit. Johnny enjoyed it. The black people shouted, "Hallelujah!" and "Amen!" as John told them,

"Treasure love. For it is more precious than silver and gold, diamonds and rubies, emeralds and pearls. Love cares, forgives, is humble and delights in pleasing others. It is love that created you . . . love that has saved you, love that sustains you. Until you truly know love, you will not truly know life."

It was a good thing they had faith, for after the war came more troubled times, trials, and tribulations. All of their children were born during that twelve-year era following the Civil War known as the Reconstruction Period. It was one of the most controversial times in the history of America. While farms and industries in the North prospered during the war, the opposite was true in the South, where entire cities and railroads had been destroyed. Many Southerners were immersed in bitterness as federal officials and profiteers from the North invaded the South, imposing and enforcing new rules of social, economic, and political reform. Hard-line Southern Democrats called them "Carpetbaggers" because many of them carried suitcases made of carpet material, and implied that Northerners were low-lifers who carried everything they owned in a single carpetbag. Some of the carpetbaggers were former Union soldiers who decided to stay in the South after the war, opening small businesses or working the rich farmlands. The embittered Southerners used the term "carpetbagger" in a scornful manner to encourage hostility toward those who sought to change the social mores of the South. Most of these changes affected the status of Negroes or "Darkies," as black people were often called back then.

During the Reconstruction Period, three amendments to the Constitution of the United States were passed. The Thirteenth amendment abolished slavery, and was ratified in 1865. The Fourteenth Amendment, ratified in 1866, made former slaves citizens with full civil rights. And the Fifteenth Amendment, that became law in 1870, gave them the right to vote.

Many former slave owners were incensed by the prospect of their previous slaves having a say in running the government, holding office, or helping to pass laws contrary to their interests. As early as 1865, a secret white supremacist group was formed to oppose the move to give blacks their rights. It was the Ku Klux Klan. They spread terror across the South, killing over five thousand blacks by 1866. They beat and lynched blacks and their white sympathizers, as they wore white robes and hoods, and covered their horses with sheets to conceal their identity.

Johnny and Molly, Jay and Glo avoided most of the hatred and strife of those years, content to live a quiet, loving life on the farm. They wanted no part in hatred. They had experienced love, and that's all they wanted out of life. But one summer evening in 1871, they would face a trial to test their love and their faith.

As the sun was fading in the Western sky, Aunt Elsie, Johnny, and Molly were on the front porch of the farmhouse with the children, enjoying the cool of the evening, singing and telling stories. They were joined by Jay and Glo, who were gathered around with their children, when a half dozen armed, hooded riders came galloping up to the house. The sight of them was terrifying. The children whined and ran to their parents or hid behind them. One of the hooded riders yelled, "Well! Looks like we done caught us that niggah right heah!"

Johnny could tell by the man's nasty tone of voice that these were men saturated with hatred. His heart began to pound heavily in his chest, fearing for Jay and his family. But he remained calm as he slowly rose to his feet, staring at the clandestine figures under the sea of white sheets, while praying in the back of his mind, "*God help us!*"

"I'm John William Van Worth. I own this property. What business do you gentlemen have that brings you here at this hour?" The man who seemed to be the ring leader of the group said, "We know who you are, Mistah Van Worth. We got no cause tuh trouble you none. We're heah tuh settle a little political mattah. Now, if you'll just step aside, we'll take this heah niggah and show him some Southern justice." The man started to get off of his horse as Jay screamed, "Help me, Mistah Johnny!" Outraged, Johnny held his palm up, and in a stern voice said, "Hold it right there, mister! Nobody comes in here to take anyone from my property without dealin' with me first!" The man sat back on his horse and spoke in a syrupy, sickening tone, "Ah thought we already dealt wid you. Ah done said, we ain't got no cause tuh trouble you."

The children started crying. Aunt Elsie ushered them into the house, urging the adults to do the same. Molly led the children in, but stayed on the porch intent on not leaving Johnny's side. As Glo and Jay started into the house, the leading Klansman saw them and angrily blurted out,

"Hode it right therah, niggah boah! Just wherah da hell you think you're goin'?" Jay froze and looked at John. It was all Molly could do to hold her anger. Johnny said, "I think it's high time you state your business or get off my property!" The hooded spokesman of the group said, "As ah wuz sayin', we don't have no quarrel wid you, Mr. Van Worth. Just let us have tha niggah and save ya'sef' a lotta trouble." John barked, "Just what do you want with him?" The hooded leader turned to his comrades and said, "You heah that, gentlemen? Mistah Van Worth heah wants to know whut we want with tha niggah!" He and his men broke into a nasty laugh. "Ah'm afraid we need tuh lynch 'im."

"Don't you know it's against the law to hang people for no reason?" John retorted.

"No reason? Hell! We got plenty uh reason. He's a niggah! That's reason enough! Beforah it's ovah, we need tuh lynch 'em all! It's the right thing tuh do! Besides that, we heah this uppity niggah's been tryin' tuh register his kind tuh vote." Molly exploded, "You filthy cowards! If what you're doing is so right, why are you hiding your evil faces under those sheets? You may think you're hiding from the law, but God sees what you're doing!"

"Shut up, lady!" the hooded one yelled. Molly continued as her adrenaline flowed, "Almighty God sees you! He sees the evil in your hearts! You won't get by with anything!"

"Hey, mistah! You bettah tell that woman tuh shut up! Wimmen ain't got no business stickin' therah noses in politics."

Johnny had been stunned but pleased by this sudden outburst of righteousness from Molly. He was inspired by her courage. He felt the same righteous outrage welling up in him.

Molly declared, "By all that's holy, no weapon formed against us shall prosper!"

Johnny realized that only God could save them now. He strongly prayed in his mind, *God! Give me strength! Show me what to do*! He bristled like angels were standing beside him, ready to take on these demonic forces he faced. The Klansman yelled out, "Did you heah whut ah said? You bettah shut her up!" Johnny was so enraged they were intimidating Molly that he just stared daggers at the hooded figure before him, calculating what he should do. Hesitating caused the voice behind the hood to grow cold and sarcastic.

"Oh! Whadda we have heah? Are you one of those stinkin' niggah lovahs? Well, maybe we ought to lynch you, too!" One of his men shouted, "Yeah, that's right!" As they started to dismount, Molly rushed into the farmhouse. Jay fell to his knees and prayed.

Johnny pointed his finger at the Klansman, and like a dynamic preacher making a profound statement at the climax of a dramatic sermon, he poured out his words in a strong, deliberate voice that seemed to echo up to the heavens.

"She's right! Almighty God sees your evil intentions! You'll pay for the hatred that engulfs your souls!" John never stopped preaching as the Klansman yelled, "Shut up! Shut up, ah tell ya!" Another Klansman shouted, "Let's hang therah asses right heah under this tree!" Two of them grabbed Johnny. Three surrounded Jay. They started pulling them toward the nearby hickory tree. But the leader of the group said, "Naw! Let's drag 'em into Summerville and lynch 'em therah, where everybody can see what happens tuh niggahs and niggah lovers around heah!" Johnny yelled, "Let go of us, you freaks of the devil!" Another Klansman shouted, "Build a fire! Throw them niggah babies in it! That oughtta show 'em!" Jay screamed at the top of his lungs, "No! Fo' god's sake! No!" Johnny continued his condemning diatribe, "You fools! You kill us and you'll be killin' yourselves. You'll spend your eternal lives in hellfire and damnation."

The hooded leader again shouted, "Shut up! Shut up, dammit! You don't know what you're talkin' about!" Johnny's voice grew bolder and bolder, louder and louder, as he felt the desperate need to penetrate their evil hearts and souls with a truth that was larger than life. "I know what I'm talkin' about! As sure as there's a God in heaven I'll request that he let me come back and haunt every one of you until you wish you were dead. You'll never sleep again for fear I'll sneak up on ya in the middle of the night and choke the very life out of your evil souls! In the name of Jesus Christ, the King of Kings and Lord of Lords, I will prevail over you! I will bring his judgment down upon your heads! So help me, God!"

Johnny had spoken with such determination that they were struck with the fear of God. They were afraid that somehow what he was saying might come true. They were stony quiet as chills ran up their spines at the speculation of justice in the spiritual world. In their hearts they knew they were wrong and became fainthearted. Johnny continued his verbal attack, "He who lives by the rope will die by the rope! You know I'll do it, don't ya! You know I'll haunt every last one of you until you die, don't ya! As God is my witness, I'll see to it that true justice is done!"

The leader of the Klansmen said, "You crazy som-bitch! You're too damn mean tuh kill! Let's get outta heah!" The Klansmen holding John and Jay pushed them to the ground, and Molly saw the action as she came running out of the house, holding Johnny's pistol.

That's why she had gone in the house to find it and load it. She held the gun with both hands, aimed at the leader of the group, and fired. Not being accustomed to firing the weapon, she didn't allow for the force of the recoil when she aimed. The pistol jumped upon firing, causing the bullet to hit above his head, blowing off his hood. She immediately recognized him.

"Buford Grant! You, of all people! A preacher's cousin! You outta be ashamed of yourself!"

Buford's face turned red. He was a member of John and Molly's church and was embarrassed that his identity had been revealed. He and the rest of the Klan ran toward their horses and Molly yelled out to them, "It's never too late to repent, you know!" As they galloped away, Johnny and Jay were still sitting on the ground, trembling from the adrenaline rush they had just experienced. Johnny waved at them as they disappeared, saying, "Y'all be good now, ya heah!" mocking their Southern accents. They slapped their knees and fell back flat on the ground, laughing hysterically, relieved that they had survived this close call with disaster.

Molly ran over to them, fell on the ground with them, hugged, and kissed Johnny, laughing in between the smooches. As they sat up, Johnny noticed Molly was still holding the gun. She was on her knees and sat back on her heels, the gun arm limp, with the weapon resting on the ground. He laughed and said, "Gimme that gun, Molly! Don't you know you could kill somebody with that thing?" Molly was now in shock over all that happened and the courage she had. "Oh my god! What came over me? It's a miracle no one was killed tonight. We need to thank God for this miracle."

Indeed it was a miracle. And Molly didn't get the full impact of it until they filled her in on what took place while she was in the house. It became another one of the stories they would talk about whenever they had company or visited family and friends.

The story was told again for a grand occasion the following year, a visit from the Wilburn family. It was in May of 1872. The Wilburns made the train ride into Charleston, where Johnny and Molly met them at the station. Major Wilburn was now in his midsixties and his gray hair had turned closer to white. Libby Wilburn was still the elegant lady, though her hair was now showing strands of gray. The Wilburns looked very distinguished. Rebecca was now a young lady also, having just passed her nineteenth birthday, and Michael Jr., who was barely five when Johnny first met him, had grown into quite a young gentleman at twelve years old.

They had been invited to stay the first night at the Mitchell home in Charleston and visit the the farmhouse the following day. There, they would visit the Van Worth children and Aunt Elsie who was babysitting. It was quite a thrill for Molly to meet the Wilburns since she had heard so much about them. They were delighted to meet Molly and the rest of her family too.

They all enjoyed home-style, Southern-cooked cuisine and exchanged many stories, including the tale of the frightful visit by the Klan. Molly told them, "I still don't know what came over us to speak out like that." Major Wilburn said, "Reverend Prather would say it was a spirit of righteousness, I'm sure." They all agreed it was a miracle of some kind that they survived the ordeal unscathed. Molly summed it up by, saying, "I must say, I believe it was the best thing that could have happened to Buford. He's been walking the straight and narrow ever since." They all chuckled at the thought.

Mentioning Reverend Prather brought to Johnny's mind his experiences with him and his daughter Nellie. Johnny had told Molly all about how Nellie and Fanny had changed their lives, and how they helped to nurse him back to health. Johnny inquired, "You mentioned Reverend Prather. How's he and Nellie doing these days, Major?"

"Well, about a year after the war he performed the ceremony for Nellie's wedding. The funny thing about it was, for a while, he was perplexed as to how he was going to walk her down the aisle to give her away and be the preacher too. But finally he decided it would be as easy as pie. He just did both." He laughed. Johnny was surprised but pleased at the news and said, "So she got married, huh? Well, I'm glad for her. Hope he's a good man."

"Oh, I'm sure he is. She married one of the men she nursed at the hospital, Delbert Bond. They call him Delly for short. He's studying to be a minister and plans to follow in Reverend Prather's footsteps." "Well, Nellie and Delly, Huh? Isn't that cute!" said Molly, smiling.

John asked, "What about Fanny? I'll bet she misses Nellie's help at the hospital." Libby said, "Fanny closed the hospital shortly after Nellie married. There wasn't as much of a need for it then. She moved back to Norfolk. The last we heard she was nursing at a hospital there."

They went on chatting throughout the evening about old times, old friends, and the way things had been back then compared to how times were changing. They talked about Les and Lola getting married and having a boy and a girl, and neither child appeared to be dwarfed.

James Woodward also kept in touch with Johnny over the years. They had exchanged several letters. Johnny related to Major Wilburn that the *Baby Belle* was used as a ferry boat the rest of the summer of 1865 in Buster's home town of Norfolk. She ran across the narrow strip of water between Norfolk and Portsmouth, Virginia. But on a foggy night in the fall that year, a larger ship collided with it and it was destroyed by the ensuing fire. Buster went to work at the Newport News Shipbuilding and Dry Dock Company, and James Woodward went back to Jeffersonville, Indiana, working at the Howard Shipyards on the Ohio River.

Tom Mitchell was happy to tell everyone about how successful Mitchell Mills was, and he related that he had always believed that cotton could be produced economically without slave labor. Cotton was so important to the economy of the South that it was often referred to as "King Cotton." They even wrote and sang songs about ol' King Cotton.

When the conversation came around to discussing the politics of the times, the ladies split away to clean up after the meal and talk about raising babies, men, and family life, fashions, and of course, whatever was the latest gossip of the day. Johnny almost wished he could go talk with the ladies because he had a bad taste in his mouth regarding most political attitudes of the times; attitudes that were so engulfed in hatred and bitterness.

The following morning, they all proceeded to the Van Worth farm to spend the day, where the children played among the frisky dogs and cats, and chickens roamed in the yard along with the family goat and a couple of ponies that kept the grass and weeds "mowed" by nibbling on it.

Michael Jr. was older than John and Jay's children, and he had been thoughtful to bring a special gift to give Johnny's son. He had saved the buttonlike spinning toy Johnny had made for him out of oak before they left for the trenches at Richmond. The "spin-yo," as Johnny called it, was still in good condition, and Michael Jr. took great pleasure in presenting it to John William, as they were accustomed to calling John IV. John William was about the same age now as Michael Jr. had been when Johnny first gave it to him. It brought back memories of how Johnny had wanted a son like him. Now here he was, giving it as a gift to Johnny's son. It was a sentimental moment that warmed Johnny's heart.

Of course, John was happy when Jay warmly welcomed the Wilburn family to the farm. Jay was especially proud to introduce his bride, Glo. It was an appropriate name for her. She seemed to glow with her big smile and her shy, blinking eyes that always happened when she was directly addressed, especially during introductions. Her humble shyness was charming and amusing, and always evoked a smile from those around her.

This was a special day they would all remember fondly. It was like a joyful picnic as they barbecued pork chops and ribs on the new barbecue pit Johnny and Jay had constructed out of creek stone. The hickory-smoked barbecue odors filled the air, tantalizing everyone's appetite. The ladies prepared green beans, baked potatoes, sliced fresh tomatoes, and corn-on-the-cob. The meal was topped off with tasty desserts and fresh watermelon.

How different things were from the starving days of the war. They enjoyed a good meal and each other's good company—the Van Worths, the Browns, the Mitchells, and the Wilburns. There was much chatting, brotherhood, laughter, and fun as they played outdoor games with the children afterward. Another beautiful sunset accented this day to remember.

In the evening, they sat around in the dim coal oil light, sharing memories of those special moments in their lives, such as Rebecca hiding a gun under her gown to save the family from Rowdy Roberts, and other episodes such as the raid on the gang, the miraculous appearance of Eli, saving Les Moore, and the unfruitful treasure hunt.

After staying the night, the following morning, the Van Worths and the Mitchells escorted the Wilburn family back to Charleston in their buggies and carriage, where they were to board the train back to Virginia. It was good for Johnny to see the stately, kindly old gentleman again, and he thanked Major Wilburn for all that he had done, especially giving Johnny the *Baby Belle* so he could make it back to South Carolina without too much walking.

Molly had heard so much about the Wilburns that she hugged and kissed them all as if she had known them all her life. Molly and Johnny thanked Michael Jr. once more for being so thoughtful about giving their son the spin-yo. They all had damp eyes as the steam engine slowly puffed out of the station and they waved goodbye, not knowing when, or if they would ever meet again.

Molly embraced her parents and brother Kent, thinking how lucky she was that the war years had not taken them from her. She knew over six-hundred-thousand total men from the North and South had died during the war, many of them from disease and malnutrition. It left many families with a lifetime of emptiness and embitterment. She almost lost her Johnny, but was thankful he was with her now.

It was just the two of them together as they made the buggy ride back home to the farm on this beautiful day in May. The blossoms were blooming on many of the trees and bushes. The birds were singing. After two days of chatter and clatter, there was now peace and quiet.

It would take over two hours to get home, plenty of time for their minds to reflect and reminisce. They thought about all of the activity of the past two days and how nice it was that even in spite of a horrible war, they had still acquired friends like the Wilburns.

Molly felt like her life was an island of sweetness in a sea of bitterness. But she was determined to make love the central focus of their lives, no matter what these terrible times of the Reconstruction brought upon them.

Johnny was thankful Molly's strong faith had rubbed off on him. It's what had saved them from the Klan. Never again would they face anything like that—or the Civil War.

They appreciated the fact that Jay and Glo were there to help them. It was a blessing for Jay and Glo as well. Johnny and Molly had pitched in to help build even more space on their place as Jay and Glo's children came along. Most often, work on the farm was hard. Life wasn't always peaches and cream. Every day had its trials and tribulations. But John and Molly, Jay and Glo, learned to take it all in stride, knowing that many times the things that are today's heavy load will be tomorrow's heavy laugh. They lived lives that were close to nature—and close to God.

They believed that God is love. That's what their Christian faith had taught them. That's what they thought about and talked about on their ride home. They began to get revelations about things that Eli had told Johnny and his men about love. He had said, "It was love that created you." They concluded God must have loved everything into existence. That he created man and woman out of love, and he designed it so that the love between a man and a woman created babies, the proliferation of humanity. It was a beautiful thing for them to contemplate. It gave greater meaning to the sweetness of their intimate relationship. They remembered that Eli said, "It is love that has saved you." They wondered if he may have been referring to the life of Jesus Christ.

"Greater love hath no man, than he who lays down his life for another." That's what the Bible says, they thought. Jesus laid down his life to save all of humanity. Eli had also said, "It was love that sustains you." They reasoned he must have meant it is God answering our prayers that provides our daily bread and sustains us in times of trouble as well. They also concluded this was the deepest and most meaningful conversation they ever had.

Now they understood why we should treasure love so much. But they already had a great appreciation of it. The agony of being apart so long during the war made them want to enjoy the ecstasy of togetherness all the more. Whenever they had a difference of opinion they would always resolve it before the sun went down. Johnny loved the fact that she was different from him, both emotionally and physically. And he loved the very difference itself. She felt the same way about her Johnny. They wondered if people had enough love for their differences, instead of just tolerating differences, what a difference it would make in human relations. That's how they loved Jay and Glo.

Molly and John had an unselfish love for one another. They derived their pleasure from pleasing each other and looked for ways to satisfy one another each day. They would seek to know what pleased each other in intimacy and all other things. They began and ended each day with an expression of their feelings for one another, verbally saying, "I love you." Molly would prepare the foods Johnny loved more often. Johnny would do little things, like pick a bouquet of wild flowers and bring them to her. She would lovingly mend his clothes and he would look for gifts for her when he went to town. He helped her with the cooking and washing when he wasn't working other chores. And of course, they showered the children with love, taught them the importance of it, and how to practice the "golden rule."

One of their favorite ways to please each other was to read the Bible or other books aloud by the coal oil light. They occasionally would compose love poems such as

You Are My Dream

I close my eyes and dream of you.
You're all I want out of this life.
With eyes wide open I see it's true
I'm just so proud to be your wife.
The little children we have made
Have made our lives complete.
I have the joy for which I've prayed
Loving God and you and them is sweet.

Love, Molly

A typical return poem from Johnny might read as follows:

My Dream of You

You and the children are so lovin'
I'm mighty glad to be your hubbin'

Love, Johnny

Obviously, Molly was better at poetry than Johnny. But she appreciated his feeble attempts just the same, and thought it was cute. She knew it was difficult for Johnny to do ordinary things, even writing was awkward for him. She also knew John had needed her more than ever when he came home from the war handicapped, and she knew she had the love to compensate for it.

When they arrived home, that evening John William was playing on the front porch with the spin-yo. Johnny got on his knees beside his five-year-old son and put his hand through the loop on the right. John William pulled on the left loop and together they made the toy spin. Mari, his older sister, watched with an amused smile. Molly looked on with adoring eyes, walked over to them, and put her hands on their shoulders as the men in her life went on playing and laughing. Mari wrapped her arm around her mother's arm and looked up at Molly's moist eyes, wondering what was moving her mother to tears and softly said,

"Mommy, what's the matter?" Molly looked at her daughter adoringly, gently smiled, and said, "Oh, I'm thinking how wonderful love is. It's one thing that lasts forever."

Mari embraced her mother as Molly went on thinking how much she loved Johnny and the children. She thanked God for her family and knew that through faith in him everything would be all right, in spite of life's storms, trials, and tribulations. They believed Johnny's arm, even death, was no handicap to a Christian because God promises his believers an eternal, perfect, and resurrected body someday, that no matter what happens in this life, through the love of God they would all be together again forever in the sweet by and by. They lived, not seeking treasures for today and the short life we spend on earth, but stored up heavenly treasures for the never-ending life of eternity, by conducting themselves to please their Maker with faith and love, feeling secure and fearing no evil. And so it was that they lived their lives through the years, ready to face anything, armed with love.

The End

Afterword

I sincerely hope you enjoyed reading *Call to Arms*. Was it fact or fiction? If you read the Foreword or the Preface, you know it was admittedly a fictional story. However, some parts of it were very real. The historical accounts were completely accurate, but John and his men and other characters were not there. Danville, Virginia, historically claims to be the second capital of the Confederacy since Confederate president, Jefferson Davis, did in fact set up temporary headquarters at Major Sutherlin's home on Main Street as the Confederacy was collapsing in 1865. Sutherlin was in charge of Quartermaster Supply for the Confederacy and his home today is a tourist attraction in Danville, a quaint community truly located on the Dan River in Southern Virginia, very near the North Carolina border.

The episode involving the Ku Klux Klan was based in part on a true Civil War story that was passed down in my family for several generations. I heard my grandmother on my mother's side of the family, Kathryn Fuhry, tell the story several times, although it was somewhat different from the way I portrayed it in this book. Her maiden name was Kathryn Brown. She was born in Hardin County, Kentucky, in 1897. As she told it, the story took place during the Civil War in the same Hardin County cabin where she was born, not far from the birth place of Abraham Lincoln. The Ku Klux Klan was NOT involved. According to her account, some Civil War soldiers forced their way into the cabin, making demands for food and other items. As I recall she never said whether they were Union or Rebel soldiers. That was never regarded as being a significant part of the tale. They could have been deserters or drifters for all I know.

The significant part of the story was that these men were dissatisfied and threatened to throw the baby of the family in the fire. Her grandfather was the man of the house and he was so outraged that he began cursing these men severely. They took him outside with the stated intention of hanging him. He threatened to put a curse on them and come back and haunt them if they hanged him. Apparently, he was so convincing that he put a scare into them, because they brought him back and dumped him off saying, "He was too damned mean to hang." You can see how I altered the story a bit to emphasize problems in the South during the Reconstruction Period.

Another part of *Call to Arms* that seems rather unbelievable is the episode involving Eli Proffit. That's based in part on another true story reported by a Union officer. He and his men witnessed a soldier in a Revolutionary War uniform charging against Confederate forces on a white horse. He swore that it was the ghost of George Washington and was advised to not ever tell anyone about it by a higher-ranking officer. This was reported on the Civil War series produced by Ken Burns that aired on public television. Of course, I did a spin off of that story, but made the ghost an angel who previously visited John and his men as a man. And to inject humor into this serious segment, I added the premise of him accurately predicting what the reader knows to be real future inventions, events, and popular characters of the screen and television that people of the nineteenth century would find unbelievable or ridiculous.

A part of the story that was based on reality was the inclusion of the Magnolia Plantation. The plantation truly was first built in 1676 along the shores of the Ashley River and the third building stands today as one of the outstanding tourist attractions of the South. It is very much as I described it in this book except that it doesn't have a grand ballroom. The Drayton family has always owned it and John Grimke Drayton did inherit the property and was there at the time of the Civil War just as described. He was an Episcopal minister who truly referred to his three hundred slaves as his "Black Roses." It's also true that he built a schoolhouse to educate his slaves against state law at the time and had two aunts who were banned from South Carolina before the war for being notorious abolitionists. Reverend Drayton left the property and moved to a summer residence in North Carolina toward the end of the Civil War out of fear that the Yankee's near Charleston were going to capture it. His slave foreman, Adam Bennett, stayed on the Plantation and eventually set fire to it before the Yankees did, as they were burning other nearby plantation houses, including the Oak Plantation. Even though threatened with death, Bennett refused to reveal to Union troops where he buried the family's valuables and walked barefoot over 250 miles to let the reverend know it was all right to return home after the war, and the plantation house was rebuilt. The part of my story where Reverend Drayton was involved in the dueling scene was pure fiction on my part. The late CBS reporter, Charles Kuralt, once said his visit to the Magnolia Plantation was the highlight of his Charleston tour through the South.

The depiction of the *Baby Belle* was an idea that makes *Call to Arms* a unique story. The boat actually exists. It is a pontoon boat I bought in 1995. I spent five years remodeling it to resemble a sidewheel steamboat. To use it for a movie version of the story, we would simply apply styrofoam and paint the pontoons, or use computer animation to make it look as if they are constructed out of logs.

I have been fascinated with the beauty, romantic charm, and folklore of steamboats since I was a youngster. The Howard Ship Yards were founded on the banks of the Ohio

River at Jeffersonville, Indiana, in 1834 by James Howard. He had a son, Edmund, and two grandsons, Clyde and James. The Howard family had the reputation of building the finest steamboats in America. It operated as the Howard Ship Yards and Dock Company until 1941, when it was sold to the government to produce Landing Ship Tanks (LSTs) used to land troops and tanks for the invasion of Normandy in World War II. Following the war, it was sold to private enterprises, and has changed ownership several times over the years, but still remains today as the largest inland shipyard in America, operating under the name Jeffboat.

Adjacent to Jeffboat, across Market street, is the three-story brick Howard family mansion, which was completed in 1893. Jim Howard and his wife Loretta were the last owners of the Howard Ship Yard and the mansion. Before his death in 1956, Jim Howard made it known to his wife that he would like to see the home turned into a museum to preserve the folklore of the river and boat building. Loretta Howard was the hostess and curator of the Howard Steamboat Museum and I spent many hours talking to this lovely and charming lady about those olden times. The mansion was built by the same men who turned out those magnificent old steamboats, and reflects much of the architectural grandeur of the Victorian Era. It houses many model steamboats and other artifacts of the steamboat era, including an arch from the famous Robt. E. Lee. It is a wonderful tourist attraction and I can recommend it highly. A visit to the Howard Steamboat Museum is a unique and memorable occasion.

If you are a Civil War buff you know that the Battle of Cold Harbor actually took place as described in this novel with six thousand Union troops perishing in one hour in the frontal assault ordered by General Grant on June 3, 1864. It is a little-known fact, but the portion of my novel regarding the explosion at the railroad depot during the evacuation of Charleston was based on an actual incident as depicted.

The story regarding Deacon Harold Butts was a true story, or at least it was told to me as being true by a very good friend of mine, who was actually at a church in Kentucky when it happened.

You probably noticed I injected humor into some of the names of the characters of this story. But some of the names were taken from real-life people I've known. I borrowed the name Jay Brown from a friend I worked with in TV, although he spells it Jae and has a personality quite different from that of the Jay Brown in this book. I would like to thank Jae for help he gave me proofreading the book and making suggestions that led to me adding several chapters to the story. Gloretha was the name of a black girl from Alabama I worked with at another TV station and she had the same enchanting shy characteristics I described in this novel. I went to Atherton High School in Louisville, Kentucky, with a girl named Molly Mitchell. She was the kind of person that was beautiful inside and out. She was intelligent and humble, with a charming All-American, good-hearted personality, accented with a sparkling smile that was a joy to behold. She was a cheerleader, and in my senior year I joined the cheerleading team just to be near her. I don't think she ever knew how much I deeply adored her, or what an inspiration she was to me. She was the inspirational model for the heroine in this book. I took the liberty to use the names of some of her family members as well. Her mother Marion, her father Tom, and brother Kent. They were wonderful people, too and were wonderful to me, encouraging me and taking me to church with them.

Several women have had a profound influence on my life that bear mentioning. I've already told you about two of them, Molly Mitchell and Loretta Howard. Mrs. Howard was at least forty five years older than me, but she was very spry and had such a vivacious personality and brilliant mind that there were times when she left me feeling senile by comparison. She was full of energy and was the spark that kept the Howard Ship Yards operating even when steamboats were waning. She traveled to find businesses that could use a boat, and her husband would design and build it. Then she would go along with the crew, preparing meals along the way to deliver the boat to the customer.

In more recent years, the woman that has inspired me the most is country-music legend, Loretta Lynn. In 1984, I had a born-again religious experience just from observing the honesty and humility of this very special lady. The story of this and my relationship with her is full of incidents that could only be described as miraculous and could be a book in itself. I will only say that I have been honored to be asked by her to step on stage at many of her concerts to perform live, a tribute I wrote and recorded for her in 1984. Since I'm an impressionist, I do the tribute in a Gregory Peck voice. He's Loretta's favorite movie star and the tribute is based on what I would say about Loretta Lynn if I could have been Gregory Peck when he met Loretta in 1974. That meeting was arranged as a birthday surprise by her husband, Mooney.

I would like to include my only wife, Darl Lee, among the great women in my life. She was very beautiful, and we shared many wonderful moments, love, and laughter together, as well as four beautiful and cherished children. I still love her today and miss her, even though our marriage ended in 1977. If I had the appreciation for women and the importance of love that I have today, perhaps that would be a different story.

I believe that females are one of the most miraculous engineering feats that God ever performed, as well as one of the greatest works of art. Women don't get enough credit for what they have done, bearing the pain and burden of making human life on earth possible. I can advise husbands to do what the Bible says, "Love your wives."

I sincerely believe that love is the most important ingredient of life. If you got a message of love out of *Call to Arms* then you received the main message I wanted to convey.

It is a message the whole world needs today. I enjoyed writing this book because the project involved many of the things I cherish, including spiritual values, steamboats, other charms of the nineteenth century, music, love, and laughter.

The Civil War remains today as a phase of American history that continues to fascinate all generations of Americans, and even people from other nations. I'm happy to have taken you on this unique and nostalgic trip focused on this historic period.

Claude Wayne